The Church Series Book Five

Tiya Rayne

Young Ann Publishing, LLC
Colfax, North Carolina

Tiya Rayne/ Young Ann Publishing, LLC
PO BOX 365
Colfax, NC/27235
www.tiyarayne.com

Publisher's Note: This is a work of fiction. Names, characters, places, and incidents are
a product of the author's imagination. Locales and public names are sometimes used
for atmospheric purposes. Any resemblance to actual people, living or dead, or to
businesses, companies, events, institutions, or locales is completely coincidental.

Ordering Information:
Quantity sales. Special discounts are available on quantity purchases by corporations,
associations, and others. For details, contact the "Special Sales Department" at the
address above.

Beast: Part Two/ Tiya Rayne. -- 1st ed.
ISBN 979-8-9865803-5-7

To Bumblebee

Family isn't defined only by last names or blood; it's defined by commitment and by love.

—Dave Willis

AUTHOR NOTE

Before you embark on this journey, take a moment to read this. This book deals with torture, mental health, and trauma. If any of those are triggers for you, please skip this book. Your mental health is important.

Also, I need you to trust the process on this one. I promise, it will be worth it in the end.

Happy Reading!

CHAPTER ONE

Excommunication

Priest

I never thought this dumb ass plan to get Fem back would work out for me. When Hawk suggested I needed to do something big, something that took me out of my comfort zone to win her back, I immediately thought of "10 Things I Hate About You" and the conversation Fem and I had that one night.

She told me until I loved someone so much that I would embarrass myself for them, I would never understand the movie. Well, I fucking understood it now. Which is why I'm at her home begging her to take me back.

Since the day Fem kicked me out of her hospital room, I haven't been able to function. It became blatantly clear how much I loved her. The only thing worse than being told to stay away from her was watching her bleed out in my arms, thinking she was going to die. To have her back in my arms now is the greatest feeling ever. I love this woman wholeheartedly.

Suddenly, the chiming of ringtones has me pulling away from Fem. I take my phone out of my pocket reading the message scrolled across the screen.

My heart races, causing pains in my chest. My palms immediately start to sweat. I glance up at the boys, and they all have the same ashen look on their faces.

"What is it?" Fem asks.

Standing up straight, I look at Lucien before answering. "We have an excommunication order out on us."

"What?" she gasps, shooting to her feet, but immediately sitting back down. Reminding me she needs to take it easy. Although her injuries have healed, she still hasn't fully recovered.

"What does that mean?" Brooklyn asks.

"It means the entire Church is coming after us," Lucien says. He grabs Malia around her waist and pulls her into him.

I know what he's thinking. He's afraid. He's not alone in his fear. As I look around the room, I realize we all have something special here. Something that we are now realizing we could be taken away from. The domesticated life has never enticed me. I'm a killer and I will always be one, but I won't lie as if the thought of coming home to Fem and Charlie every night did not appeal to me. However, with this new information, that may not be a possibility.

"And they have orders to kill us on sight," Lucien finishes, placing a kiss on Malia's head.

"That doesn't make sense," Hawk argues. "They haven't chosen a new Pope. The Council doesn't have the power to make that decision without a Pope."

He isn't lying. Only a Pope can make that type of call. Yes, the council must agree, but the official notice has to come from the Pope. We are still two weeks out from the ordination of a new Pope.

"What if there is someone else?" Fem asks. "Someone higher than the Pope."

We all turned to look at her. My brows pinch as I think over her words.

"Who is higher than the Pope?" Many asks the question I'm sure all of us are wondering.

She hesitates for a second. "God. And I think we're going to need Beast."

She's right. Not only would I need all my sons back home where we could work together and remain safe, I knew there was one more person I was going to have to contact. I guess it's time I cash in one of those favors he owes me.

As soon as I lift my phone back up to make the call, the device lights up in my hand. An unknown number comes across the screen. It's a New York area code, so I don't hesitate to answer.

"This is Priest," I say, as soon as I answer the phone.

"Hello, my name is Gabriel August Jones." The little voice on the other end of the phone recites as if they've practiced this phone call before. "I live at…"

"Wait," I say, shaking my head. "Who is this?"

"Put it on speaker," Lucien advises.

I quickly click the call over to speaker phone.

"My name is Gabriel August Jones. My mommy said to call this number in case of an emergency. Hulk is bleeding and mommy is on the floor."

"Oh, my goodness, that's Beast's son," Fem says clutching a hand to her chest.

My head spins, and a new fear takes over me. Someone is bleeding. Did someone from the Church get to my son before I could?

"Alright, Gabriel, this is your uncle Lucien. Where are you right now?"

I'm glad Lucien has the wherewithal to take over the conversation because I'm not thinking straight.

"Hulk told me to hide in the closet. I'm scared."

His little voice breaks at the end of his sentence sending me into overdrive.

I have no idea who this Hulk is. I'm assuming it's Beast. "Alright kid, listen to me," I say, taking over the conversation. "We're heading your way. I need you to remain in that closet until I get there. Anything changes you call me back immediately. Okay?"

"Okay. But can you hurry."

I swallow as I get choked up hearing my grandson plead for me to get to him. "I promise I'll go as fast as I can."

"Okay. Bye," he says before his line goes dead.

I hang up the phone but take a second to gather my emotions. Not only did I hear my grandson's voice for the first time, but I also just found out my son might be hurt and maybe even his girl. If that's the case, I'm not sure what version of Beast we will meet.

"Phoenix," I say to TR or should I say, Fem's father. "Can you get all the women to my ghost house?"

He nods. "Yeah, I can. Once I get them settled, I'll head out and see what I can find out about this excommunication order. I still have connections in the Church."

I dipped my chin at him without replying. We will need all the help we can get right now.

Turning to Fem, I say. "Pack quickly. Your home has been attacked once already. I don't know who is behind this Excommunication stuff, so we have to be cautious."

"I'm coming with you," she argues.

I'm shaking my head before she can finish speaking. "No, you're injured and it's too risky—"

"You don't understand," she says cutting me off. "If something is wrong with Summer, he's not going to be himself. He's going to need someone that knows her, preferably a female. Trust me, Nathaniel."

I stare at her for a moment. I want to argue, to tell her that I know my son and what he needs. But Fem has been right all this time about Beast. Had I known about his kid and girl, I would have tried to take over and in the end, he would've resented me. I'm learning to trust her more when it comes to the boys. Besides, she's spent enough time with them over the years to know what they need.

"Alright, but you stay near me and don't overwork yourself."

She agrees before turning to her mother. "Ms. Reese can you pack me a few things and make sure Charlie has what he needs."

"Yes, don't worry about us. Ya'll go get that baby."

"Let's go," I say, to Hawk, Zel, Many, and Lucien.

The six of us quickly head out the house.

"Fem and Many, you ride with me. Lucien, take Hawk and Zel with you."

"Got it." Lucien agrees, heading in the opposite direction from me.

I climb into the driver's side of the Charger. Fem gets in on the passenger seat with Many in the back.

"I hope brother Beast is okay," Many says in his British accent.

"Everything is going to be fine," Fem says in a tone that tells me she's not sure if her words are true.

"Buckle up," I announce, before pressing on the gas.

I made the hour drive in less than forty-five minutes. I defied every traffic law there was. We pull up to the Victorian farmhouse and park behind the Subaru. The house looks the same as it did the night Beast met me on the sidewalk. As soon as I climb out, Lucien and the others pull up behind me.

I take off the jacket I was wearing and toss it back in my seat.

"How do we do this?" Lucien asks, coming up beside me.

"Front door," Fem says strolling up to the porch.

She reaches for a flowerpot sitting near the front door. Picking it up, she flips it over, exposing a rotary combination lock. She rolls the dial, and a hidden door pops open before exposing a key. After placing the pot back down, she moves to the front door.

"Hold on," I tell her. She pauses, looking over her shoulder at me.

"Unlock the door, but don't walk in. Let Hawk in first."

Hawk steps to the front of our line. I turn to the others and dip my head. We all take out our guns. It's not like I plan on killing Beast, but I'm not sure what we will be walking into.

Fem unlocks the door and steps back. Hawk takes a deep breath before opening the door. As soon as he steps in, he ducks down barely missing a blade being tossed at his head. I figured Beast would be ready for us. No one's senses would be sharper than Hawk's. We all rush into the house.

Beast is standing in the doorway between the foyer and the living room. His shirt is covered in blood. But I can immediately tell he isn't the one injured. This is going to be worse than I thought.

"Beast, where is Summer?" I ask.

He turns his head slightly, his gaze shifting to the left. It's as if he's listening to something in the distance.

"Kill them all. They've come to take her," he says.

His voice is different. It's deeper than usual. Whenever Beast goes to his dark place, his mother is the one that takes over. In most cases he only replies to her commands. However, I've heard him speak in his mother's voice before when he is truly lost in his haze. This is not that voice.

"That's not his mother," Lucien says coming up behind me. He obviously notices the same thing I did.

I take a step forward. "Beast, I need you to reign it back in. Where is Summer?"

Once again, he turns his head to the side in that weird way. "Peel their flesh one by one and burn it in the yard."

"Ooookaaaay," Zel whispers loud enough for us to hear. "Is anybody else a little freaked out right now?"

"We do not like this version of brother Beast very much," Many says in his nasally voice.

Holding up my hand behind me, I try to quiet everyone down. Beast isn't himself, but he is still our family.

"Son," I say to Beast. "I need you to answer my question."

"I don't think we're going to get through to him." Fem points out from behind me. "And judging by the blood on that shirt, we don't have much time to get to Summer. Nathaniel, if she dies..."

She didn't have to finish that sentence. I knew what she was getting at. The same thing would have happened to me if Albany would've died when Luca shot her. I would've lost my mind. However, a mindless Priest and a mindless Beast are two completely different beings.

Thinking quickly, I pull out my phone and call the last number that called me. Beast has been telling us for three months that he's found his new lifelines, let's hope that connection still remains.

"Hello?" the soft voice answers.

I quickly put young Gabriel on speaker phone. "Hello, little Gabriel. This is Priest."

"Hey, Mr. Priest. Are you here?" His excitement at my voice has a thickness forming in my throat. I have to clear it before I can speak again.

I keep my eyes on Beast as little Gabriel speaks. For the first time since we walked in, he's looking at us.

"Yes, I'm here."

"Can I come out now? I want to see Hulk and mommy."

Giving Beast my undivided attention, I refer my last question to him. "Can he come out now, Beast? Your son needs you. Do you hear his voice?" I ask taking a step toward him.

"Priest, what are you doing?" Lucien asks nervously.

"We don't think that's a good idea, father Priest," Many says in his deep voice.

I ignore their pleas. I know what I'm doing. At least I hope I do. I've never seen Beast this far gone before. I have seen him in the deepest part of his haze, but to be this blind and cold that he can't determine us from friend or foe is new.

"What do you say, son? Are you ready for little Gabriel to see you?" I press forward trying to pull Beast out of his haze.

He blinks, taking a step back. He then tilts his head in that way he's been doing since we walked in, as if he's listening.

"It's a trick. Slit his throat," he says in that unfamiliar deep voice.

I don't let it deter me, I take a few more steps closer, placing myself within his reach. Beast's eyes narrow at me. For the first time since I walked in, I get a glimpse of my son. He's in there buried deep.

"Hey, little Gabriel," I call out. "What's your favorite food?"

I knew the only way to get Beast out of that dark place was to lure him back to us. When he was a kid, I used to sit and talk to him for hours when he was caught up in the haze. At times, I'd call one of his brothers in to talk. He would eventually fight off the red haze and come back to us. But the last few months he's been showing us he had found his peace with the girl and his son. So, if I wanted my son back, I needed his son to talk to him.

"I like chicken nuggets," little Gabriel says softly.

Beast shakes his head as if he's trying to lodge something out of it.

"I like chicken nuggets too," I say without taking my eyes off Beast. "Who has your favorite nuggets?"

"Chick-fil-A. Hulk likes nuggets too. But he loves pancakes."

The kid chuckles, and I laugh too.

"Mr. Priest," little Gabriel whispers my name as if he's about to tell me a secret.

"Yeah, Kid?"

"Can I come out now? I want to see my mommy. Tell Hulk I promise I'll be brave like I was with the bee. I'll use my words, and I won't cry. Can I come out?"

Jeez this kid is breaking my heart. Beast puts his hands up to his head as he pounds his fists against his skull.

"You have to fight it, son. Whatever the fuck is going on in your head right now, you can fight that shit. Your son needs you. Your brothers need you, and Summer needs you."

The moment I say her name, he drops his hands down to his side. His eyes water, and as the first tear falls, he drops to his knees. I go down with him trying to catch him.

"It's okay. I got you," I say, rocking him back and forth in my arms.

"I can't lose her, Priest. I can't," Beast pleads in his own voice.

Fuck, I'm just glad to have him back. Without letting Beast go, I hand the phone to Lucien.

"Go find the kid," I explain.

He takes the phone and immediately starts talking. "Hey, nephew. This is your uncle Lucien. I'm coming for you." He takes off out of the room.

"I'll go find Summer," Fem says walking past us. Zel goes with her.

Hawk and Many surround me and Beast.

"We got you, brother. I promise," Hawk says, his voice cracking a little. He places a hand on Beast's shoulder.

"Priest," Fem shouts, causing my heart to pick up speed. Please don't let her tell me any bad news. "We have a heartbeat. But we need a doc, now."

Hallelujah.

Beast pulls away from my embrace, his eyes are bloodshot red.

"You hear that, kid. She's still fucking fighting. We need to get her out of here."

He nods, standing to his feet. We all rush into the kitchen where Fem and Zel are. Lying on the ground in front of Fem is a tiny female with light brown skin. She's wearing a too big t-shirt and fuzzy slippers. Beast kneels beside her, lifting her head in his lap with the gentlest touch.

"Call Doc, have him meet us at the nearest Church clinic," I say to Zel.

"Isn't that risky with the excommunication order?" Hawk asks.

"She won't make it back to the ghost house. It's either there or a hospital," Fem answers for me.

"We will take our risk at the clinic. Tell Doc it's for me," I direct my last sentence to Zel.

He quickly pulls out his phone and walks off.

"Beast, we have to get moving." Beast shakes his head. "Come on, son. We need to go."

He places his hands under her body, lifting her from the floor. She lays limp in his arms.

Zel rushes back into the room. "Doc said screw the clinic, bring her to his house. He also wanted me to let you know he stands with us."

I dip my chin, feeling proud I have at least one ally in the Church. Just then, Lucien walks down the stairs. He's carrying something wrapped in a blanket.

"Remember, keep your head down, soon as we get outside you can come out."

The blanket moves. "Okay, uncle Lucien," a small voice says underneath the cover.

As bad as I wanted to see little Gabriel, I knew that Lucien made the right decision. The kid didn't need to see this.

"Let's go," I say to the others.

We left the farmhouse. Fem and Beast—along with Summer's limp body—climb in my Charger. While the others go with Lucien.

Just as fast as I got to Summer's home, we left. Once again, I break all road laws. We are up against time. Yes, we have an excommunication order on our heads. And yes, I should be connecting with my source about said EO. There is so much shit about to rain down on us that we need to prepare for it. However, I push all of that to the back of my mind. We must save Summer, because if we don't, all hell will break loose.

CHAPTER TWO

Family Ties

Beast

The sound of the clock ticking is the only noise in the all-white waiting room inside Doc's make-shift hospital inside his house. His home is a brick Tudor-style house. He transformed the entire basement into a hospital, while the upstairs remained his regular living space.

Glancing down at the blood covering my hands, I shut my eyes and take a deep breath.

"Break the blind one's neck, and then slit the throat of the old guy," the deep voice in my head whispers.

Fisting my hands at my temple I fight to get the sinister voice back in its box. Despite coming back from that dark place back at home, I can't seem to shake the voice now. I never thought I'd miss the sound of mother's voice. But I'd much rather hear her than this one.

"Hey, you alright?"

I open my eyes at the sound of Hawk's question. I'm no longer sitting across from him as I was moments ago. Now, I'm standing in front of him with my hands clenched at my sides.

11

The deep voice laughs in my head. I take as many steps as I can away from my brother. My heart is pounding in my chest. I don't miss the look of concern on Hawk's face.

"Have a seat, Kid," Priest says. "Doc will let us know something in a few."

Before he finishes speaking, I'm shaking my head no. I need to get out of here and put as much distance as I can between myself and my family. At least until I get a handle on the voice in my head.

"I need fresh air," I lie as I turn to walk out the door heading back outside.

"Beast, sit," Priest demands.

I blink, and when I open my eyes, I have Priest pressed against the wall with one hand around his neck and my blade pointed at his chin. Hawk is at my shoulder trying to pull me away. I don't even recall moving.

"Let me out, Gabriel," the sinister voice pleads.

Pushing away from Priest I shut my eyes and focus on breathing. In through my nose, out through my mouth. The same way I learned as a kid in the training program.

"Where are you, mother?" I call out to the now silent voice.

"Mother's not here anymore," the other voice taunts.

I slam the palm of my hand against my forehead. "Get the fuck out of my head," I growl.

Sudden movement behind me has me looking over my shoulder.

"Everything alright?" Lucien asks, as he scans the room thoroughly.

"Yeah, everything is fine," Priest answers rubbing at his neck.

Hawk looks over to me, tilting his head to the side. "Are you good, brother?"

I nod before I answer out loud. "I'm good."

"Liar." The word is followed by laughter.

Just then, Zel, Many, and Albany walk into the room.

"Where's Gabe?" I ask immediately. I need him to keep me sane. His presence silences the voice in my head.

"We have him situated upstairs. He's watching one of the Spiderman movies. I already have Iron Man loaded to play next. He's good," Zel explains.

I nod, thankful for their help. Albany walks over to Priest. She touches his reddening neck. He shakes his head at her and whispers something that I can't hear. My face heats and shame turns my gut.

When Priest looks to me, I look away. My gaze focused on the white plain walls.

"How are we looking on surveillance?" Priest asks Lucien.

Doc's place was already secure, but when we got here, Lucien added a little more protection. Technically, we are still on Church property considering Doc is a working member of the Church.

"I have every camera in a 20-mile radius working for me," he looks down at the tablet in his hands. "So far, nothing looks out of place."

"Alright, the place is locked down, my grandson is entertained, and Summer is in Doc's care, it's time to regroup," Priest says taking a seat. "First, Beast, I want to know what happened? How did we get here?"

Sighing, I run my hands through my hair. "It started five years ago. I got a menu about a John Doe. Turns out he was an ex-agent. He called himself Gambler."

Priest's eyes narrow. "I've heard of him. He went rogue when I was still a young Deacon. What does he have to do with anything?"

I quickly explain the conversation I had with Gambler and the information I got from him. I tell them how I tracked Jason Averil and how it led me to Timothy Smith. And how that ultimately led me to Corbyn.

"So let me get this straight. The Church has been taking hits for rich assholes?" Zel asks sounding disgusted.

"Yes," I sigh.

The room goes silent. They are all reflecting. I don't blame them. Learning that information messed with my head as well.

I took pride in what I was doing. Knowing that I was killing people that deserved it, helped sate the evil inside me. However, finding out that I may have killed an innocent person just for the personal gain of an entitled prick, makes me feel like the vile demon mother always said I was.

"So, you think this Corbyn guy is god?" Albany asks, folding her arms over her chest.

"I have a feeling this god isn't just one person. Any of you heard of the Royal Crown?"

"I have," Albany says. "Hawk, you should remember them too. It's how you found out about Heimlich's experiment and his daughter."

Hawk leans up in his seat. "I remember. Brooklyn and I went to the club the night they had that secret meeting."

"The Royal Crown is a dangerous organization," Albany goes on to say. "Some of the most powerful men and women in the world run that group."

"Not only that group," I add. "But I think the Church as well."

Silence fills the room once again. After looking over all that I'd discovered recently, I had come to the conclusion that the Royal Crown was the hands behind the Church. I knew they had enough power to have the Church kill for them. That alone was enough to make me believe they were behind everything.

However, the most convincing part was how they all referred to the members of the Church. They thought of us as puppets. Just mindless pawns that could easily be moved around. It was in the way Timothy spoke to me about his transaction with the Church. It was as if we were discussing a business deal. He had a healthy amount of respect in his tone, but no true fear.

The other leading factor was my encounter with Boris and Blue Eyes. Not long after killing those two, I got the call from Maksim and then the attack on Summer.

"How much power are we talking?" Hawk asks, breaking the silence in the room.

"The type to get an excommunication order put on us," Priest replies instead of me.

"I think my searching for them and killing a few of their members pissed them off."

"A bit of advice, be careful when you kick a hornet's nest, when they swarm, they attack everyone around you." Maksim's words play back in my head.

"I should've listened."

"Sorry about that," I say, ducking my head. "I risked your lives, and that wasn't my intention."

"You failed," the sinister voice in my head says. *"But I can help you. Set me free."*

A soft touch on my shoulder has me looking up into Priest's gray eyes. "Don't start feeling sorry for yourself. This isn't all on you. We've had to be on this group's list for a while. And you didn't do anything any of us wouldn't have done."

"He's right, Beast. None of us blame you," Lucien adds.

"They are liars. Kill them all."

I swallow and nod my head, hoping to drown out the voice.

"Well, what now?" Albany asks. "Trying to hide all of us forever is going to be difficult. Lucien is good, but he's not that good."

In this we all agreed. However, I wasn't worried about that decision. I had my own plans. I was going to make sure that they all survived this, and it very well might be the last thing I do.

Before anyone can answer, Lucien's tablet sounds an alarm. Everyone jumps to their feet. Lucien scans the screen in his hands.

"Who the hell is this?" He asks, before flipping the tablet around.

Leaning against a sleek black car not far from Doc's house is a man with dark brown hair. He's wearing shades and a long sleeve white shirt. He's holding up a sign that reads; Hello Beastie.

I nearly snarl as I push away from the wall and head to the door.

"Where are you going?" Someone asks behind me.

I don't answer as I rush out of Doc's place. I reach the street just in time to find Maksim leaning up from the car. I'm on him faster than I've ever moved before. I have him pinned against the trunk of his car; my hands fisted in the collar of his shirt.

"Easy, Beastie. I'm not your enemy," he says in that accented voice.

"If you're not the enemy, then who are you?" Priest questions. I don't take my eyes off Maksim or the smirk on his face.

"My brother," I growl, snatching the shades off his face.

Just as I suspected, he has the exact same eyes as I do. The day I mentioned Gabe not having my eyes, Maksim told me not to worry, most don't. That's when I knew he was connected to me in some way. Although all the others I've met including, Victoria, Yohan, Boris, and Blue Eyes, all have different physical characteristics, there were some very familiar features, height, being one. Considering they all considered themselves siblings, I put the pieces together.

"Wait, Colleen had another kid?" Lucien asks.

I let go of Maksim, putting space between us. He's right, he isn't my enemy. In fact, if not for his warning, I wouldn't have known to get to Summer.

The moment I think her name, I get a pain in my chest that has me rubbing the area as if I've been shot there.

Her smile and those freckles that scatter over her nose pop in my head. I reminisce on the last image I have of her before everything went to shit. She was standing at the stove wearing my shirt, fixing my favorite food. She looked at me and her brow dipped. *"Everything okay?"* her soft voice had asked.

"I fucking need you, Summer," I whisper to myself.

"No, Beastie and I do not share the same mother," Maksim replies to Lucien getting my attention back.

"I would like to tell you all about it, if we could just go inside. It's not safe out in the open like this. We are all wanted men, are we not?"

"He's right, Priest." Zel says.

It's then I notice they all have their guns out and aimed at Maksim.

"What do you say, Beast. Can we trust him?"

I look to Maksim after Priest's question. I don't really know him, but my gut hardly ever steers me wrong. For the past few months, Maksim has done nothing but help me. Even in the beginning, he warned me to take care of my loose ends. And if I remember correctly when the PI was telling me about the benefactor, he told me that the benefactor wanted him to watch over Summer. He said that Summer was the benefactor's sister-n-law. At the time I chalked his words up to the benefactor lying to the PI. However, now that I think about it, he wasn't. He did hire him to find Summer and keep her safe.

Turning back to Priest, I answer, "Yeah, he's good."

Maksim dips his chin at me. He then pops the trunk of his car and pulls out two duffle bags. We all head back into the waiting room at Doc's.

"How is she?" Maksim asks as soon as he takes a seat inside.

"We still don't know yet. Doc has been in there working on her since we got here." Hawk answers.

Maksim looks at me solemnly. "Yohan took the shot. When I called you, I was trying to get to him before he did it. I might have injured him, but he's not dead."

The full image of Yohan pops into my head. I think back on all his details, from the caramel color of his skin to his hazel eyes, his curly hair, even the smirk on his face the last time I saw him. I categorize it all, because once I get my hands on him, he will never look that way again.

"Start talking," Priest says, folding his arms across his chest as he leaned against the wall.

Maksim sighs and leans back in his chair. "Corbyn got the idea from the Church."

"Who is Corbyn?" Zel asks.

"Elliot Corbyn," Maksim replies.

"Wait, the same Elliot Corbyn that owns one of the largest international investment companies in the world?" Lucien asks.

"Yes, Elliot Corbyn is Beast's father. He's also the father of myself and twenty others. There are only eleven of us left, not including Beast. Well, nine now since little brother took two of them out at the club." He tips his head to me. "Nice work, by the way. I've always hated Boris and Freddy."

I don't respond.

"Why so many kids?" Zel asks, bringing the conversation back to the topic. "Was he trying to start an army?"

Hawk and Many laugh at Zel's joke, but I don't.

"Yes," I answer for Maksim.

From everything I remember about the two I met at the club along with Victoria and Yohan, they were all well trained. Almost as well trained as me and my brothers. And they were loyal to Corbyn. As if he were their very own Pope.

"Corbyn really underestimated your intelligence." Maksim smiles at me before continuing. "Like I said, he got the idea from the Church. When he was younger, he went on a spree, dropping his sperm off in any woman that was willing and able. Once the babies were born, he swooped in and took us the moment we were no longer dependent on our mothers.

"From the time I was three years old, I was trained to be a killer. He raised us to be his own personal bodyguards. He stripped us of our identities and brainwashed us, turning us into mindless, loyal drones. Many of my siblings have laid down their lives for our father."

"It sounds like a cult," Albany says.

Maksim nods. "Oh it is. Thankfully, I stopped drinking the Kool-Aid and started to see Corbyn for what he truly is, a narcissistic psychopath."

One would think hearing about their father for the first time would elicit some type of emotion. However, I felt nothing hearing about Corbyn. If I'd died and never knew who my real father was, I wouldn't have cared.

"What got you off the mind control juice?" Lucien asks the question that was on my mind as well.

I've met the others. The way they speak of Corbyn is like hero worship. As if he's some god or something. Even when Maksim and I first started communicating, I noticed that even though he was warning me against the "bad guys" he was still protecting them. The loyalty to Corbyn runs deep. So, what changed?

"Four months of the worse torture you can think of." The darkness that clouds Maksim's face tells a very dark story. One I know all too well. Whatever he went through in those four months pushed him to the point of almost breaking.

"I was captured by one of my father's enemies. Daily they took me out of my cell to…" he pauses before clearing his throat. "Play with me. Thankfully, I was able to escape."

No one needs further description of what play means. We've seen and done some terrible things for information.

"Why change your loyalty?" I ask. "If you were able to escape and go back to Corbyn, why go rogue?"

"I survived," he says. "The rule is, if you are captured, we are supposed to end ourselves. Because I didn't die, he felt I betrayed him. I was sentenced to three years in lockdown."

"Lockdown?" Zel asks.

"It's similar to what Beast had to do for those five years. But imagine a small pit dug into the earth that is only wide enough to lie down in. No sunlight and only a hole to shit and piss in. Twice a day you'd be fed bread and water. I refuse to be locked down, so I broke out."

"And then you found Beast?" Priest asks. "Why?"

A slow smile spreads across Maksim's face. "Little brother has always intrigued me. Corbyn would often mention the son that got away. He often pits us against you by telling us of your accolades and our failures. He made you our enemy without us ever meeting you.

"When I left, I went in search for you. At first, I thought I'd kill the chosen son and find favor with Corbyn again. But the more I discovered about you—about all of you—I realized I didn't want to go back to Corbyn."

The room goes silent. I look at Priest, and he's watching me closely. I can't understand the look on his face. My emotional Rolodex is no use to me right now. Does he want to know how I feel about this? I'm not even sure how I feel yet. Right now, I'm numb.

"I have a question for you," Maksim says to Priest. He leans up in his seat placing his elbows on his knees. "It has always interested me how you were able to get to Beast before Corbyn. How did you do it?"

There is a second of hesitation before Priest speaks. "When I was a kid, I broke into the Church headquarters. They had just come and recruited my little brother. I wanted to know more about the organization, and admittedly, I wanted in."

This is the first time any of us have heard the story of how Priest came into the Church. I always thought they recruited him the same way they recruited us.

"I made it all the way to the top floor of the building before they caught me."

"You broke into one of the most secure buildings in NYC? How old were you?" Hawk asks.

"Ten," Priest replies with a grin. "When I reached the top floor, I stumbled upon something I should never have seen." The Pope was bent over his desk, with who I later realized was a well-known judge behind him. Let's just say they were getting really acquainted with each other."

"Oh shit," Lucien blurts. "That's how you found favor with the Church?"

Priest grins. "The Judge had just been appointed an associate justice on the supreme court by a very conservative republican president. The judge himself had a very public stance against homosexuality. His entire platform was based off him being a devout Christian and family man. If I were to have exposed him, well it wouldn't have ended well."

"Why not just kill you?" I ask. "You knew their secret. It would have been easier."

Priest nods. "I'm pretty sure it crossed their minds, but the judge wanted to know how I got up there. I explained it to him, and I told him that I didn't give a shit who took what up the ass, I just wanted to know how I could join their organization."

"I could see a young Priest saying that." Zel laughs. My brothers join in.

"Both the judge and the Pope took a liking to me." Priest continues. "The judge told me if I vowed to never tell a soul what I saw, he would make sure I made it into the organization. The rest was history. I did favors for him and the Pope throughout my time as Deacon. One of those favors was when I was sent to kill Fem's mother."

I knew this story. It's why I was trying to keep the information from Albany as long as possible.

"Turns out," she says to me. "He killed the wrong person, and my mother is still alive." Now that's news.

"How does this relate to you getting my brother before Corbyn?" Maksim asks, bringing us back to the original topic.

"Well, while I was recruiting my first class, I got a call from that judge. He told me he had a location for a recruit. Someone I needed to get to fast. He told me about Gabriel Taylor. The only reason I think this Corbyn guy didn't find Beast is because he didn't know of Colleen's mental issues. After she got pregnant is when she came off her meds. She went completely off her rockers and ended up moving off the grid with Gabriel. Corbyn wouldn't have known where to find her."

"Who is this judge?" Maksim asks. "How did he know about Gabriel?"

"His name is Robert Shelton, and he is who I need to talk to in order to figure out how we got this excommunication order."

Maksim shakes his head. "Well, I'll be damned. All this time, the answer was under his nose."

"What are you talking about?" I ask.

He grins. "Robert Shelton's real name is Robert Anderson Corbyn. He changed his name when his mother remarried, breaking ties with the Corbyn men. He's your uncle, Beastie."

"Did you know that?" Lucien asks Priest.

We all turn to a shocked looking Priest.

"No. He never told me how he knew you. He just told me that you needed me."

Maksim stands to his feet. "We need to get to Robert. If Corbyn finds out that he has ties to you, he will kill him. And if we're going to get your names cleared, we're going to need him."

Priest pulls out his phone, I'm assuming to call Robert. However, the white door to Doc's operating room opens. I immediately push away from the wall to face Doc. The room grows silent. I hold my breath as I wait for the short man with bushy eyebrows to speak.

Doc removes his gloves and sighs. "She's a very lucky woman. Had that bullet traveled a little further down she would've been gone."

"Thank goodness," Albany gasps, placing her hand on her chest.

Someone pats my shoulder, but I don't turn to look and see who. My heart is racing in my chest and my head fills with white noise. She's alive. My Summer is alive.

"We're going to keep her here for a few days," Doc goes on to say. "She's going to need some blood, so if anyone has A or O type blood, we could really use a donation."

"I'm A+," Zel volunteers. "I can donate."

"Me too," Albany adds.

"As can I," Priest says.

I look down at my hands feeling inadequate. Not even my blood is useful to her.

"If everything goes smoothly, she should be back on her feet in a week or two."

"Thank you, Doc. We appreciate this," Priest walks over and shakes Doc's hand.

"Can I see her?" I ask.

Doc looks to Priest, who subtly nods his head.

"Right this way," Doc steps back, allowing me access to the door.

Before I can take a step forward, Priest steps in front of me. His eyes narrow as he searches my face.

"The moment you step in that room, shit's going to get real again. Quiet your head," he warns.

I dip my chin and walk around him. I needed to see her. Pushing the door open, I enter another stark white room. This one looks like what I imagine an operating room would resemble. Two bright lights shine over her body on the table. Large machines surround the bed. Discarded on the floor are bloody cloths.

I walk over to Summer's body lying on the table. The two dark-haired females that helped Doc with the surgery smile at me. A blanket covers Summer's body. She looks pale, her golden-brown skin looks dull. But most importantly, her chest is rising and falling underneath the cover.

There is blood smeared on her face. I use my hand to wipe it away.

"They tried to take her from you, Gabriel. We should kill them all. Everyone," the sinister voice says in my head.

"We should," I mumble.

"Did you say something?" One of the females in the room asks.

"There's a knife right there. Cut out her heart and watch as she bleeds out. Just like Summer bled out."

I don't realize my hand is on the scalpel until the bite of the blade digs into my palm.

"Oh my goodness, you're bleeding," the woman closest to me says.

I toss the blade back down on the metal tray, causing a clanking sound. Once again, I lost control to the monster in my head. I have to get out of here. I have to get away.

The voice in my head laughs as I quickly make my way out of the operating room. The moment I step back out into the waiting room, all eyes turn to me and silence fills the space.

"Beast, are you okay?" Albany asks.

I don't respond. Instead, I turn and run for the door. The shouting of my name behind me doesn't stop me or slow me down. I run for their lives.

CHAPTER THREE

Allies

Priest

"Have you heard anything?" Lucien asks as soon as I walk into the kitchen at the ghost house.

It's been three days since Beast stormed out of Doc's makeshift hospital.

"No, nothing yet." Even though I've called Robert and left countless voicemails in the last three days, I have yet to get a call back from him.

I'm starting to worry a little. It's not like Robert to disappear without a trace or to go without responding to my calls. I admit, I've never had to call in a favor before, but he would still answer for me.

"Any luck finding Beast?" I ask Lucien.

He's been on Beast duty since he left that day. Although I would've liked to have followed him and brought him back immediately, my intuition and years of dealing with Beast told me to give him his space. Something is off with my son. I've seen him amid his haze many times. I've watched him battle his mother and although she is ruthless, he's always been able to control her. But whoever is in his head now is proving to be a much stronger adversary and much more dangerous.

"No," Lucien says answering my question. "But so far there have been three disciples, and two deacons reported dead. At least we know he's still around the area."

"When will they learn," I say shaking my head. "Approaching Beast now is a death warrant. He's not himself."

Lucien nods his head. Hearing about the brutal ways those Church members have been showing up shows me that Beast is far from okay.

"How is little Gabe?" Lucien asks, distracting me from my thoughts.

Pulling the chair out across from him at the table, I take a seat.

For the first time since I walked into the kitchen, a smile spreads over my face. The best thing about these three days has been the time I've spent with my grandson. Other than the first night he got here, he's adapted well to me and his uncles.

We don't fault him for his breakdown that first night. He was in a new house with strangers and off his routine. It was a lot of change in a short period of time. Not to mention his mom hasn't woken up and his father is missing. Anyone would have struggled with that.

The kid is super fucking smart, funny, and easy to hang with. He's not demanding and doesn't talk much. He seems to just enjoy being in someone's presence.

"He's good," I answer Lucien's question. "A lot happier now that his mom is back under the same roof as him."

Yesterday, we were finally able to move Summer from Doc's to the ghost house. The pain meds she's on have her in and out. She sleeps most of the day.

Lucien and I both turn to the kitchen door at the sound of footsteps. Maksim walks in. He's wearing a black tank top and basketball shorts. It's a bit weird how much he and Beast favor. It isn't just their looks that are so much alike. Yes, they share the same eyes, but it's more of their demeanor that is alike. He even walks the same way Beast does. However, one thing is completely different, Maksim isn't as standoffish as his brother.

"How's Summer?" I ask.

Even though Beast has not shown up, Maksim has proudly taken his brother's place at Summer's side. He sits with her every day, talking and reading to her.

"Same as the day before," he says in his accent. "Doc says he will wean her off the meds tomorrow. She's going to be asking for him."

He doesn't have to explain who *he* is.

"She's still calling out his name in her sleep?" I ask.

It is the most heartbreaking thing to witness. She cries for him and he's not there to console her.

"Yes. More frequently now," Maksim says grabbing a water bottle out of the fridge. He twists off the top before guzzling the liquid down.

I understood Beast's need to be away from us. Whatever is in his head wants to kill us. It was made clear at Doc's when he nearly stabbed me. I know he's keeping his distance for our safety. But I also know that he needs to be here. His family needs him.

"I feel like we need to be doing something," Lucien says pushing his laptop away from him.

"So far, we can't find Beast and you haven't been able to get in contact with Robert. I feel like we're just twiddling our thumbs."

"We are being smart, Twin. Rushing out there now with no plan and no idea what we're up against is stupid. We're smarter than that."

"Yeah, well you don't have a pregnant wife that needs to see her OBGYN." I turn at the sound of Hawk's voice.

He, Many, and Zel are at the entrance of the kitchen.

"He's right, Priest. Malia and Ari both need to see their doctors too. Malia is in her second trimester and Ari isn't far behind," Lucien adds.

"Not until we figure out what we are up against."

The guys sigh, letting out their frustration.

"Look, in all honesty…" Lucien's words get cut off when my phone rings in my pocket.

I quickly pull the device out and hold it up to my ear.

"This is Priest."

"Well, hello, young Nathaniel. It's been a while." Robert's voice comes through the phone.

"Where the hell have you been?" I say through clenched teeth.

He chuckles. "I was out of the country. I'm assuming you're about to cash in one of those favors."

"You bet your ass. We need to talk about—"

"Not over the phone." He cuts me off abruptly. "My flight just landed. Meet me at the house in Boxwood in an hour."

The phone goes dead, letting me know he's disconnected. Placing my phone back in my pocket, I turn to the boys,

"You want action, we got it. Suit up, we're going out."

We were out of the house in twenty minutes. Hawk and Many stayed home with the women. Even though Albany, Ari, and Ms. Reese are highly trained, I still didn't trust leaving them alone at the house. As I told the boys, we still have no idea what we are up against.

Exactly an hour after getting off the phone with Robert, we pulled up to his Tudor style mansion in the suburbs not far outside of NYC.

I step out of the Charger, and button my suit coat. Glancing around, I check out my surroundings. Everything looks clear. The street is mostly vacant. A white Hummer is parked on the side of the road two houses down, but there is no one inside.

Seth comes over to stand beside me by the front of the car.

"Is it just me, or does it seem exceptionally quiet out here?"

It definitely wasn't just him. The silence and the empty street caught my eye as well.

"Let's get inside," I say.

The three of them followed me up to the front door. Before I knock, I realize the door is slightly ajar.

I look over my shoulder, and without a word, I tell them to get out their guns. Pulling my Beretta out of my back holster, I slip the safety off and hold the gun out in front of me. We frame the door, two on each side.

Using my foot, I open the front door. Silence greets us. I give the nod that I'll go in first. I walk through the door, my gun pointed out. Seth comes in behind me.

At first glance the house looks normal. Nothing seems out of place. However, on closer inspection I notice a single drop of blood in front of the closed office door.

"This doesn't look good," Maksim says, standing behind me.

I didn't respond. Instead, I push the door open and step into the office. The sight before me is so graphic, if I didn't know better, I would've thought Beast had been here.

"Oh shit," Zel says, turning away from the sight.

"Not bad work," Seth adds, stepping up beside me. "A little overkill with the tongue."

Nailed to the wall, as if he was portraying Jesus on the cross, is a naked and bruised Robert. His head hangs down between his shoulder blades. His tongue has been removed from his mouth and is now nailed to the wall beside his head. But the most alarming part are the words written in what I assume is his blood on the wall above his head. No More Allies. The initials VC are signed beneath it.

"Victoria," Maksim says somberly beside me. "Outside of me, she and Yohan are Corbyn's most trusted. He must have found out his brother has been the one helping you."

"How did he figure that out?" I ask.

"I'm assuming the phone call." I turn to look at Zel. He's holding up a smashed cell phone in his hand.

"Fuck," Seth roars. "That was our only hope of getting out of this shit."

Staring up at the mutilated body of a person I once considered a friend, I don't have the heart to tell my son that he's right. If we were ever going to get our names off that excommunication order and figure out how to take down Corbyn, Robert was it. Now we are back to ground zero.

Before I could say anything, the large, picturesque window in Robert's office cracks and bullets fly in.

We all take cover. I jump behind the solid oak desk. Maksim slides behind the end of the bookshelf to my right. Seth leaps over the bar in front of me.

"Zel," I call out.

"I'm here. I'm good."

I can't see him because he's somewhere behind me.

"Maksim, Seth?"

"I'm good," Maksim says.

"Flesh wound," Seth groans. "But I'm good."

"Did anyone get a visual of the shooter?"

"No," all three say at the same time.

I peek around the side of the desk and once again bullets fly through the window, this time shattering the glass. I slide back just in time to avoid being shot.

Fuck, who the hell is shooting at us. Flipping around onto my knees I keep my body blocked by the side of the desk as I hold my gun up ready to aim if I need to. Slowly, I peek over the top of the desk.

"Is that a drone?" Maksim asks at the same time I get sight of the shooter.

Sure enough, a black drone hovers over the front yard. It's unlike any drone you would find in a store. The size of a large remote-control car, it's shaped like a rectangle with three sets of spinning blades. The damn thing looks like one of those military choppers.

"Fucking, Tech," Seth grumbles.

"Who is Tech?"

"A member of the Church," I explain to Maksim. "He's most likely here to collect on the excommunication order."

"Wait, I thought you guys were popular at the Church?"

At this, Zel, Twins, and I all laugh.

"You guys were poorly misinformed," Zel says shaking his head. He's standing on the other side of the window, his back to the wall.

"We were hard to digest for most," I try to explain. "Some hated us for our unconventional bond and others hated us because they simply couldn't compare."

"Well, Tech hates us because Lucien hacked into one of his drones when we were kids and found a video of him jacking off to My Little Pony porn. He broadcasted the video in the cafeteria the next day. We all called Tech, Twilight Sparkle Cock for the next few years," Seth shakes his head. "Don't know why he would still be mad though."

I roll my eyes at Seth. Turning my attention back to the window and the drone, I keep my focus on the machine.

A crackling sound like the pushback from a microphone comes out of the drone before a computerized voice speaks.

"Twins, Priest, and Zel, come out with your hands up. Don't make this difficult."

I scoff. One of the things I expected with this excommunication order was that a lot of agents would bank on gaining clout from capturing us. Agents that usually wouldn't get any respect would attempt to make a name for themselves by taking us down. It's why so many keep approaching Beast even though they know they shouldn't. They think the benefits outweigh the risks. They will learn their lesson the hard way.

"Twin, how the hell do we get rid of that thing?" I ask over my shoulder as I keep my eyes on the drone. For now, it continues to hover outside the window.

"According to Lucien, the entire body is made from indestructible metal. Trying to get a bullet to penetrate the body is useless. However, he says there is a small hole on the top of the drone. It will be where the red light is."

Peeking over the top of the desk, I get a quick glance at the red light before the bullets start to fire once again. I duck back down.

"Can anybody get a clear shot of that damn light?"

"Not me," Zel says from his spot from the side of the window.

"Anytime one of us peeks out that damn thing shoots," Maksim growls.

It takes me a second to come up with a plan.

"Seth, feel like being a target?"

Seth grumbles. "Fine, but you got only one chance at this."

"It's all I need," I gloat.

Repositioning myself behind the desk, I prepare to get up.

"Now," I shout to Seth.

I can only hear the movement of Seth behind me as he draws the attention of the drone. The drone starts to shoot at Seth. I jump up from my spot and fire my weapon. Immediately, the drone stops shooting and then starts to spin in circles before dropping to the ground.

"Are you good Seth?"

"Yeah. It missed," he replies.

Before I could get excited and celebrate in our victory, two more appear, firing round after round at us. I drop back behind the desk.

"Fuck, how many of those things does he have?" Maksim shouts over the noise.

"Knowing Tech, probably fifty," Seth replies.

This time the bullets continued to rain into the room.

"How the hell are we going to get out of here?" Zel asks over the loud sound of gunshots pinging off the walls and furniture.

Before I can reply, the bullets suddenly stop. I look up over the desk and the drones have both dropped to the ground.

"Are they malfunctioning?" Maksim asks.

Just then a body comes flying into the office knocking the rest of the glass out the window. We all duck down. Once the coast seems to be clear, I stand back up, gun aimed at the window. Lying on top of the desk is the body of Tech. The claw edge of a hammer is lodged in his mutilated face.

"What the hell?" Zel asks.

I look back up at the window to find Beast standing there. He still has on the same clothes he wore the day he walked out of the hospital. His blonde hair is hanging down in his face, covering most of his features.

He doesn't speak for a long moment. He just stares back at us, breathing heavily.

"You okay?" I finally ask.

He turns his head to the side slightly. The same way he did back at the house when we found Summer. I glance over to Maksim. He's staring at his brother as if he too is trying to get a read on him.

"I need to come home," Beast finally says.

My shoulders immediately drop. I had no idea how much tension I was holding until he spoke.

"Absolutely, son. You can come home."

He nods his head and steps through the window, ducking down to get his large body through the shattered glass.

"How did you find us?" Zel asks Beast.

He takes a small black phone out of his pocket. "I took it off one of the Disciples I killed. They broadcast any sightings of us through an app. Tech spotted your car from a traffic light. He sent out the message, but told everyone it was his kill."

I run a hand over my head. "Fuck, can they trace us back to the ghost house?"

"No. They've only been watching the city, but we should definitely dump your car."

"Wait. Dump whose car?" I ask. "Not my got damn Charger."

Seth pats me on the shoulder. I turn to glare at him. "Sorry, old man. You're going to have to get rid of your first love."

The shit I do for these fuckers.

"Fine. But we're going to need some new wheels to get back home."

"I got us covered," Beast says.

As much as I hated to get rid of my Charger, I knew that it was too well known in the Church community, and it could jeopardize all of us. Despite knowing all of this, it still pissed me off that I had to get rid of the car.

"I think we can chalk this outing up to a bust," Maksim says coming up behind me. "I can guarantee that Victoria swept this house clean. No need to linger. There will be no information left behind."

I assumed as much. Corbyn didn't seem like the type of person that would leave something behind to make it easy for us. I glance over at Roberts' body sprawled across the wall once again. The man was good to me. From the moment he got me into the Church to the moment he sent me to get Beast and my many years as a member of the Church. Despite how we were introduced, he was a good man. He didn't deserve the death he was dealt. I would do all that I could to make the person responsible pay for it.

True to his word, Beast had his chop shop guy come and get the Charger and bring us another car. After glancing over my shoulder one last time at my baby, the five of us loaded into a got damn minivan and headed back to the ghost house. On the way back home, Lucien swept all the traffic cameras in the city clean of us.

CHAPTER FOUR

Wake Up

Summer

The slow beeping sound is driving me crazy. I first noticed it in the dream I was having. It was low at the time, but the more the dream started to fade the louder the noise grew.

Slowly, I open my eyes hoping to find the noise and turn it off. The moment my eyes open, I immediately close them again. The lights are extremely bright. I groan as I try to lift my arm to shield my eyes.

"Whoa. Take it easy," a deep male voice says.

However, the voice isn't foreign to me. I've heard that voice a lot lately. It's in those brief moments when I'm lucid, it's even in my sleep talking to me.

Opening my eyes, I turn my head toward the sound. It takes a moment for my sight to adjust. My breath catches in my throat when I take in the man sitting beside me.

I recognized him from that day in my school parking lot. He's the guy that appeared when that asshole refused to move for me. He's attractive with his square jaw, broad nose, and dark hair. But it's the eyes that have me gasping. I never saw his eyes the day in the parking lot.

"Your eyes?"

He smiles. "I'm Maksim. I'm Beast's brother."

"That explains the parking lot," I croak out.

He chuckles. I attempt to sit up and immediately cry out when sharp pain goes through my shoulder.

"Hey, take it easy." He shoots out of his seat. Wrapping his arms around my waist he helps me sit up. He then places three pillows behind my back.

"Doc said you should move slow for the next few days," he says as he retakes his seat. "He left these pills." He picks up a bottle of medicine and shakes it in front of me.

"No, no meds," I quickly say. He looks confused by my outburst. Apparently, his brother did not tell him about my past.

"I used to be an addict. Opioids were my preferred drug of choice. I try to avoid them as best I can."

He nods his head. Not an ounce of judgement on his face. "Alright, we can get rid of these, and I'll get you something less addictive."

I smile, liking his energy already.

"So, how did you end up on babysitting duty?"

He grins showing off his white teeth. "Actually, I volunteered for it."

I must've looked shocked cause he again laughs before continuing. "Everyone else had their hands full, and I didn't want you to be alone. Beastie was going through some things, so he couldn't be here."

The moment he mentioned Gabriel my heart started racing and so did that beeping sound.

"Is he okay?"

"Relax," Maksim runs a hand through his hair. "Beast is fine."

"And Gabe?"

A wide smile spreads over his face. "Gabe is doing well too. He asks about you every day and even comes to sit with you sometimes."

That makes my heart smile. I can only imagine the fear my baby felt watching me lying here unresponsive. Not only that, but he wasn't home in his normal domain, I know it was probably an adjustment for him.

"What happened to me?" I ask the most obvious question. The last thing I remember is standing at the stove flipping pancakes when all of a sudden, the patio door shattered and then I don't remember much after that.

"You were shot," he says point blank, pointing to my left shoulder. "The way the bullet traveled, you're lucky to be alive."

Damn, that cat analogy must be still in effect, because I'm still using up lives. It's like I owe death something and he keeps trying to collect. It's even more alarming that I was shot in the same shoulder my dad hit. This is the most unlucky shoulder ever.

Scrunching my brow, I ask. "Who shot me?" I want to add 'this time' but I leave that part out.

"Our other brother."

I'm so confused. "I thought Gabriel was close to all his brothers?" I remember the stories he told me about Hawk, Zel, Seth, Lucien and Many. Every story led me to believe they were a tight group.

Maksim shakes his head. "Not those brothers."

For the next twenty minutes, he fills me in on their father and his other siblings, along with the excommunication order on Beast and his brothers.

I feel like I've missed a lifetime of information rather than the four days he says I've been out. Even though there has been a lot going on, and I should be more concerned about the fact that I was shot and nearly killed, my only concern is Gabriel.

"How is Gabriel taking all of this?" Like his son, Gabriel also doesn't do well with too many changes. Finding out that not only does he have a father and a bunch of siblings, but they're also trying to kill him, is probably messing with his head.

Maksim scratches his chin. His gaze bouncing to the wall over my head. I've only known this man for a few minutes, but I can already tell whatever he's about to say isn't exactly the truth. The way he looks over my head and avoids eye contact is a dead giveaway.

"He's doing fine."

I didn't have to see the lie on his face to know it was one. I know Gabriel enough to know he's not alright.

Before I could respond, the room door opens, and I see the sweet face of my baby boy.

"Mama!" Gabe shouts before running into the room.

I prepare myself for him to leap onto the bed. However, just as he gets close, the deep voice that has my heart beating and my thighs squeezing calls out his name.

"Gabe. Easy. Mama's still hurt."

I look up toward the open door and my eyes connect to Gabriel's. Every time I see him, it's as if the air in my lungs is being sucked out. Seeing him now feels like the time I first saw him at that restaurant after five years. I can't take my gaze off him.

He stares back at me just as hard as I look at him. Gabe climbs up in the bed and gently wraps his arms around my neck. I shut my eyes, basking in the joy of my son hugging me without me asking or hugging him first. He leans back on his knees and smiles up at me.

"You were sleeping a lot."

I hold back the tears that are fighting to fall. "I know. I'm up now though. What's been going on?"

He smiles as he starts to tell me about his papa Priest and his uncles along with his cousin Emory.

The entire time he's talking, my eyes keep going back to the doorway where his father is still silently watching me. He has not once made a move to come into the room.

Finally, Gabe takes a break in his conversation. "Wow, seems like you've been having fun."

He smiles at me.

"Yeah, I have a lot more family now, mama."

My heart cracks open at his words. Even when he was spending time with my mother and sister he never once referred to them as family. He knew who they were. He understood that my mom was his grandma and

Raina was his aunt, but he never called them family. Hearing him say this about Gabriel's brothers and father really warms my soul.

"You're right," I say, my voice cracking. "You do."

"Hey, nephew," Maksim says getting Gabe's attention. "How about you and I go find papa Priest and let your mom and dad have a few minutes."

Gabe nods before climbing off my bed. Maksim stands and holds out a hand for Gabe. Gabe takes the outstretched hand and they both walk side by side to the door. Maksim stops in front of Gabriel. Although nothing is said, they stare at each other for a moment letting me know something is being communicated. Finally, Gabriel moves aside, and Maksim and Gabe walk out the room.

Gabriel still does not enter. I study his face. A sinking feeling hits my gut. I know that look in his eyes. He's scared. Gabriel and I have had many conversations about his fear of losing me and Gabe. He always feared he would be the one that would hurt us unintentionally. Even though he didn't pull that trigger, I already know he is taking the blame for it.

The look on his face tells me he wants to run. But he won't. He can't, because he promised me he would stay.

"Summer," the way he says my name, as if it pains him, makes my heart beat erratically. The beeping in the room matches the rapid thumping against my chest.

"You know getting shot hurts like hell," I say, my brain going into overdrive. The mouth diarrhea is about to spew.

"Summer," he says again pushing away from the doorframe.

I continue as If I didn't hear him. If I don't let him speak, he can't say anything I don't want to hear.

"But at least I have another story to tell. I can now retire the 'my daddy shot me story.' Plus, this one sounds better anyway. I got shot by my boyfriend's brother has a better draw to it than daddy issues." I chuckle at my own dark joke.

"Summer." He stands at the foot of my bed. Those gorgeous eyes staring at me with so much regret and pain.

"Talk about an ice breaker right. I'll be all the rave at parties."

"Summer," he calls my name once again. This time I shut my eyes unwilling to see that look on his face.

"Stop it," I demand.

Silence fills the room.

"Whatever you think you're going to say to me, I don't want to hear it." I finally open my eyes and glare at him.

"I love you," he says. However, those words don't bring me the joy they usually would.

His tone is off, and that pain and regret are still in his eyes.

"I love you too, Gabriel."

He shakes his head. "You will never understand how much I love you. I love you more than I love my own life. You and Gabe are the best things that have ever happened to me. But."

Just that one simple word has tears spilling down my face. He hasn't even said anything else, but pressure starts to build in my chest. My breath seems to be caught in my lungs.

He continues, ignoring my tears and pain. "We can't be together."

I shake my head refusing to accept his words. "No. No. I will not accept that. I won't let you run away from us."

He shoves his hands down the front pockets of his jeans. "It has to be this way."

"It doesn't," I shout. "Yes, I got shot. But I'm still here. Gabe and I are both still here."

He turns away from me, staring at the wall to my left.

"This is over."

I gasp as my hands begin to shake. The tears fall faster now. My brain runs through so many emotions. I question myself and my values. I question if I'm at fault and what makes me so disposable to so many people. How can you tell me you love me and then toss me aside in the same sentence.

"You promised," I choke out through my tears. "You promised you wouldn't leave me again."

He still doesn't turn to look at me. His eyes are bloodshot red, and his shoulders are almost touching his ears they are so tensed.

"I know," he simply replies.

I wait for him to say something else. For him to explain how he can so easily throw away what we have. Yet, he doesn't say anything more.

"Please, Gabriel. Please don't do this." I hated that I'm reduced to begging this man. My pride is yelling at me to let him go if he doesn't want to be here. But my heart is much louder right now. It is hemorrhaging in my chest.

"It's done," he says it as if it's so easy for him.

Is it that simple for him to walk away from me? My entire world is crumbling because the man I love, the man I saw myself spending the rest of my life with is telling me we can't be together. How is he able to walk away from me so calmly.

Gabriel turns and walks to the door. My tears continue to flow down my face as I fight to catch my breath.

He stops at the door without turning to me. "If you need anything, I'll be here."

"I need you," I whisper.

He turns and looks at me over his shoulder. "I would give you the world, Summer. But I can't give you that."

Fighting back my tears, I lift my chin. "Then you have nothing to offer me."

Gabriel is silent for a moment. He then dips his head and walks out of the room shutting the door behind him.

And just like that, I fall apart. My shoulders shake as sobs rake through my body. My wound burns but I don't care because my heart hurts worse.

Not even seconds later, the door opens and Maksim walks in. He doesn't say anything as he shuts the door and makes his way over to his chair. He takes a seat, hands me a tissue and sits back without saying a word. I now know what that look was about before he left. He knew this was going to happen. Which is also why he took Gabe out.

For longer than I'd like to admit, I cried. I cried until there were no more tears to fall. I cried until my head and my injury hurt so bad I could no longer take the pain. When Maksim finally left my room that night, I took one of the pain pills the doctor left.

Oblivion pulled me into its embrace. Darkness took me under, and the joy of dullness swallowed me. The feeling was everything I remembered it to be. Why did I ever give it up?

CHAPTER FIVE

Demon

Beast

I pound my bare fists against the bag, ignoring the smeared blood I leave behind and the pain in my knuckles.

"You're a fool," the demon in my head growls.

I've grown to call the voice a demon. That's what it reminds me of. An ungodly being that only seeks destruction and death.

"Shut up," I grumble as I once again slam my fists into the bag.

It's been a week since I left Summer's room after calling it off. Since then, I spend my days down here in the gym trying to quiet the demon in my head. At night, I sit outside her door listening to her soft crying. For the longest I fought every urge I had to go in that room. Five nights ago, I'm glad I broke down and finally went in. Finding her kneeling in her bathroom crying as she poured the pills doc gave her down the toilet was hard to witness. But I needed to see it. I walked in that room that night to take back everything I said, but seeing the damage I do to her reminded me why I can't have her back. I quickly slipped back out without her ever knowing I was there.

"You broke up with her allowing her the chance to find another. He will love her, touch her, and make her cry out his name while he fucks her raw."

43

Shutting my eyes, I fight hard to quiet the demon. The vision of what he just said plays in my head. An unseen man strokes inside of Summer as she moans with pleasure. Her eyes take on that glazed look it has whenever I am buried deep inside her. She whispers the words I love you to the faceless man.

When I open my eyes, I'm standing outside the gym with a barbell in my hands. I drop the weight and stumble backward. My back hits the wall as I slide down to my ass.

The demon laughs in my head. "*Kill her so that she may never know another man.*"

Placing my hands to my head I beat at my temples. "Mother, where are you?" I again find myself begging for the voice of my mother to return.

"*Mother is not here.*" The low chuckle of the demon floats through my head.

Shutting my eyes, I slam my head back against the wall. "Get out of my fucking head," I growl.

"You okay, son?"

I open my eyes to find Priest standing before me. He has on workout clothes. His brow is arched as he stares at me.

I swallow, fighting back the demon in my head. "I'm good. I was just...ugh... letting off some steam."

"Hmmm," he hums. "Is that why your knuckles are bleeding?"

I look down at my hands, seeing the damage I've done to them. I don't answer Priest. There isn't much I can say.

"Let's go get them bandaged up," he says turning his back to me.

Standing up from the floor, I wipe the bloody knuckles on my shorts. "I'm good, Priest."

"No, you're not," he snaps turning back to face me. "But I'm not going to beg you to tell me what's going on. However, I am going to take you upstairs and clean those wounds."

I go to argue with him again and he holds up a hand to cut me off.

"You have a son here, Beast. One that's going to notice your hands. And although he will see the bandages too, it won't be as shocking as looking at your raw knuckles."

Feeling like an idiot I drop my head. I didn't think about how my actions would affect Gabe. I don't want to traumatize him any more than I already have. I'm already the reason he had to see his mother lying on the kitchen floor.

Nodding, I reply. "Okay."

I follow Priest up the stairs toward the kitchen. We all thought Priest was crazy when he had this house built. It's an architecturally contemporary home with clean, minimal lines. The house is three levels with ten bedrooms and ten and a half bathrooms. It has a theater room, home office, full gym, shooting range, panic room, and a sex room for Priest.

The house is surprisingly quiet for a Sunday night. It's nearly eight o'clock. There is no one out in the hallways. Even the dogs are missing.

"Where is everyone?" I ask as we enter the kitchen.

I take a seat at the island. Priest goes to the sink and reaches under the counter. He pulls out a fully stocked first aid kit before coming over to where I'm sitting.

"Fucking," he says without thought. "The kids and the dogs are in the theater room with Fem and Ms. Reese. Zel and Maksim are probably relaxing. But everyone else is doing what grown folks do when there's not shit else going on."

Nodding my head, I don't reply to that. The image of Summer and the unknown man pops in my head again along with the laughter of the demon.

"Whatever the fuck is going on in your head, you've got to fight it."

I open my eyes to look at Priest, wondering how he knows where my thoughts went. Looking down, I realize my hand is wrapped around his wrist with a tight grip. I release him and shake my head.

"I'm trying," I simply say holding my hands out to him palm side down.

Priest uses a small spray bottle and sprays my knuckles. The sting lets me know there must be some type of antiseptic in the bottle.

"It's different from your mother?" he asks.

I nod before replying. "Yes."

"Is it new?" He puts away the spray and grabs the ointment out of the box.

"No," I admit. Although the voice was mostly silent, it's not new.

He dips his chin placing the ointment away, he brings out the bandages and starts to wrap my hands.

"And what does it want?" he asks, looking into my eyes.

"Everything that I love."

I don't have to explain that to Priest. He understands what I mean. If the demon only wanted destruction, I could manage that. But this voice wants to take everything from me. It isn't strangers that I'm brutally murdering when I close my eyes. No, it is the death of my brothers, Priest, and Summer that plague me. The demon does not want me, it wants those around me.

Priest sits back in his seat watching me closely. "How much control do you have over it?" he finally asks.

"Right now, I'm managing."

He's silent again. "And when you can't?"

"I'll be so far away from this house Lucien will never be able to find me."

He nods his head. "I'm not going to tell you how to deal with this because I don't know what it's like. But I know you, Beast. I know what you're capable of. You can win this battle. The moment you realize that your greatest weapons are behind these four walls, you will be unstoppable. It doesn't matter if the voice belongs to this thing or your mother."

He stands taking the first aid kit back to the kitchen sink. I sit with his words. If only it was that simple. The best thing I can do for everyone in this house is leave.

"Coward," the voice whispers.

Approaching footsteps has my head lifting toward the open doorway of the kitchen.

"Is every room in this house this bright?"

Her voice has my heart racing and my cock twitching in my workout shorts. The way this woman has complete control over me should be studied. Even when I know I don't deserve her. It's been so long since I've heard her speak. I shut my eyes to revel in the sound of it.

"Yes they are," Maksim's voice has my eyes popping open. "You will get used to it."

I stand from my seat when I spot Maksim walk into the kitchen carrying Summer in his arms. She's wearing a long T-shirt and tiny shorts. She hasn't noticed me yet, but I haven't been able to take my eyes off her. The way her legs dangle over his arms. The way her good arm wraps around his neck as her injured arm rests against her chest.

My nostrils flare as I watch them.

"He wants to fuck her. You should skin him alive," the demon growls.

I take a step in their direction, ready to do as the demon says.

"Beast," Priest barks my name.

I turn to glare at him. His eyes narrow as he slowly shakes his head.

"Hey brother," Maksim says getting my attention. Summer has yet to look at me. In fact, she is looking everywhere but at me.

"Summer was getting a little stir crazy and wanted to come out of the room," Maksim explains. "She tried to walk, but after standing she got a little lightheaded, so I carried her in here."

I don't miss the fact that he's trying to explain why he has his hands on her. I'm grateful that he was looking out for her, but I still didn't like to see her in his arms.

Summer pats Maksim's shoulder. "Thanks, Sim. You can put me down now. I think I can take it from here."

"She's given him a nickname," the demon points out. *"She's fucking him."*

Taking a deep breath, I ignore the demon's words in my head.

Maksim lowers her legs to the ground before letting her go. She walks over to Priest, holding her hand out.

"Hi, I'm Summer. I'm assuming you're papa Priest?"

Priest grins before shaking her hand. "That would be me."

"It's good to finally meet you. Gabe talks about you a lot."

It hurts to see her ignoring me the way that she is. I want her to look at me. I need her to see me.

"He's a good kid," Priest says letting her hand go. "I would've come in to meet you sooner but I was giving you your....space."

Everyone in the house knew I had broken up with Summer. I guess they all felt her sadness and were giving her a wide berth. Although, the women of the house have been in to introduce themselves and see her multiple times. My brothers have all been reluctant except for Maksim.

The kitchen grows silent.

"How are you?" I ask.

Her body goes ridged at the sound of my voice. I watch as the smile falls from her face.

She turns to me. Although there are no tears on her face, her eyes are still red and puffy.

"I'm good, Beast," she replies coldly. "So, Sim, how about—"

"What did you call me?" My question silences the kitchen once again. I can feel Priest's gaze on me, but I don't turn away from Summer. She isn't looking at me, she's facing my brother.

"Like I was saying," she ignores my question. "I want to see the rest of the house."

"Don't *ever* call me that," I growl.

There was something wrong hearing her call me that name. I am not Beast to her. I am not the man the Church made me when I am with her. I'm Gabriel. She is the only person that knows the real me.

"What should I call you then, Beast?" She turns to me and glares. "Obviously not Gabe, because that's what I call my son and since you opted out of being an active father in his life that doesn't seem to fit."

"Uh, Summer maybe we should stick a pin in this till later—" Priest says.

But in true Summer fashion she's not listening.

"I would call you Gabriel, but I shout that out while we're fucking and since you decided you no longer wanted to be with me, I felt that might not be appropriate either. So, what should I call you, Beast?"

I growl before charging toward her. Maksim steps in front of me. I go to shove him out the way when a piercing alarm goes off through the house.

"Fuck," Priest shouts. "Someone just got through our security."

All my anger drains. I forget about Summer and our argument. Right now, our house could be surrounded by Church members ready to shoot first and ask questions last. Or worse, Corbyn has found us.

"Go to the basement," I say to Summer. "Don't come out until one of us comes to get you."

Before she can comply or argue, Lucien runs into the kitchen with nothing but his underwear and a gun. He's soon followed by Hawk and Zel. We all headed toward the front door.

"How the hell did this happen, Twin?" Priest asks as he stops by the staircase. He twists one of the banisters counterclockwise and then clockwise. The fourth step opens up. Priest pulls out a drawer filled with guns and knives. He tosses me a knife and gun and then hands Maksim a gun before grabbing one for himself.

"I was a little occupied. My apologies," Lucien says as he goes into the living room and turns on the TV.

We follow him inside. He presses a few buttons on the remote and the outside of Priest's house comes on the screen. The first view is the backyard. It's empty. He then checks the side of the house and when he doesn't see anything there, he pulls up the camera on the front of the house. Parked in the driveway is a silver BMW with its driver's door wide open.

"Who the hell pulls into the driveway to do a hit?" Zel asks.

Suddenly, banging at the front door has all of us turning that way.

"I'm giving you five seconds to open this door and tell me where my best friend is or I'm calling the cops," the familiar voice shouts through the door.

I groan, causing everyone to look at me.

The banging comes again. "I have a bat, and I know how to use it."

"You might as well let her in. She's not going to go away," I say.

"Who is it?" Hawk asks.

"Trina," Summer's voice comes from behind me. Apparently, she did not listen to my directions.

"I'm guessing my cellphone is somewhere in this house," she asks.

"Yeah, Gabe has it," Lucien replies.

"We always share our location. Sorry guys," Summer apologizes.

"I'm about to bust the windows out this big fancy ass house," Trina yells once more through the door.

Summer cringes, and says, "We really should let her in. She will definitely break your windows."

CHAPTER SIX

Bestie

Summer

I'm sitting on the couch facing Trina. Gabe is fast asleep with his head in her lap after he spent an hour telling his godmother all about his new family.

Once Gabe fell asleep, I was able to give her the watered-down short version of what's going on. I'm now waiting for her to say something.

"So," she starts. "You mean to tell me you're trapped in a house with nothing to do for an unknown amount of time with all those fine ass men I just met?"

I shrug, not sure where she's going with this. "Yeah, I guess so."

She shakes her head, and then looks up at the ceiling with prayer hands. "God, I'm just asking that the blessings you give to others you will give them to me."

I shove her arm as I laugh. "Really, girl? That's all you took away from what I said?"

"Summer, did you see those men?" She whispers lowering her voice. She glances over her shoulder. Even though we are alone, I'm pretty sure they aren't far away from us.

"Especially the older guy with the gray hair. You know I like older men."

Shaking my head, I roll my eyes. "I think he's married. Just like you."

Maksim has been giving me the rundown of the house. I know that mostly everyone here is either married or dating. I've yet to officially meet any if the guys outside of Maksim and Priest. Emory and Malia came to see me the day after I woke up. Apparently, the brother her boyfriend was looking for was Gabriel. The other ladies of the house have also introduced themselves.

Trina waves me off sinking back into the sofa. "I know how to look and not touch."

She gets comfortable before she looks me over. Her eyes narrow.

"Are you okay? You look off." One of the issues of having a best friend that knows you so well is that she knows when something is wrong.

Slowly, being careful with my shoulder, I lean back on the couch beside her.

"I relapsed."

Trina leans up so fast she almost knocks my baby on the floor. She readjusts him in her lap before speaking. "Bitch, What?"

"Relax," I say holding up my good hand. "The doctor prescribed me Percocet. I initially turned them down, but I had a weak moment and took them for two days. But I fought the demon and flushed them down the toilet on the third day."

Flushing those pills was harder than getting out of that bed by myself. However, I knew it was what I needed. When I found myself impatient for my son to leave the room for the night so I could toss back a pill, I realized I was losing a battle. And no matter how much my heart hurt, no man was worth going back down that dark road again and jeopardizing my son.

The next morning after flushing the addictive pills down the toilet, there was a bottle of extra strength Tylenol beside my bed. Someone knew my struggles with opioids and got me a safer alternative. I'm still not sure who placed those pills there, but I was thankful.

Trina cuts her eyes away before looking back at me. "I'm proud of you for tossing the pills and telling me."

I nod, happy that I had a friend that had my back.

"What caused you to fall off the wagon?"

Sighing, I reply. "He called it off." I can feel the tears ready to fall again. I look up to keep them at bay. "I know it's a stupid reason to let five years of hard work wash down the drain just for a man."

"Not just any man," she says placing a hand on my knee. "Your child's father, and the man that you love. Broken hearts hurt like hell. I can vouch for that."

She leans back. Our shoulders touch. She gently slides her fingers between mine on my injured hand while her other strokes Gabe's curls. Just having her touch and her strength eases me a little.

"I know why he's running away from us. He blames himself for me getting shot."

"Rightfully so."

"Trina," I turn and glare at her.

"What? Look, one of his looney half siblings tried to kill you over some beef between the two of them. I'm not saying he's fully to blame, or he should beat himself up over it, but I understand why he is blaming himself."

With a shake of my head, I understand his thought process too, but that doesn't mean I agree with it. Like I said, he didn't pull the trigger and him not being with me didn't stop making me a target.

I explain this thought to Trina.

"You're right. But you know men think differently. Besides, I believe him breaking up with you is more of his punishment not yours."

Turning to look at her, I lift my brow. "What do you mean?"

"The very few encounters I've had with baby daddy told me that not only is he madly in love with you, but he's also very cautious around you. Like, he thought that at any moment he would wake up and it would all have been a dream. He looked at you as if you were a gift he wasn't worthy of. You getting shot by one of his enemies proved his theory right. Because you were injured, he thinks he doesn't deserve you."

"That's insane."

"Duh," she shrugs. "But he's a man. You know they're all stupid."

I don't argue or correct her for generalizing men.

"How do I change his mind?"

"You don't," she says bluntly. "You let him stew in his stupidity until he realizes he can't live without you."

Knowing what I know about Gabriel, I don't think that plan will work. He strikes me as the type that even if he realized he couldn't be *without* me, he would still never be *with* me. He's stubborn.

Sighing, I lay my head back against the couch. "I don't know. Part of me wishes I could just take my baby and run."

She laughs. "We both know he'd hunt you down and drag your ass back."

At that, I had to laugh because she's right. No matter what Gabriel says about our relationship status, he wouldn't let me disappear from him.

"Besides," she goes on to say. "If what you said is true, you need to be here with these people where it's safe."

"You mean to tell me you and Mr. James wouldn't keep me safe?" Although I had no plans of running, I still make the joke.

Trina waves my words off. "You know James and I would go to hell and back for you and Gabe. But sexy grandpa and fine ass uncles seem to be better suited for the job."

I chuckle but sober quickly. Leaning a little closer to her I whisper. "I feel a little out of place here. I don't know these people and the only connection I have is to their son and brother who I am no longer with. Maksim has been really great to me, but even he is new to them. What if they realize I'm not worth the headache to keep alive. They might toss me out on the street."

"If that's the case, you call us and we'll come get you, but Summer, you're overthinking. You're going to be fine. What's not to love about you?"

I look at her and quirk a brow. Trina has known me all my life, she knows who I am. She tosses her head back and laughs.

"You might have a point. But just remember, they'd never get rid of Gabe and you two are a packaged deal." We both laugh at her joke.

For another hour and a half, I spent time with my best friend. Before she left, Priest reminded her that she can't tell anyone where I am. She doesn't even need to let them know she's spoken to me and under no circumstance should she come back to this house. Lucien even showed her how to wipe this last location from her GPS and he set up an app on hers and my phones where our calls to each other can't be tracked.

Before she left, Trina told me that she wasn't the only one looking for me. Apparently, my mother has been trying to get in touch with me too. She even called Trina looking for me. I'm not yet ready to speak to my mother.

By the time I was climbing into my bed, it was close to midnight. Gabe decided to sleep with me tonight instead of in his shared room with Emory. He was fast asleep on the other side of the king size bed.

Maksim had not too long left the room. He usually sits with me until I am ready to call it a night. Movement underneath my door has me climbing back out of bed and walking over to it. I pull the door open only to come face to face with Gabriel.

No matter how hurt or angry I am with this man, the sight of him will always have my heart hammering and my breath catching in my throat.

He doesn't speak or move a muscle. He only stares down at me. Without speaking a word, I know what he wants. I roll my eyes as I turn and head back for my bed, leaving the door open. Everything inside of me is telling me to send his ass on his way. I shouldn't allow him his comforts. Yet, I don't say anything. The soft sound of the door closing behind me and then the ruffling of his shoes against the carpet tells me he entered the room.

Once I climb into bed, I spot him taking a seat in the corner of our room. His back is to the wall, and he can see the entirety of the room along with the door. I don't know who he is protecting us from considering we are in a house full of his family and 80% of them are trained killers. Still, I don't deny him this small access to us.

Sliding down in bed, I wince at the pain in my shoulder.

"Move slower," his deep voice says.

I scoff. "Now I'm supposed to believe you care about my pain?"

He flinches at my words, his light eyes staring at me.

"I'm sorry—"

"Don't," I cut off his apology. "I'm only allowing you to sleep in here because I know it comforts you and unfortunately your presence still calms me. But I don't want to talk. And I definitely don't want to hear your meaningless apology."

Even though what Trina said made perfect sense and I know he's torturing himself, I didn't want to hear his apology. He chose to run when he promised he wouldn't. No, he didn't leave like he did the night we made Gabe, but he is still running.

Turning off the lamp, I shroud the room in darkness. The only sound besides the whirring of the ceiling fan is the soft snoring of my baby boy.

"You know you can't leave, right?" he says, letting me know he was somewhere listening to my conversation with Trina. The way he says it, it was almost like a threat. It wasn't just a reminder, but a warning that what Trina said was true. No matter where I went, he'd find me and drag me back.

Sighing, I reply into the dark. "I know."

He doesn't say anything else.

I try to quiet my thoughts. This was the hard part of the day. It's why I started taking those pills. The last three months play back in my head. The time I spent with him, the way he made me feel so seen and desired, the way he knew me better than most people in my life. The way he held me at night when we would lay in the bed together. The way he made love to me like our souls were connecting or he was afraid he'd never get the chance to do it again. Even the way he looked at me when he asked me to have another baby for him. All of it plays back in my head like one of those sad romance movies no one watches more than once.

My heart again feels like it's breaking. The tears come anew. I know what Trina said, but his refusal to be with me still feels as if I'm the issue. As if I'm the one not worthy.

As silent as I try to be, my sniffles fill the room. He never says a word. Eventually, I fell asleep, my face soaked in tears.

same room with them. Not like I've been able to be around anyone.

CHAPTER SEVEN

Royal Crown

Beast

The last three nights, Summer has allowed me to sleep in her room. And although she hasn't cried since that first night, I can still feel her sadness. It feels as if my skin is being peeled back inch by inch. But it is what I deserve.

Gabe's giggles have me tuning back in. He and Emory are in the backyard chasing bubbles from Emory's new bubble machine along with a small dog and four German Shepherds.

Although we are all locked in this house, it has been harder for the kids. Especially Gabe. He doesn't understand why we can't leave. So, everyone has tried to accommodate him and Emory. We've purchased balls, board games, movies, toys, anything we can think of to keep them happy. Even Summer, who still needs her rest, spent all day yesterday watching Disney movies with them.

"Are you guys ready for some lunch?" I ask.

They both stop in the middle of the yard and run up to me.

"Hulk, can we have chicken nuggets?"

"We have to see what Emory's mom is cooking."

Emory starts moving her hands. "My mom is making cookies just for you." she signs to Gabe.

I relay her message to him.

"Yay, come on doggies," he cheers and rushes into the house. Emory and all five dogs follow close behind him.

I step into the home and make my way into the kitchen. All the women are here. I haven't really spoken to any of them. Other than Albany, I don't actually know them. I know who belongs to who, but I haven't talked to them.

Albany's twin with the red hair seems the most skittish around me. I know she is Hawk's wife. The woman with the soft curves belongs to Seth and Lucien. Only thing I know about her, is that my son adores her and she's Emory's mom. The girl with the blue dyed tips in her hair is Many's girlfriend. She talks a lot and blurts out random facts. When we were first introduced, she told me every famous person she knew with the first name Gabriel. The older woman is Ms. Reese, who I found out is Albany and Hawk's wife's mother that was supposed to be dead.

The most important woman in the room draws my gaze. Summer is sitting at the island. Her long braids with the curly pieces hang down her back. She's in another oversized shirt that clearly doesn't belong to her. For the first time, it stands out to me that the shirt isn't hers.

"Whose shirt are you wearing?" The kitchen gets quiet when I ask my question. All eyes turn to me except hers. She continues to look down at her phone.

"I asked you a question."

She still does not look up at me.

"Mommy, Hulk is talking to you," Gabe says standing beside his mother.

She turns to him with a beautiful smile. "I hear him, baby. But Hulk has no right to worry about me or what I'm wearing." She looks up at me and glares. "I am no longer his concern."

"Look how she treats you. She's flaunting another man's clothes in your face. She doesn't respect you. Cut her throat out," the demon whispers. *"Cut all their throats out. They're laughing at you."*

"Gabriel, what are you doing?" Summer's voice brings me out of my haze.

Somehow, I'm no longer standing at the doorway like I was. I'm right beside her now, crowding her space. When did I move? Glancing around the room, all the women seem to be watching me cautiously. When I look to Albany, her eyes are narrowed at me as if she's expecting me to do something.

I take a step back, placing space between myself and Summer. I need to get out of the kitchen.

The demon in my head laughs. I escape around the corner, placing my back against the wall. I shut my eyes and fight to quiet the voice.

"Okay, I don't care what any of you say, that man scares the s.h.i.t out of me," Hawk's wife says.

"He's not bad," Summer quickly comes to my defense. "He's actually a good guy. He just isn't himself right now."

"Yeah," Albany adds. "He's not himself."

Pushing away from the wall, I head for the front door, needing to get far away from this house and Summer.

"Beast?" Priest stops me before I can leave.

I turn to face him. He eyes me wearily.

"You okay?" he asks.

I nod.

"Well, come on. Phoenix is back, we need to talk."

I follow Priest into his downstairs office. Already inside are Lucien, Hawk, and Zel, sitting on the leather sofa in the corner of the room. Many is sitting on the windowsill with his back against the glass. An older black man I've never met is sitting on the edge of Priest's desk. Maksim is sitting in one of two chairs in front of Priest's desk. Priest takes his seat in his office chair. I close the door behind me and lean my back against the wall beside it.

"Okay," Priest starts. "We're all here. What did you find out?" he directs his question to the older man.

"Looks like this has been in the making for a while. That order was in the works nine months ago."

"What would've triggered them to put out an excommunication order on us nine months ago?" Zel asks leaning up from his seat.

"Hawk," Lucien answers. "Nine months ago, Hawk went rogue. Pope was on our ass to bring him in."

"It would explain that feeling I kept getting around Luca. I always felt as if he had something up his sleeve those last few times we met. It would also explain why he threatened to retire me. Luca did this," Priest says.

Maksim shakes his head. "Your Pope might have sent out the decree, but I'm telling you he didn't have the power to make that call alone."

"So, we're back to Corbyn putting this in action?" I ask.

Maksim leans forward, resting his elbows on his knees. "Possibly, but no one person owns the Church. As much power as Corbyn has, not even he could make that call alone. He would need approval from the family heads."

"You're telling me the entire Royal Crown has it out for us?" Lucien asks.

"I doubt it," the older guy I'm assuming is Phoenix says. "I run in the same circles as these people. Most of them have their heads so far up their own asses they couldn't care less what's going on around them."

"He's right," Maksim adds. "To get a bill like an excommunication passed, you need two things. First, you need a handful of the family heads to sign the bill. Once you have your signatures, the bill goes before the committee, which consist of the family heads, to agree on it.

"However, if there is no opposition, the bill may only need two or three signatures to get passed. And Beast can confirm, though the RC used the

Church for their crimes, they didn't really care about you guys. Killing off six of you wouldn't lose them any sleep."

"Okay," Lucien shrugs. "Now we just have to haunt down everyone on that committee and kill them."

"Whoa," Phoenix says holding up his hands in surrender. "I don't doubt you guys are capable, but that's not wise."

"What would you have us do then?" Hawk questions rubbing a hand through his hair. "We can't just sit here like this doing nothing."

Priest holds his hands up. "He's not saying that, Hawk. He's saying we need another approach."

"Absolutely," Phoenix cosigns. "You don't need to go after all the heads, you just need to talk to the ones that signed that bill. If you can convince them to withdraw their signatures, the excommunication order will get tossed out."

For the first time, we seem to have a plan. For the last two weeks it feels like we've been twiddling our thumbs around this house. No matter how big this home is, it will never be big enough. I need to get out of these four walls.

"Yes, you need to feed me before I feast inside this home," the demon voice in my head grumbles.

"Do you really think we can talk them into withdrawing their signatures?" Zel asks.

"In my dealings with the RC, I've learned there's one thing they value more than anything else."

"What's that?" Many asks.

"Secrets and favors. These people have more money than they know what to do with. But what they don't have around them is loyalty. And the talents you boys offer is something they will want greatly."

"He's right," Priest says. "It's how I got on Robert's good side. I did him favors and was always loyal to him and he made sure nothing happened to me in the Church."

"Alright, then how do we find out who signed that bill?" I ask, stepping away from the wall.

I was optimistic about this new plan. It gave me something tangible I could do.

"Your Pope would have a copy of the bill," Maksim says.

Zel sighs and Hawk sinks back on the couch.

"Well, we're back to square one," Many says in his nasally voice.

"We killed the last Pope six weeks ago," Priest explains to Maksim.

"Wouldn't the new one know," Maksim suggests.

"He would, but they haven't appointed a new one yet. Some type of delay," Phoenix says rubbing his chin. "But what about Fox's records keeper? Don't they still have those?"

"What's a records' keeper?" Lucien asks.

"Every time a new Pope is chosen, he picks a record keeper. No one knows who he is. It's the person that would keep all the Pope's dealings and secrets. This person is appointed so that nothing important ever dies with a Pope," Priest explains.

"How do we find the records' keeper?" Zel asks.

"Luca would have a copy of the contract the record keeper signed. It would be kept outside of the Church since it's supposed to be top secret."

"He's been dead six weeks. I'm sure they cleaned out his apartment," Lucien states.

Priest shakes his head. "No, they haven't."

"How do you know?" I ask.

Priest rolls his eyes as he stands to his feet. "Because I'm that asshole's next of kin. Hawk, Maksim, Beast, and Many, you're with me. Zel and Lucien, I need you guys to watch the satellite. You see any heat coming our way you let us know."

"We got you," Lucien said.

"I'm heading back out," Phoenix says getting to his feet. "I'm more helpful to you out in the streets. I'll keep my ear to the ground for any more information."

Priest and Phoenix shake hands.

"Thanks for all the help.

Phoenix grins. "We're family now. That's what we do. Speaking of," he winks at Priest. "Let me go speak to my daughters."

Phoenix nods to all of us before exiting the room.

"Alright, the goal is to go out and get back in as quick as possible. Let's go."

We head out of Priest's office. Hopefully, this outing turns out better than their last one.

CHAPTER EIGHT

Disciples

Beast

Pulling the van up to the curb, I turn the car off. We all climbed out. I step onto the sidewalk beside Priest.

"I hate that fucking minivan," he grumbles. "I have five other cars in my garage at home. We could take any of those."

"We like the minivan," Many says in his British voice. "We have a lot more room in the back."

Priest glares at Many.

"Plus, we need transportation that isn't traceable back to any of us and one we don't mind losing," I say.

"Yeah, because I highly doubt you want your Bentayga in a shootout," Hawk chuckles.

"Damn right," Priest says leading the way inside of the high-rise apartment.

The front doorman greets us as we enter. We take the elevator instead of the stairs this time since we're going to the 20th floor. As soon as the doors to the elevator close, we all pull out our weapons. Just in case that door opens, and someone is on the other side waiting for us.

The elevator stops at the top floor. Priest is the first person to walk out. I follow along with the others.

We pass a few doors until we arrive at the very last apartment. Priest stops in front of a red door that's slightly ajar.

He turns and looks over his shoulder at us. Dipping his chin, he lets us know to be ready. We hold our guns down but alert. Hawk takes the lead. He pushes the door open with his gun out in front of him. He then steps into the house first.

As soon as we walk in, we can tell that someone has been here looking for something. The place has been tossed. The furniture is turned over and all cabinets and drawers are spilling out.

"Looks like someone beat us to the punch," Many says, stating the obvious.

"Watch your step, Hawk," Priest tells Hawk right before he nearly bumped into a turned over vase. "We're still going to look," he goes on to say. "Everyone spread out. Many, take Hawk with you."

We all follow the directions Priest laid out. I head into the back of the apartment. The place looks thoroughly examined. I doubt we will find anything here. However, I don't argue that point.

The bedroom I chose looks like it is the primary. The mattress and box spring have been flipped off the bed and sliced up. The nightstand has been emptied out and most of its content is on the floor at my feet. Same thing with the closet. Sifting through the mess, I don't find anything that would help us.

Leaving the primary, I head into the hallway. I come face to face with Maksim.

"Any luck?" he asks.

I shake my head.

He runs a hand down his face. "This was thoroughly swept," he says looking around at the mess on the ground. "Looks like something Corbyn orchestrated. My only question is, what were they looking for?"

"I'm guessing the same thing we are."

He looks at me for a moment as if he's mulling over my words.

"You might be right. He's trying to keep you guys from finding those names."

Which is even more an incentive to find them. Corbyn doesn't seem like the person to care if we just find the names. There has to be a reason he's trying to keep them from us other than us trying to get the ones that signed to withdraw their signatures.

"We need to find that document," I say letting my inner thoughts out.

We both make our way back into the living room where we find the others. Priest kicks a box lying on the floor. It flies into the wall making a loud thud.

"Fuck," he shouts running a hand through his hair. "This was our best shot at figuring out who signed that order."

"We will figure something out, Priest," Hawk says. "Besides, we already know Corbyn signed it. Let's just focus on him."

I fully agreed with Hawk. Although, I thought this plan to reach out to the others to get the excommunication order dealt with was the smarter and less violent plan, I was always still going after Corbyn.

Priest shakes his head but doesn't say anything. I don't think he likes the idea of going after Corbyn. For some reason, Priest is being hesitant. It isn't like him. He's always taught us to go after the source and not be afraid of any enemy. So why the change and hesitancy now?

"This is a bust, let's just go," he says before turning and heading to the door.

"Wait," Hawk stops him.

We all turn to look at Hawk. His head is tilted to the side as he stares blankly.

"Take three steps back, Priest."

Priest looks confused but follows his commands. The moment he takes his second step, the floorboards make a creaking sound. I press on the floor beneath me, and it doesn't make that sound.

"Do you hear that?" Hawk asks. "The floor is different there."

Priest immediately gets on his knees. He presses around the seams of the hardwood floor. As soon as he presses on one particular spot, we realize there is a slight gap between one wood panel and the other.

"Anyone got their knife?" Priest asks.

I take mine out of my leg holster and hand it to him. He uses the tip of the knife to wedge between the seams. It takes only a minute for the floorboard to pop up. Priest hands the knife back to me before lifting the wood panel. Underneath the floor is a lock box. He pulls it out and carries it over to the kitchen counter. He looks over the key lock thoroughly.

"Hand me that knife back," he says holding out his hand toward me.

I take my knife back out and place it in his hand. He sticks the tip of the knife in the lock before reaching into his suit coat and pulling out a long skinny tool. I've seen Priest break into many locks, it's how I learned to do it. It's a trait he learned from his father.

He fiddles with the skinny tool for a few seconds before a soft click is heard. He hands my knife back before opening the box. The first thing we spot are pictures. The first few Priest flips through are of a young Pope and some older hard faced looking woman.

"That's his mom," Priest explains passing the pictures around.

"I'm hoping she had a lovely personality," Maksim says as he grimaces.

"No," Priest replies. "That bitch was as ugly inside as she was outside."

The next picture Priest comes to has him going rigid. He flips through the next few without showing us.

"What is it?" I ask noticing his change.

"That muthafucker," he growls, stuffing the photos in his front suit pocket. "He had cameras hidden in Fem's home bathroom."

He didn't have to explain anything else. We did not want to see those pictures. Albany was like a sister to us. It pisses me off that someone had invaded her privacy. If Pope wasn't already dead, this would have made me pay him a visit.

The next thing Priest pulls out of the box were three black notebooks and a hard drive.

"We can go through the notebooks back home. And Lucien will have to check the drive," he says placing everything back in the box and closing it up. He tucks it under his arm and we all head for the exit.

"Time to turn those earpieces on," Priest directs us as we get on the elevator.

Pulling out my earpiece and turning it on, I place it back in my ear. "Are you there, Lucien?"

"Yeah, I'm here," he replies.

"Are we still clear?" I ask Lucien as we step off the elevator.

"Yeah. Nothing's been reported yet," Lucien replies.

We head for the minivan. Maksim takes over the driving this time. Priest is in the front passenger seat. Hawk and I are on the second row with Many in the back.

We pull away from the curb and into traffic.

"Zel and I are following your route on the traffic cam," Lucien reports. "Did you guys find anything?"

"The place was trashed when we got there. But Priest found a lock box underneath the floorboards that contains some notebooks and a hard drive," Hawk explains.

Maksim fights his way through traffic for ten minutes. When we pull up to a red light, Zel's voice comes over the earpiece.

"At this light, turn left," he directs.

We all look confused. In order to get home, we need to keep straight.

"You see something?" Priest asks. I immediately scan the street up ahead.

"White work van five cars back. It pulled out the same time you guys left the apartment. It had been sitting there since you pulled in, but no one ever got in or out."

Turning in my seat, I look out the back window trying to get a view of the suspected van. Unfortunately, I have no luck.

Maksim makes the left turn. We wait to see if the van does the same.

"Yeah, you guys got a tail," Lucien says.

"Can you tell who's driving?" Priest asks.

"No. I don't have a clear view."

Maksim speeds up. The work van does the same before speeding off around us. For a moment we thought that maybe we were paranoid for nothing. That is until the van turns and stops in the middle of the road. The side door opens, and someone points a huge gun at us.

"Fuck," Maksim shouts. Right as he turns the car at the last minute. Bullets start to ping against the back half of the minivan.

"Get down, Many," I shout.

Thankfully he was able to get to the ground before being hit. The work van follows behind us. Maksim does his best to lose it in traffic. He plows through red lights and flows in and out of traffic only clipping a few cars as he goes.

"Take the next right," Zel says through the earpiece.

Maksim follows his lead. Bullets fly through the back window. Looking over my shoulder I notice a familiar face hanging out the passenger window firing an AR- rifle.

"Disciples," I say.

"I hate those fucking guys," Hawk says ducking down in his seat.

"I can take the shot," Priest says glancing out the side mirror. "I need a better angle."

Maksim speeds around a mail truck blaring his horn. "Get out of the way," he shouts as bullets continue to ping off the back of the van.

"Up ahead, take a right. That should give you a clear enough shot. But you will only have a few seconds," Zel says.

"It's all I'll need." Priest lets his window down.

"Brace yourselves," Maksim shouts as he takes the turn without slowing down.

Priest leans out the window and takes one single shot. Looking over my shoulder out the back window I watch the bullet hit its mark dead in the center of Shaw's forehead. Proving once again that a true marksman only needs one bullet to get a job done.

The reprieve is short-lived when another disciple climbs up from the back and shoves the dead body out the way before taking his place firing rounds. He's joined by the first gunman that leans out of the side of the van and opens fire. The glass over Hawk's head shatters, raining pieces down over him.

"Shit," he says, touching his ear and pulling back a bloody hand.

"Is this as fast as this stupid ass van can go?" Priest shouts.

"I'm flooring it. As long as they have those rifles, we're in trouble."

Unbuckling my seat belt, I pull my knife out of my holster. "Turn around," I say.

"What?" Priest asks, looking over the front seat at me.

"Turn around."

Maksim glances at me through the rearview mirror.

"Switch sides with me, Hawk," I say climbing over the seat.

Before Hawk can deny or confirm, I have him in my vacated seat. Placing my gun in my dominant hand, I hold my knife in my other.

"This is stupid, Beastie," Maksim shouts. Yet, he turns the car around. Bullets come flying at the front of the car. I slide the door to the van open.

We play a game of chicken, until Maksim turns the wheel slightly and drives beside the van. I leap out of the door of the minivan and into the worker van's open door. The disciple with the AR is too stunned to react. I hit the floor of the van with a thud, tucking my body, I roll twice before coming to a crouch position. The guy with the AR turns his gun toward me, but I shoot him in the head. Another guy is behind me, I aim at him, but he crashes into me sending my gun flying.

The disciple lands on top of me, and I recognize him. Nyx came in during the same time we did. He didn't have the skills to be a Deacon, so they made him a Disciple. Nyx wraps his hands around my neck, trying to squeeze. I thrust my blade into the side of his neck twice before turning the handle and yanking it out.

I shove his limp body off me. Rolling over, I grab my gun and quickly place a bullet in the driver's thigh. I then charge to the front of the van.

The man in the front passenger seat attempts to turn to aim his gun at me. The problem with AR's is that they are too big and not good for confined spaces. Using the hand with my knife in it, my blade shoves the end of the gun up. He fires off rounds into the back of the van. I then place my handgun at his chin and pull the trigger blasting his brains onto the roof of the van.

The driver is losing control of the vehicle since I shot him in the right leg. The van is careening onto the sidewalk and heading into a building. Opening the door on the opposite side of the one I used to get in, I tuck my body and fall out of the moving vehicle. I hit the pavement hard earning some road rash. The van hits a pole and nearly folds in half.

Standing to my feet, I hobble over to the passenger side of the van. The driver groans as he leans up from the steering wheel. He looks to the left and then to the right. His eyes widen when he sees me.

I fire one shot into his head, splattering his blood on the window behind him.

"You got a lot of cleaning up to do," I say in the earpiece to Lucien as I walk away from the scene.

"Already on it," he says.

The minivan pulls up at the curb in front of me.

Priest shakes his head at me. "I swear you boys are going to give me a fucking heart attack."

The van door creaks open. I climb inside and take a seat. Slowly and with a lot of effort the door starts to close again as Maksim pulls away.

"We're going to need another vehicle," Maksim announces.

Pulling out my phone, I call Pharrell and let him know we're on the way.

CHAPTER NINE

Clothes

Summer

"It looks good," Doc says, reapplying the dressing on my shoulder.

Maksim gives me a thumbs up over his head as if I'm doing something spectacular. This was my first time meeting the short man with the bald spot they call Doc. All my other interactions with him I've either been sleeping, or too drugged up to remember.

You'd think I'd be a little more concerned about how my healing is going but I can't seem to focus on anything except my exchange with Gabriel this morning.

This morning, like every morning since I let him in my room that night, I woke up with him in the corner of my room.

I rolled out of bed and ignored him, even though his presence always makes me giddy. Walking into the bathroom, I switched on the light to do my morning routine. After washing my face and brushing my teeth, I look up to find him in the mirror watching me intently.

His gaze roamed over my bare legs causing an ache to form in the pit of my stomach. Even with an injury I miss the feeling of him pressed against my body. I'm pretty sure if he hadn't broken up with me, I would be riding his face right now, arm bandaged up and all.

"Whose shirt are you wearing?" his deep voice brought me out of my naughty thoughts.

Glaring at his reflection in the mirror, I roll my eyes. He asked me this same question three days ago.

"I thought we already discussed that. What I do or who I do, doesn't concern you."

Obviously, I was being a bitch, because there was no one in this house that I would be sleeping with. But Gabriel doesn't get to break up with me and then still act like a jealous lover.

He steps into the bathroom, his arms falling from across his chest down to his side. He stops himself, shutting his eyes, he shook his head as if he was trying to force something out of it.

He takes a few deep breaths before opening his eyes and staring at me.

"Please answer my question."

Even though I still want to be mad and refuse him this one little request, I give in. It's something about the desperate look on his face and him pleading for a response.

Sighing, I turn to face him, leaning my ass against the sink.

"It's Sim's, alright."

His gaze narrows and his head cocks to the side. If I didn't know any better, I would say his eyes darkened.

"It's not his fault," I find myself saying. "When I was brought here, I didn't actually get a chance to pack clothes. And although I am very thankful someone purchased clothes for Gabe, I don't feel right asking anyone to order me something. I also don't have my debit card to order my own. So, Sim's shirts have to do."

All the women in the house offered to loan me clothes and they did give me bottoms, but all their shirts are a bit too snug to comfortably fit my injured arm.

He remains silent, staring at me blankly. He then turns and walks out of the bathroom and out of my room. That was four hours ago, and I haven't seen him since.

"All done," Doc says as he finishes replacing the bandage on my shoulder successfully pulling me out of my memory.

"How long before I can really shower?" I ask.

Although I've been making the quick showers and sink baths work for me since I woke up from the meds, it's definitely time to get a thorough clean in.

Doc takes off his gloves and tosses them in the trash bin in the corner of the room.

"You are free to shower like normal."

Feeling giddy, I do a little shimmy in celebration.

"But you still want to be careful with your movements though."

Admittedly, it's hard to reach certain areas with a busted shoulder, but thankfully the bullet hit my left side and not my dominate right one.

"And how long before I should be completely healed?"

Doc comes back over to the bed. He pulls three packages of gauze and a tube of ointment out of his black bag and places them down beside me.

"You have about four more weeks before you can move that arm freely again."

Nodding, I don't comment. Four weeks feels like a long time away, but when I realize I could have died, limited mobility is nothing.

"Do you need any more pain meds?"

I shake my head before he can finish his sentence. "No. I'm good."

"Well, alright. I'll see you in about two weeks. Take care, Summer."

Doc walks out of the room leaving me and Maksim alone.

"You'll be back to normal in no time," Sim says, walking over to the bed.

He picks up the t-shirt I had on earlier. I continue to hold the towel up to my chest with my right arm. Carefully, Sim slides my injured arm into the sleeve of my borrowed shirt and works it over my shoulder and head before I stick my other hand into the last sleeve.

Once my shirt is back on and covering my breasts, I pull the towel out and toss it to the bed.

"Good news, right?"

"Yeah. I guess."

He steps back, narrowing his eyes, he looks me over.

"You've complained for a week about needing to shower and now you don't seem as happy?"

Being around Maksim has even further shown me how toxic my relationship with my sister is. Although he's Gabriel's brother, I swear he feels more like mine. He's truly become a friend since I've met him. He starts every day knocking at my door to see if I need help with anything. If something is going on in the house, he always makes sure I'm included in the details. I like the women I've met here. They are all really nice, but Maksim is who I talk to most.

"Did Gabriel say anything to you today?"

Maksim shakes his head. "No. He stormed out the house early this morning and hasn't been back yet. Priest asked him where he was going but he simply told him 'Out'."

He holds out a hand to help me down from the bed.

"I thought we couldn't leave?"

"*You* can't leave," he laughs. "You and all the other women. Until we figure out who is behind the excommunication order and get a hold of Corbyn, it isn't safe for you all to be out roaming freely. From my understanding, the Church has no idea any of you exist. Except for the female that Priest is with and her twin sister. But you're different. Corbyn knows you, so you definitely can't leave. We should all be keeping a low profile, but Beastie, well, he seems to do what he wants."

I kind of figured that. Most of the women here are terrified of him with the exception of Fem. However, even she is giving him a wide berth lately. Especially after that situation in the kitchen the other day. Something is off with him. I've seen him go dark before. There is a look in his eyes when his mother takes over. But that day the look felt different, darker, more vacant. Even his movements when he walked over to me were different. Gabriel has always been stealth and quick, but it was like he was on autopilot walking over to me.

"Can I give you some advice, big brother to little sister?" Maksim asks.

I smile and nod. He walks over to the door and holds it open for me. I make my way over to him but stop in front of him.

"Give him some time and space. I know his decision to call off the relationship hurts, but I think he needs it."

I'm all for giving Gabriel his space, but I will never give up on him. It may make me sound crazy, but I know him. The more I back down from fighting for us the more reason he will believe that his decision was the right one. But more importantly, he needs to know he is worth the fight. Between his mother and his psycho biological father, he needs to know that I will have his back. There is nothing he can do that will make me walk away. Even though that's what he believes.

However, I don't tell Maksim this.

"Fine," I say, rolling my eyes with a smile. "I'll give him his space."

"Good." We walk out of the bedroom side by side.

"You know, you're doing good at this self-appointed big brother role."

He chuckles. "You're a lot easier to deal with than my other siblings."

We part ways in the hallway. Maksim heads to the gym in the basement. I head into the heart of the home. The kitchen is the hot spot for the house. There is always someone in there.

Today, Malia is here with her boyfriend with the glasses. I think his name is Lucien. Apparently, my friend is dating twin brothers. And as fine as they both are, I don't blame her. However, I do notice that I never see them together. Usually if Lucien is with Malia, the other is nowhere in sight.

"Hey, Summer. What did the doc say?" Malia asks.

"Everything looks good."

"That's great," she says. "I got grazed by a bullet a little over three months ago. I can't imagine what it feels like to actually get shot."

She comes over to the sink and washes her hands. I take a seat at the island.

"It's not great, I can tell you that."

"Fuck," her boyfriend growls before going back to doing something on the computer.

"Is everything alright?" I ask Malia as she places ingredients down on the island to make a sandwich.

She looks over at him then back at me.

"Lucien's frustrated because he can't crack some type of code," she whispers.

"Your whispering skills are very questionable, baby," Lucien says without glancing up from his computer. "And it's not a code, it's an encrypted hard drive."

When I look back at Malia she shakes her head. I'm guessing she's as confused as I am about his explanation.

Taking the top off my water bottle, I take a sip.

"Brook, you need to lie down." I turn to the entrance of the kitchen as Brooklyn and Hawk walk into the room.

Of all the women in the house, Brooklyn has to be the funniest. I swear whatever comes to her head comes out of her mouth. And the jabs between her and Priest have me in stitches.

Brook wobbles over to the bar stool beside me. Her round belly is poking out beneath her tank top. She's only five months, but her stomach is more pronounced than mine was at that stage. Gabe was huge, but he was by himself in my belly, unlike Brooklyn's situation.

"Walker, if you tell me to lay down one more time, I'm going to legit leave your ass."

He walks up behind her and helps her climb onto the barstool. He is the most attentive man I have ever met. He's constantly helping Brooklyn and making sure she's safe and comfortable.

"You said your back was hurting. Something could be wrong," he says rubbing her belly.

She rolls her eyes. "My back is hurting because you fucked me up against the washing machine ten minutes ago."

I nearly spit out the water I just took a sip of. Malia tosses her head back and laughs. Hawk's face turns bright red.

"No matter how grown you are, I'll never get used to you talking about sex around me."

Fem walks into the kitchen and marches over to the fridge. Even though she and I have known each other for five years, the woman still scares the shit out of me.

"Don't act like the weird shit you and Priest do down in that sex room is easy to digest," Brooklyn says to her sister.

"Wait, there's a sex room?" I whisper to Malia. It's the first I've heard of it.

"Not for you," Priest says walking into the kitchen.

Does everyone have bionic ears in this damn family.

He goes straight to the table with Lucien and takes a seat.

"I thought you were watching *The Avengers* with the kids?" Fem asks leaning against the island with a water bottle in her hands.

"I was until twiddle dee and twiddle dumb walked in asking stupid ass questions."

I'm finding out that twiddle dee and twiddle dumb are Ari and Many. Although Ari seems harmless, her boyfriend is a bit odd with that whole three voice thing. Fem says that he's harmless. Brooklyn says he's crazy and nobody wants to take her concerns seriously.

"About that," I announce to the room. "Sorry about my son forcing you guys to watch *Marvel* all day. He kind of gets fixated on things."

"Don't apologize for that," Priest says sternly.

"What grumpy father time means," Brooklyn says getting my attention. "Is that we don't mind watching those movies with Gabe. It beats the hell out of the shit Ari had us watching."

"Please don't mention it," Malia says holding up a hand. "I'm still traumatized." Brooklyn, Fem, and I chuckle at the face Malia makes.

"You know it's really hard for me to focus when all of you are talking?" Lucien says glaring at all of us.

"Still no luck on Pope's encryption," Priest asks.

Lucien takes off his glasses and rubs his eyes. "No."

Malia plates the sandwich she just made and takes it over to Lucien. She moves the laptop from in front of him to the side before placing the sandwich down in its place.

"Babe, I have to work," he complains.

"Eat first. That file can wait a few minutes."

She turns to walk away but he wraps an arm around her and pulls her into his lap. She giggles as he places kisses all over her neck and face. I smile at the interaction as I turn away.

Although my love life is in shambles, I enjoyed watching people love each other. However, being surrounded by so many loving couples does sting a little right now.

My thoughts go back to Gabriel. The look on his face this morning when I told him I was wearing Sim's shirts stood out to me. Even though I'm mad and hurt by his decision to call it off between the two of us, I didn't like the idea of him being upset.

Malia comes back over to the island to clean up the mess she made with the sandwich. Ms. Reese walks into the kitchen with Charlie on her hip.

"Malia, let Seth know I placed that order for him," Ms. Reese says handing Charlie over to Fem.

"I'll let him know," Malia hums.

"Can ask you a question?" I lower my voice in hopes only Malia can hear.

"Sure," she says as she reties the bread bag.

"Do Lucien and Seth get along?"

Malia quirks a brow at me.

I rush out my next words, not wanting to offend her. "I'm just asking because I never see them with you at the same time."

She tosses her head back and laughs. I notice the others at the island join her.

"What am I missing?" I ask glancing around at their amused faces.

"Sweetie, Beast didn't tell you? Lucien and Seth are the same person." Brooklyn chuckles.

My jaw damn near unhinges, it opens so wide. A feather could knock me on my ass. I would have never guessed that. I mean, they are identical, but they give off two completely different vibes. Not to mention one wears glasses and the other doesn't. Plus, the tattoos are different.

"Lucien has a split personality disorder," Malia explains pushing her hair behind her ear. "But I assure you he's safe and will cause no harm to you or Gabe."

I wave off her concerns. Has she met my child's father?

"No, no need to explain. I'm just...." I pause trying to find the right words to express my shock. "So, it's like a two for one special?"

This time Brooklyn, Malia, and Ms. Reese howl in laughter.

"I guess I never thought about it that way," Malia laughs.

"If you think that's crazy, wait until you figure out Hawk's superpower," Brooklyn jokes.

Twenty minutes later we are all caught up in our own conversations. Ms. Reese, Malia, Brooklyn, and I are discussing their pregnancies so far. Hawk, Priest, and Fem are talking about their former Pope. Lucien interjects every now and again before going back to his laptop.

However, all conversations stop when a looming shadow falls over me. Brooklyn's eyes widen when she looks up over my head.

"Beast, son, are you alright?" I turn around at Priest's words and gasp.

Gabriel is covered in blood. It's in his hair, smeared on his shirt, and on his face. My gaze rakes over his body trying to see where the blood is coming from. However, there isn't a mark on him.

Immediately, he's surrounded by Priest, Hawk, and Lucien. However, he's too focused on me to notice them as he stands over me.

"Gabriel, baby, where is this blood coming from?" I reach out to touch him, but he leans back. It's then that I notice the shopping bags in his hands. There are four bags total from one of those well-known retail stores that sell everything.

He drops the bags at his feet. "Change clothes."

"You're bleeding. You need to—"

"Summer," he growls my name in a way that has my heart stuttering in my chest. "Go take off his shirt."

Before I could open my mouth, Priest spoke.

"Fem, take Summer into her room and help her change out of those clothes."

"But—"

"It's not his blood, Summer," Priest reassures me.

Fem comes up beside me. "Let's go, Summer."

I hesitate to stand from my chair. I can't take my eyes off Gabriel, and he's staring right at me. The man is confusing. One minute you're telling me you don't want to be together and then the next you go out of your way to bring me clothes just so I can't wear another man's shirt.

I guess this shouldn't be too unusual. He did spend five years in lock down without communication with me, but still paid every bill in my house. I think it's just second nature for him to take care of me.

Finally, I allow Fem's incessant tug of my arm to get me out of my seat.

"I'll help," Brooklyn volunteers.

"Malia, you go too," Lucien says.

"I'll take Charlie and put him down for his nap," Ms. Reese adds.

Malia and Brooklyn grab the bags at my feet and carry them out of the kitchen.

As soon as we step out into the hallway, I hear Priest ask?

"Who's blood?"

"Disciples," Gabriel says. "Two of them. They tried to attack me after I left the store. I need you to wipe the cameras at the back of the building."

I don't get to hear the rest of what he says because Fem drags me back to my bedroom. Although I allowed her to lead me away, I can't help the nagging feeling in my soul that something is wrong with Gabriel.

As soon as we enter the room, Malia lays my clothes out on the bed.

"Something is wrong with him," I tell Fem as soon as she shuts the door.

"No shit," Brooklyn says rubbing her belly. "He is like fucking Micheal Myers."

"Brook," Fem warns before turning back to me. "I think your near-death experience triggered something in him. Priest says he's not hearing his mother's voice anymore."

"Wait, that should be good," I explain as I lift Maksim's shirt up and slide my good arm out of the arm hole. "His mother tells him to kill."

Fem shakes her head. "No, his mother is who Beast allows to guide him while in that dark place. Notice I said guide." She helps me pull my injured arm out of the arm hole before tossing the shirt on the bed.

"He has always had control over his mother in his head," she goes on to explain.

Malia holds out a large black t-shirt with a well-known rock band printed on it. Fem takes the shirt from her.

"I still don't see how her being gone is a problem."

I've seen how bad it could get when Gabriel's mother took over. I've witnessed it firsthand. Could there be anything worse than her?

"Priest thinks someone else is taking her place."

"Someone like who?" The memory of the other day in the kitchen flashes back in my head. There was something different about him that day. The way he stood over me and seemed to move across the kitchen without even realizing he was moving.

"We don't know," Fem says helping me put my injured arm in my shirt before sliding it over my head. "But whatever it is, Beast is struggling to control it."

Placing my good arm into the other sleeve, I was unsure how to take this information. I don't think I've ever doubted his ability to fight through his mother's voice. Even on that first night we met. Maybe that makes me naïve. But I truly believed that he could conquer anything.

"So, you mean to tell me we're locked in this house with a real-life jigsaw who at any moment could lose his shit and kill all of us?" Brook asks, placing her hands on her hips. "No offense, Summer. I know that's your man and all."

I don't take offense to Brooklyn's words. She doesn't know Gabriel like I do. He would never hurt us.

"He wouldn't do that," I argue. "I know he looks menacing on the outside and is capable of things you couldn't imagine. But that man is the kindest, gentlest, most loving and thoughtful man I've ever met." My throat clogs up with tears just thinking about the man I've grown to know and love.

To some, Gabriel would be too hard around the edges. The way he communicates would drive others crazy. Not to mention his many quirks and brooding presence. To anyone else he may be too imperfect to be considered worthy, but to me he is perfection.

"Aww, baby," Malia says walking up to me and giving me a hug. "I can tell you love him."

I wipe my eyes as she lets me go. "I understand how you feel. Seth's a little different. He's more volatile and rougher around the edges than Lucien. He's an acquired taste."

"You got that right," Brooklyn mumbles.

Malia only playfully rolls her eyes at her before turning back to me. "But I know the kind, loving, and protective side of Seth. I know that he adores his brothers and Priest and wouldn't do anything to hurt them or us."

I nod. She's right. That's exactly how Gabriel is. No one is calling my man a saint, but he is a good person.

"Look," Brooklyn says coming up beside me. "I'll just take your word for it. But if he goes all Jason Vorhees on us, I'm using you as a shield."

Despite the topic and my tears, I laugh at her joke. At least I think it's a joke.

"We will all be alright. There's nothing to worry about." Even though Fem said the words, she didn't sound the least bit confident. But that's okay. I had enough faith in my man for everybody.

CHAPTER TEN

New Class

Priest

"Take my cock to the back of your fucking throat, Fem," I growl out over her head as I shove more of my length into her mouth.

She gags, her eyes watering, as she sucks me off. I reach over her body and smack her ass. She's tied down to my bondage bench. Her ass is in the air with a medium-sized butt plug inside of it. Pulling out of her mouth with a wet plop, I stuff my cock back in my sweats as I slowly walk around her, admiring how her body is spread out for me.

I don't touch her as I stare at her soaking wet pussy as it leaks around the vibrating yoni balls.

Moaning, she arches her body off the bench. Her arms and legs shake. Her pussy pulses. She's orgasming.

"What number was that?"

"Nathaniel," she whines.

I know what she wants, but she doesn't get it yet. I readjust my rock-hard cock in my sweatpants. There are a thousand more pressing matters at hand. It's been five days since we found that lock box in Luca's home.

Every time I think of the pictures he had of Fem, I'm tempted to dig his ass up and put three more holes in his corpse. Most of the pictures were taken from one of her play home's bathrooms. It only calmed me a little to know he didn't have her real address. But still, it pissed me off to know he had those pictures locked away in a shrine like she belonged to him.

"Please, baby, I need you," Fem whimpers, getting my attention back.

Not being able to wait any longer, I slip my joggers and boxers down my hips as I step up behind her. Snatching the yoni balls out of her, I toss them behind me. She screams as she cums again. Lining my head up to her opening, I push forward loving every single inch of the tight fit.

She whimpers my name as I make room inside her. I work my hips behind her chasing an orgasm that is so close to the edge I'm nearly falling over as soon as I slide in.

"Fuck, Fem," I growl as her walls squeeze my cock for dear life.

I smack her ass and watch it jiggle.

"Fuck me back," I demand.

She does the best she can, rocking back to meet my thrusts while being strapped down. My nut was rising up in me like a tsunami.

Reaching up I slide the plug in her ass out to the tip before pushing it back in. She arches like a house cat. I continue to slide in and out of her as I use the plug to fuck her ass. This is as close to a threesome as she will ever get.

Her cries of passion are music to my ears. She's so fucking wet, her juices slide down my balls to my thighs.

My nut is surfacing so fast, my back locks up. However, I refuse to come before she gives me her fifth.

"Give me another one," I grit out through clenched teeth as I continue to fuck her asshole with the plug.

"No, I can't. I can't," she cries.

"Don't tell me what you can't do. You will fucking cum for me," I growl

Her body jerks against the leather bench. She screams as she erupts like a volcano. Her cream oozes out around my dick as her walls lock down on me like I'm a prisoner inside her warmth.

Tossing my head back, I roar as I bathe her walls with my nut. I go so hard and long I lose my hearing for a second.

I pull out of her completely spent. While I pull my pants up, I admire the semen that drips from her slit.

I have a brief image of her belly full again. This time, a little girl with her entire face. The vision is so strong I can almost smell the powdery scent of a newborn. Opening my eyes, I come back to reality.

"Soon," I say out loud. Charlie is still too young, and we have enough problems right now.

The image of Beast coming home covered in blood two days ago pops in my head. I needed to do something fast to save my youngest son.

After pulling out the plug, I unstrap Fem from the bench. Lifting her up, I carry her to the bathroom. Before sitting her on the edge of the tub, I kiss her lips.

"How're you feeling?"

I had planned to make her wait a little longer before I brought her down to the room again. Although she's healed from being shot, she still isn't fully recovered. Which is one of the reasons I tied her to the bench and not to the swing.

She stretches, lifting her arms over head. "I feel thoroughly sexed." She chuckles.

"Good." I test the water for her making sure it's the perfect temperature. I then add her bath bomb and relaxing oils. Once the tub is full, I help her climb inside.

Fem sinks down into the water, closing her eyes. I pull up the small stool beside the bath and take a seat.

"I need your help," I say.

She laughs. "I should've known when you brought me down to this room you wanted something."

"I have to have a reason to give you this top-notch cock?" I lift a brow at her.

She shakes her head. "Nobody said it was top-notch."

"It's the only cock you've ever had. How do you know it's not the best?"

She taps her chin as if she's thinking. "You're right. I need to sample more dick so I can test your theory."

"Don't get fucked up in here."

She laughs as if I've told the world's funniest joke.

"I'm just kidding," she says sobering. "Tell me what you need from me?"

I scratch at my beard. "I need you to keep a close eye on Summer."

Her brows crease. "Why? You think something's wrong with her?"

I shake my head. I've been around the girl for two weeks now. She seems genuine. Maybe a little talkative and awkward, but definitely harmless. Most importantly, she's an amazing mom to my grandson and she's head over heels in love with my son.

"No. She's good. I just need you to keep an eye on her. Whatever is going on with Beast, she is the catalyst for it. If he goes off the deep end, she might be the only one to pull him back."

Fem lifts from the tub, tucking her knees to her chest. "You think it will come to that?"

I'd like to think it wouldn't. I've worked with Beast for twenty-five years. I know how dark he can go with his mother in his head. But this new thing is alarming. It doesn't guide him, it takes over him.

A memory plays back in my head. It was the day I picked Beast up from Colleen. When I walked in that house and saw his naked body lying on the floor of that too little cage covered in feces and bruises, I was livid. I almost choked his mother to death in her home. I'd never tell anyone I put my hands on a woman that way, but watching her stare at him in disgust as if she wasn't the cause triggered me.

After pulling him out of the cage, I wrapped his little body in a blanket. I marched down those porch stairs with Colleen hot on my heels.

"You don't know what you're doing!" She screamed at my back.

I placed Beast in the back seat of my brand-new Charger and slammed the door. Turning to glare at Colleen, I marched back up the stairs. She didn't even back up as I approached her.

"You better be glad I've had my fill of killing women. Because if not, your ass would be dead right now."

She smirked at me. "You still think he's a little boy." She shook her head. "You don't know what's buried inside him. He is evil."

Done with her bullshit and not trusting my restraint, I turned and headed back down the steps. I needed space and distance between me and her.

"You're fucking insane. You should get whatever mental disorder you have checked," I shouted over my shoulder.

She laughed. It was the most diabolical laugh I'd ever heard. It stopped me in my tracks. I turned to face her. Right before my eyes, the glaze of delusion falls from her face. From the moment I walked in, she'd been overly cocky and smirking as if she was out of her mind. But for the first time she looked completely normal. Almost like a scared mother.

"If you let it out, you will never be able to put it back in again."

"Let what out?" I asked truly confused.

"The real him," she said stoically before turning and walking into the house.

At that moment, I chalked her words up to the ramblings of a schizophrenic. But after seeing him the day Summer was shot, I'm not so sure I can dismiss her claims anymore.

Then two days ago, the look on his face as he pleaded with her to take Sim's shirt off was almost desperate. I think she is his trigger and his cure. It sounds insane, but I'm pretty sure I'm right.

"If you're worried about her running off, you can relax. The girl is in love with him. She's not going to leave him."

"You loved me, but you still left."

She tilts her head, watching me closely. "You know why I did that, Nathaniel. That's not fair."

I hold up a hand to stop her. "I didn't say that to be an asshole. I'm pointing out that sometimes love will make you do something crazy even though you think it's the right thing."

She sighs. "All right. I'll keep an eye on her. But I also think Beast needs to see someone. This new thing feels wrong."

I shake my head. "He will never do it. Even trying to get him to see the shrinks at the Church when he was a kid was hell. The moment he suspects anyone trying to get into his head he will lose his shit."

She's quiet for a few seconds before she speaks again. "I guess you're right."

The way Fem cares for my boys makes me love her more. I know they'd never consider her a mother figure considering they are all older than she is, but I know they view her like a sister.

I nod, before standing up. I drop a kiss on her forehead.

"I'm going to shower. I'll get you out when I'm done."

I go over to the walk-in shower and turn on the water ready to wash the smell of sex off my body.

After getting out of the shower and getting Fem out, I put her to bed. She was too tired to go back up the stairs, so I put her in the bed in the playroom. I made my way down the hall heading toward the staircase when noises from the gym caught my attention. I head in that direction.

When I walk into the room, I freeze in place.

"What the hell is going on in here?"

Standing, with a big ass bowie knife in his small hand, was Gabe. Puzzler is standing in front of him showing him how to grip it.

Gabe drops his head looking down at the floor.

Emory immediately starts to sign. "Don't be mad papa Priest. Gabe wants to learn how to fight. I just wanted to teach him a few things."

I walk into the room and kneel in front of Gabe.

"Is that true, Gabe. Do you want to learn how to fight?"

He nods his head as he starts to flick his forefinger against his thumb.

"Hey," I say getting his attention. "Lift your head and look at me."

He slowly lifts his head, his fingers still flicking. Slowly, I place my hand over his, halting his flicking. He doesn't turn to look at the action.

"Why do you want to learn to fight?"

Emory waves, causing me to turn to her. "He says he wants to—" I hold up a hand to stop Emory.

"I want him to answer," I wink at her. She smiles and nods at me understanding my reason for stopping her explanation. If Gabe wants to learn to be like us, he has to be able to speak up for himself.

Gabe looks over my head.

"Look at me, son." I wait until his gaze falls on me. "The first lesson you need to learn about being able to fight is looking your opponent or anyone in the eye. Even if it feels weird. Okay?"

He nods.

"Use your words."

"Yes," he finally says.

"Now, tell me why you want to learn to fight?"

He looks at Emory before turning back to me. "I want to be brave like Hulk."

"Being able to fight doesn't make you brave."

"I know," he says pushing out his little chest. "But I want to learn so that I can be brave and I won't have to hide when something bad happens to mommy."

My heart goes out to him. I know the feeling of being unable to save or help someone you love. It's how I felt when I walked in on my mother lying on my kitchen floor. Watching her body slowly shrink due to the cancer ravaging her was one of the most helpless moments I've ever felt. So, I can imagine how terrified Gabe felt in that moment with Summer. Although, me nor his father would have allowed him to do anything in that situation, I understand his need to learn.

"Alright," I say standing up straight. "If you want to learn how to fight, I will teach you."

He cheers. While Emory does the sign for excitement.

"But you have to take it seriously. Both of you," I turn to include Emory even though I know she doesn't need any lessons. However, it will help Gabe catch on faster if he has Emory here to learn with him.

"You will meet me here every single day at this time. No excuses, okay?"

They both agree.

"Hand me that knife," I say taking the Bowie from him. "We don't learn to fight with weapons yet." I hand the blade to Emory.

She picks up a yellow stuffed rabbit off the ground, twists its head off, and then places her blade down into the body of the rabbit.

"Can we start today?" Gabe asks, getting my attention back.

I shrug. "We sure can."

"Yes!" he cheers.

"If we do this, we have to keep it between us. I'll tell your mother and father eventually."

I doubt Beast will mind me teaching his son how to protect himself, but I can imagine Summer wouldn't quite understand.

"Okay, papa Priest. Can I get a nickname too?"

Placing a hand on his shoulder I shake my head. "Nicknames are earned," I told him. "But I promise, when you've earned it, I'll give you one."

With his chin up and his chest out, Gabe nods making me feel prouder than I've felt in a long time. I loved my boys, and they have made me proud more times than I can count. However, it was something about seeing the children of my boys do great things that made me feel ten feet taller.

"Alright, the first lesson you need to learn is whenever you walk into a room, you need to check for all the exits."

After nearly twenty-plus years, I finally had my new class of Deacons.

CHAPTER ELEVEN

Records' Keeper

Beast

I watch her from my spot in the kitchen. She's laughing at something Hawk's wife says. She seems to find her funny. I notice that Brooklyn makes Summer laugh often.

I watch the way Summer moves while cradling her arm. She's being very cautious of moving it wrong. She reaches for a cookie Twin's wife tries to hand her. Her brow pinches slightly as she leans back in the barstool.

Climbing up from my seat, the room suddenly goes silent. It does that whenever I enter or move too quickly. I don't let it get to me.

"They fear you," the demon taunts. *"Show them why they should fear you. Start with that bitch of a baby mother of yours."* I stop walking as I shut my eyes to quiet the voice in my head.

The demon laughs. *"Let me out, Gabriel. Let me free."*

"No," I growl.

The voice laughs as it drifts away.

"Beastie, are you well?" Maksim asks.

I open my eyes. Everyone is looking at me as if I'm losing my mind. I feel as if I am. I don't reply to him. Instead, I go to the kitchen sink and pull the first aid kit from underneath. The room goes back to chatting again. I take out some pain meds and then go over to the fridge. After grabbing a bottle of water, I take it over and place it and the pills in front of Summer.

"Thanks, babe," she says with a smile, and then it quickly is replaced with a frown. "I meant, Gabriel."

I never thought hearing her use my name would hurt as bad as it does right now. When she called me Beast the other day, I thought I would lose my mind. I wanted her to call me Gabriel. But hearing her use the endearment and then take it back, I no longer wanted her to use Gabriel.

I don't know how long I stand there in front of her trying to calm the rage inside me.

"The bitch toys with you. Cut off her skin and wear it in front of her."

Pressing my hands to my head, I try to shove the demon out.

The moment I feel a soft touch on my arm, I open my eyes. She's touching my elbow. She tugs at the arm. I drop both hands back down to my side. Summer threads the fingers on her good arm through my fingers. Her thumb rubs the back of my hand soothingly.

"Brooklyn, I'll send you the oil I used for my stretch marks. It worked wonders," Summer goes on to say as if her simple touch isn't doing something I haven't been able to do since she was shot. She's quieted the demon.

Without removing my hand from her grasp, I glance around the room. Maksim is standing closer to me now. Apparently, Priest had also entered the room. He looks at Fem. She glances over at him. They have a quiet conversation with their eyes without speaking one word.

The entire time, I stand beside Summer's chair as she holds my hand.

I've almost completely zoned out, when suddenly Lucien rushes into the kitchen.

"I did it," he announces, looking frazzled. "I broke into the hard drive. I know who the records' keeper is."

It's been a full seven days since we broke into Pope's house and found that lock box. Lucien has been frantically trying to crack into that hard drive. It must have been locked down tighter than a military base.

"Fucking, finally," Priest grumbles. "Who is it?"

"Cardinal Jefferson 'Gutter' Watson."

Priest chuckles, but it isn't a funny laugh. "Grab Seth," he tells Lucien. "Beast, you and Maksim come with me."

"We should grab Zel too," Lucien adds. "We can use some eyes up high."

I agreed. We didn't need any last-minute surprises like the last time we went out. It took Lucien three days to wipe all the cameras completely. The news talked about the incident but had no viable footage of it. The Church did a supreme job of cleaning up the mess the disciples made.

Even two days ago when I went to grab Summer's clothes was a messy day. I lured those disciples behind the building and next to the trashcans, then let my Bowie do the work. I tossed the bodies in the dumpster and then called a clean-up crew before I left. I searched the web every day to make sure there was no sign of the event anywhere. So far, nothing has come up.

Before long we are cruising the streets in the black Suburban we got after trading in the minivan. I'm sitting in the second row. My hand still tingles from where Summer rubbed it.

"You alright?" Priest's voice has me looking up from my hands in my lap.

"Yes," I answer. "I'm capable of doing my job without you holding my hand, Priest."

He watches me for a long moment before holding his hands up in surrender. "Fine, I won't hold your hand."

He turns to face the front of the SUV. The car goes back to silent.

"But if it was Summer," Seth says from the back seat.

I turn to glare at him. However, he and the rest of the group laughs. In the past, this would have bothered me.

I don't like people laughing at me, but I get the joke now. Seeing how all my brothers have softened for their women lets me know that even though they are cracking on me, they understand my actions. I've watched them all bend over backwards for their significant others. I've even seen the calmness and serenity they get being in their girl's presence. Especially Seth. They aren't mocking me to be cruel, but out of love.

So, instead of getting angry, I turn around in my seat and go back to staring at my hand. Her touch is no longer present, but the warmth is still there.

Not long after, we pull up to a high-rise apartment complex. Before getting here, we stopped at the building across the way to let Zel out. Closing my door behind me, I scan the street around us. Nothing looks out of place, but I pay attention to all the cars parked near the front of the building. They are all vacant and there are no work vans anywhere around.

Priest walks up to my left adjusting his jacket. "Are you sure Lucien got the cameras on loop?"

Seth pulls out his phone and looks down at something. "Yep, we're all clear," he says replacing the phone in his pocket.

"Good. Beast and I will take the elevator up. Seth, you and Maksim wait about five minutes and take the stairs."

"Got it," Seth replies.

"Zel, you keep your eyes open and let us know if anything looks out of place," Priest says leading the way into the building.

We break off once inside. Priest and I go to the elevator leaving Maksim and Seth in the lobby. We make it to the top floor and then march down the hall toward the Cardinal's apartment.

I didn't have many dealings with Cardinals. Most of the people at the Church wanted as little interaction with me as possible. I didn't blame them. I do know that the Cardinals tend to get soft in their later years. Being so far removed from the fieldwork of Deacons, it made sense they weren't as sharp as we were. However, I also know that once a killer always a killer. It's like riding a bike. So, by no means will this be easy. Which is why the moment Priest, and I stopped in front of the door, I pulled out my weapon.

Priest puts his ear to the door and listens. He gives me a subtle head shake letting me know he didn't hear anything. He then steps back and reaches into the pocket of his suit jacket to retrieve two sharp tools. He sticks them both in the lock and starts to fiddle. It takes him less than three seconds to jiggle the handle and for it to click. Replacing his tools in his pocket, he pulls his gun out his back holster.

Slowly opening the door, he steps into the apartment with me on his heels. It takes only seconds to realize no one is home.

"The place is empty," he says out loud for the others to hear.

"I say we wait it out," Zel replies. "Lucien has recent footage of him still using the place as his main residence. He'll come back."

"I agree with, Zel," Seth adds and from the way his voice echoes you can tell he's in a stairwell.

Priest looks around at the apartment. It's obvious the place is occupied and judging by the empty wine glass on the side table, he's been here recently.

"Alright, we'll wait."

Before Priest could finish his statement, I hear footsteps outside the door. Placing a finger to my lips, I turn in the direction of the door. An older man with dark blonde short hair and brown eyes steps into the apartment carrying a paper grocery bag. The moment he spots us, true fear crosses his face.

"Hey, Watson. It's been a while," Priest says.

Watson drops the bag sending vegetables and canned goods across the floor. He takes off running. I follow.

"He's on the move," Priest's voice comes through my earpiece. Cardinal Watson looks over his shoulder as he fires a shot at me.

"Gun," I shout to Priest as I easily dodge the barrage of bullets.

Watson goes to the elevator and jabs the down button. However, I guess he realizes that it would never get here in time before I catch him. He shoots at me again, slowing down my pursuit as I have to dodge being shot. The bullet lodges in the wall near my head.

He takes off around the corner. Picking up my pace, I round the corner but quickly jump back as another bullet comes flying in my direction.

Peeking my head around the side of the wall, I notice he's running again. I take off after him. He looks over his shoulder, eyes wide in fear.

However, he's not paying attention and runs smack into Seth who has just emerged from the stairwell. Watson falls to the ground, his gun hitting the floor and sliding away.

"Well, hello, Cardinal." Seth sneers down at him.

"You are no longer a member of the Church. You have no authority here," Watson spits out at Seth.

Seth snorts before pulling his gun out and pressing the barrel to Watson's forehead. "You think I give a fuck about your protocols?"

"Easy, Seth," Priest says, stepping up beside me.

Watson looks over his shoulder and glares at Priest. "You never did have control over these mongrels."

Priest smiles. "I'm going to make this simple. All you have to do is answer a few questions and we will be out of your way. That's not too hard, is it?"

"I'm not telling you shit," Watson snarls.

Priest laughs. "Oh, you will tell me. You won't be happy about it, but you will tell me. Get his ass up."

Seth grabs Watson off the floor and hauls him to his feet. He shoves him in the back and Watson falls into my chest. He looks up at me and cringes before stepping back. Seth grabs his arm and drags him back to the apartment. Once inside we shut the door. Seth pushes Watson down onto the recliner in the living room.

Priest takes a seat on the end of the coffee table right in front of him.

"I always knew you were Luca's lap boy. I should have known you were his records' keeper. You two rode each other's dicks so hard I was always amazed neither of you got pregnant."

Watson's top lip pulls back showcasing his teeth. "Don't you speak our Pope's name. I know you had something to do with his death. Even if this excommunication order wasn't already in play, I would have made sure the truth was revealed."

Priest chuckles. "You think I killed my brother?"

"Half-brother," Watson snarls. "He told me how your mother was a whore."

Priest tilts his head to the side. It's the only tell he has when he's beyond pissed.

The smile on his face contradicts how I know he really feels. "I'm going to let that remark pass only because I know how your day is going to end. I'm still on the fence on which son I'll let finish you."

Watson's eyes balloon once again when he looks over at me. He thinks I'll be worse than Seth. I most likely will, but Seth won't be a day in the park.

"I won't tell you anything," he declares, lifting his chin higher.

Priest leans back and pulls out his cellphone. He clicks a few buttons, and it starts to ring with a FaceTime call.

"You found him?" Albany says as soon as she answers.

"Yep," Priest replies. "He's all yours." He flips the phone around.

Watson shoots up from his seat when he realizes who is on the other end of the line. Maksim shoves him back down in the chair.

"This can't be. She's dead," Watson shouts.

"Surprise," Albany laughs. "I've been resurrected. Now, Watson, an excommunication order was signed on my husband and his sons. Who signed the bill?"

Watson shakes his head. "I don't know."

"You do know," Albany argues. "You were there the day it was signed."

He scoffs shaking his head. "You don't know anything. A record keeper doesn't sit in on meetings of the Pope. That's not how that works."

"Then tell me how it works?"

He shakes his head again. "I'm not telling *you* anything. Your skills won't work on me."

They all say that. Everyone likes to believe that Albany's talent will never work on them. They think they are immune. They are always wrong.

"You're right," she sighs. "I'm sorry Priest, but I don't think he's going to crack. You're going to have to find the copy of the EO to figure out who signed it. Watson is just too loyal to Pope to give us anything."

"Maybe we should start looking here," Seth says.

"No, I think we should check his office at headquarters," Priest adds.

The entire time they are talking, Priest keeps the phone facing Watson.

"I would never hide important documents in my home," Watson laughs as if we are all idiots. "You are wasting your time here. And if you think you will be able to waltz into Church headquarters—"

"They're at his house," Albany says cutting him off.

"Wait, what?" Watson looks confused.

Albany groans over the phone. "Men are idiots. You never corrected me when I said there was a copy of the EO. If I were wrong, you would have proudly pointed that out just like you did when I mentioned you being present. The moment Seth mentioned your house you started to panic. It was subtle, but it was in your eyes. In fact, you looked to the right. I'm not sure what's over to his right, babe, but you might want to check there first."

The entire room turns toward the large framed picture on the wall. I don't know why everybody uses pictures to hide shit.

"You also gave yourself away when you told us you wouldn't hide anything at your home," Albany finishes. "Cardinal Watson, thank you for your assistance."

Priest turns the phone back around and smiles into the screen.

"You know my dick gets hard every time you do that."

The sound of Albany's soft chuckles fills the room. Seth makes a gagging sound.

"Yeah, well you hurry up and bring that hard dick home and maybe I'll let you touch my tonsils again."

Priest's face turns red before he ends the call and tucks the phone in his pocket. I won't lie as if the thought of my cock in Summer's mouth doesn't flash in my head. I miss the way her mouth felt wrapped around my length. It wasn't the only thing I missed about her.

"You know, there is a lot of fucking in that house. I'm starting to get jealous," Maksim pouts.

"You and me both," Zel adds into the earpiece.

Priest stands from the coffee table ignoring Zel and Maksim. He walks over to the picture and takes it down. To no one's surprise, a safe is hidden in the wall. It's a fancy one that will require a retinal scan.

"We're going to need his eyeball," Priest says over his shoulder as he places the picture on the ground.

Without thought, I pull out my knife. Place a hand to Watson's chest and with the tip of my blade under his right eyeball, I shove forward. Watson howls in pain and thrashes against my hold. The eye falls forward. I use the knife to cut the tendons before tossing it to Priest. He catches it but looks down at it horridly.

Watson continues to cry out in pain.

"We could've just taken him over to the safe." Maksim points out.

"Admittedly," I shrug. "I didn't think of that."

Priest turned back to the retinal scan and placed the eyeball against the device. It beeps as a red light scans the eye and then it turns green. He tosses the eye over his shoulder. It flies toward Maksim, but he quickly moves out of the way to dodge it.

Priest opens the safe and sitting inside are stacks of paper. He brings the papers over to us separating them out between us.

I flip the pages in my hand before coming to a crisp white sheet with the official seal of the Church.

I read the paper out loud. "By decree of Pope Luca Otella, it is thereby set forth that Priest Nathaniel Otella, Deacon Killian Hawk Walker, Deacon Hiroshi Zel Tanaka, Deacon Luciano Seth Twins Gramble, Deacon Milo Many Beckett, and Deacon Gabriel Beast Taylor are henceforth no longer members of the Church. They have been excommunicated. Anyone found harboring or aiding them will be punished. Set price of excommunication is ten million per head. Signed into effect by Elliot Joseph Corbyn, Franklin H. Smith, Samuel Mason O'Cleary, and Dominique J Katz." I finish.

I hand the paper over to Priest who quickly scans over it before passing it to the others.

"Damn, ten million for each of us?" Zel says through the earpiece. "They weren't playing about wanting our heads."

A strained laugh comes from Watson. "There's nothing you can do," he says as he holds a hand over his bleeding eye. His voice is weak and frail, and he can barely hold his head up. He won't last long.

"The bill has been signed by people more powerful than you will ever know. I'll die peacefully knowing you will finally get what you deserve, Priest."

Priest turns to face Watson. He laughs. "The funniest thing about of all this, is that you believe you will die peacefully."

The smile on Watson's face falls immediately.

"Have your fun, Seth," Priest says without looking at Seth.

Seth rubs his hands together. "This is going to hurt, Cardinal. It's going to hurt a lot."

Maksim, Priest, and I make our way over to the kitchen. Priest places the document down in front of us.

"What are we up against, Sim?"

He shakes his head before answering. "I think we all knew Corbyn's name would be on this document. However, I don't think it's wise to go after him."

"Are you still trying to protect your father?" I ask.

Maksim glares at me. His eyes narrow and darken. "I'm going to let that dumb ass comment pass, little brother. If my loyalty isn't clear to you by now, let me know?"

Priest holds up a hand. "No one is questioning your loyalty, Maksim. You've proven it." He then cuts his eyes over to me. "Right, Beast?"

"Why do you want to wait to go after Corbyn?" Loyal or not, I wanted the answer.

Maksim rakes a hand over his head. "You're underestimating him. No matter what you think you have planned, he is prepared for you to come for him. Corbyn has more money, more guns, and more allies than you. It would be pointless to take him head on. Especially without the backing of the Church."

I nod, content with his answer. It wasn't going to stop me from going after him in the end, but that was my battle with Corbyn.

Watson's screams break through our conversation. I glance back into the living room to see Seth chop off one of Watson's fingers and then stuff it in his mouth.

I turn back to the document in front of me.

"What about the other names on this list?" Priest asks Maksim.

"The most alarming name I see is Dominique Katz. He and Corbyn disagree about everything, so it's strange he'd agree to sign this bill."

"How much of a problem is he?" Zel asks over the earpiece.

"His pockets are deeper than Corbyn's which means he has the means and time to defend himself. He has trained men around him just like Corbyn, I'm talking military special ops trained."

Not promising records' keeper, but still nothing will keep me from making sure my family is safe.

Watson's scream cuts into my thoughts once again. I turn to see what caused this one. Seth is now slowly carving something into his chest.

"An amateur," the demon snarls. *"He sent an amateur to do the job you're more qualified to do. You should check the kitchen drawers for something to pull his spine out of his back."*

"Beast, what are you doing?"

Priest's voice brings me out of my haze. When I come to, I'm looking through the cutlery drawer. I slam it closed causing the silverware to clink together.

"Get out of my head," I growl.

The demon laughs at my request. Once I gain control, I open my eyes to find Priest and Maksim staring at me. Priest narrows his gaze before turning to Seth who is still working. When Priest turns back to me, he studies me for a second longer.

"Hey, Seth," Priest calls out without taking his eyes off me.

"Yeah," Seth replies.

"Wrap it up. We need to go." Priest says nothing else as he goes back to the document.

"So, who do we go to first?" Priest asks.

Maksim looks down at the bill once more before answering. "O'Cleary," He points to the name Samuel J. O'Cleary on the paper.

"We'll have Lucien track him down and find the best way to approach him," Priest says taking the paper and rolling it up before sticking it in the inside pocket of his suit jacket.

We walk into the living room where Seth is sitting on the table watching the life slowly drain from Watson.

"All good?" Priest asks.

Seth stands and wipes his blade off on the arm of Watson's chair.

"Yeah, I'm good." He replaces his blade in his holster.

106 • Tiya Rayne

Priest makes a call to the cleaning crew as we head out of the apartment.

When we make it back downstairs to the lobby, Priest stops me right as we walk outside.

"I know you want to know why I didn't let you kill Watson."

I scratched my chin. Until now, I didn't want to think about it.

He goes on to say. "That thing in your head, do you trust it enough to let it roam free yet?"

I look away from him. "No."

"Did it come out while we were standing in the kitchen?"

"Yes."

Priest nods. "We're going to figure this out, Beast. First, we're going to handle this EO shit, and then we're going to get your mother's voice back."

I dip my chin to my chest as if I'm agreeing, but deep down I know it's a lost cause. There is only one way to silence the demon.

It laughs in my head. *"You're too pussy to ever do that. Don't make idle threats, Gabriel."*

"Come on," Priest says tapping my arm. "Let's go grab Zel and get out of here."

As he turns, a familiar whistling sound hits my ears. I shove Priest to the side and step back. An arrow comes flying and landing in the concrete where Priest was once standing.

"Archer," I shout. "Seth, get to the truck." I don't have time to check and see if he listens, because I take off for the lobby of the apartment building. I'm a little too late as an arrow narrowly misses my arm, cutting into my flesh.

A second after I'm under the awning of the apartment, Priest joins me.

"Fuck, that came out of nowhere," he says checking my shoulder.

"I'm good," I tell him. "Zel, do you have sights on Archer?"

"No, he's on top of the building. He had to be waiting there since we got here. He hasn't been in any of the cars that pulled up."

"We are getting swamped out here," Maksim shouts. Glancing back toward the truck, I can see the many arrows puncturing the vehicle.

"You said he's on our roof?" I ask Zel.

"Yeah, I think so."

Turning around, I stomp back into the building.

"Beast, where are you going?" Priest shouts.

I don't answer as I stop the first person I see. "Where is your maintenance elevator?" I growl.

The man carrying his small dog shakes as he points around the corner. I march off leaving him there. I find the elevator and climb in. Pulling my gun out of my back holster, I take the safety off. As soon as the doors open, I step off ready to fire. However, I don't see anything. The top of the building is open except for a few large air conditioner units. I use the first one as a shield as I peak around the other side of the building. That's when I spot Archer.

He came in after us. Many other priests tried to duplicate the magic that Priest had. There were so many blind recruits the year after Hawk came in, it was crazy. However, most failed because they couldn't understand the real reason we were as successful as we were. It had nothing to do with our gifts but more to do with the man that raised us.

Archer is blind in one eye, but he turned out to be a decent recruit unlike most others they brought in. He's nowhere near as talented as Hawk though.

Archer's back is to me as he rapidly fires off one arrow after another. It reminds me of one of the superheroes my son likes.

Before I can aim my gun, Archer turns around with an arrow docked and fires straight at me. I duck behind the metal unit before I get hit.

"Beast is that you?" he calls out. "Why don't you step out of the shadows. Let me get a good look at you."

Slowly, I glance around the air unit. An arrow comes whizzing by again as I slide back to avoid getting hit.

"Beast, I need you to get me a clear shot," Zel says in the earpiece.

"Where are you?" I whisper.

"To the left of that large green square thing."

I move to the other side of my unit and peek around to see where Zel is. I spot a flash of light reflection. We've used the technique before. Zel usually holds up a mirror and reflects it off the sun so we can find him.

"Alright," I say. "I'll draw him out."

I listen closely trying to find where Archer is.

"Archer," I say once I don't hear him. "We don't have to do this. I'll come out."

It's silent for a moment, and then I hear the slight sound of gravel underneath feet right on the other side of the unit. Seconds later, Archer rounds the corner, his arrow docked. I only have a split second to react as the arrow flies clipping my ear.

I move fast, knocking the weapon out of his hands. Archer drops down and sweeps my legs out from under me. I stumble to the ground falling on my back. He does a backwards flip heading toward his weapon. Getting back to my feet, I pull my Bowie out and toss it in his calf.

He groans as he stumbles to the ground. I march over to him and grab his leg. He turns to the side and there is a small object in his hands. Too late, I realize what it is. The small dart launcher shoots off, hitting me in the chest.

I stumble back before yanking the little dart out of my chest. The moment I pull it out, I start to feel woozy.

Archer gets to his feet and charges at me. Even though the vision of him keeps getting blurry before clearing up, I can see him well enough. As soon as he's close enough I reach out my hand and grab him by the throat. He pulls out a small blade and slices at my arm.

I groan. "Fuck."

I toss his ass to the ground a few feet away from me. Immediately, my world becomes more and more blurry.

"You feel that?" Archer asks rolling to his side. "It won't kill you, but it's enough tranquilizer to knock your big ass out."

I stumbled once again. I have to prop my hand up against the air unit to keep my balance.

"I've been.....poisoned," I say out loud knowing someone in my earpiece will here.

"Stay put, we're on our way, Beast," It's Seth's voice I hear in the earpiece.

Archer leaps up from the ground and charges at me. His shape is too blurry to make him out completely. He yells as he draws closer.

My vision clears long enough to watch the bullet from Zel's rifle blow a hole in his head. It's the last thing I see before I go crashing to the ground. Only one thing crossed my mind. Summer.

CHAPTER TWELVE

D.O.E

Beast

I have no concept of time. My world is a mix of excruciating pain and vivid nightmares. There is a small reprieve in the mix. The sweetest voice I've ever heard calls out to me and soothes me in between the pain and the dreams.

"Summer," a female voice says. It is not the voice of the angel I hear in my dreams. "Sweetheart, you haven't eaten all day. You need to eat."

"I'm not hungry," the angel says. Her tone is sad as if she's crying.

The brief reprieve is over, and the pain is back. It feels as if my body is burning from the inside. I groan as my muscles began to spasm.

"Gabriel, baby, please. I'm here," the angel cries before the soft touch of something wet and cold touches my skin. I want to go to the angel, to reassure her I am alright, but the nightmares pull me back.

The dream world tries to pull me under. I clamber from its fingertips, resurfacing once again. Low humming has me turning my head to the sound.

"How is he today?" This voice belongs to a man.

The humming stops. "The same," the angel is back.

A deep sigh fills the room. "It's been twenty-four hours. You need to get some fresh air and eat something."

"I'm not hungry, Sim."

"Please, little sister."

"I said I'm not hungry." Someone has angered my angel. I fight to gain control of my body. I want to get up and rip the culprit's head off. But nothing moves on me.

Suddenly the pain comes rushing back. My moment of clarity is gone. This time, the fire in my body seems to rush to my head making it feel as if it would explode. I yell out. Trying to fight the feeling of my brain melting. Without my consent my body thrashes from side to side.

"Oh my goodness, Gabriel," the angel shouts.

"Fuck," the male voice says. "Priest." It shouts.

Suddenly hands are covering me trying to hold me down. In the distance I can hear her sobs. My angel is crying. It is the last thing I hear before the nightmares suck me back under.

I'm not sure how much time has passed. The dream world has set me free again. I am no longer back in the house with my mother. This time when I resurface, everything is much clearer. The softness of the sheets underneath me tickles my skin. The scents of lavender, vanilla, and the distant scent of stale food assails me. Even the coolness of the room stands out. I've never been as aware of my surroundings as I am right now.

There is silence in the room. I flex my foot and for the first time it actually moves.

A loud bang echoes. It sounds like a door slamming against a wall. Fast, heavy footsteps approach.

"Alright, that's it," Priest shouts. "It's been three days. You haven't left this room, nor have you eaten any of the food we've brought you. Get your ass up, get some fresh air, and eat."

"I'm not leaving him," Summer argues. "His fever just broke two hours ago. It could come back."

"Summer, if you don't get your ass out that chair and go eat, I'll drag you out and force feed you. I know you're worried about my son. But when he wakes up and realize we let you starve to death I'm going to have to fucking kill him."

"But," she starts.

However, I cut her off. "He's right." My voice sounds raw, and my throat burns like hell.

"Gabriel," Summer screams before something soft and solid hits my chest.

I wrap my arms around her, happy to be able to do it. Finally opening my eyes, I spot Priest standing over my head. His hair is disheveled and his white button up shirt is wrinkled all to hell. He looks as if he hasn't slept in several days.

His eyes are red as he stares back at me. Summer lifts from my chest, tears falling down her face.

"Why aren't you eating?" I ask.

"We thought you were going to die," she cries.

Slowly, and with a lot of effort, I lift my hand and wipe her tears. There is so much I want to say to her. Like, never in a million years will I let anyone take me off the face of this earth without making sure her and Gabe are taken care of. I know that at some point I'll have to go after Corbyn and it might just be the last thing I do, but I will make sure that Summer and Gabe will never have to be concerned about their future or what will happen to them.

But I don't say any of that because I'm trying to do the right thing by her. Even if it's the last thing I want to do.

"You need to eat, angel."

"I just sat here for three days thinking you would die. I don't want to eat."

Cupping her face in my hands I stare into her brown eyes.

"Do it for me. I need you to eat something."

I can tell in her eyes she wants to argue, but my only concern is her health. Priest is right, if I'd woken from this and something had happened to Summer, I'd lose my shit.

"Okay," she finally says.

She pushes up from the bed and walks to the door. She stops before walking out and turns to look at me again. I can see the words I love you in her eyes. She wants to say them to me, but I can also read the uncertainness in her stance. I think she knows that saying the words won't change our status. Our love for each other is not the issue.

"I know," I say, replying to her unsaid statement. "Go eat," I demand.

Nodding, she walks out of the room. The moment she's out of sight, I sink back into the bed. The little energy I held on for her is now sapped out of my body.

"That woman loves you to death. She never left your side the entire three days."

I don't reply to him.

Priest walks over to the side of the bed. "A love like that is hard to come by. You should cherish it—"

"What happened?" I ask turning to look at him.

I didn't need relationship advice. I already knew everything he was saying. Our love for each other wouldn't change the fact that I am a hazard to Summer. Because I love her too, I will never risk her life.

Running a hand over his short hair, Priest takes a seat in the chair I'm sure Summer spent most of her time in.

"Some type of plant-based poison. Doc said you had enough in your system that probably would have killed a normal sized man. Thankfully you're not normal size."

He tries for a laugh, but it doesn't sound authentic.

"You scared the hell out of me, kid."

Glad to be off the topic of me and Summer, I push up from the bed and place my back against the headboard.

"You and I both know my death will be a lot more brutal than plant poison."

"As long as it happens after mine, I won't argue." He tugs at his chin hair.

"What did I miss?"

Priest sighs, leaning back in the chair. "Not much. We kind of put everything on hold until you got better. Fem is getting help from the DOE. They should be coming in today."

"Help with what?"

"Tracking down these Royal Crown signatures. We need all hands on deck to get to these people. Lucien can't do it by himself."

I nod in understanding. My brother is talented, but juggling his pregnant girl, a daughter, and this work, it's not easy on him. It took him days to break into Pope's hard drive.

"How's you mental?" He asks hesitantly.

Pushing the cover back, I swing my legs over the side of the bed. "You don't have to ask me that every ten minutes."

"I know I don't, but I will." He stands up from the chair and holds out a hand to me. Reluctantly, I take it. He helps pull me to my feet. My head swims momentarily, but I remain on my feet.

"It will always be my job to protect you and make sure you're okay. If that means I have to ask you every ten minutes if that damn thing in your head is fucking with you then I will."

Although I want to argue, I don't. I needed to know I had him on my side. Since I was a boy Priest has been the one to truly care about me. He has accepted everything about me since the first day he met me.

The memory of him pulling me out of that cage at mother's crosses my mind. I was so embarrassed when he lifted me up. I was covered in piss and shit, but he didn't care. Instead of taking me back to the others smelling awful, he stopped at a truck stop and took me inside the bathroom where he bought me things to bathe and clean myself. He purchased me some cheap clothes and some of those rubber slip on shoes for showers. This man has always had my back.

It's because of that, I answer his question. "It's silent right now."

He nods. "Any reason you think that is?"

"My head's still a bit too muddled from the poison, maybe."

He seems to take that in. "Okay. Let's keep track of when it's more active."

I agree before heading into the bathroom. Before I shut the door, Priest calls out one last time.

"Come to the dining room once you get done in there." He walks out the room.

I shut the door to the bathroom to get cleaned up.

Feeling more alive than ever, I make my way outside. I know I told Priest I was going to come see him when I was done, but I needed to make a more important stop first.

"Hulk," Gabe shouts as soon as he sees me. He runs up to me and wraps his arms around my lower half.

Stepping back, I squat down to get to his height. He then wraps his arms around my neck. I relish in the feel of his tight embrace. Summer explained that hugs from Gabe were rare and should be cherished.

He steps back from my embrace with a large smile on his face. I also notice a slight bruise on his cheek. It's old and almost healed, but I've had enough bruises to spot them at any stage.

"What happened to your face?"

He looks down before responding. "Emory and I were playing. It was an accident."

I look over his head at Emory. I go through my emotional Rolodex to read the expression on her face. Guilt. I can immediately tell that whatever happened, she did not mean to hurt him.

Her hands move rapidly as she signs. "I'm sorry. I apologized to him."

I hold up a hand to stop her. "It's okay. You both should be careful when playing."

They both nod in understanding.

"I've missed you, Hulk," my son says fully distracting me from his bruise. "Mama said you were sick."

"I missed you too. And I was sick. But I'm much better now."

He reaches out slowly and touches my ear. The wound is still pretty red from the stitches, but it doesn't hurt. The arrow cut the top of my ear, slicing it into two pieces, but I'm assuming Doc stitched it back together.

"Does it hurt?" Gabe asks.

"No. Not anymore."

He pauses for a moment, then looks over his shoulder before turning back to me. He lowers his voice as he asks, "Are you scared when you get hurt?"

Although his question is odd, I answer it anyway. "Getting hurt is part of my job. It isn't about being scared. It's knowing that it's part of the risk. Firefighters, soldiers, and police officers all know that when they go to work, they risk getting hurt. But you must be brave enough to do what needs to be done."

Gabe is quiet for a moment as if he's thinking over my reply. I wonder does his question have anything to do with the accidental bruise under his eye.

"Why do you ask?"

He looks over his shoulder at Emory before turning back to me. "No reason," he says.

A trained deacon left a bruise under my son's eye and now he's asking about fearing getting hurt.

Shaking my head, I sigh. "Just remember when you are playing this game, one of you are trained and one of you are learning."

Emory nods and gives me a thumbs up.

I lean into Gabe and whisper. "Learn how to block."

He grins and puts his arms up in a blocking form in front of his face. I stand and ruffle his hair. I spent a few more minutes outside with him, Emory, and the dogs, before going back inside.

The house seems to be buzzing with energy. Walking into the dining room, I pause. It looks like a high-tech conference room. The table and chairs are still here, but at the front of the room is a large whiteboard. On the side of the room closest to the door, is a small table with a large flat screen TV. A rectangular folding table is in the back of the room and there are four computers set up on it.

Everyone is already here. Priest and all my brothers along with Albany, Many's girlfriend, and three other women. One is dark-skinned with gray eyes. She's talking to Albany near the whiteboard. The other girl has a deep brown complexion the same color as Albany. Although not as dark as the first girl, it's nowhere near as light as Summer's. She's tall, has to be at least six feet. Her glasses are perched on the bridge of her nose and her straight black hair hangs past her shoulders. When she spots me, she smiles brightly at me as if she's known me all her life.

Mother said they would all run from me.

The other girl in the room has a golden tan complexion. Her hair is long and curly with brown and blonde highlights. She's too busy setting up a computer system to pay attention to me.

"Oh, Beast, you're finally here," Priest says coming over to me. "These are the ladies of the Daughters of Egypt. They are friends and colleagues of Fem and Ari. That's Kyra," he says pointing to the girl with gray eyes talking to Albany.

"The one working on the computer is Deidra. And that's Alicia," he points to the tall girl with the pretty smile. She walks over to us and holds out a hand to me.

"Hi," Alicia says, voice light and friendly.

Looking down at her offered hand I slowly reach out my hand to shake hers. Her fingers are skinny compared to mine. They seem too fragile. I quickly remove my hand from hers hoping I won't hurt her.

She pushes her straight hair behind her ear before rocking back on her heels.

"So, have they told you why we're here?"

Instead of answering, I dip my chin to my chest.

"Good, well come on, I'll show you the setup." She turns and walks away. Her skirt, though it touches her knees, hugs her curves tightly.

"Kid," Priest says beside me. "I promise you don't want those problems."

I'm not sure what he's getting at. What problems? I shake off his words and follow the woman to her computer.

"We have every satellite we own searching for Sam O'Cleary." She points to the map on her screen. She then points to the bigger monitor at the front of the room. The big monitor has the same thing as her computer, only much bigger. There are small glowing circles covering most of the map on the screen.

"The moment his face is recognized, it will alert us on here. We will then pinpoint his location."

"What then?" I ask folding my arms over my chest.

"Well, we track him down, follow him, and figure out the best way to isolate him so that you and your brothers can confront him."

It seemed simple enough, but I knew it wouldn't be that easy. These people had access to travel all around the world. Trying to track them down would be like finding a needle in a haystack.

"So now we just wait while your satellites play Where's Waldo," I say.

Alicia laughs. It's soft and airy like her voice. She touches my arm.

"Wow, handsome and funny. A rare combination."

I look down at her hand on my arm. I wait for it to give me that ick feeling. The one that would usually make me step out of her grasp. However, it doesn't come.

Priest clears his voice causing me to look up at him. He swings his head to the doorway where I find Malia and Summer. Malia is smiling as she brings in a tray of sandwiches. Summer is watching me closely. Her eyes glued to where Alicia's hand is lying on my arm. The ick feeling finally hits and I subtly step away from Alicia's touch.

When I turn back to the door, Summer is no longer standing there.

Where did she go?

"I swear you boys are going to cause me to have a damn stroke," Priest says shaking his head as he walks away.

I ignore him as I walk out of the room. I needed to find Summer. She wasn't too far. I find her pacing in the kitchen. On the island are all the ingredients used to make those sandwiches.

"Did you eat?" I ask as soon as I enter.

She turns and glares at me before turning back to the counter. She picks up the bag of bread and ties the end.

"Yes, I ate," she says curtly.

I have no idea why she's being so cross with me. An hour ago, I had to force her out my room and now she won't look at me. Her anger seems as if it has come out of the blue.

She continues to tidy up the food while slamming the cabinets closed.

"Are you going to tell me why you're angry with me?"

She stops what she's doing to glare up at me. "Are you fucking serious right now?"

I narrow my gaze, but don't respond.

She rolls her eyes. "What the hell was that in there?" She points toward the wall.

"They were showing us the set up for their satellites."

"Don't play with me," she says through clenched teeth. "I'm talking about you smiling all up in that chick's face."

She had me completely stumped. I had no idea I was smiling at all. Even if I was, what's wrong with smiling?

"I made a joke, and she laughed."

"Oh really," she crosses her arms over her chest. "Let me hear the joke. I want to laugh too."

I watch her for a moment trying to read her expression. Although her words say one thing, the frown on her face and the way her brows pinch tells me she is not in the mood for a joke at all.

"I don't know what you want from me, Summer." I admit truthfully.

She shakes her head dropping her arms. "I spent three damn days by your bed praying that you don't die, and you don't know what I want from you?"

Running a hand through my hair, my frustration grows. She keeps saying everything but what she wants. It's like she thinks I'm supposed to know why she's vexed without her telling me.

"She's become mouthy," the demon says making a reappearance. My breathing picks up as I fight to silence the voice.

"Are you listening to me?" Summer shouts.

"Maybe if you cut out her tongue, she'll be a little more obedient."

Shutting my eyes, I take a step away from her, trying to put distance between us. The things the demon wants me to do to her are hard to block out.

"Gabriel," she calls my name, and her voice seems to grate my nerves.

"Kill this bitch already. We don't need her, Gabriel."

"Babe, look at me." Summer touches my arm. I snatch away from her and step back.

"Don't touch me," I growl.

Her eyes widen momentarily as she watches me. Her features go from pinched in concern to sadness.

"So, I can't touch you now?"

The demon laughs. *"She wants you to kill her. It's why she keeps taunting us. Let me out."*

I need to get away from her. I need Summer to never want to be near me again. Lately, the demon has seemed to only focus on hurting her. It's in every vision and every word that it says.

"No," the word comes out like it's coated in acid.

Her mouth falls open and she looks stunned. "Wow," she simply replies.

"Do I need to remind you, we aren't together anymore, Summer." I choose my words carefully. I need them to sting. The more she hates me the more she will stay away from me.

She looks away, her gaze going to the wall. A tear tracks down her face. She quickly wipes it away before turning back to me.

"You will never have to remind me again." She turns and walks out of the kitchen, squeezing past Priest as she goes. I have no idea when he walked in. Priest watches me for a moment. His gaze is penetrating.

"I hope you have a good reason for that," he says.

I don't reply verbally. Instead, I dip my chin to my chest.

"I won't ask you to elaborate right now. We got a hit on that O'Cleary guy. Come on." He turns and walks out of the room. For a moment I stand in my spot thinking over my actions. It eats me up to know I hurt Summer, but it's for her own good.

"It won't last long," the demon says before laughing. *"She'll be back. And I will slit her throat then."*

I shake off his words as I make my way back to the dining room.

CHAPTER THIRTEEN

S. O'Cleary

Beast

Although Alicia and the D.O.E were able to track down Sam the same day I woke up, it took us two weeks to set up a plan to get close to him.

Those two weeks have been hell. My plan to keep Summer away worked. However, I didn't realize how miserable it would make me to have her so close yet so far away. She no longer allows me in her room at night. The first two nights after she kicked me out, I would wait until she fell asleep to sneak into her room and sit in the corner.

Unfortunately, she woke up in the middle of the night to use the bathroom on the third night and kicked me out. Since then, she's locked her door. I'm back to sitting outside the room all night. During the daytime, she speaks to everyone but me.

As hard of a pill it is to swallow, it is still for the best. The demon inside of me is still fighting to take her away from me.

"I will bleed her slowly and then fuck her corpse," the demon growls in my head.

Shutting my eyes, I fight against the monster's pull. It gets harder and harder each day.

"Beast?" Priest calls my name causing me to open my eyes and look at him.

We're disguised as a lawn care service outside of Sam O'Cleary's million-dollar mansion. The regular guys couldn't work today due to some truck issues. We've been tampering with their trucks for a week.

"Focus," Priest says reminding me we had a job to do.

A rock flies through the air, nearly hitting me in the face. I turn to Many and glare.

"We are sorry brother, Beast," he says in his British accent. "We are not really good with a weed eater."

I can't fault him because none of us know what we're doing. Hawk has dug up two flower beds. Seth is going in circles on the lawn mower and I'm not sure if he has cut a blade of grass. The mulch Zel is spreading looks as if he's just tossing it in the air. Many and I are supposed to be weed eating while Priest is trimming back hedges.

Maksim is home today. Because of his relationship with Corbyn, O'Cleary would recognize him immediately.

The garage door opens, and a Hummer backs out the driveway. Inside is O'Cleary's wife and two boys.

"The wife is on the move," Priest says, his voice coming from beside me and through the earpiece.

"Is the house clear now?" Priest asks Albany. She's back home keeping visuals on the cameras inside. It took the girls from DOE no time to hack into O'Cleary's camera system.

"Yes, only O'Cleary and two staff members are left in the home. You still have that bodyguard at the door and the one outside with you."

Priest and I both turn to the large burly man that's standing at the top of the yard watching us wearily. He has yet to leave us alone.

"Alright, Zel. Take care of the guard," Priest instructs.

Without a word, Zel walks over to the guard, he's still spreading mulch as he goes. As soon as he's close enough, he tosses the mulch bag to the ground, pulls out his gun and fires a tranquilizer into the guard's neck. The guard is too slow to react. The tranquilizer guns were provided to us by D.O.E. We didn't want to kill any innocent bystanders if we didn't have to.

The guard drops to the ground. Hawk joins Zel, and they pull the man into the bushes before covering him with the mulch. The tranq should knock him out for four or more hours.

I toss the weed eater I'm carrying to the ground. Seth climbs off the lawn mower without cutting it off. The noise will serve to keep up the charade and distract anyone inside from knowing we aren't still working.

We move as a unit toward the back of the house.

"Unlock the door," Priest says to Albany.

There is a second's delay before her voice comes through the earpiece. "Alarm is off, and the door is unlocked."

People will never know how easy it is to break into computer-controlled alarm systems. Zel leads the way inside. We stay low with our tranquilizer guns out in front of us.

"You have a bogie coming around the corner to your left, Beast," Alicia's soft voice says in my earpiece.

I turn the corner and fire off a tranq. It hits the maid in the chest. She drops quickly.

"Thanks," I say in response to Alicia.

"You're always welcome," she hums.

When I look to my right, Priest is looking at me shaking his head. He doesn't speak as he goes back to moving through the house.

We quickly take down the second guard and the butler.

"Where is O'Cleary?" Priest asks.

"Upstairs in the shower. His room is on the second floor. Last room on your left."

We follow the directions Albany gives us. Keeping our ears open and staying alert. The sound of the shower tells us he's still in the bathroom.

Priest enters the room first with me bringing up the rear. We take up the full space of the room. I stand close to the door keeping my eyes on the exit. Priest sits on the bed. He will be the first person O'Cleary sees when he walks out. Hawk is on the wall beside the bathroom. It will put him behind O'Cleary. Seth is leaning against the wall behind Priest's head. Many is beside me and Zel is on the wall across from me. We have every inch of the room covered.

The shower water cuts off and I'm brought back to the night I killed Andrew. It was the night I promised Summer, I'd never leave her again. A promise I've had to break.

"It's for her own good," I remind myself.

The sound of drawers closing in the bathroom brings me back to the moment. We wait another five minutes for the door to open.

Samuel O'Cleary steps out of the bathroom in a fluffy white robe. He's in his early forties. A businessman that inherited his family's billion-dollar, multinational, confectionery, food, holding, beverage and snack food company. Their products are in every grocery store worldwide.

"Who the hell are you people?" he asks alarmed.

"You signed an excommunication order on us, and you don't even know who we are?" Priest asks.

Sam's eyes narrow before a slow smile appears on his face. I'm used to his reaction. The Royal Crown did not fear the Church.

Sam chuckles. "Oh, you're part of that little Church thing," he sneers walking further into the room. He goes over to his dresser and pulls out some boxers. Without a care in the world, he slips on his underwear underneath his robe before turning back to us.

"What can I do for you men?" he says cheerfully. "But make it quick, I have things to do."

Priest turns to look at me. "You weren't lying. They don't fear us."

I shake my head.

"Fear you," Sam says laughing. "Why would we fear what we own."

Seth starts to chuckle. Priest follows along with Hawk, Zel, and Many all joining. Priest stands from the bed, tugging on the sleeve of his jumpsuit.

"You own the Church," he says walking up to Sam.

"Of course we do."

"Except, you forgot something," Priest says stopping in front of Sam.

"And what's that?" Sam folds his arms over his chest.

"Thanks to you, we no longer work for the Church." With those words, Priest pulls his actual gun out and places it at Sam's cheek.

"Whoa. Whoa," Sam says, the humor from his earlier tone is no longer there. "Wait a minute."

"No, we won't wait." Priest slings Sam by the collar of his robe to the middle of the floor. He lands flat on his back.

"Let me tell you something about the Church." Priest walks slowly over to where Sam is lying. "The Church, for all its flaws, creates damn good killers. They have a way of desensitizing you from the fear of death and the outcome of it. They teach you that pulling the trigger on a female begging for her life in front of her children is no different than stepping on a spider that somehow got lost in your bedroom."

He squats down in front of Sam. Placing his gun at Sam's knee cap.

"The Church creates perfect monsters. It's why they have such strict rules. For instance, rather than letting one of its members go, they'd rather kill them off. They know that once you've been trained to kill you can't shut it off. Once you've been conditioned to take a life without remorse or second thought, you cannot survive in the real world. It's too dangerous.

"Now the part that you play in this story, is that you helped set free seven of the deadliest motherfuckers the Church has ever seen. And right now, six of them are in the room with you and they are pissed the fuck off."

"I'm sorry. I'm sorry," O'Cleary claims.

"I don't want your got damn apology, O Cleary."

"What do you want then?" he asks the million-dollar question.

Priest stands and then nods for O'Cleary to do the same. Slowly the man gets to his feet.

With a polite smile, Priest says. "I want you to withdraw your signature on that order."

O'Cleary's eyes balloon. "Are you mad?" he scoffs. "Corbyn would—"

"Corbyn isn't here right now," Priest says cutting him off. "So, you need to make the decision. Would you rather die now at the hands of my sons or face Corbyn's wrath later?" Turning his back to O'Cleary, Priest walks over to the dresser and leans his back against it folding his arms over his chest.

He stares at O'Cleary waiting for him to make the decision. O'Cleary looks around the room, his eyes bouncing off all of us. When they land on me, he pauses. He stares at me as if he's seeing a ghost.

"Yes," Priest says. "That is Corbyn's son. We also have Maksim with us."

O'Cleary swallows then turns back to Priest. "I'll withdraw my signature."

Priest nods. "Smart decision."

"May I ask one favor?"

"You're not really in the spot to be asking favors," Seth says what we're all thinking.

Priest quiets Seth with a hand in the air.

"What do you want?" I understand why Priest asked this question. Phoenix explained to us that the RC loved favors. He also explained owing one or having one owed to you wasn't a bad thing. These were some of the richest people in the world.

"When you return to the Church, may I call on your services personally?"

Although the thought of doing kill for hire doesn't sit well with me, we knew this would be one of the things that the RC would want in return. And seeing that we've been doing it for them all this time without knowing, there is no reason to stop now.

"As long as your kill is within our standards, we have a deal," Priest says. "Now make that call."

We didn't leave O'Cleary's home until he'd successfully called all the heads of the family's that didn't sign the EO and withdrew his name. He did warn us before we left that Corbyn, and the others would know something was up. We explained, we didn't give a shit.

We walked back into the ghost house two hours later. Her laughter is the first thing I hear when I enter the home. It even overpowers the Soca music. Like a moth to a flame, I follow the sound of it. She's in the kitchen. As soon as I step into the room, I freeze as fury wraps me up in a tight embrace.

She's at the stove cooking. Maksim is beside her trying to steal something out of a pot she's stirring. She playfully shoves him away, but he doesn't budge. He tickles her, causing her to bend and laugh. He sneaks his fork into the pot sampling what looks like spaghetti.

"Kill him," the demon growls. I lose my control.

It's as if I can see myself moving but can't stop it. Charging over to Maksim, I yank Summer away from him and sling her behind me. My gun is out and at his temple in seconds.

"Easy, Brother," Maksims says, his electric green eyes glaring up at me.

"Beast, stop this," Priest shouts.

"You are trying to take her from me." When I speak, I notice the voice is different. It sounds nothing like me. The laughter in my head tells me who is talking. *"Pull the trigger,"* the demon whispers.

"Look at me, Beastie," Maksim speaks slowly. "I would never do that to you."

"He's lying," the demon snarls. *"Blow his brains out."*

"Son, listen to him," Priest states. He's standing beside me now. "Fight it," he says lowly.

Closing my eyes, I try to take deep breaths. I have to regain my control.

"Fight this," I repeat in my head.

"You will never win this battle. I am who you are," the demon taunts. When I open my eyes all I see is Maksim tickling Summer. It quickly turns into a

vision of him fucking her against the kitchen counter. I bring my gun back and slam it across his face.

"You fucked her," I bellow.

Maksim spits out blood onto the floor at my feet. I'm still holding my gun to his head, my hand at his throat.

"I would never disrespect you like that. That's just that voice in your head talking nonsense."

"Listen to him, son. Maksim has been nothing but a brother to Summer."

I once again try to clear my head. To get the demon out of my thoughts.

"He's lying," the demon purrs. *"Kill him and her."*

"It's lying to you, brother," Maksim pleads. "Summer isn't even my type. I prefer my women like that of the twins."

"Hold the fuck up!" Seth shouts. I cut my eyes over to him. He's standing behind Maksim along with Zel and Many. I imagine Hawk must be somewhere in here as well.

"Relax, crazy Twin," Maksim says. "I will not steal your girl from you."

"You know what, I think I'm on the voice in your head's side," Seth says holding his arms up in surrender. "Kill his ass, Beast."

"Seth, will you shut the fuck up," Priest argues. "Let your brother go, Beast. He's telling the truth."

"Kill him," the demon shouts. *"Kill them all."*

I shut my eyes fighting to regain control. I was losing this battle.

"Summer, are you okay?" Someone in the room asks.

My eyes spring open and I turn to find Summer clutching her arm close to her chest. My stomach sinks down to my feet. The memory of me grabbing her and shoving her behind me pops up in my head.

The demon recedes and I successfully push him to the back of my head. My arms fall to my side. Priest quickly grabs the gun from my hand. Without acknowledging him, I go to Summer. I try to touch her, but she flinches. Everything around me freezes.

The demon laughs. *"She's afraid of you now. You'll never win her back."*

I start to feel claustrophobic. Glancing around, I notice everyone is watching me. They aren't looking at me like I am their brother or friend. They stare at me as if I'm a monster. In this moment, I fear that I am. Without another word, I storm out of the kitchen.

"Gabriel," Summer calls after me.

"Let him go. He needs the space," Priest says.

I don't stick around to hear anyone else. I leave out of the house, putting as much distance as possible between me and the people I'm fighting to protect.

CHAPTER FOURTEEN

Bonds

Priest

Three days have passed since Beast stormed out of the house. His absence is like a heavy wet blanket over the home.

Summer mopes around most of the day, keeping her distance from everyone. Maksim is just as upset. He blames himself for Beast's outburst. He barely looks in Summer's direction. I wish I could say that's the only disruption in the house right now.

Being cooped up like this is starting to really take its toll on everyone. Small bickering is starting to spread like wildfire. Just this morning I had to damn near pull Many and Zel apart.

Walking into the kitchen, I spot Summer at the counter. She's making a cup of tea. The bags under her eyes could store enough clothes for a family of six. I guess that's what happens when you stay up all night waiting for Beast to return.

"I hope that tea has something to help you sleep in it," I say making my way over to the fridge to grab something to drink.

"I'm not tired," she lies.

I turn and place my back against the refrigerator. Popping the top to my seltzer water, I take a sip.

"You need to sleep."

"I'll sleep when he comes back."

"And if he doesn't?" I ask watching her face closely.

I had no reason to believe that Beast wouldn't return. He can't stay away from this woman any more than I can stay away from Fem. But I needed her to understand that risking her health wasn't wise.

She sniffles and wipes her eyes. "I just want him to come back. I need to tell him that I'm sorry. I shouldn't have flinched like that. He thinks I'm afraid of him and I know that hurt him." She breaks down in front of me.

Placing my drink on the island I go over to her and place a hand on her shoulder. She turns and buries her face in my chest.

At that moment Fem walks into the kitchen holding Charlie. I look at her and mouth 'help'. I don't do well with women and tears. I'm a bit too blunt to be the one to console someone.

Fem winks at me and then turns and walks back out. I'm going to turn her ass red for that.

"Okay. Alright," I say to Summer leaning her back so I can see her face. "I know you love my son. I know that you think you have to be understanding of all his flaws but let me tell you something." I pinch her chin and hold her head in place. "Don't ever deny how you feel around Beast. You're not helping him by doing that. If you are afraid, tell him. And it's alright to be afraid. He needs to learn how to treat you, and more importantly, if you explain that something scared or hurt you, it teaches him how to deal with those emotions. I don't coddle my son, and I never will."

She looks away. I let go of her chin. Summer has to understand that if she's going to be with Beast, she needs to advocate for herself. Beast will swallow her up if she doesn't. Of course he's not doing it on purpose. But he will never learn what's an acceptable behavior and what's not if she continues to hide her emotions from him.

"I understand. I just don't want him to feel as if he can't be himself with me."

"You're not changing who he is by voicing your concerns. You are making him aware of his actions. Beast will always suffer with understanding emotions and social ques. It is who he is, but he's smart and can learn to adapt."

She nods and wipes over her cheek clearing the drying tears.

"Do you think he's okay out there?"

I chuckle. "If anyone can survive out there right now, it's him. Trust me." I move back over to the other end of the island to grab my water.

"I'm sick of these fucking dogs."

Shouting in the hallway has me heading in that direction.

Brooklyn is leaning against the wall as Many pulls Kraken, Ari's German Shepherd, off her.

"He did not mean it," Many says in his British accent getting the dog to sit. "He is very protective of pregnant women."

"I don't give a shit if he's part of Paw Patrol, keep the dog out of the way."

"Walker, it's fine," Brooklyn says. "He just caught me off guard."

"No," Hawk barks at Brooklyn. "I'm sick and tired of this. You're already high risk, we're barely able to take you out the house to get checked, and now you have a 90-pound dog nearly knock you over. Many and Ari need to do something about this."

"Hawk!" I shout. He swings his head in my direction. "I understand your frustrations but taking it out on Many and Kraken is not called for."

Hawk tosses his hands up in the air. "So my concerns don't matter to anyone?"

"I'm not saying that. I'm saying shouting at your brother because you're frustrated isn't the answer."

"Honestly, I think we're all just a little tired, Priest," Zel says behind me. I had no idea when he walked into the hallway. Maksim is standing behind him.

Shutting my eyes, I take a quick breath. Look, don't get me wrong, being locked in this house, despite how large it is, for this long is starting to drain me as well. And truthfully, there isn't enough fucking in the world to distract from the fact that these walls are closing in on us. But we have to remember why we are here.

"What do you suggest, Zel?" Fem asks, coming down the stairs. She's still holding Charlie in her arms. "Should we say forget it and just go our own way and hope that no one is killed?"

Zel runs his fingers through the front of his hair. It's starting to grow again.

"Of course not. That's not what I'm saying. I'm just pointing out this isn't working."

"Well, I am all for suggestions. Maybe you know something we don't?" Fem asks.

"No one is leaving," I say, making that clear.

"Unless you're Beast. In that case you can come and go whenever you want," Hawk says.

"What's that supposed to mean?" Maksim asks folding his arms over his chest. "My brother is having some mental issues. He's leaving to keep the peace."

Zel scoffs. "You've known him for two months. Don't act as if you're an expert on Beast. He's throwing a tantrum."

"Exactly," Hawk adds. "He knows that if he acts out, Priest will let him leave."

"That isn't true. Gabriel is battling something right now," Summer says in his defense. "He isn't just abandoning you."

Hawk scoffs. "Says the ex-girlfriend he's left behind."

"Whoa. Watch it," Maksim growls dropping his arms down from his chest.

"Walker, that was uncalled for." Brooklyn fusses.

Summer turns and rushes in the other direction toward her bedroom. The door slams shut moments later.

"I'm going to go talk to her," Brooklyn follows Summer into the bedroom.

Hawk looks away. "I didn't mean that," he says.

"Frustration and annoyance, is one thing. But attacking each other is completely off limits," I say. "We are all locked in this house together, equally tired and ready to get this shit over with. It doesn't give us the right to be assholes." I turn my attention to Hawk. "Kid, I know your anger stems from the fact you did not see the dog before it jumped up on Brooklyn. I get it, but this isn't who we are."

Before anyone could say anything else, Seth and Malia walk down the stairs laughing. I assume Seth feels the vibe in the room. He pauses and scans over everyone.

"What did we miss?" he asks.

I don't answer, instead I turn around and head for the basement. I love my boys, but I needed a break. I'd much rather spend my time with my two new favorite people.

"Papa Priest," Gabe shouts as soon as he sees me. He and Emory are downstairs in the living area of the basement playing board games.

Emory waves when she sees me.

"What are you doing?"

"We're playing Candy Land. Do you want to play?" Gabe asks.

I take a seat down on the floor beside him. Emory has Frenchie in her lap. Hydra, Cerberus, and Echidna are all surrounding Gabe. It seems like Ari's guard dogs have chosen a new owner.

"Yeah, I'll play."

"Me and Charlie want to join too," Fem says stepping into the room. She takes a seat beside me, placing Charlie in my lap. He looks up at me and smiles.

"Yay," Gabe sings. He hands out the color pieces for all of us and then helps Emory gather the cards.

"It's going to be alright," Fem leans into my ear and speaks.

I nod but don't respond. At the rate everyone is going, I can't make that promise. We need to handle that excommunication order and fast. I don't think we can survive much longer living in the same house.

CHAPTER FIFTEEN

Apologies

Summer

"You mean to tell me, not only is he fine as hell, but he's wise too?"

I sigh and roll my eyes. "Trina, will you please stay focused?"

It's been hours since the incident in the hallway. After Brooklyn calmed me down, Hawk walked in and apologized for his hurtful words. He explained he was speaking out of frustration. Although I accepted his apology and don't hold what he said against him, his words still hurt like hell.

"Look, Zaddy is right."

I place my hand to my forehead at her calling Priest Zaddy. After telling Trina all about the hallway incident, I then told her about the conversation Priest had with me in the kitchen.

"You guys don't understand," I argue. "Gabriel is vulnerable right now. Telling him he scared me will send him off the deep end. I don't want to trigger him."

Truth is, he already has one foot out the door due to me being shot. I'm trying to prove to this man that he needs to stick around. That I am

137

someone he needs and wants in his life. Telling him I'm afraid of him is going to give him more ammunition to run.

"No," Trina says with a chuckle. "You don't want him to run for good."

Have I mentioned how much I hate how well my best friend knows me? Sinking back in the chair in my borrowed bedroom, I tuck my knees to my chest.

"Maybe you're right. But that's a good reason to not tell him."

"Girl, coddling his feelings in order to make him stay is probably the most basic bitch thing I've ever heard. That's the shit my mama did for my daddy for fifteen years. And guess what, he still left. If baby daddy is going to love you correctly, he needs to know how to treat you."

That's easy for her to say. James doesn't have a condition that requires her to be patient with him. I know at the end of the day Gabriel would never hurt me. Even with the incident in the kitchen he wasn't intending to hurt me. It's not like I'm trying to protect an abusive man.

"Funny, that's exactly what it sounds like." The thought pops up in my head. I shake it away.

"I understand what you're saying."

"You don't," she says with a laugh. "I can hear it in your tone. But eventually you will realize what me and my man are saying to you will help."

I snort in laughter but quickly quiet down. Looking over to the bed, I check to see if I woke Gabe. He's still sound asleep.

"You need to stop claiming that man as yours. His wife will literally kill you."

She groans. "Let me have my delusions." I chuckle at her antics.

"Anyway," she goes on to say. "How are you feeling about being there now? Do James and I need to keep the private jet fueled?"

I think back over the last few weeks. They haven't been great but mostly for the fact that I'm desperately trying to win back my man. The house doesn't feel so foreign to me now. I do, however, still feel like the outsider that doesn't contribute to shit.

"I don't know. It still feels like I'm in the way here. But I guess I'm not in a rush to leave."

"What makes you feel as if you're in the way?"

Sighing, I push my braids over my shoulder. "Obviously, the brothers and Priest are all here because they are part of that organization. Even Maksim, who isn't a member, is helping them track down people and going on assignments with them. Then Ari, and Albany are in their own ass kicking organization. They often get called in to help with the computer stuff.

"Brooklyn is even useful because she has this crazy memory. Malia keeps Lucien fed and happy while he works nonstop. Hell, she even bakes sweets to make everyone happy. Even Ms. Reese is useful with helping with the kids and relaying messages from her ex to Priest. I'm just kind of here. What can I offer other than making everyone a fucking bracelet?"

"Hey, you make damn good bracelets. Don't downplay yourself."

I laugh at Trina's joke. I know this all sounds crazy. Everyone has been nice and welcoming to me, but I have this unshakeable fear in my head that eventually I'll be just an extra mouth to feed, and they will vote me off the island. I'm not sure if it's because of the way Gabriel is making me feel with this break up or what, but I feel as if I'm on borrowed time in this house. I'm trying to find ways to be helpful.

"Maybe I'm over thinking."

"Of course you are," Trina says. "But that doesn't mean your feelings aren't valid. Maybe you should do something nice for the house. I mean it seems as if you guys are going stir crazy. Maybe try to have a party or host a date night. I know you and Gabe aren't on good terms, but at least it would be something nice to get everyone involved."

That was a brilliant idea. Not only will it be a good contribution to the house, but it could also help me remind Gabriel that he wants me. The more I think it over, the better the idea forms.

"Trina, you're brilliant."

"I know and you're welcome."

A voice in the background of her phone catches my attention.

"Alright, Summer, I have to go. Hair and makeup are here. I think the date night is a great idea, but I also want you to understand you are enough. And if they don't like it, fuck them."

I laugh. "Okay, girl."

"Kiss my baby for me. Talk to you later."

I hang up the cellphone and glance over at my sleeping baby. It's after two in the morning here, but almost nine a.m. in Paris where Trina is.

Climbing out of the chair, I go over to the bed and drop a kiss on Gabe's head before heading into the kitchen. The house is quiet this early in the morning. Which is a lot different from what it sounds like most of the day.

Heading over to the Keurig in the kitchen, I brew myself some hot water for my tea. Ms. Reese has been making grocery runs for us. She was able to grab some of my favorite teas, along with Gabe's favorite snacks.

The conversation between Priest and I, plays back in my head. Despite what Trina said, I did understand their logic. I can't keep downplaying my feelings and fears to make Gabriel stay. But I truly felt awful for how I responded to him that day. I don't want him to think he can't come back home.

I'm lost in my thoughts when his voice comes out of the blue and startles me.

"Why are you still up?"

I spin around to face him with a hand over my chest. Raking my eyes over his body, I check for any injuries. The last time he disappeared from the house to get me clothes he came back covered in blood.

"You scared me," I say without thinking.

He lowers his head. "I didn't mean to."

"I know that, Gabriel." This is what Trina and Priest don't see. It's the utter remorse and sadness in his eyes when he does something to me. Just like the night his mother took him over and he choked me in my kitchen. The next day he could barely look at me. It would be different if he knew what he was doing or if he had no remorse, but he does.

"*Sounds like the mindset of a true battered woman.*" The voice in my head says again. This voice is really starting to piss me off.

"Where've you been?" I ask to change the subject.

"Around. Trying to clear my head."

"Is it cleared?" I hold my breath as I wait for his answer.

Those sea-foam green eyes stare back at me. They rake over my body with precision. If I didn't know any better, I would think I saw desire staring back at me as he takes in my T-shirt and cotton shorts. But I think the lack of sex is starting to cloud my brain. Being in a house where you can hear everyone else fucking, yet you haven't had any in weeks, is catching up with me.

"It's clear enough," he says in response to my earlier question.

I'd gotten so sidetracked thinking about his dick and all the ways it makes me ache so good when he's inside of me, I almost forgot what I asked him.

"Well, that's good. I'm glad," I say lamely. Clearing my voice, I speak again. "And just so you know, there is absolutely nothing going on with me and Sim. He is truly like a brother to me. And he would never do anything to cross a line with you."

He nods saying nothing further.

I feel as if there is an enormous mountain between us. Even though Gabriel was never the talkative type, we had a chemistry when we were together. Conversation, although mostly led by me, was always free flowing. Now, I feel as if I don't know what to say to him.

Silence fills the kitchen. I can't find anything else to say that would make it less awkward.

"I'm going to go crash in one of the extra rooms in the basement," he finally says breaking into the quietness.

"Yeah. Of course. Sleep is important. It's right up there with drinking your water and eating vegetables," I say. "Eight hours a night is ideal. More if you're younger." I physically have to tighten my lips to keep from rambling any further.

He stares at me without speaking. There is no emotion or expression on his face. It's as if I'm a stranger to him and not someone that he shares a child with. Or Someone that he once told he loved.

I look into his eyes hoping to find something that lets me know the man I love is still there. The man that once held me so close to his body and whispered how much he loved me. I have no problem fighting for Gabriel as long as I know there is something there for me to fight for. However, staring in his green eyes, I see nothing. Hell, at this point I would even take that dark vacant look he gets when his mother or whoever takes over him. But there is nothing.

Turning away and glancing at the wall, I fight back the burning sensation in my throat that signals tears are approaching.

"Goodnight," I say barely over a whisper.

"Night." He walks away. The sound of his boots thumping across the tile floor in the kitchen is the only sound around us.

I shut my eyes as the first tear falls. Rubbing a hand on my cheek I wipe it away.

"Come lay with me."

I spin around to find him right behind me. His gaze staring down into my face. I had no idea he had moved around the island to me.

"I need to sleep. And I can only do it if you're near me."

I look down at the hand he has held out to me. Part of me is excited. I feel as if this is the sign I needed. But there is another part of me that warns not to read too much into it.

Placing my hand in his, I allow him to lead me out of the kitchen, my tea forgotten on the counter. He leads me down the basement stairs and into a room with a king size bed, two nightstands, and a chest of drawers. There is no other furniture in the room.

Gabriel pulls the covers back and allows me to get in first. I climb on and slide to the other side. He gets in behind me, switches off the lamp, and then pulls me into his chest. My back tucked up against him.

He doesn't speak at all. Within minutes he is breathing steadily, letting me know he's fast asleep. I lay there for a while, listening to his soft snores. By the time I finally fall asleep, the sun is starting to touch the sky.

CHAPTER SIXTEEN

Beast

"I ordered the food. I think everyone will be happy with the options." Summer says to Ms. Reese as she diligently goes over her checklist for the date night she's planning.

She's been bubbling ever since she walked in the kitchen this morning announcing to everyone her plans for a date night she's hosting in two weeks. She wanted everyone to come. All the females seemed happy for the news. The guys didn't put up much of a fuss, but I can tell they weren't all that elated.

I've watched her all morning go to everyone and ask their food and flower likes and dislikes. She seems happy to be doing something.

I'm just glad to see her smile. I wasn't there when she woke up in my bed this morning. Even though I laid there and watched her sleep for an hour. I knew that if she awoke in my arms it would lead to questions. Questions that would lead to answers she didn't want to hear.

Feeling as if I was stalking, I leave Summer and Ms. Reese in the kitchen and head down to the gym. We have another hour before Alicia and the other ladies of the D.O.E show up to go over their satellite findings today.

The moment I step off the last step, Maksim walks around the corner. He stops in his tracks eyeing me.

"How's your lip?" I ask.

He touches the cut gently. "It will heal. How's your headspace?"

I nod. "Clear for the moment."

We stare at each other in silence for a few seconds. After calming down and spending a few hours outside of the house, I was able to think more clearly. Everything Maksim has done with and around Summer has led me to believe he sees her as a friend. There has been nothing to suggest otherwise.

I scratch the back of my head. "Look," I start, but he stops me from speaking.

"You didn't do anything I wouldn't have done if I'd thought someone was pressing up on my girl. But I want to make myself perfectly clear, Summer is my sister. I would never disrespect you or her in that way."

As I said, after having time to think it over, I already knew this to be true. But I respect him for making it clear.

"I know," I say.

"Good. But I will also tell you, little brother, that will be your last time pressing a gun to my head without me kicking your ass."

A slow smile spreads over my face. "You could try."

Maksim laughs. He walks over and pats me on the shoulder. We part ways. I spend my downtime in the gym, working out before showering and heading upstairs to join the others in the dining room.

Everyone is already there when I walk in. Hawk and Zel are sitting beside each other talking. Albany, Priest and Lucien are at the end of the table looking at something on Lucien's screen. Many is talking to Maksim as they lean against the wall. Ari, Kyra, Deidra, and Alicia are going over something on the large computer monitor. As if she could feel my gaze on her, Alicia looks up from the screen. The moment our eyes connect she sends me one of her warm smiles.

She walks away from the others and over to me. I meet her halfway.

"How are you?" she asks.

"Good. Thanks again for letting me crash at your place those three days."

Ten minutes after I stormed out the house that day, my phone rung. I was expecting it to be Priest. I was shocked when I answered, and it was Alicia. She was calling to get help with searching for the other two names on the excommunication order. She said that she could hear in my tone I was stressed and invited me to come to her place to get space. I initially wasn't going to do it, but she promised me I wouldn't be disturbed. She and I ended up talking for hours that first night and every day after. She's easy to talk to.

"No problem," she places a hand on my arm. "You are always welcome. I'm usually the last person my sisters come to for help in situations like that, so it felt good to be able to offer it to someone."

I fully understood that. My brothers would call on me for certain things, but none of them really leaned on me for comfort. The only one that would go out of their way to spend time with me is Seth. I have no doubt all of them loved me, but they all had their favorites amongst each other. Hawk and Lucien were most alike. Zel would often seek out Many or Hawk for company. And of course, Lucien always had Seth.

"Well thank you for opening your door for me."

She smiles up at me and I notice not for the first time how pretty and straight her teeth are.

"Let's get focused," Priest says drawing my attention from Alicia's face.

"I guess that's my cue," Alicia says walking back over to the other ladies.

I watch her leave until she's standing beside Kyra. A burning feeling on the side of my head has me turning in that direction. Maksim is watching me, his brow arched. He looks over to Alicia and then back to me. He narrows his gaze but doesn't say anything as he places his attention on Priest.

"What do you have for us, Deidra?" he asks the caramel skinned girl with the curly hair.

"It looks like our next confrontation will be Franklin Smith."

"What do you know about him, Maksim?" Albany asks.

Maksim shakes his head. "Not much. He didn't have many dealings with Corbyn. I know he's the CEO of a multinational holding company and conglomerate specializing in luxury goods."

"That he is," Kyra says. "And at the moment, he's in Paris. However, he will still be easier to get to than Dominique Katz."

"So what, we wait for him to come back state side, or are we going to Paris?" Hawk asks.

"We have his business calendar pulled up and it looks like he will be back stateside in a few weeks. I think it best we wait to get him when he's back here. Trying to get to Paris allows for a lot of things to go wrong and out of our control," Alicia says.

Plus, being that far with the excommunication order on our heads and not knowing where Corbyn is didn't seem like a smart move.

"I agree with Alicia on this."

She turns and grins at me.

"Oh, I bet you do," Maksim sneers rolling his eyes.

I'm confused by his tone and his actions. Alicia had a good point, why wouldn't I agree?

"I'm with Beast and Alicia," Priest says. "We're all anxious to get this done, but we will always move smartly. The end goal is to come out of all this alive and with as few enemies as possible."

"Alright," Kyra says. "We will keep track of Franklin. The moment he's back in the states we will let you know."

That concluded our meeting for the day. I hated that it felt as if we weren't getting much done, but in a short period of time we've gotten at least one person to withdraw their name and we're on the way to the next one. In no time, we can put all our effort into killing Corbyn and then I will disappear for good.

Even though I know the plan and what I need to do, I still find myself heading outside to the back patio. Summer is here with a tape measure and her notebook. I don't say anything to her, and she doesn't notice me. But I sit in the chair watching her, just needing to be near her.

CHAPTER SEVENTEEN

Date Night

Summer

Tonight was the big night. It took me the full two weeks to set my plan up. If everything goes smoothly, not only will I remind Gabriel of how good we are together, but it will also cut down the tension in the house and show everyone I can be an asset.

Although there hasn't been another blow up like that day in the hallway or when Gabriel accused Maksim of trying to get with me, there is still a bit of hostility in the air. I'm hoping this will smooth everything out and help ease some of that tension.

"Where do you want these lights?" Maksim asks as he steps onto the back porch with the string lights I ordered.

I was able to convince Maksim and Zel to not only help me, but to join us tonight as well by bribing them with some of Malia's fudge brownies.

"I'm going to hang them up in that tree where the fire pit is."

He takes the lights over to the area I have designated for tonight. The plan for the evening is to enjoy dinner, dancing, and play some couple games. One of the reasons I'd planned it for two weeks out was because I wanted to make sure when we ordered everything it had time to show up. Everyone places their orders under Ms. Reese's name.

"Summer, you have a package," Ms. Reese says stepping onto the porch holding a small box.

I drop the flowers I was gluing to the arch and rush over to her.

"Is it my dress?"

Ms. Reese smiles. "I think so."

I was so nervous my dress wasn't going to make it here in time. The thing I'm most excited about showing tonight is this dress. Although green is my favorite color, black is Gabriel's. Trina and I spent hours over the phone trying to find the perfect black dress. Something sexy, but not slutty. I wanted something that would make Gabriel's jaw hit the floor but not too inappropriate that anyone else felt uncomfortable.

Taking the package from Ms. Reese I look over the label. It was indeed my dress.

Ms. Reese chuckles. "I can't wait to see you in that dress. You've been dying for it to come for a week."

I blush. I know I tore this poor woman's nerves up about checking the arrival. All the other ladies ordered their dresses through Ms. Reese as well and they got theirs back quickly.

"It's gorgeous," I say shyly.

"Mmhmm," she hums putting her hands on her hips. "Gorgeous enough to have a certain someone ready to strip you out of it?"

My entire face heats up. I clutch the package to my chest as embarrassment fills me. Does everybody know how desperate I am for Gabriel? I wonder do they think I'm crazy or delusional for even trying.

Ms. Reese places a hand on my arm. I look up into her soft eyes.

"Everyone in this house has done crazy things for their menfolk. Don't be ashamed."

"You think this is all for nothing?"

She chuckles. "Sweetheart, it's as obvious as night and day that man loves you. He's just being hardheaded like most men. Trust me, I know," she says rolling her eyes. "Now, what do you need me to do?"

I appreciated how much help she's been. Not only has she been crucial at watching the kids for us. Gabe loved Granny Reese. But she has also been good at keeping us all straight.

"I still need help with this flower arch."

She smiles. "Then let's get to work."

It takes me, Ms. Reese, Maksim, and Zel only two hours to get everything set up in the backyard. The other girls offered to help, but I wanted it to be a surprise for them.

Standing in front of my bathroom mirror I examine myself once again. My braids are parted down the middle and hanging down to my waist. The curly hair coming from the braids have been revived and are looking full. My make up is very light, but the black liner on my eyelids accentuates my almond shaped eyes. Trina calls it a cat eye look. The deep red lipstick has my lips looking fuller than usual. The black dress is simple. The hem falls to my mid-thigh. The sleeves and entire back down to the top of my ass is peek-a-boo lace cut outs. The neckline is heart shaped which is perfect for my small boobs. However, the beauty of the dress is the sides. Both sides are cut out and the peek-a-boo lace design continues there as well.

"I don't know. This isn't too much?" I ask Trina over the Facetime call.

"Girl, hell no. You look absolutely fuckable."

I cut my eyes to her. She knows the overall goal of this night. But that doesn't mean I'm not trying to be classy.

"I'm serious, Trina. Do I look sexy but elegant?"

She rolls her eyes. "Summer, you look good. I mean I would have done way more make-up but that's just me. Now, you're going to put those heels on, go out there and enjoy the night you worked hard to create. And regardless of if baby daddy gets his shit together or not, you are going to have a good time. You need it. Hell, the whole house needs it."

In that she was right. Even though I was hoping tonight ended with me and Gabriel back together, if we got nothing else from this night but good vibes and laughs, it would all be worth it.

"You're right," I say. "I should be going. I still have to set the food out."

"Alright. Call me tomorrow and let me know how it went. Love you."

"Love you too." I pick up my phone and disconnect the Facetime call.

After putting my heels on, I head out the bedroom. Ms. Reese is watching the kids tonight while we enjoy our time. For dinner, I ordered a simple surf and turf platter from a steakhouse.

After Gabriel bought me clothes, Priest gave me a credit card with an alias name. He told me I could use it to get whatever I wanted. Until now I haven't touched the thing.

I finished putting the final touches on the food table and stood back to admire my work.

"Wow," Brooklyn says behind me. I spin around to take her in. She looked absolutely stunning in her red romper. Brooklyn had the kind of shape that looked good in anything she wore. Not even pregnancy can take away from her figure. Hawk was standing beside her in a button up and dark wash jeans. He looked very nice with his shaggy hair back from his face.

"You are wearing that dress," Brooklyn says, eyeing me.

"Thank you." I push my braids over my shoulder. "You're looking gorgeous too."

She flutters her lashes at me in a joking manner as she rubs her belly.

"Thanks for doing this, Summer," Hawk says, pulling Brooklyn into his side.

"No problem," I wave him off. "You guys can take a seat at the table underneath the flower arch."

Brooklyn grabs Hawk's hand and leads him to the table in the yard.

Ari and Many are the next to show up. Ari is wearing a burgundy skater skirt with suspenders and a white turtleneck. Her curly hair is in a high puff at the top of her head. Many has on a T-shirt that matches her skirt and black slacks. They look adorable.

Malia and Seth walk out next. Malia has on a black body-hugging dress with a deep V-front. She also had one of those bodies that could wear a brown paper bag, and she would be stunning. Seth is wearing a simple white Tee with a leather jacket and dark jeans.

Fem and Priest walk out together. Fem is wearing a black catsuit that makes her seem like she's six feet tall. Priest is wearing a gray button up with his sleeves folded up and black jeans.

Zel and Maksim walk out next. It brings me joy that they also got dressed up for the event. Maksim is wearing an actual blazer over his crisp button up. Zel has on a black turtleneck and gray dress pants.

"Little sister," Maksim says in his gruff voice. "I do not know how I feel about this dress."

I do a spin. "What? You don't like it?" I tease.

"You're going to get us all killed tonight," Zel says plucking a grape off the fruit tray and popping it in his mouth. "But I'm here for the entertainment." He walks away with his hands stuffed down in his pockets.

"Should I change?" I ask Maksim.

He chuckles. "I'm with Zel. I'm here for the entertainment." He heads to the table with the others.

Now I was feeling very insecure about my dress decision. Maybe I should go in and change.

"Summer, come sit," Malia calls out.

Fuck it, I'm here now. I head over to the table with everyone else.

"As soon as Gabriel gets here, we can eat," I say to everyone.

"Is he here?" Seth asks. "I thought he left."

My heart falls to my feet. Did I do all this for his attention, only for him not to attend? Yes, I wanted us to have good night in general, but this was for him.

"Oh," I say shaking my head. "Well, I guess we don't have to wait. We can eat."

"It's okay," Maksim says. "We can wait."

"No. really. Go grab food."

"You don't have to tell us twice," Ari gets up. "We are starving."

Many stands and joins her. Everyone else gets up and heads over to the food table.

"For what it's worth, you did a damn good job with this," Malia says placing a hand on my shoulder.

"And you look drop dead gorgeous doing it. It's his loss," Brooklyn adds as she makes her way over to the table with Hawk at her heels.

We all fill our plates with food. The chatter is pleasant, and everyone seems to be happy at the moment.

"Steak and potatoes," Priest says. "You're my type of girl, Summer."

"Only thing she's missing is your Jello cup for after your meal, grandpa," Brooklyn jokes.

I laugh. Suddenly everyone seems to go quiet. I look up to find them all staring at me. However, I quickly realize it isn't me they are staring at. I turn around to find Gabriel behind me. He's wearing a dark green Henley with a black leather coat. The buttons of the shirt are undone showing his chest. His black jeans are pristine and his usual black combat boots are on. His long dark blonde hair is hanging down with a messy side part. He looked so damn good if I'd had panties on, he would have melted those bitches off.

I notice way too late he's holding a bouquet of sunflowers in his hands.

"You got me flowers," I say even though it's obvious.

He doesn't answer. Instead, he stares down at me, his nostril flare as if he's having a hard time breathing.

He shuts his eyes and the paper around the flowers crinkle underneath his death grip.

"Your dress," he groans.

"I knew it," Zel says behind me. "We're all about to die."

A few chuckles sound off from behind me.

Gabriel opens his eyes, and his shoulders drop a little. "You look beautiful." Although the words leave his mouth, his face looks as if he's in pain.

"Thank you," I say. "And thanks for the flowers." I hold out my hand to take the flowers from him. He places them in my palm. I place my plate down on the table behind me.

"I'm going to go put these in water. You guys can finish fixing your food."

I walk into the house and into the kitchen. A few days ago, I saw a glass vase in the cabinet. I pull it down and fill it up before unwrapping the flowers and putting them in the water.

When I turn around, I'm startled to find Gabriel behind me. His jacket is off and in his hands. My mouth waters at the way that henley fits snugly over his muscles. I'm so busy staring that I don't realize he's holding out his jacket to me.

"What's this for?" I ask.

However, he doesn't reply. He just holds it out toward me. The strain on his face and the pleading in his eyes tells me that he's battling something.

Finally, he says. "Please."

Zel's words comeback to me. *"We're going to die."* It's obvious Gabriel is battling the voices in his head. I didn't want to do anything to trigger him. Without question, I take his jacket and slip it on.

"Thank you," he says.

We head back out to the others. As soon as I slip out the door everyone turns and stares. Seth groans and Zel laughs.

"Pay up," he tells Seth.

Seth pulls out a twenty from his pocket and hands it to Zel. Gabriel and I quickly fix plates and join the others at the table.

The night is going smoothly. We've eaten, laughed, and danced. Now, we were all sitting around the fire pit. The lights in the trees over our head setting the mood.

Fem is sitting in Priest's lap, his hand resting on her thigh. Brooklyn is sitting on one end of the double couch with her feet in Hawk's lap. Ari is sitting on the arm of Many's chair. Zel and Maksim are sharing the other couch. Malia and Seth are sitting in two chairs beside each other. Gabriel is sitting in another chair across from where I'm standing.

"Alright," I announce. "Priest this question is for you and Fem. What's your significant other's favorite color?"

"Not fair," Zel says. "You gave them an easy one?" For the game section of the night, he and Maksim teamed up.

"She asked you if Maksim is left or right-handed. It doesn't get any easier than that," Priest tells him before turning back to me. "Her favorite color is blue. But more specifically turquoise."

"Aww baby," Fem says leaning down pressing a kiss on his lips.

"Now what's his favorite color?" Brooklyn asks. "I'm guessing it's that retro green color all the appliances were colored in the 70's."

Using the index cards my questions were written on I cover my laugh.

"Shouldn't you be flying off into the night to kidnap children from their beds?" Priest asks Brooklyn.

She rolls her eyes at him and gives him the middle finger.

"His favorite color is black," Fem says before her sister can reply. "And gray."

I glance over at Gabriel. I wonder if that's why his favorite color is black as well. When I look at him, he's already watching me. His gorgeous eyes staring deeply into mine. It takes everything for me to look away from him.

"Okay, Seth and Malia. What's your partner's favorite movie to watch?"

Malia giggles when Seth turns to her. "Star Wars. Preferably Star Wars, The Empire Strikes Back, and Return of the Jedi," he says.

"For Lucien, it's the same," Malia answers. "Although he likes the newer ones as well. And Seth's favorite movie is American Psycho."

"That doesn't surprise me," Brooklyn mumbles before taking a sip of her sweet tea.

"Alright, Many and Ari."

"Hold on," Fem says. "You aren't asking Beast any questions. Beast, what's Summer's favorite color and movie?"

"Yeah," Zel adds. "And which is her dominate hand."

"Zel, give it a fucking rest," Priest argues.

"Her favorite color is green," Gabriel answers. He's watching me closely. "Her favorite movie is Love and Basketball, and she's right-handed." He cuts his gaze over to Fem.

"Okay, Micheal Myers, you better prove you know your woman," Brooklyn jokes.

"Alright, I have a question for the men," Zel says leaning up in his seat. "If you really want to prove you know your girl, what's one thing you know about her that she doesn't know you know."

"Oye," Maksim grins rubbing his hands together. "That's a good one."

"Hawk and I have no secrets," Brooklyn says with her head held high.

"Does he know you slip into men's dreams and suck out their soul?" Priest says taking a sip of his bourbon.

She flips him off again.

"Brook watches Harry Potter movies when no one is around."

Brooklyn gasps as she swings her head toward Hawk.

"Yay," Ari sings as she claps. "We can do a marathon tomorrow. I have an extra Hermoine wig you can wear."

Brooklyn groans and shoves Hawk shoulder.

"Malia watches threesome porn in the bathtub at night."

"Seth!" Malia shouts. Her entire face turns red.

"Fuck, that's sexy," Maksim groans.

"Ari was born with an extra finger," Many admits in his nasally tone.

Ari swings her head in his direction. "How do you know that?"

He shrugs. "We found your baby picture hidden at the bottom of your closet."

"A third finger doesn't surprise me," Zel says shaking his head.

"Fem made out with her twelfth-grade science teacher."

Fem's jaw drops as she looks back at Priest.

"Wait," Brooklyn gags as if she's about to vomit. "Are you talking about Mr. Getty? He kept smiling at me in the hallway once, I thought he was crazy."

"How did you find out about that?" Fem asks Priest ignoring her sister.

"Hold on," Brooklyn says leaning up in her seat. "Didn't he die in a car crash that year?"

"Oh, he was dead before that car crashed," Priest shrugs.

I don't even want to know how he knows that.

"Summer feels like she isn't contributing to the household. Which is why she went out of her way to make this night successful. She feels like she's useless and in the way."

Part of me is shocked that he knew this, but I should always suspect that Gabriel is somewhere around. Of course he overheard my conversation with Trina that night. When he mentioned me not being able to leave, it should have dawned on me he heard all of the conversation no matter how low I said it.

Now, I'm standing in front of everyone feeling naked and bare to them. It's like they can see every insecurity I have. I look away from their faces.

"Well," Brooklyn says getting my attention. "Summer needs to know that she is part of this family and even if she does nothing but take up space, she will never be useless to us. We are a group of misfits. She doesn't have to do anything other than be herself to belong."

"I second that," Malia adds.

"As do I," Priest says. One by one the others agree with Brooklyn.

I fight back the tears of being so completely vulnerable and then having them all tell me I was part of the group. When I look at Gabriel, he's watching me. He studies my face and then subtly winks at me.

He didn't reveal what he did to be mean or to make me look crazy. He knew my fears and wanted me to understand that I was accepted. It was the sweetest thing he could have done.

"Alright, my turn," Zel announces. "Maksim sings love songs in the shower."

"You slimy worm," Maksim shouts.

I toss my head back and laugh as Maksim gets up and chases Zel around our chairs. Eventually, we get back to the game. We talk and laugh until about midnight.

Beast

I shouldn't be here. I should go to my room and put space between us. However, from the moment I saw Summer in that dress, I've wanted to be exactly where I am right now. In her room away from everyone.

I watched her for weeks stress over making tonight the best night for everyone. At first, I thought it was only about her plans to get my attention, as if she's ever lost it. But after paying closer attention to her tonight, I realize how much Summer was trying to be the perfect hostess. I realized it wasn't just me she was trying to appease.

I know what I said in front of everyone seemed rude, but I needed her to see that my brothers, Priest, and their women thought of her as family. She thought she added nothing to this household. I know that stems from her insecurities about her past of being a drug addict. But we all had jaded pasts. She didn't have to walk on eggshells around us to make herself fit in.

The shower water cuts off and my cock hardens further. It took all my strength to keep me from walking in that bathroom and pinning her against the shower wall.

The bathroom door opens and Summer steps out with a towel wrapped around her body. She startles when she sees me.

"Gabriel, what are you doing here?" she asks.

My breathing picks up. I shut my eyes as I imagine the beautiful deep tawny skin that stretches over her body. The memory of how her hot, wet center squeezes my cock so snuggly it feels as if it was made for me. I can almost taste her sweet essence on my tongue.

"Tell me to leave," I croak out as I imagine all the ways I want to fuck her.

Her head tilts to the side as she stares at me. A slow smile lifts her beautiful lips.

"Why would I tell you that?" She walks over to me stopping between my legs.

The smell of her body wash hits my senses along with the heat from her recent shower.

She doesn't move, she just stands there, her legs wedged-between mine. Her chest right at my eye level.

"You should leave," I tell myself.

"You should cut her open and lay her spleen on the fucking floor," the demon encourages.

I shut my eyes to drown out the voice in my head. If there was no other proof that being in her room right now was a bad idea it's hearing that voice. He's a reminder that I'm not stable enough to be here. I thought it was bad when I realized she was wearing that dress around my brothers. In no way did I think my brothers were looking at Summer, but the voice in my head was relentless.

"Look at me, Gabriel," her soft voice pleads.

I open my eyes to find Summer's deep brown ones staring at me. She reaches out and touches the side of my face. Her touch feels like heaven. It nourishes me as if I've been starved of it for years.

"Are you alright?" her brow creases with concern.

Not being able to resist myself, I slowly move my hands up her sides until I get to the top of her towel. Pulling at the tucked ends, I unwrap the fabric and drop it at her feet. She stands before me bare. Her dark chocolate nipples sticking out. I exhale sharply, causing her peaks to pucker even more.

With my eyes locked on her I lean forward and take one nub into my mouth. Summer moans and rolls her head back.

I take my time lapping her breasts. Sucking one into my mouth while I tug at the other with my fingers. She buries her hands into my hair, pressing my face into her flesh. I grab the back of her thighs and drag her onto my lap. She straddles me, grinding her center into my pants-covered crotch. I dip my tongue into her mouth, swallowing her whimpers.

Her flavor bursts across my tastebuds as I take command of her tongue with mine. Needing more of her, I stand, turning her around so that she is closest to the bed. I then lie her on her back and lean up. She is fucking breathtaking lying on the crisp white sheets. Her brown skin standing out in contrast. Her lips swollen and slightly pink from my kisses.

I rake my eyes down her body until I get to the triangle between her legs.

I grab her leg under her knee and lift it up until her foot is planted on the bed. Grabbing the other leg, I do the same until she is spread wide open. My mouth waters at the sight of her glistening lower lips.

"Open your pussy for me," I demand as I tug at my aching length behind the confines of my jeans.

She slides her hand down her body until her thin fingers slide between her fat lips, parting her folds.

She moans as she rubs circles around her nub.

"Please," she begs when I make no move to touch her.

I still don't trust myself, but I can't allow her to ask me for anything I know I can provide. Getting to my knees between her legs, I bury my face into her center and inhale. Her sweet scent has me releasing my cock. I bury my tongue into her warmth. She cries out when I latch my mouth around her nub and suck. I tug at the head of my dick, before wrapping my hand around the shaft and jerking off.

Summer buries her hands in my hair and pulls at the strands as I eat her pussy as if it is my only nourishment. She creams over my face as I continue to roll my tongue over her nub. Her body squirms underneath me as I take her to her heights. I know immediately when she cums. Her legs lock around my head and she screams. Her essence rains down on me. I drink every drop, slurping at her center.

When she goes limp, I stand to my feet. Her eyes widen as she looks at my length. My cock is so hard it's an angry purple. She lifts up from the bed, sliding off the edge she gets on her knees.

With her eyes locked on me, she places my dick in her mouth and immediately takes it to the back of her throat.

"Fuck," I hiss. Watching the way her full lips look around my pole has me ready to explode.

Summer does her best sucking me off. My toes curl at the suction she has around me. Even though I know I should stop now, I don't. I've come too far. Grabbing her braids, I tug her off me. She stands up. I kick out of my boots and shrug my pants off my ankles using my feet. Once I'm left in nothing but my shirt, I lift her up. She wraps her legs around my waist. I walk us backward until the back of my legs touch the chair in the room. I take a seat.

Summer straddles my lap. She lifts up slightly and lines my cock to her opening. We make eye contact as she lowers her body onto mine. Nothing, and I do mean nothing feels as good as Summer's pussy.

She starts a slow ride. Rolling her hips up before dropping them back down. Not once do we break eye contact, nor do we speak. I think we both know that saying anything would destroy the moment. This doesn't fix anything between us. I still couldn't be with Summer. And I know that she was hoping that's what this meant. However, I couldn't make myself stop. I know that made me selfish, but I couldn't think about it right now. Not while her warmth had me trapped inside her.

Cupping her ass, I pull the cheeks apart as I direct her up and down my shaft in a much faster pace.

She coos when I start to fuck her from the bottom. The wet sound her juices make has the room sounding like we're cooking something creamy. Still, we do not look away. In her eyes I see how much she loves me. I see the desire, the hope that we will find our way back to each other. I hope that in my eyes she sees my desperation. She sees how hard I'm working to protect her. I hope she can glimpse how much she means to me despite not being able to be with her.

She stops moving and cups my cheeks in her hands. Her brown eyes narrowing.

"I love you too," she whispers.

At her words, I shut my eyes, hold her body to mine and lift my hips pushing all the way in her from the bottom. I fuck her hard and fast. She cries out, tossing her head back. She cums on my shaft once again, squeezing it so tight my nut shoots from me like a cannon.

I growl as I fill her womb with my seed.

Still holding her, I lift up from the seat and carry her over to the bed. I lay her between the sheets. In no time, Summer falls asleep. I watch the rise and fall of her chest. Crushing guilt rains down on me. I fucked up. Without a second's delay, I redress, then turn and leave the room. I have to let her go.

7. Smith

Beast

Her scent still lingers on my fingers, along with her taste on my tongue. I should've known better. I should've kept my distance, but seeing her in that dress and fighting my urges to be with her for nearly two months had pushed me to the breaking point.

I went into that room to just be near her, to sit in her presence, to calm the demon inside me. But when I walked in that room and heard her in the shower, I got caught up. I craved the sweet scent of her like a drug. However, seeing her in the kitchen this morning with that hopeful look in her eyes made me feel more guilty than I did last night.

Dragging the heavy body of the last guard into the utilities closet, I drop him on top of the other six men.

"Ugh," Seth groans arching his back. "I miss the days when we could just kill these assholes and leave them for the clean-up crew. Carrying these heavy muthafuckers is damaging my back."

It took a little over two weeks from the day Kyra and the others from D.O.E first told us about Franklin. One week for him to get back to the states, and another week to plan out the best way to approach him.

"I don't know. It's kind of relaxing not having to worry about killing anyone. Don't you guys get tired of it?"

Both Seth and I turn to Hawk. "No," we say at the same time.

Hawk shakes his head but doesn't complain.

"You can ride off in the sunset with Brooklyn all you want when this is done," Seth goes on to say as we all head out of the utility closet. "But I will always and forever be a killer. It's in my blood. I won't give this up."

"Not even for Malia?" Hawk asks. "I know Lucien wants out."

I close the door and place the padlock back on it.

"Malia knows who I am, and she accepts me," Seth explains as we make our way back to Priest and Many. Zel is once again being our eyes in the sky. "Besides, I can't do the domestication thing."

Hawk scoffs. "What about you, Beast?"

I turn to glare at him. Did he really need to ask me that question? Seth laughs.

"I don't even need to see you to know you're giving me a face," Hawk jokes.

We make our way back into the restaurant of the private golf course. The place is mostly vacant, but with the price of membership fees to get in here, I understand.

"Everything's all cleared up?" Priest asks as we head over to the table he's sitting at.

"All guards have been handled," Hawk explains.

"How do we look out there?" He asks Zel through the earpiece.

"Looks like Franklin is heading in your direction. If you can keep him in the spot across from you, I have a clean shot.

"Okay, but hopefully it won't come to that."

Priest was adamant about not killing any members of the Royal Crown. I can't say that I agree with that stance, but I did understand it. We need to keep our enemy count down.

I stand directly behind Priest's chair. Seth sits in the seat to his right and Many to his left. Hawk leans his back against the wall behind Many's chair.

Once again, we left Maksim at home. He's too well known amongst the Royal Crown.

"Heads up," Zel warns.

Seconds later, two men walk into the restaurant attached to the golf course. Both men look to be in their mid-sixties. They were in good shape for their age. Both turn to our table and glare. The shorter man with the bad hair plugs scrunches his face. Franklin Smith, the taller of the two, eyes us suspiciously as they make their way over to us.

"Excuse you, but this is our table," the short man complains.

Priest ignores him completely. "Hello, Franklin. My name is Priest, and I would like a moment of your time."

The first man turns bright red. I'm assuming he didn't like being ignored by Priest. I'm not the best with reading emotions, but the way he glares and tightens his fist seems pretty obvious.

"Look here you, degenerate asshole. You don't run—"

Franklin places a hand on his friend's shoulder stopping his tantrum that was sure to get him killed.

"Actually, Walter, I think I'm interested in this conversation," Franklin says, never taking his eyes off Priest.

"Are you sure?" Walter asks, turning to Franklin. "We can have your security toss their asses out."

Seth chuckles and Many snorts. People that are not in the killing business have no sense of awareness. If Franklin's security could have kicked us out, we, one, wouldn't be here, and two, they would be standing here. Although Walter doesn't seem to recognize this, I think Franklin does.

"It's alright. Besides," he says pulling out the chair across from Priest. "I don't think they would be much help now."

Walter hovers around the table.

"Move the fuck on," Seth growls to Walter.

The man nearly trips over his feet trying to scurry away. Once he's gone, we get down to business.

"Is my security dead?" Franklin asks.

"No," Priest replies. "Not at the moment."

Franklin doesn't speak as if he's taking that information in. "You do realize this place has cameras from the front entrance all the way to the golf course."

"They have been on a loop since I pulled into the parking lot."

Franklin smiles. "And I'm assuming there are more of you somewhere around here?"

This time Priest smiles. "You have a sniper aimed at your head. But I assure you, the time it will take his bullet to travel to your skull, one of us could already give you a third eye."

Franklin's face never changes. The smile remains. "Obviously you don't want me dead," he shrugs. "If you did, I'd already be bleeding."

"You are correct."

"Then what do you want, Mr. Priest?"

Priest takes a second before speaking. He leans forward in his seat, unbuttoning his coat jacket. "Let me formally introduce myself. My name is Nathaniel Priest Otella. These are my boys, Many, Seth, Hawk, Beast, and Zel, who you won't be seeing." He points to each of us as he says our name.

"So, this is about Corbyn's excommunication order?" For the first time, the smile fell from Franklin's face. He seems shocked more than anything else.

"Yes," Priest answers. "We need you to withdraw your signature."

Franklin laughs. However, we don't join him.

Holding up a hand, Franklin says, "I'm sorry. I'm not laughing at your request. I'm laughing because I wasn't even going to sign that bill. It took some convincing. But now I'm glad I did."

"Why is that?" Hawk asks.

"Because now I see the importance of partnership."

Once again, we knew that this was what we would need to offer up in order to get the EO dropped. Maksim and Phoenix said as much. Even O'Cleary proved this point.

"What do you want?" Priest asks.

"Access," Franklin says.

Unlike O'Cleary who only wanted a single favor from us, Franklin seems to be a lot smarter. He sees the importance of having an ongoing partnership with us. Can't say that I'm excited about it, but I'm smart enough to know that a partnership with one of the richest men in the world was beneficial.

"We have limits. There are some things we will not do."

"Women and children?" Franklin questions.

"Children definitely. Women if necessary and for a valid reason."

Franklin nods. "I can agree with that completely. Is this unlimited or do I have a set number of calls I can make?"

Priest stalls for a moment. I wonder what he's thinking. We didn't really discuss the negotiating part of this. We all just understood we would have to do some fucked up shit for these people to get them to withdraw their name.

"You got five calls," Priest says. "Anything more than that, you will need to barter."

The smile on Franklin's face tells us he is happy with that deal.

"Should we write it down?" Franklin asks.

This went a lot faster and smoother than I thought it would. I had no doubt they would all withdraw their names, but I figured we'd have a lot more convincing to do for it.

"My word is my law," Priest says. "If I say I'll do it, then it's done."

"And you're not worried about me reneging?"

This time, all of us laughed. We didn't need to tell him how unwise it would be to go back on his word with us or what we would do if he did. He's intelligent enough to read between the lines.

Franklin dips his chin. "Understandable."

See what I mean?

He reaches a hand across the table to Priest. "You have a deal."

Priest stares at the hand before shaking it. "I'm going to need you to make that call."

We left Franklin Smith after telling him where he could find his security guards.

Summer

My body hums with every move I make. Last night was incredible and exactly what I needed. Looking into Gabriel's eyes as he fucked me in that chair told me that he still loved me, he still wanted me. There was hope for our relationship. Hope is all I need.

"Summer, did you hear me?" Malia asks.

"No, I'm sorry. What did you say?" I've been so caught up in my head, I wasn't paying attention to anything.

Malia, Brooklyn and I were in the kitchen preparing lunch. We were making homemade pizzas. Maksim, Fem, Ari and the other ladies from D.O.E were in the dining room. They were making sure the guys didn't need help while they were out.

"Someone is extremely distracted," Brooklyn says with a smile.

Malia turns to face me. She stares at me, looking me over. I get a little self-conscious at how hard she's looking.

"What?" I finally ask.

"You're glowing," she hums.

"Wait," Brooklyn says, getting my attention. She looks me over. "Oh shit, you got dick last night."

My entire face heats up. I place my hands on my cheek in an attempt to cool my body down.

"Okay. You're right. I did."

I love how excited both women get for me.

"I bet he can fuck," Brooklyn says nodding her head. "The crazy ones always have good dick."

"You might be on to something," Malia says. "Lucien is the sweetest most compassionate lover in the world. But Seth will have me sweating out my perm."

We all laugh.

"Gabriel is…" I shake my head as I try to think of the right words. "He's incredible."

"Awww," Malia says wrapping an arm around me. "I'm so glad you two worked it out and got back together."

I wipe at the tear that fell from my eye. "Me too. I guess that dress really paid off."

Malia laughs stepping back from our hug.

"What paid off?" Albany asks as she and Ari enter the kitchen.

"Summer and Leatherface got back together."

I roll my eyes at Brooklyn's joke.

"That's great, Summer," Albany says taking a seat at the island.

"I agree," Ari says, skipping over to me. "When Many and I heard you two last night, I thought he was killing you. Glad I didn't charge into the room like I wanted to."

Once again, my face heats up.

"Let me get this straight," Brooklyn asks. "You thought you were overhearing a murder, and you didn't go in the room to check?"

Ari shrugs. "I figured if he was killing her, he'd have no issues killing me. So, we just waited it out until the morning." She turns and walks over to the kitchen table.

Brooklyn shakes her head. Malia just watches her with her mouth open. Oddly enough, I understood her.

We all get caught up in the next couple of minutes talking about our men. I learned some interesting things about the guys. As soon as Malia and I pop the pizzas in the oven, the guys all walk into the kitchen.

Hawk comes in first.

"Hey babe," Brooklyn greets him as soon as he enters. He walks over to her, wraps his arm around her waist and rubs her belly.

Many comes in next. He lifts Ari out of her seat and spins her around. Seth and Zel walk in together. Zel goes over to the fridge. Seth plants his face in Malia's neck. She giggles as he embraces her from the back.

"How did it go?" Albany asks as soon as Priest and Gabriel enter.

I keep my eyes on him. The moment his green gaze lands on me, I get a flashback from last night. I clench my thighs together at the memory.

"It was good," Priest says, bringing me out of my naughty thoughts. "It went better than expected." He drops a kiss on Fem's forehead before leaning on the back of her chair.

I look around the room and notice all the couples hugged up together. It's then that it dawns on me that Gabriel is still in the doorway.

I look over at him and pause. My stomach drops to my feet. That look is back. The same one he had when he walked into my bedroom the morning I woke up and told me we couldn't be together.

The burning in my throat starts. I'm such an idiot. I thought last night meant something, but I should've known. No matter how much he loves me, he's too stubborn to see we should be together.

Everyone around me is talking and laughing, but I can't make out anything they are saying. It feels as if I'm caught in a vortex, lost in the depths of his emotionless eyes.

Gabriel turns and walks back out of the kitchen without saying a word to me. Pushing away from the counter, I follow behind him, needing to talk to him. I just needed to remind him of what we shared. I step out into the hallway. He's there talking to Alicia. The tall girl from D.O.E.

She says something that makes him smile. A sharp pain hits my chest and my eyes blur. Alicia turns around and walks back into the dining room. Gabriel turns to me as if he knew I was there all along. We lock eyes right before he follows her into the dining room.

I stand there for a second, processing what I've just witnessed. My eyes sting as they blur with tears. Before anyone can walk out and ask me if I'm okay, I rush into my borrowed room and shut the door. Leaning my back against the barrier, I allow the heartbreak to run its course.

CHAPTER NINETEEN

D. Katz

Beast

"I'm serious, Beast. I painted this," Alicia says with a chuckle.

We're standing in the dining room looking at the image of the artwork on her phone that she painted.

I shake my head at the picture. "It looks like a severed foot," I tell her.

She tosses her head back and laughs. "It's actually the horizon."

I turn and look at her before going back to the image on the phone. I turn her screen sideways, trying to find the horizon in her artwork.

"No. It's a foot."

She giggles before taking her phone from me and sliding it into her pocket.

"It's safe to say I am not an artist," she jokes. "But I love artwork. It was all around me when I was a kid. Did your parents have a lot of artwork in the house?"

I rub the back of my head. "No," I say hoping she leaves it there.

She stares at me expectantly. She has a way of looking at you waiting for you to say more without her ever asking for it.

Sighing, I answer. "I wasn't raised by my father and my mother didn't believe in art. She had a few pictures of Jesus on her walls but that was it."

173

Alicia nods. "My grandmother was a religious nut. She could recite the bible front and back. It made it hard for me to talk to her. She believed that God and the Devil were behind everything. Was your mom the same?"

Mother was absolutely like that. She believed everything was either of God or the Devil. Unfortunately for me, everything I did seemed to stem from the devil. My entire existence was evil. The things that I couldn't control like hunger, fear, sadness, anger, she believed were some kind of spirit in me.

"Yes," I simply say in response to Alicia's question.

"Would she—" before she can say anything else, Summer walks into the dining room.

She stops at the door. Since the day after the date night fiasco seven days ago, she has refused to speak to me. It doesn't stop my breath from stalling the moment I see her. It doesn't make me crave her any less. That night with her has replayed through my mind so much I can describe in detail every moan, every face, and every sound her pussy made as I drove into her.

I crave her more now than I did those five years we were apart. But every time I think I can have her back, the demon in my head reminds me why I should stay away.

"Cut out her heart and watch it slowly stop beating," the demon growls. I shake him out of my head.

Summer looks between Alicia and me. We are sitting side by side, leaning into one another. It's how we were able to share her phone.

Before I can say anything to her, Summer spins on her heels so fast she nearly runs Maksim over. She doesn't stop to speak to him, she just scurries away.

"Little sister, are you alright?" he asks, but she never answers. When Maksim turns back to us, he shakes his head. He walks into the room and takes the open seat on the opposite end of the table.

Moments later, the rest of the gang joins us.

"Alright, have you ladies had any luck with Dominique Katz?"

"He's a slippery man," Kyra says. "It isn't hard to find him, but finding a way to get you guys close to him is the problem. His security is very tight."

"I told you, Dominique is not an easy man to get to," Maksim says leaning up in his seat.

"Maybe we can make an appointment?" Zel suggest. "I mean, that's one way to get face to face with him."

Priest goes to reply, but his cellphone goes off in his pocket. He pulls it out and answers it then places it on the table.

"This is Priest," he says out loud.

"Hello Nathaniel. I've heard you were looking for me."

Priest looks to Maksim, his brows bunched together.

"Who is this?"

A deep chuckle comes through the phone. "This is Dominique Katz. I figured I'd save you and your boys the trouble of planning a visit. How about you come to my office today at noon?"

Not once did we expect Dominique to reach out to us. We knew that word would spread after we met with O'Cleary and Franklin and they both withdrew their names. We still didn't think it would be this easy to meet Dominique.

"Alright," Priest says. "We will be there."

"Good," Dominique replies. "Oh, and tell Maksim to come with you. I'd love to catch up with him." Silence greets us on the other end of the phone suggesting he's hung up.

The entire room glances around at each other.

"That was too easy, right?" Hawk asks. "Do you think it's a setup?"

"No," Maksim answers. "Dom doesn't play games. If he called to set up a meeting, he wants the meeting. But why?"

"Didn't you say Dominique and Corbyn weren't friends?" I ask Maksim.

He nods.

"There was a reason Corbyn was searching Pope's house for that records' keeper's information. He didn't want us to find it. Maybe Dominique is why."

Maksim leans forward in his chair. "You could be on to something, brother. Dominique has a lot of power in the Royal Crown. He's someone you would definitely want on your side."

"Then let's meet him," Priest says. "Maksim, Beast, Zel and Many you four are with me. Hawk and Twin, I want you to stay with the women. Twin, check and see if you can break into his camera system. Even though Maksim doesn't think he's a threat, I'd still feel comfortable having your eyes on us."

"I got you," Lucien answers.

We all climb to our feet. If we were going into downtown Manhattan to meet Dominique at noon, we needed to head out. The others clear out the room quickly.

"Be safe," Alicia says to me.

I tip my head at her before walking out of the dining room. On the way to the front door, I spot Summer. Her head is down while Maksim is saying something to her. I can't see her face or hear what they are saying. As if she can feel my gaze on her, she looks up and our eyes connect. Her face is flushed, and her eyes are red. She's been crying. She looks away from me, saying something to Maksim, she then walks away.

Maksim looks back at me and shakes his head. He doesn't speak to me as we head to the garage to grab the borrowed Suburban.

We make the ride to Dominique's office building in good time. It's not hard to believe with Priest behind the wheel. I doubt he ever drives the speed limit. We find a parking spot a block away and feed the meter for an hour.

"Twin, do you have eyes inside the building?" Priest asks through the earpiece.

"All is clear. He has two guards outside his office door but that's it."

We make it to the building, but Priest stops us at the door.

"Is Fem watching the camera?"

"I'm right here," Albany answers.

"Good. I want you to keep your eyes on Dominique. Tell me if I can trust him or not. Everyone else stay vigilant," he warns. "I don't trust these people. When we get in let me do the talking."

No one was going to argue with that. We all entered the building. The guard at the door took our names and quickly advised us to take the elevator up.

We followed his directions after Lucien told us there was nothing waiting on us on the other side. So far, Dominique has kept his word about this being a casual visit. However, I agreed with Priest. I didn't trust these people.

When we stepped on the top floor where Dominique's office was, we followed the directions the front doorman gave us. There was no need to knock on his door. Standing outside the office to greet us was Dominique Katz.

He was tall but not as tall as me. He stood eye level to Zel which makes him 6 foot 2. He was not much older than us. Maybe late thirties or early forties. He was a bit of a pretty boy. His dark brown hair was wavy and long. Not as long as mine or Hawk's but it fell to his neck. He had a chin strap beard with a goatee. His dark blue eyes were intelligent but shrewd. He smiles when he sees us, but it still doesn't put me at ease.

"Nathaniel Otella," he says walking up to Priest with his hand out. "It's nice to finally meet you."

Priest shakes his hand. "You speak as if you know me."

Dominique chuckles. "Oh, I do. Nice to meet you, Hiroshi, Gabriel, Maksim, and Milo." He says to all of us.

"Is Killian, Lucien, and Seth not joining us?" his gaze narrows in confusion.

"I don't know about this guy," Lucien says through the earpiece. "How does he know all of us?"

Good question. Priest asks the same thing out loud.

"Come inside," Dominique says holding out his hand toward the office door. "I will explain everything."

"After you," Priest says.

Dominique chuckles but leads the way into his office. The inside is like most billionaire offices, large, stunning views, and dark furniture. Dominique leads us to the seating area on the left side of the room. Priest sits in one of the wingback chairs. Dominique sits on the other one beside him. Many takes a seat on the couch. I stand with my back against the wall where I can see everyone and everything. Zel is behind Priest's chair. Maksim is near the door. The one guard that entered the room with us is standing opposite of Maksim on the other side of the door.

"I've been dying to meet you since I was a young boy and heard all about you," Dominique says.

"And how did you hear about me?"

"My father. He was close friends with Robert Shelton."

By now we all knew who Robert was. Priest's ally in the Church. The man that got him in.

"How close of a friend?" Priest asks.

"Not as close as you're thinking," Dominique laughs. "They went to law school together. Robert talked about you and your skills often. He boasted about you as if you were his own child. For a while, I thought you were."

"If you knew him so well, why sign the order?" I ask.

"Good question, Beast," Hawk says through the earpiece.

Dominique stands up and walks over to the wet bar in his office. He pours brown liquor from a glass decanter into two whiskey glasses.

"Would you believe me if I told you, I signed the order so that we could do exactly what we're doing right now," he says bringing the glasses back over.

He sets one on the table in front of Priest and then takes the other back to his seat. He leans back in the chair placing his right ankle over his left knee.

"He's telling the truth," Albany says, "At least half of the truth."

"But that's not the only reason, right?" Priest picks up the whiskey and takes a sip as he sits back in his seat.

Dominique watches him with a grin on his face. He chuckles as he leans forward and puts his glass down.

"Everything Robert said about you is true," he says gleefully. "You are correct, that isn't the only reason I wanted to meet you. Let's get down to business. I have no issue withdrawing my name. I'd planned to do it in the first place. However, I will be honest and tell you it will not solve your problem."

"How so?" Priest asks.

"Corbyn already has three other members ready to sign a new order. The moment I withdraw my name, another order will go into action."

"Fuck," I hiss.

"I should've known Corbyn had something like this in place," Maksim says shaking his head.

"Your father is a smart man, Maksim. But I think we can outsmart him." Dominique smirks. It's easy to tell that he dislikes Corbyn. He grimaces every time he mentions his name. I'm still not sure if we can fully trust him yet.

"And how do we do that?" I ask.

Dominique's gaze lands on me and stays for an extended time. He doesn't speak or react, he just stares.

Finally, he turns back to Priest. "As long as my name stays on that order, the other one can't go through. That gives you time."

"Time for what?" Many asks.

"To kill Corbyn." The grin that spreads over Dominique's face is slow and malevolent. The boardroom suit and tie façade fall away, and we see the real diabolical man.

"That was your plan the entire time." Priest states what we've all come to realize. "It's why you signed the order."

Dominique chuckles. "Yes. I have plans. And those plans consist of Elliot Corbyn being out of the way. He has run his course. I am not the only member of the committee that feels this way."

"Then why doesn't the committee kill him?" Maksim asks, pushing away from the wall. "You all have the means. Why put Priest and his boys through this bullshit just to kill Corbyn?"

Maksim is right. If they wanted him dead, they could have done it and left us out.

"Politics," Dominique shrugs. "Mostly."

"He's lying," Albany says in the earpiece. "There is something he's not telling you."

Before Priest can ask anything else, Dominique speaks again. "Look, I'm not your enemy. Corbyn wants you all dead. He's not going to stop signing those excommunication orders until he gets what he wants. The next three may not be as willing to agree as myself and Franklin."

"You convinced Franklin to sign the order?" I ask thinking back to what Franklin Smith said. He admitted he had no plans to sign the order until someone convinced him.

"Yes," Dominique replies. "I knew we needed to buy time. In all honesty, you are doing us a favor, but you're saving yourselves as well. You were always going to have to kill Corbyn," he says the last part directly to Priest. "You took something from him. Something he wanted." Dominique's gaze flashes to me before going back to Priest. "Corbyn is a jealous and prideful man. He will not give up."

We all knew at some point we had to go after Corbyn. We thought if we could clear our names, we could possibly have the resources of the Church in our corner. However, it seems as if we won't have that luxury.

"When we kill Corbyn," Priest says. "You will withdraw your name and get the excommunication order lifted?"

"The moment Corbyn takes his last breath, I will make the phone call and withdraw my name before his body temp drops. You have my word."

We all remain quiet, waiting to see what Albany will say.

"He's telling the truth," she says reading Dominique.

Priest stands and tugs at his suit jacket. Many stands too.

"You have a deal."

Dominique smiles, getting to his feet. We all start to make our way over to the door.

"Uh, Priest, may I speak with you alone for a moment?"

"No," I say.

Priest holds up a hand toward me. He eyes Dominique. "Give us a minute, boys."

I hesitate to leave. I still didn't trust these Royal Crown people totally.

"We got eyes on him, Gabriel," Lucien says in my earpiece.

Nodding, I follow the others out of the room. I turn to look at Priest once more before walking out. He dips his chin briefly, signaling he's alright. The guard that was in the room with us steps out behind me and shuts the door.

"For this conversation," Dominique says. "You're going to need to turn that earpiece off."

Seconds later, we can no longer hear what Priest hears.

"What's going on?" I ask Lucien.

"They are just talking. I can't hear them, but Priest doesn't seem pressed."

"What do you think about this Maksim?" Zel asks walking over to us so that we can speak without being overheard by the guards.

Maksim places one hand over his chest and rubs his chin with the other. "I've always known that Dominique hated Corbyn. I should've known when his name appeared on that order it was something like this."

"Can we trust him?" I ask. I didn't care who did or didn't like Corbyn. I was going to kill him anyway. This just expedited it for me.

"Dominique has always been a man of his word. He does exactly what he says."

"Good," Zel says. "Because if he fucks us over, I'll kill him myself."

Not long after, Priest walks out of the office. He doesn't say what they spoke about. He just said that Dominique can be trusted.

Later that night, I walk out of the gym after a long workout. Lately, I spend hours down here at night until I'm sure the rest of the house is down for the night. I shower, and then camp outside of Summer's door.

However, tonight, when I step out of the gym, I'm greeted by Maksim. He leans against the opposite wall, his arms folded over his chest.

"We need to talk."

I narrow my gaze at him. "About what?"

"Summer."

I freeze, my body going rigid.

"You should cut off his tongue and stuff it down his throat," the demon says. *"He wants her for himself."*

After the last talk I had with my brother about Summer, I didn't expect to have another one. He assured me he had nothing but brotherly love for her.

"Your concern with Summer is starting to rub me wrong."

"And you questioning my intentions is doing the same," he replies.

We stare at each other for a long moment. I have to fight the voice in my head to not kill my brother and leave his corpse at Summer's door.

"What do you want, Maksim?"

"Are you sleeping with Alicia?"

All the earlier anger fades away. Confusion has my brows nearly touching. "What? No."

He watches me for a moment before dropping his arms down by his side. "Then maybe you want to make that clear to the mother of your child." He turns and walks away without anything else to say.

Does Summer truly think I want anyone else but her? Has she questioned this? I forgo a shower and walk up the stairs taking them two at a time. This time when I get to her door, I don't pretend as if the locked barrier deters me. Over the door sill is the generic bedroom door key. Priest has one over all the doors. I use the key to unlock the door and step into the room.

It's dark and quiet. Underneath the mound of covers is a slumbering Summer. Walking over to the bed, I look down at her. The only light is the moonlight streaming through the blinds from the two windows. I stare down at her sleeping form. Her silk bonnet covers her braids. Her mouth is parted slightly. The dusting of freckles that scatter over her nose draws my attention.

She is the most beautiful being I have ever seen. How could she ever think I wanted anyone other than her.

"She doubts you because you failed her. Slit her throat so she can no longer question you," the demon cackles in my head.

As quickly as I entered, I back out of the room. Placing space between us. If Summer has to believe I am interested in Alicia in order to keep her distance from me, then that is what I will allow her to believe. I will do anything to keep her safe, even if I am the one she needs to stay safe from.

CHAPTER TWENTY

Boils Over

Priest

It's been three days since my private talk with Dominique.

"You need to make a choice, Nathaniel. A hard one." His words swam in my head. He was right, I was going to have to make a choice. The first of many choices is the reason I called this meeting.

The children were outside with Ms. Reese, along with all five dogs. I look around my dining room, which we've turned into our very own headquarters. Twin and Malia are sitting at the head of the table. His two laptops are in front of him, but he's focused on her. Ari and Many are standing against the wall. She's whispering something in his ear that makes him laugh. Hawk and Brooklyn share a side of the rectangular table. His hand rests on her rounded belly.

In the chair beside Brooklyn is Summer. Her gaze keeps flicking to Beast who is standing beside Alicia at the other end of the table. She's showing him something on her tablet. As if Alicia could sense my gaze, she looks up at me. Our eyes lock and I'm reminded of the conversation she and I had earlier this morning. She gives me a subtle reassuring smile before going back to her conversation with Beast.

Maksim is sitting in the chair in front of Summer. Zel is beside him and Fem is on the other side of Zel. The only other person in the room is Kyra, who is leaning against the back wall.

I clear my throat to get everyone's attention. All eyes turn to me.

"I brought you all here because, going forward we will need everyone on the same accord. Until this moment, we've been trying to figure out the best approach to handle the excommunication order. It seems the only way to clear our name is to go after Corbyn."

"Finally," Lucien grumbles.

"It's about time," Hawk says, leaning forward on the table.

Part of me feels guilty about their stance on this. I've made my boys believe they are invincible. I've taught them to fear no one, but they haven't fully grasped what we are up against.

"You may want to save your excitement," Maksim says. "This won't be easy."

"There you go again," Beast states glaring at his brother. "Every time we mention Corbyn, you try to steer us in another direction. Are you sure you're clear on where your loyalties lie?"

I can feel this going left, I quickly interfere. "Maksim is right. Everything I've learned about Corbyn tells me we are up against a monolith. One that has the time, means, and resources to fight back."

The next part of this conversation is not going to go over well, but they need to hear it.

"Because of that," I continue. "We're going to need all our focus on Corbyn. No distractions. I've been talking to Kyra and D.O.E has agreed to hide the women and children for as long as it takes. There is a home out in Georgia that is as safe as this one."

"Absolutely not," Hawk says.

Shaking my head, I try to get him to see reason. "The moment we make our first strike against Corbyn, he will counter. It's exactly what happened to Beast and Summer. Corbyn will not play fair, and he will try to hit us where it hurts the most. That puts the girls at risk."

"Which is why we need them close to us," Lucien argues. "I'm not being that far away from Malia and Emory."

"He's right," Hawk states. "Brook is nearly seven months pregnant, I'm not leaving her alone."

"She won't be alone," Kyra chimes in. "The D.O.E will have them highly protected. They will be more guarded than the president. I promise."

Hawk is already shaking his head.

"I don't understand the problem," Zel says. "We're finally going after Corbyn and finishing this. What's a few days or weeks without your wife?"

"Easy for you to say, you don't have one." Lucien scoffs.

"I'm glad," Zel counters. "Maybe if you weren't so busy up Malia's ass 24/7 we could've found Corbyn already."

"What the fuck did you just say to me?" Lucien stands, pushing his chair back.

"Babe, calm down," Malia grabs his arm and tugs him back in his seat. "If it means keeping you guys safe, I don't mind leaving."

"You're not going anywhere," he says as if it's final.

This is getting out of hand. "Everyone is sacrificing something for this," I say.

"Except for you," Ari says. "Is Aurora being sent away?"

"They will need my help here. But Ms. Reese is taking Charlie, which means Nathaniel and I are sacrificing."

Many scoffs pushing away from the wall. "So, you would have us send our women away, but you would keep yours here."

I run my hand down my face. "Can we please stop looking at this with our cocks. Fem is staying because Fem is a highly trained killer. And although Ari is too, she's pregnant, and I wouldn't risk her or her baby on this."

"I don't care what the rest of you do, but Brook isn't going anywhere."

"Neither is Malia."

Zel tosses his hands in the air. "For fucks sakes. I hope I never find pussy that has me acting so irrational and selfish."

"Fuck you, Zel," Hawk shouts. The room goes up in commotion. Maksim is trying to keep Zel in his seat as Many, Hawk, and Lucien go in on him.

Fem is trying to explain why my idea is for the best. Even Kyra is trying to assure them all.

"Summer can go."

Even through all the shouting, I hear his voice. The room goes silent. I drop my gaze to Summer who is staring at the wall over Maksim's head. Her face is stoic, but her eyes tell a different story.

"She and Gabe can go. When do they leave?"

No one speaks. Although this is what I want, I have a feeling this is not going to end well.

"The house in Georgia is ready. We can have them all moved in within two days," Alicia explains.

"Beast," Maksim starts.

"No, Maksim. He's right." Summer cuts him off. She stands to her feet, running her hands down the front of her yoga pants. "Send me. I'll leave. After listening to all of you guys fight to keep the women you love by your side it has become blatantly obvious, I have no business here."

"Don't say that, Summer." Brooklyn places a hand on her arm. "You belong here."

"She's right, we don't want you to leave either," Lucien adds. "I think we should all stay together."

"That's not your call," Beast argues. "What you do with Malia is your business. But Summer is—"

"Nothing to you," she says cutting him off. "Because if I was, you wouldn't feel the need to toss me away like trash every chance you got."

"I'm trying to protect you."

"Fuck you, Beast," she snarls.

Beast goes completely rigid. His hands are tightly fisted at his side, his breathing is labored and his nostril flare with each breath he takes.

"Let's all take a breath," I try to calm the room down. There is too much tension right now and with Beast being unstable we didn't need to set him off in this tight space.

"I think we should send the women out and try this conversation again," Fem says getting to her feet. She must also hear the bomb that is Beast, ticking.

"When can I leave?" Summer turns to me and asks crossing her arms over her chest.

Before I can reply, Beast speaks. "You're not going anywhere."

Summer scoffs. "Oh, now you want me to stay. No thank you. I'm going to leave so you and Ms. Computer whizz can continue to rub your relationship in my face."

Beast brows bunch. I understand Summer's concern. My son has an issue with reading cues, so he hasn't picked up that a lot of the things he's been doing with Alicia seem like flirting.

Alicia looks to me for help. Before I could say anything, Summer starts talking.

"Don't act shocked," Summer goes on to rant. "I just want you to know that two can play that game." The moment the words are out of her mouth, I push away from the wall.

I look at Lucien and tilt my head to the door, letting him know to get Malia and the others out of here. Lucien whispers to Malia and she stands up. Ari joins her after whispering to Brooklyn. All three women quickly walk out of the room.

"What did you say?" Beast asks the simple question, but it isn't his voice.

"That's enough, Summer," I say, trying to reel this shitshow back in.

"I said," she continues as if she didn't hear me. "I'm not waiting for you anymore. I will make it my soul purpose to find a man that will love me. All of me. One who won't throw me away every time his emotions get the best of him. One that won't abandon me like a little boy with an old toy."

"Try it," Beast snarls. "And I will kill him."

I make my way over to Beast, moving Alicia out of the way.

"Calm down, son." I place a hand on his arm, but he quickly snatches it away.

"No worries," Summer goes on to say as tears pour down her face. "I'll find another man and another one. And every night when I'm fucking his brains out, I'll look him in the eyes and remind him that I belong to him."

The next few things happen so quickly it almost looks simultaneous. Maksim leaps over the table to stand in front of Summer. Beast lifts the wooden table and tosses it into the wall on the opposite side of the room. The laptops and papers that were once sitting on top are all on the floor.

"Oh shit," Zel shouts.

I grab Beast, but he tosses me aside as if I weigh nothing. He charges at Maksim, grabbing him by the neck, he smashes him against the wall before charging for Summer. She backs up, but he continues to rush her.

Lucien pulls out his gun.

"No," I shout. Although I understand his actions. They have never seen their brother like this before. Beast has been swallowed up by the red haze many times, but never to the point he has attacked those he loved.

Summer's back hits the wall. Beast grabs her neck and lifts her off the floor.

"Tell me why I shouldn't snap your fucking neck?" he asks her in a voice that isn't his.

It's proof he has lost control of the demon in his head. I remain calm even though my heart is racing.

"Son," I say, keeping my voice level. "Fight through the haze."

He ignores me, placing his face in Summer's neck.

"I should've split your skull months ago," Beast hisses at her. "Tell me why I shouldn't do it now."

"Gabriel, please," Summer pleads. I notice she's able to speak which means he's not choking her.

"Gabriel's not here," he mocks.

"We need to step in," Maksim says. He's clutching his shoulder as if something's wrong with it.

"Not yet," I tell him. "Beast, you are in control. Fight through your haze."

His hand tightens around Summer's throat. Turning her face red.

"He's right, Beast," Alicia says, stepping up beside me. "You can fight this."

Beast peers over his shoulder at Alicia. "You think I don't know who you are? I've known since the first time you spoke to me. Be quiet before I kill you next."

Alica looks at me and we both are a little confused by that admittance. When Fem first mentioned the idea of Beast talking to a psychiatrist, I shut her down. I knew he would never willingly speak to anyone. However, Fem told me about a highly trained member of D.O.E that would be able to talk to him without him knowing. Alicia has been working on Beast since she got here.

"You're not going to kill anyone," Alicia goes on to say. "Because you don't have control here."

A sinister laugh comes from Beast. "Is that what you're banking on? I run him."

"No, you don't," I argue. "You are a hallucination, a made-up part of him. The same way his mother and I were. Beast is in control. You are a weapon his mind has created to deal with his emotions."

"You don't know shit about me," he grits out through his teeth as he turns his attention back to Summer.

Sighing, I take a step forward. The conversation Alicia had with me earlier today weighed heavy on my heart. I thought of how and when to tell Beast. I know that it would devastate him. But he needs to know. All of them needed to know.

"You have schizoid personality disorder, Beast," I say.

Alicia explained to me that Beast had a mild version of schizoid personality disorder along with traces of schizotypal personality disorder as well as signs of sociopathy. He is the perfect storm of disorders to make him the greatest killer in the Church organization. All of his conditions are treatable and manageable with meds when needed and by talking to a psychiatrist on a regular basis.

Beast turns and looks over his shoulder glaring at me. Immediately, I can tell his hold on Summer's neck loosens by the way the redness in her face slowly recedes.

"The Church misdiagnosed you when you were younger. And you are not possessed by a demon. Your mind is just creating things. But you are in control."

Lucien looks over at me, his gun lowering to his side. "When did you find this out?"

"Today," is all I say in response.

"How do we help him?" Zel asks.

Although this meeting did not go as planned and lately, they have been bickering back and forth with each other like cats and dogs, it made me proud to see them rallying behind Beast now. He's going to need it.

"He just needs to remember who he is and what's real," I explain. "And right now, he needs to remember that he is hurting the woman that he loves."

I make sure I look at Summer pointedly when I say those words. She needed to remind him that he loved her, but she also needed to be reminded too. I don't fault her for her outburst. She was hurting and in return wanted to hurt him. But they both needed to understand that they love each other. And for this diagnosis, they would need to be each other's backbone.

"Gabriel," Summer gets his attention back. "Baby, you're hurting me. Whatever this thing is in your head, it's hurting me."

He releases Summer so quickly she drops to the ground. He steps back, his hands are in tight fists by his side.

"Get out of my head," he growls to himself.

"You got this, Beast," Hawk says.

"We're all here, brother," Many adds.

Eventually, Beast's breathing slows, the tension in his shoulders' wain, and his hands relax. The moment he opens his eyes, he goes straight to Summer. He lifts her off the ground. She wraps her arms around his neck and her legs around his waist, burying her face in his neck.

He doesn't speak to any of us, instead he storms out of the dining room carrying her in his arms.

We all watch as the two lovers slip away.

"I'm not going to lie, I almost pissed my fucking pants," Zel says breaking the silence.

Hawk snorts and the rest of us chuckle. I go over to Maksim to check on his arm.

"You good?" I ask him.

He rolls his shoulder, suggesting he might be injured. "Between him and my other siblings, I'm really starting to second guess this brother thing."

I shake my head. He's only joking. We all know how much he loves Beast.

"He should be fine for now," Alicia says getting my attention. "Beast is very intelligent. I'm not completely shocked that he subconsciously knew what I was doing. Most of his battle will be reminding himself what's real and what isn't. His schizotypal disorder is mild. We want to keep it that way. He needs to start seeing someone on a regular basis before it turns into schizophrenia."

"Thanks, Alicia," Fem says coming up beside me. "We appreciate your help."

She nods. "And can you let Summer know that I was never trying to take her man. I don't want her to think I'm that type of person."

"I'll let her know, but I don't think any of us will see her for the rest of the day." Turning to the rest of the room I say, "Speaking of, let's put a pin in this conversation. We need time and clearer heads before we discuss it again."

They all seem to agree.

"Now, let's get this room back in order." Though they all groan, we help right the dining room. Even though we had a name for Beast's condition, I know that we still had a long road in front of us.

CHAPTER TWENTY-ONE

Levels Out

Summer

I hold on to Gabriel until I hear the soft click of my bedroom door. Even then, I don't let him go as he carries me over to the bed.

He places me on my feet and pulls away from me, cupping my face in his large hands. His green gaze roams all over my face. When his eyes lands on my neck, he looks disgusted.

Look, I won't lie as if that wasn't the scariest thing that has ever happened to me. Even the time he lost control back at my house, it wasn't as terrifying as this. He looked deranged, evil almost, as he told me how much he wanted to kill me.

However, I hide that fear. Tuck it down inside me. Now was not the right time to bring it up.

Gabriel leans his forehead to mine. He takes a deep breath and blows it out before placing a kiss where his head once was.

He lets me go and steps away.

"I'm going to finish this mission with my brothers and Priest and then I will disappear for good. You and Gabe will always be taken care of. And you don't have to—"

I cut him off with a belly laugh. I don't know what's so funny, but I laugh. I laugh until my laughter turns into tears.

"Summer," he calls my name and tries to reach for me, but I step away.

"I have got the be the dumbest person in the world," I tell him. His gaze narrows and his brow pinches. "I mean here I am trying to hold back my feelings and emotions after being nearly killed and you can stand in my face and tell me you want to leave. Everyone was right."

"Did you not hear what they just said? I am a defect. I have a disorder."

"And you think because they gave it a name, it changes anything?"

I won't lie. Hearing Priest tell me his diagnosis was scary. Hearing words like schizoid, schizotypal, and sociopath aren't easy to digest. Hell, they are downright the things of nightmares.

But giving his condition a name doesn't change how I feel. I loved him when it was just his mother's voice in his head. I loved him when we thought it was autism that had him void of emotions sometimes. I loved him even though I watched him beat a man with a hatchet, stab my ex, and shot gambler. I loved him when there was no diagnosis. Giving his condition a label does not change the love.

"I am not safe. Why don't you understand that? No one around me is safe when I don't know what's real and what isn't. I'm fighting voices in my head," he roars.

"And I'm fighting them with you," I shout.

He grabs the back of his head and looks up at the ceiling.

"Look at me, Gabriel?" he shakes his head, refusing to look at me. "Look at me," I demand.

When he lowers his head, his eyes are red, and tears linger on the lids.

"I have been choked, cursed out, and threatened by you," he turns away, but I continue on.

He needed to hear this. I finally fully grasp what Priest said to me that day in the kitchen. By holding back how I felt about the things Gabriel was doing made him think he had to walk on eggshells with me. If he never knew how I was feeling, then he would never know that I can accept him for who he is.

"There are times you scare the hell out of me. I'm not afraid to admit, there are moments I am terrified of you." The tears he was holding falls down his cheeks.

"But even in those times, I never question if I want to be with you. Your diagnoses do not change how I feel about you. They do not make me want you any less. I will stand up to every voice in your head. I will battle them for you until I take my last breath. But I will not fight you to love you. I will no longer beg you to stay if you don't want to. You can leave." I hold my hands out at my side.

"I love you," he growls.

"I'm not questioning your love. I am simply asking you if you will stay."

I realized the night we had sex and his eyes spoke volumes of his love for me, that love was not our issue. It is and will always be Gabriel's urge and desire to run from us.

He shakes his head. "It's not that simple. I will die for you. I will kill anyone—"

"You were killing before you met me, and you will kill after I'm gone. That isn't the flex that you think it is. My question is simple, Gabriel. Will. You. Stay for me?"

He backs away, placing space between us.

"I don't have this under control. I don't even know what it is. I could snap and—"

I was done with the excuses. I was done begging this man to choose me. He had valid points. We didn't know what his diagnosis meant or what all it would require. However, all I need him to understand and accept is that no matter what, we face it together. I needed him to know that even though the world would be difficult, as long as he was willing to stay, I'd face the difficulty with him.

Turning away from him, I head to the door. I didn't need to further this conversation. It was yes or no. His inability to answer was answer enough. I make it all the way to the door before his voice stops me.

"I'll stay," he shouts desperately.

I turn to face him to find tears streaming down his face.

He takes a step toward me. "I'll stay despite my madness and the voices. Even when the world gets so dark I can't see any light, or when everything inside me begs me to leave, I'll remain. I will stay by your side until you take your last breath, and even then, I will follow you into the abyss." He stops in front of me and cups my face in his large hands. "Baby, I will stay for you."

My heart knocks against my chest as tears spill down my cheeks. I lift on my tiptoes and place my lips to his. His mouth opens immediately and allows my tongue to dive inside. Our kiss is needy, reckless, almost violent in our desperation to show how much we need each other.

"I love you," I moan against his mouth.

He grabs the back of my thighs and lifts me off my feet. I wrap my legs around his waist. He pins me to the door behind me. When he pulls back and stares down at me, there is darkness in his gaze. But this darkness doesn't scare me. It excites me. It tells me I'm in for a long night.

He grabs the collar of my shirt with one hand and tugs it, ripping it off my body in tattered shards. My breasts fall free. He lowers his head and suctions his mouth around my right nipple. I hiss as I arch my back pushing more of my breast into his mouth. My nipple feels a bit sensitive, but I enjoy the ache.

He snakes his tongue from my breast up my chest, to my neck where he bites softly at the flesh before placing his lips back on mine and pushing his tongue into my mouth.

I dig my nails into the hair at the back of his neck. He carries me over to the bed and gently lays me down. When he lifts his body from mine, he stares down at me. He grabs the waist band of my yoga pants and tugs them down to my hips along with my panties. I lift up so he can drag them down my legs until he tosses them to the floor.

Gabriel spreads my legs into a wide v. He runs a hand through my pussy lips smearing my wetness over my nub. He watches his fingers separate me as if he's watching his favorite movie.

"Ooh, yes," I moan as he slowly strokes my sensitive clit.

Removing his fingers, he then places them in his mouth, sucking my essence off. Once he's cleaned his digits, he lets spit dribble from his lips onto my mound. He then inserts his finger into my warmth using a scissoring motion. Flipping them around, he motions in a come here gesture while his thumb circles my bud.

My eyes roll to the back of my head as pure pleasure has my limbs tingling. I can feel my orgasm fast approaching. My body starts to shake.

"Keep those legs open," He demands. His green eyes never looking away from where his fingers are making magic.

"Gabriel," I cry out when my orgasm crashes. My body convulses, feeling as if is malfunctioning.

He pulls his fingers out of me and then unbuckles his jeans. I sit up in the bed, ready to place his length in my mouth. He shoves his pants and boxers down to his ankles. Getting up on my knees, I wrap my hand around his large erection. Returning the favor, I spit on the head of his cock before using my hand to rub it into his length getting it wet. Before I could put it in my mouth, he gives me different orders.

"On your back, head off the side of the bed."

I obey his command, flipping around. Once I'm in place, he pinches my chin and tilts my head back. I open my mouth as he places his dick inside. At this angle, I can manage to get more of him down my throat. He pushes in until his balls brush against my chin. I choke, causing my eyes to water. He pulls out, allowing me to breathe.

"Relax your throat," he suggests. "Let me touch your tonsils."

Like the obedient freak I am for him, I do as he says. He pushes into my mouth so deep I fight to breathe.

"Through your nose," he advises.

Again, I listen to his command, and it becomes much easier. Gabriel rolls his hips as he pushes his length in and out of my mouth. He tosses his head back and moans.

Seeing how good I'm making him feel and hearing him moan has my thighs rubbing together, I move my hand down my stomach toward the apex of my legs. I find my nub slippery wet with my essence. I twirl my fingers around it. Even though it's sensitive from the last orgasm I had, I don't stop.

Suddenly, my hands are knocked away.

Gabriel's fingers replace mine as he continues to fuck my face. He plays with my clit, making it harder as I get close to coming again.

I moan around his cock when he slips a finger inside me. The sounds my pussy is making should be embarrassing. But it feels too good for me to care. He pulls his digits out and pinches my clit. I shoot off to Mars. This time, I scream as the orgasm shakes me to the core. I don't even know when he took his dick out of my mouth. Once I come down after my second orgasm, Gabriel grabs the back of my neck and lifts me up.

"On your knees," he orders.

I get to my knees. He pushes my upper body down into the mattress. My ass is so up in the air my pussy farts. Without a warning, he enters me with a strong thrust that has me crying out and rocking forward.

His hands come down on my ass with a hard smack before he rubs the ache. "Don't run." He doesn't stop his strokes as he makes the command. His hips smack against my ass. He's feeding me every inch of his dick.

"Uhhhhh, shit" I cry out, placing a hand at his thigh to keep him from going too deep. He grabs my arms and holds them behind my back as if I'm being arrested.

"I've been craving this pussy since the last time I was in it," he grumbles. "You think you're keeping me from it now? This shit is mine, Summer. Mine."

"Fuck, yes. It's all yours."

He pulls out of me. Before I can ask a question, I'm on my side with a knee under my chin and the other one straight out. He places one knee on the bed before directing his length back at my opening. He pushes back in. I cry out at the new angle. He strokes me slowly and deeply.

"I love you, Summer. I fucking love you," he moans as he works my body.

Sweat has his hair sticking to his flushed face. He looks absolutely handsome. I reach out a hand for him. I want to feel his skin against mine.

He pulls out and climbs on the bed. I roll over onto my back. As if he knew exactly what I wanted, he pulls his shirt off before getting on top of me. His body fits snugly between my thighs. He adjusts himself back inside me before pressing his chest to mine. I cup his face as I stick my tongue into his mouth. Our kiss is back to that desperate one from earlier.

From this angle he doesn't get to pull out as far, instead he does a simple pull out and grind. The move has his brittle pubic hairs brushing against my sensitive clit. He lifts his upper body up a little, caging my head between his hands. His strokes are deep and slow. My eyes roll back into my head, my nails dig into his back as he fucks me so deep my lower stomach moves with his motion.

Gabriel has fucked me every which way but loose, he has sexed me so good I couldn't walk the next day. But this time, we make love. He's not fucking me, he's making love to my soul. He's tying his fate to mine.

When I open my eyes and my brown clash with his green, I see everything he is trying to tell me. He's showing me he means what he said. He will stay. He lowers to his elbows and seals our lips together again. His heavy pants meet mine.

"Come for me," he whispers against my wet lips. "Leave your mark on my back and fucking come for daddy."

I erupt like a volcano. My scream bounces around the room, my vision goes out, and I wet his dick up. Gabriel lets out a growl that turns into a loud moan as he releases inside of me. His hot semen bathes my walls. Once he's done, he falls to the bed, turning me onto my side.

Panting, I try to catch my breath, feeling weak. However, the head of his cock presses to my opening. He lifts my leg over his hip and pushes back into me.

I whimper at the intrusion.

"You thought this shit was over," he chuckles as he starts to stroke in and out of me again.

I guess I won't be going anywhere for a while.

CHAPTER TWENTY-TWO

Corbyn

Beast

I watch her as she sleeps. Her mouth open slightly, her braids scattered across her pillow like a waterfall. She is my peace.

"She is a whore," Mother says in my head.

Hearing her voice is the sweetest sound in the world right now. I shut my eyes and take it all in.

After fucking Summer to sleep, I went out and talked to Alicia for a bit. She gave me the basics of my condition. She also told me I had a long road ahead of me but she believed I'd be alright. Basically, the voices are my conscious. My mother's voice is the voice of the things I was taught. They are the impressions of the beliefs and lessons I learned from her. Priest's voice is my true feelings. His voice is the beliefs I've established myself. Which is why most of the time those two voices are combative and disagree.

The demon in my head is the subconscious part of me. The part that does not feel or have emotions. It's always been there. It is the part of me that will require the most work.

Another thing I asked Alicia to do is speak to Gabe. When Priest told me I was misdiagnosed, I thought of my son. Not always, but sometime the disorders I have can be passed down. I think mine are a combination of getting it from my mother and the condition in which she raised me. Either way, I want to make sure my son is okay.

Summer moves in her sleep, alerting me that she's going to be waking up soon. Her eyes pop open and she looks right at me. She smiles before yawning and stretching.

"How long have I been sleep?"

"Five hours."

Her eyes widen and she sits up in bed. "Seriously? Why didn't you wake me up?"

"Because you needed the sleep." I stand from the chair I was sitting in and climb into the bed with her. She scoots over making room for me.

"You might not want to get too close," she giggles. "I haven't brushed my teeth."

I don't reply. She narrows her gaze at me.

"What's wrong?"

"I don't think you believe me when I say I'll stay."

She watches me for a second without a word. It feels as if she's studying me, trying to see where my thoughts are.

"I mean, you're right. You did make a promise to me once before and broke it."

The guilt of her words hits me hard. The night I made love to her before I killed Andrew, I did make that promise. And at the time I had no intention of ever breaking it. But I did. I broke her trust in me.

She continues. "But I am a believer in second chances, so I have to believe what you say is true."

I nod. "Or, I can prove that it will never happen again."

Her brow pinches. "How would you do that?"

"Because you're going to marry me."

Her mouth falls open, but no words come out. I lift her hand and show her the solitaire five carat pear-shaped diamond ring I'd placed on her finger. She gasps at the sight.

I never had plans of getting married. I never had plans of having a kid either. Never knew either of those was an option for me. But as I watched Summer turn away from me and nearly walk out that door, I knew then that I couldn't live without her. I knew I would fight every instinct in me that told me to run in order to be with her. I want to belong to her and only her.

One day, when Corbyn is gone and we've been reinstated into the Church, I will have to go back to reality. I love Summer and I would give her the world, but I have to feed. That will always be a part of my life. But even then, I need her in my world. I will not give her or my son up.

"How? When did you get this?"

I shrug. "Today, while you slept. The ladies and Maksim helped me pick it out. The women thought you'd like the shape, and Maksim suggested the carat size. We picked it out online, and I went and got it."

Her eyes water as she looks down at the ring. "Gabriel, it's beautiful."

"What do you say?"

She stutters for a moment. Her mouth opening and closing. "I mean, it didn't really sound like you gave me an option." I pull her into my chest.

"I'm glad you know."

"I swear, Gabriel, if you try to walk out on me after we're married, I'm going to pull a you on you."

I chuckle before flipping her over and lying her underneath me. She squeals, but it quickly turns into a sigh when I brush my erection against her pantie-less mound.

"Gabriel," she moans.

"I will teach you how to do it. That way you will know I'll never leave." With one hand, I free my erection from the confines of my pants. I barely get them to my ass before I push into Summer.

She digs her nails into my back as she gasps beneath me. I would stay here for the rest of my life if I could. Wrapped between her thighs, buried deep inside her.

"I found him," Lucien's voice yells into the intercom in the room. "I found Corbyn."

I look down at Summer. Having her tight heat wrapped around my cock has me second guessing if I want to stop or not.

"You should go," she says, touching the side of my face.

"Fuucckk," I growl as I pull out of her.

Climbing off the bed, I pull my jeans back up on my hips, readjusting my still hard cock, so it won't be as obvious. I wait for Summer to dress and brush her teeth before leaving the bedroom.

Summer and I both walk into the dining room. When I got up the first time, I noticed that they had fixed the table and put the room back in place. I apologized to everyone for the destruction. Thankfully, the laptops weren't damaged due to my outburst.

Already in the room are Lucien, Malia, Hawk, Brooklyn, Many, Arie, Zel, and Sim.

"Did she like the ring?" Maksim asks as soon as he spots Summer.

She holds up her hand with a huge grin on her face. "I love it. Thank you guys for helping pick it out."

"We're glad we could help. Congratulations." Malia sings as she walks over and hugs Summer. Brooklyn is the next person to hug her, then Ari takes her place.

My brothers all congratulated me and patted my back.

"See, I told you. The bigger the carat, the more the forgiveness," Maksim says in my ear.

I dip my chin to my chest at him. To be honest, he's turned out to be not too much of a bother. I'm kind of starting to like the guy.

"Thank goodness you guys worked it out. I don't think that table could've survived another argument," Hawk's wife says.

Her comment makes Summer laugh, so I don't take offense.

Just then Albany and Priest walk in together. Both are looking frazzled and disheveled.

"What took y'all so long?" Lucien asks.

"We were fucking. You think you kids are the only ones that can get some pussy in my house?"

Summer buries her face into my arm. Embarrassment. The emotion pops into my head instantly.

"Ugh, please spare us the details of your elderly activities. Your grandchildren can't stomach it," Hawk's wife says turning her nose up and rubbing her stomach.

"Don't you two start," Albany stops them with a hand up. "What do you have for us, Lucien?"

"He just showed up on my radar. He's back in the states attending a fundraiser tonight. This is our chance."

"I didn't tell you to start tracking him yet," Priest says rubbing at his chin.

Lucien shakes his head. "Look, I understand your concern, but we have him, Priest. We can take him out tonight and get our lives back."

Priest shakes his head. "It's too soon. We need more time."

Lucien scoffs, tossing his arms up in the air.

"More time for what?" he argues. "To sit in this house and drive each other crazy?"

"I'm with Lucien on this," Zel adds. "For the last two months, we've been chasing after these leads, only to find out we have to go after Corbyn. I think this is our opportunity."

"This feels like a setup," Maksim says. "He knows you're looking for him. Why would he come back?"

"Exactly," Priest states. "He seems smarter than this. More calculated. I think we should stick with my plan of sending the women away and then figure out the best approach."

"We've already told you we aren't sending the girls away," Hawk says with a shrug.

"Exactly," Lucien adds. "Plus, I'm tired of waiting. There isn't enough space in this house for Emory to run around. Malia needs to see a doctor, and Brooklyn has had to miss her last check-ups. We can't keep living in hiding. I think Corbyn underestimates us. That's why he's come out. He doesn't think we can take him. This is the right time."

"I'm with brother Lucien on this," Many says in his deep voice. "This is the time."

"And you all agree?" Priest asks.

"Yes," Hawk says. "It's time."

"What about you, brother? What do you say?" Sim turns his attention to me.

I can understand everyone's side. My brothers were ready to be done. But, Priest is correct. Corbyn was too smart to make this so easy. However, even I know how much they underestimated us. This could be just another example of Corbyn being cocky. And we can't waste an opportunity like this.

"I say we strike."

Summer's grip on my arm tightens.

Priest sighs, shaking his head. "I guess no one is listening to their old man. So, let's do it."

The energy in the room shifts. We all go from family men to killers in a split second. Lucien takes off his glasses letting us know Seth is now with us. Tonight, we were taking back our lives.

We are across the street from the fancy ballroom the fundraiser is held in. Priest rented a room under an alias. Right now, we are checking our weapons.

"What do you see, Fem?" Priest's voice comes over our earpiece.

We sent Fem in before us to scout out the place.

"Your guy is here," she replies. "He has a lot of bodyguards with him. They are wearing suits with red ties. There're at least fifty of them all around the room."

"Those are his regular guards," Sim says as he places a .45 in his back holster. "They're ex-military. We need to take them out quickly. Do you see anyone with tattoos like mine?"

I wait for Fem to reply. I still owe Yohan for taking that shot at Albany.

"No. no one with tally mark tattoos," Fem says.

I look over to Maksim. His brow is bunched up.

"I'm not liking this," he says. "Corbyn always travels with at least one of us."

For the first time, I'm starting to get that feeling too. Maybe we are moving too fast.

"No way we are backing out now," Seth says. "We're too close."

"He's right, new brother Sim," Many adds. "We have to at least try."

Maksim looks over at Priest who shakes his head. He still isn't trusting this decision, but he's going through with it. I can see it all over his face. He's doing this for us.

Maksim nods his head, then places a knife in his side holder. "Okay, I'm with you guys."

"Alright, boys," Priest says to everyone in the room. His gaze rakes over Many, Hawk, Me, Seth, and Maksim. "We make this quick. In and out. No showboating. Do you understand?"

A chorus of yeses goes up. After making sure we had all our weapons, we filed out of the room. Priest has the duffle bag with extra guns. We take the stairs down to the lobby.

"Alright Zel, you're our eyes at this point," Priest says into the earpiece.

"I got you. Good luck in there, brothers."

He's on top of the roof of the hotel we just exited. He has a perfect view into the ballroom.

We step outside onto the sidewalk. The street is busy. We aren't worried about cameras catching us because none of those work. Kyra and Ari are back at the ghost house manning those. Our black suits allow us to blend in with the other attendees of the party.

"Alright, Fem," Priest says. "Time to clear the room."

"You got it, baby," She purrs.

"Won't we have to worry about the fire department coming?" Maksim leans over and asks me.

"No. Lucien cut the connection between the sprinklers and the fire alarm."

As soon as the sentence is out my mouth, we hear the shrill of screams coming out of the building.

"That's our cue. Let's go," Seth says.

We all cross the street and enter the building before splitting up. The sprinkler system makes it slightly hard to see. We fight through all the people in their fancy suits and gowns rushing out of the building. Maksim is right on my heels.

"Corbyn's on the move," Zel says in the earpiece.

"Keep him in here," I growl out.

I spot the first of Corbyn's bodyguards out in the hallway. Our gazes lock at the exact same time. He reaches for his gun, but I'm faster. I shoot him in the neck, and he goes down. Chaos ensues after that. Gunfire goes off everywhere.

I rush into the actual ballroom. Quickly scanning the room, I take note of all the exits. Hawk and Many are on the farthest side of the room making sure no one makes it out the back entrance. Seth is behind a table and firing off rounds. I lost track of Fem and Priest. But if I know him, he's with her.

"On your left, brother," Maksim yells as he fires at someone in front of us.

I turn and fire at the guard coming up on my left. He goes down quickly. Maksim and I move further into the room. Our guns aim in all directions scoping out the scene.

One of Corbyn's guards runs up on me from my side. I spin in time to dodge the bullet whizzing by my head. Maksim, fires and kills the man that attacked me. I turn just in time to shoot at the guard behind Maksim. We quickly move through the room gunning down guards that cross our path. When we run out of bullets in one gun, we toss it and grab for another.

I aim at the man in front of me and fire, but the gun clicks. I'm now out of guns. Tossing the gun to the ground, I reach for the knife at my back. Before I can pull it out, a harpoon shoots through the guard's body, impaling him. He falls to his knees. Across the room, Many waves at me before going back to shooting.

I duck my chin at him, even though he can't see me.

"Here you go," Fem says as she rushes pass, tossing me another gun.

She fires a shot at one of the guards, rolls across the floor at the feet of another one and comes up behind him, putting a bullet to the back of his head.

"That is a very talented woman," Maksim says behind me.

"You got no fucking idea," Priest says through the earpiece in our ears.

Maksim and I get back to work clearing everyone on our side of the room. Guns are not my favorite weapon, but Priest made sure we were all good with them.

"Corbyn is on the run. He's heading to the parking garage," Zel warns. "I'm going to lose sight of him if he gets that far.

"Beast come with me," Priest yells. "The rest of you finish up here and clear us some space."

"You got it," Seth adds.

"Be careful, brother," Maksim warns me.

I take off back out the way I came in. Maksim fires shots over my head clearing my way.

I run into another guard, but easily dispose of him. As soon as I step back out to the foyer of the building, I meet Priest.

"Let's go," he says. We both take off in the direction of the underground parking garage. We take the stairs two at a time.

As soon as we come out of the doors and enter the garage, a bullet whizzes past our heads. Corbyn is in front of us with his weapon drawn. He turns and takes off running. We follow.

"We see Corbyn. We're on his tail," Priest says.

Running through the garage, we reach a point where there's nowhere else to go. There is a wall in front of Corbyn. He stops and turns around with his hands above his head. A smile planted on his face.

"You've reached the end of the road, Corbyn."

"That I have. But I must admit, I'm glad to finally meet the great Nathaniel Otello."

I keep my gun aimed at Corbyn. It's startling to see how similar we look. I've met some of my siblings and none of them resemble Corbyn as much as me. Even his dark blonde hair matches mine, although not nearly as long. The eyes are the exact same.

"My brother talked so highly of you. That should have been my clue to what he did. I guess I should thank you for raising my son."

"I didn't raise your son," Priest argues. "I raised mine."

The smile falls from Corbyn's face for only a moment before he plants it back in place.

"I hope there are no hard feelings about the whole excommunication thing. Really, you guys had outgrown that organization. Honestly, I did you a favor."

"If you wanted to do us a favor, you and your royal club would keep your hands out of the Church."

Corbyn laughs. "You think it would make a difference? Even if we left the Church to its own devices, we would still have power over you. Money rules the world, Nathaniel. Have you not realized that? Your own government is run by the Royal Crown. The American people haven't picked a president since Washington.

"The Crown has always handpicked your leaders. When you get in that booth to decide Democrat or Republican, it never matters because we have already chosen. We have always made the laws and the rules. We are the power behind the world. Even if you kill me, we will still reign supreme. You are fighting a losing battle."

Nothing Corbyn said came as a shock to me. I've always known money and power ran the world. Corbyn is correct, the Royal Crown will always have a hand in the Church. There is nothing we could do to change that. Even if we killed Corbyn and got reinstated, we can't take down the Royal Crown.

So what do you do?

"Priest, we're heading to you," Seth says in the earpiece.

"Your time is up, Corbyn," Priest announces. "I hope your money serves you well in hell."

I go to pull the trigger, but something catches my attention out of the corner of my eye.

"I think you might be mistaken, Priest," Corbyn sneers as I spin around.

"Priest get down," I shout the words as Victoria fires her weapon.

I fire back at her, hitting her in the chest. She stumbles but doesn't fall, letting me know she's wearing a vest. The sound of screeching tires has me turning just in time to see a red Hummer nearly barrel into me. I jump to the side to avoid being hit.

Corbyn and Victoria run to the truck and jump in.

"You should have stuck with me, son," Corbyn shouts before shutting the door.

The truck pulls away. I leap to my feet and fire the gun at the back window. The glass doesn't even break. I chase after the Hummer.

Just then, Seth, Hawk, Maksim, Many, And Fem run around the corner. They see me shooting and fire at the truck as well. It never slows as it disappears out of the garage.

"What the hell happened?" Seth shouts. "I thought you had him?"

I ignore him as I spin on my heels and rush back to Priest. I come up short when I spot the blood surrounding his head.

I freeze in my spot. My body becomes numb. It's almost like I'm having an out of body experience. It isn't until Fem screams beside me I finally rush back to myself.

"What's going on? What's happening?" Zel pleads through the earpiece.

"It's bad, brother. It's really fucking bad," Seth replies somberly.

CHAPTER TWENTY-THREE

Hospital

Summer

Last time I was in Doc's makeshift hospital, I was the one behind those swinging doors. I had no idea what it looked like in the waiting room, but if it felt like this, I'm glad I wasn't there.

Hawk called Brooklyn and told her to get here. All he said was Priest was shot. He didn't tell us how bad it was or anything. We left the kids with Ms. Reese while Brooklyn, Malia, Ari and I came right over.

We've been sitting in this waiting room for hours hoping to hear something soon. Seth is pacing the floor like a raging bull. Fem hasn't stopped crying since we got here. Malia and Brooklyn were by her side the entire time. Hawk is sitting with his arms across his chest, and his head leaning back against the wall with his eyes closed. Zel is beside him with his head down, his leg hasn't stopped jumping yet. Many and Ari are beside each other. For once neither of them has anything to say.

Maksim is standing across from me, his back is against the wall. His gaze keeps sweeping the room as if he's waiting to see who is going to fall apart first. However, the one I am most concerned about is the one that is silently sitting on the floor beside me. His back is against the wall, one knee is bent and the other is out in front of him. He has not spoken a word.

When I walked into the room, he didn't even look up. He seems unaware of his surroundings and Gabriel is never unaware.

It isn't his lack of response that is bothering me, it's the vacant look in his eyes. It's like staring at those glass doll eyes. I've seen the vacant look those few times when that dark voice in his head took over, but this isn't that. I've never seen him so out of it. He's scaring me.

"Fuck this," Seth shouts, picking up one of the chairs and hurling it across the room at the wall.

I jump at the sudden sound.

"Seth, please calm down," Malia pleads.

Seth grabs his hair and tugs it so hard I think he's about to pull it out by the roots.

"Brother, calm down," Many says in a voice I don't think I've ever heard him use before. It's hollow.

"This is stupid. We're sitting here twiddling our thumbs when we should be out there looking for Corbyn."

"We're not just sitting here," Zel says lifting his head. "We're here because Priest is in there." He points to the swinging doors that have yet to move.

"And why is that? Huh? Why is he in there? Because Corbyn put him there," Seth continues to rant. "We should have taken him down from the start instead of all those dumb-ass side missions."

"We were doing what Priest wanted. What we should have been doing," Maksim says, putting his two cents in.

Seth turns and glares at him. "Why the fuck are you still here?"

Maksim pushes away from the wall. He stops when Malia leaps up. She grabs Seth's face between her hands.

"Baby, you're upset. Rightfully so, but you can't take it out on everybody."

He yanks away from her touch. "This is bullshit. Bullshit," he shouts so loud I once again startle. I look beside me at Gabriel and he still has no reaction.

"Yo, where is Lucien?" Zel says. "We need him out here because I can't deal with your dumb shit."

"Fuck you, Zel? Where were you when they were putting a bullet in Priest?"

Zel shoots to his feet. "Doing what he told me to do. Where were you, Seth? Since you have all the got damn answers."

"Guys please," Malia pleads.

Hawk and Many both hop to their feet. Hawk is standing between Zel and Seth while Many tries to hold Zel back.

"We're not doing this," Hawk says, looking between the two. "We're brothers. We don't argue like this."

"Fuck him," Seth yells. "He's not my fucking brother, none of you are."

I gasp at his outburst. I've never heard them argue like this. Even in those two and half months when they would get into petty arguments it was never like this.

"You're just angry. Don't say that," Many says still using that hollow voice. "You don't mean it."

Seth tugs at his hair. His eyes are so red that it looks as if he took a hit off a good blunt.

"I've got to get out of here." Seth tries to walk around Many and Hawk, but they block him in.

"You're not leaving. We're staying together," Hawk demands.

"Let him go. If he's going to act like a lunatic, then let him go. We don't need him," Zel yells.

"Fuck you," Seth shouts. Now instead of trying to leave, he's trying to get to Zel. Sim pushes away from the wall. He gently moves Malia out of the way as he grabs Zel and holds him back.

I glance at Gabriel. He's so unbothered you would think he wasn't in the room right now. He doesn't even look over at his brothers.

"Hey," Brooklyn stands up and shouts. "We are not doing this shit here. Seth, calm the fuck down and stop being an asshole. Zel, take a seat. You're not the only ones in here hurting." She points at Fem.

Both men seem to come to their senses. Zel walks away and retakes his seat. Seth runs a hand over his head.

"Sorry," he mumbles before sitting down. Malia quickly takes the chair beside him. She rubs his shoulder as he leans forward on his knees. Hawk and Many both retake their seats.

We sit in silence for another hour before the doors swing open and Doc walks out. His scrubs are covered in blood and sweat is pouring down his face.

Everyone stands on their feet. Well, all except Gabriel.

"Talk to me, Doc?" Seth says.

Doc removes the little surgical cap off his head and twists it in his hands. He turns to Fem.

"I'm so sorry. We did all we could do."

I gasp before covering my mouth. A piercing scream leaves Fem's lips before she drops to her knees. Brooklyn goes down with her, trying to console her. Malia pulls Seth into her arms as he weeps onto her shoulder. Many is silently staring off in space with tears streaming down his face. Zel has his face buried in his hands while Hawk is back sitting with his head leaning against the wall as tears fall from his eyes.

I've only known these men for a short period, but never have I seen them so broken. Their father is gone. Although Priest had no blood tie to any of these men, he was their father. And nothing can change that.

Out the corner of my eye, I watch Gabriel climb to his feet and walk out of the room. I've been giving him his space. Something told me that he needed it. However, now my gut tells me he needs me.

"Gabriel," I call his name as I follow him out the waiting room and into the hallway. He stops but doesn't turn around to face me.

"Go back inside, Summer."

"No." I walk up on him slowly until I'm standing right behind him. "You promised me you wouldn't run anymore."

His breathing is so labored his shoulders and back expand with every deep breath.

"I'm not running. I just....I need to get out of here." He tries to walk away again, but I rush to stand in front of him. I place my hands on his chest to stop him. His eyes are red and they glisten with unshed tears.

"You can't run off every time things get hard. You have to face it."

"I can't," he whispers. "Not without him."

I cup his cheek guiding his gaze to mine.

"Yes, you can. Because he taught you how."

He shakes his head, but I keep talking.

"Your brothers need you right now. You all need each other. You have to stay for them."

"He's gone." He shuts his eyes. "He's gone." His voice breaks, and he falls to his knees, burying his face in my stomach. His body shakes with his sobs. The tears fall down my face as I hold tight to the man I love. The man that has been everything I needed him to be when I've needed it.

"I'm here for you, baby. I'm right here," I say as I stroke his hair and place kisses on his head.

Maksim walks up. His blood-shot eyes stare at me. He goes to his knees beside his brother and wraps his arm around him.

"I got you, little brother. No matter what. I got you. Priest was a good man."

We stand there for what feels like eternity. Gabriel cries into my stomach while Maksim continues to inform him he will be with him until the end. I fight my own emotions as I try to wrap my head around the fact that Priest is dead.

CHAPTER TWENTY-FOUR

New Allies

Beast

The car ride to the cemetery is silent. It's been four days since Doc made the announcement about Priest.

The ghost house has not been the same. Many hasn't spoken a word since that day. We haven't seen or heard from Seth. Zel has been locked away in his room. Even Hawk has been quieter than usual. And Albany.... I've never seen anyone as broken as her.

I've been so thankful for Summer and Malia. They both stepped in to handle all the arrangements. Priest had mostly everything taken care of as far as the burial went. He even picked out the cemetery and the plot. But there were a few things that needed to be dealt with, and Summer and Malia were the only ones in a clear enough mindset to deal with it.

"I miss Grandpa Priest," Gabe says in the quiet car.

I swallow hard. The bond Priest and Gabe formed in such a short time was incredible. I never thought he would ever get the chance to experience the relationship we had with him.

"I know, baby," Summer says behind me.

"I never got my nickname."

My heartbreaks even more. I shut my eyes and try to breathe. *"You failed them,"* the dark voice whispers. *"You should have taken the shot. You let them all down."*

The guilt of my actions has weighed heavy on me in the last few days. The demon voice is back. I've been trying to talk to Alicia to keep it at bay, but my guilt seems to bring him out. It's how he came out the first time after Summer was shot. Although no one has said anything to me, I know they all feel it. I know they all think that I was the one with Priest when it happened. I should have protected him.

"Are you well, brother?"

I look over to find Maksim watching me. He's been doing it a lot lately. I don't open my mouth to respond. Instead, I dip my chin to my chest.

He turns back to the road before glancing in the rearview mirror.

"Do not worry, little nephew. I will give you a nickname when the time comes."

I glance over my shoulder to look at Gabe. He nods, but I can tell he isn't happy about Maksim's words.

"If his father had done his part, he wouldn't have to settle." Fisting my hands in my lap, I shut my eyes to once again fight against the dark voice in my head.

"Who are all these people?" Summer's voice brings me back to the here and now.

One of the biggest issues we had with burying Priest, was keeping everything quiet. We still had an excommunication order on our heads. But there was no way we weren't going to bury our father.

Maksim pulls the black SUV to a stop behind the one in front of us. In the car with me are Maksim, Summer, and Gabe. In front of us, Many, Ari, Zel, Emory, and Phoenix who flew back three days ago. Brooklyn, Fem, Hawk, Lucien, Malia, Charlie, and Ms. Reese are in the first SUV.

"Do you know these people?" Maksim asks.

Glancing around at the men and women in all black, I growl.

"Stay in the car, Summer." I grab the gun at my back and climb out of the SUV.

"Gabriel, please," she pleads.

Yes, I could be climbing out to my death. But the rage brewing in me right now seeing these members of the Church at Priest's funeral had me ready to face death head on.

"I got him," I heard Maksim say. "Stay down."

He climbs out with me. The doors to the SUVs in front of us open. All my brothers climbed out. I can tell by the expression on their faces they are just as pissed as I am. Maksim rounds the car to my side.

Bishop Gates leads the pack of Church members. Alongside him are three other men that I have never seen before. My brothers and I draw our weapons, aiming them at the crowd.

Gates holds his hands up. "We come in peace," he says looking at all of us. We have yet to drop our weapons. "Today you are burying a friend, a brother," his voice catches on the last word. "A father, and a damn good man. We are here to make sure that he gets the burial he deserves. You can relax, boys. You are amongst allies."

Hawk's arm drops first, followed by everyone else. I'm the last to put my arm down.

The three guys I've never met before step forward. All three are tall, but not as tall as me. One has short blonde hair and scars on his face. The second younger looking one has dark brown hair and as many tattoos as Seth. The other one is a business type guy with the same dark hair with brown eyes.

The business guy holds out a hand toward me. I shake it.

"My name is Niccolo Basille, I'm a friend of Priest. These are my brothers, Salvito Delgado and Kazimir. Our oldest brother Mason couldn't make it. However, he sends his condolences and his own personal guards." He points to the men up on the hill with large guns.

"We wanted to make sure that Priest was put away with all the respect he deserves."

I nod, thankful for their help.

"How long have you known Priest?" Lucien asks beside me.

Niccolo smiles. "We all met him when we were young boys. What age do you think we were, Vito?"

The guy with the tattoos chuckles. "I might've been about five or six."

Church recruits? But they aren't members of the Church and they damn sure didn't come in under Priest because he never had another class.

"We appreciate the fire power and you guys joining us today," Maksim says.

"Between their guys and ours," Cardinal Taylor says. "We have the cemetery covered. If anybody steps on this land with the intent to cause problems, they won't live to see another day."

"Thank you," Lucien says. "I know Priest would appreciate this." His voice cracks at the end of his sentence.

"He would do the same thing for all of us," Bishop Gates says.

They step back making a pathway to the burial site. I turn around and open the back door. Summer steps out first and then she turns to get Gabe out. She picks him up and he buries his face in her shoulder. After shutting the door, I take him from his mother. He looks me in the eyes as the first tear falls. He swipes it away.

"I'll be brave, Hulk."

I shut my eyes and inhale before opening them back up to stare at him.

"Not today, Gabe. Today, you don't have to be brave."

He nods his head as his tears start to fall freely. Grabbing Summer's hand, I walk over to my brothers. Brooklyn is on one side of Albany and Pheonix is on the other side of her. She's holding onto Charlie as she visibly shakes with her sobs. We follow behind her as we walk over to Priest's casket.

I didn't hear most of the things the priest said. I don't even know if anyone got up and spoke on his behalf. My mind was blank as I stared at the black casket with gold trim. My father, the man that made me who I am, was gone. A part of me was going with him.

As I stared, I made a vow to him. I vowed that I would avenge him, and then I would join him. If my father could not be here to be with his family, then neither should I. I was the reason he was there. I didn't deserve the happiness he couldn't have.

Summer's hand tightens around mine. I look over at her. Her eyes are red, but they stare at me with so much concern. It's almost as if she could hear my thoughts. As much as I loved her, I knew that I would have to break my promise to her. I told her I wouldn't leave her again, but I had to. I couldn't stay on this side with her. My guilt would never allow it.

Instead of telling her that, I squeeze her hand back and drop a kiss on her forehead. When I lean back up, I shift Gabe in my lap. I would make sure they were taken care of before I go.

We all stand when the priest tells us to. The cemetery workers hand the women with us a rose. They all walk over to the casket and toss them into the hole as they lower Priest's body down. Summer walks back over to me and grabs my hand. I set Gabe down when Emory comes up beside me. She takes his hand after handing him a rose. They both walk hand and hand over to the hole and toss their flowers inside. The last one to walk over to the casket is Albany.

She still has Charlie in her arms. She clutches her rose to her chest. Her body shakes as she sobs. When the cries break away from her closed lips. My tears start to fall.

"Please, God. I can't," she pleads. "You can't leave me, Nathaniel. You can't," she sobs.

Her body starts to tremble. I recognize it before it happens. Releasing Summer's hand, I rush to Albany's side. My self and my brothers all get to her at the same time. She collapses to the ground, but we are all there to grab her. She lets out a gut-wrenching sob.

"You can't leave us. You can't leave Charlie," she repeats.

We wrapped our arms around her. I looked into my brothers' faces and there was nothing but pain and determination staring back at me.

"We got you," Hawk says. "You and our brother. No matter what. We got you."

"Forever," Lucien adds.

We held Albany just like that until she was able to stand on her own. I don't know how much time passed. But by the time we climbed back in those SUV's I was determined to set things right.

CHAPTER TWENTY-FIVE

Plans

Beast

We'd been back at the ghost house a few hours after the funeral. Everyone was in their own space.

Summer was trying to keep Gabe occupied. He went into a shell after the funeral. Not even Emory and the dogs could get him to come out of it.

I was in the dining room sitting at the table staring at the wall. My mind was blank but full at the same time. I was trying to turn over in my head how I was going to leave and finish this fight alone.

"Plotting your escape?" Maksim asks, drawing my attention to him.

I had no idea he had walked in. He was leaning up against the doorframe with a water bottle in his hands.

"I'm not escaping."

He shrugs before pushing away from the door. "Do you know I am only three months older than you?"

I don't respond. Maksim and I have yet to talk about anything personal about ourselves. Not sure why he thinks it appropriate now.

"I never really felt close to my siblings. I loved them, but there was always a disconnect. The first time I spoke to you on the phone, I felt as if

I was speaking to someone I'd known all my life. Do you want to know why?"

Leaning back in my chair, I run my hand down my face. "No."

He laughs as he takes a seat across from me. "It's because we are more alike than you know. I know I would've questioned myself if I had seen my father shot dead in front of me. I would have tried to figure out what I could have done differently. And in the end, I would've been so blinded by guilt that I wouldn't be able to think straight. Might have even considered a suicide mission."

Maksim's eyes narrow at me. I clench my teeth together, not liking how well he just read my thoughts.

"Someone has to pay," I grit out.

"And it better fucking not be you."

I turn to the doorway to find Hawk, Lucien, Zel, and Many watching me. Looking away from them, I stare back at the wall.

"It's my fault. I should have taken the shot. If I had, Priest would still be here. I don't get to survive when he didn't."

"And so you'll leave Gabe to feel like us?" Zel asks, walking further into the dining room. "That's bullshit, Beast, and you know it."

"I can't look at them," I say slamming my hand down on the table.

"Who?" Hawk asks.

"Albany and Charlie. I can't face them knowing what I did?"

"And what did you do?"

We all turn to the sound of Albany's voice. She hikes her brow at me.

"I'm not in the mood for a pity party, Beast. I'm going to say this one time and one time only: you did nothing wrong. You taking the shot at Corbyn or not wouldn't have prevented that bitch from shooting Nathaniel. Before you even showed up at the function, that was the plan. They lured you and Nathaniel to that parking lot for that reason. It's why he came back. It was a setup from the start."

We all looked away, feeling guilty.

"I shouldn't have pushed us to go after him," Lucien says in a low tone. "Priest was right, we weren't prepared."

"But now we are," Albany says lifting her head. "What's the first lesson Nathaniel taught you? Before he told you to check for entrances and exits. Before he ever put a weapon in your hand, what did he teach you?"

"That we were a team," Many speaks for the first time since the day Priest died. "He taught us we were brothers."

Albany nods. "The reason the Church hated him so much was because he had the secret formula. You guys aren't great killers because you're blind, or have a split personality, or forms of schizophrenia. You're great killers because a man that loved you, a man that thought of you as his sons, poured into you. He made you believe that you could do anything in this world."

We all look away from her. She's right. Every time a new Priest tried to bring in a blind kid, or an autistic kid, or a kid with some form of mental disorder, they never turned out like us. Everyone tried to copy Priest's formula. But they never understood what made us so great.

"Even Corbyn tried to duplicate what Priest did with you guys," Maksim says. "He thought he got close, but me and my siblings never cared for each other the way you guys do. We don't work like you do."

Albany steps further into the room. "The last three months you guys forgot the first lesson he taught you. I know you all have families and your own people to look out for, but to Nathaniel you were still his boys and his priority. Every decision he made was not just for me and Charlie but you guys and your families.

"The house in Georgia, came fully stocked with a nursery and around the clock care for Malia, Brooklyn, and Ari. He made sure that they would have the best OBGYN in the city at their beck and call."

Hawk drops his head. Lucien and Many both look away from Albany.

"The last three months all any of you could think about were yourselves. That's not what he taught you."

She's right. Every decision we've made since the excommunication has been for our own benefit. We weren't working together. Hell, I was so caught up battling the demon in my head I didn't think about anything else.

"If we need to, we can send the girls away," Hawk says.

"It's too late for that," Albany sighs. "Besides, we all need each other right now."

"So how do we fix it?" Zel asks.

"By doing it together," I say looking up at the faces around me.

"Exactly," Albany agrees. "We need to put our heads together and come up with a plan. Not just making decisions based off our own emotions. Yes, we are angry and hurt right now, but that's not going to help us win this battle. We need a solid plan. What do we know about Corbyn?"

"He's smart," Hawk says. "And patient."

That's been proven by how long it took him to come out of hiding. We were so ready to go after him after Yohan shot Summer. However, he never showed himself even though he had the upper hand. He waited until we were so desperate we wouldn't stop to think if it was a setup or not. We ran headfirst into his scheme.

"His money and influence run deep," Lucien says dropping down in a seat.

"But he's not the muscle," Zel states, leaning against the back wall. "He surrounds himself with his paid bodyguards and his kids. I bet if you get him by himself, he's defenseless."

"How do we do that?" Lucien asks. "He will never be without his guards or one of his kids."

Maksim rubs his chin. "Then we eliminate his protection."

We all turn to look at him.

"You sure you're up for that?" I wasn't dumb. Although Maksim and I have grown somewhat close over the last few months, I won't act as if he doesn't have a connection with his siblings. What he is suggesting means we take them out. He has to draw a line in the sand and decide which side he's going to stand on.

He shakes his head. "If I thought I could save them, I would. Trust me, I tried before I left. The damage Corbyn did to them can't be undone."

"Yours was," I reply.

He nods. "Torture does that to you. Also, like I told you, I've always been different. If you want to know what side I'm on, I'm with you. I'm with all of you." he says looking around at all of us.

"Good," Albany says pulling a chair out and taking a seat. "Because I want to know every sibling you have, and I want to know everything about them. Many, grab that dry erase board."

Many goes to the corner of the room and rolls out the giant whiteboard we'd been using to keep track of the names on that excommunication order. He wipes off the words on the board before grabbing the black marker.

"There are eight left," Maksim says. "Micah, Zeke, Adam, Nolan, Archie, Evan, Yohan, and Victoria."

Many writes all eight names on the board.

"I want Victoria," Albany says with a growl. "No one touches her."

Maksim shakes his head. "Don't set your sights on the last two. They are Corbyn's favorites. He will keep them closest to him."

"Then we start with the others. Who's the easiest target?" Lucien asks.

"I know what you're capable of," Maksim says. "But I don't want you to get ahead of yourselves. My siblings are well trained. Just as well as all of you. This won't be easy."

"Yeah, but didn't Beast take out two of them by himself?" Hawk asks.

"I did, but that's because they were arrogant. They weren't expecting me to be a step ahead of them. We won't have that advantage this time."

"He's right," Albany says. "We take nothing for granted. We have to be smart about our attacks. The goal is to pin Corbyn against a wall. A trapped rodent will always make a mistake."

"If we take away his protection, he will tuck his tail and hide and you will never be able to figure out where he is," Maksim says. "Corbyn owns properties all over the world. He can go from one house to another. I know about most, but he has one or two that no one knows the location to. It will be like trying to find a needle in a haystack."

"Then let's remove some of the hay," I say as the thought hits me. "The goal is to trap him where we want him. Let's lure him into his own trap. We burn down all his hideaway houses that you know leaving only one or two. It will force him to take refuge in one of those two houses."

"You said there are only two you don't know right?" Lucien asks. Maksim nods.

"Then we eliminate all the others. It will give him a sense of false protection. If we can narrow the search down to one or two places, I promise me and Kyra can track him down."

"Who are we going to get to attack the homes? It's not smart for us to separate, plus Maksim said some of those places are overseas," Hawk states.

"D.O.E has already offered their services," Albany says. "They try to stay out of Church business. But this is personal. They will do it for me."

"Cardinal Thomas and Trigger Gates both offered their services as well. They said they are here for whatever we need," Zel offers.

It's good to know that Priest still had some true friends in the Church. It wasn't just our lives he impacted.

"I'll give you the list of all the safe houses I know," Maksim tells Albany.

She dips her chin at him.

"With that out of the way, who's our first target?" Lucien asks.

Maksim rubs a hand down his face as he looks over at the whiteboard. "We will start with Zeke. He's the most likely to be alone. It won't be easy, though. He lives a solitary life."

"He has to come out of his house for something," Hawk says.

"Running," Maksim replies. "He does it every night, but he always picks random times and spots around the city. Corbyn always taught us to never form routines."

"So, all we have to do is track his movements and follow him to wherever he runs."

"Still won't be easy," Maksim says, responding to my statement. "The moment he spots anyone near him he will be tipped off. Zeke is paranoid. He doesn't trust anyone, man, woman, or child?"

"There has to be some way to get close enough to him," Zel says.

Maksim shrugs. "He likes animals."

Many chuckles, pulling my attention to him. "I think we will take care of this one."

CHAPTER TWENTY-SIX

Dog Lover

Many

Leaning back on my hands, my feet dangle over the edge of the playground equipment. We're sitting on the very top of the play set.

It took us over a week to set this night up. We needed to make sure Zeke came to this particular park. So, we started subliminal advertising. We paid for billboards and signs to go up all around his home advertising the running trails at this park. Not only did we put up signs, but Lucien was even able to tap into his home camera system. For the last two days, we've been playing a repeat of the park's name through a loop on his speaker system while he slept.

It took a lot to get us here, but we all believed tonight our efforts would finally pay off.

"You're so cute when you're focused."

We look down into the face of Ari. She's standing on the platform underneath where we're seated. We get that fluttery feeling in our stomach like we always do. It takes our breath away every time our eyes land on her.

"She shouldn't be here. It isn't safe." We think in my social worker's British accent.

"Women are at a higher risk for miscarriages in the first trimester," Our Phyllis voice says.

"She's smart and well prepared. She will be fine," Priest says in my head.

"You will stay here and out of sight," we warn her in our Priest voice.

Climbing down from the roof of the playground, we plant our feet back on the monkey bars. We then swing our body onto the platform she's standing on. Lying at her feet are Kraken and Hydra. We left Cerberus and Echidna home.

Ari grins. "Don't worry, Milo. I won't do anything to endanger the baby. That's what these two are for." She points to the dogs before taking a seat in front of the slide as if she's about to slide down.

We occupy the spot right beside her.

"We know, but we still want you to take it easy."

"You do know I am not the first agent of D.O.E to take a mission while with child?"

She reminds us of this constantly, but it does nothing to ease our concern. We know what Ari is capable of, we just don't like the idea of her risking herself. However, it wouldn't be right to ask her to step down when we are not willing to stop either.

We know Lucien and Hawk are hoping that after we clear our names that we will be able to walk away from the Church. We feel at odds with them on that. We don't want to stop. Although we don't have a driving force to kill like our brother Beast, we do enjoy what we do. It is part of who we are.

It gives us a purpose and makes us feel as if we're protecting those in need. Unlike what we did as kids.

The memory of our mother and sisters pop up in our head. We shut our eyes to fight against the vision. We failed them.

You will fail Ari and this baby too. Our thoughts are loud and hard to ignore. They have been harder to fight since Priest was taken away from us.

"Stop it," her soft voice pulls us out of our head. We look over at her, her fuchsia tipped hair hangs past her shoulders now. "You're thinking about failing me again, aren't you?"

We didn't answer her. Instead, we push her hair behind her ear to get a better view of her face. People think Ari and I don't have deep conversations. They think we only talk about movies, anime, and books. But she is our other half. She knows our deepest fears and the thoughts that haunt us.

"You are my world, Ariane."

"And you are mine, Milo. But don't change the subject."

A smile lifts our lips. She never lets things go. "We failed them. My sisters, my mother, Priest. We failed them all."

She places my face between her hands. Her brown eyes staring into mine. "You were a child when your family was killed. You did what any sensible child would have done."

We pull our face from between her hands. We have to look away from her.

"She is right. We were too young to fight Papa," our social worker voice says.

"He outweighed us by nearly a hundred pounds. We would have been defenseless against him," our Phyllis voice responds.

"We could have outsmarted him. I could have saved Natalia. She was the youngest and easy to carry. We could have gotten her to safety," Our Priest voice argues.

"We could have saved one of them," I say in my Priest voice.

Ari turns my face back to her with a finger under my chin. "She could have fallen and broken her neck. You could've gotten caught and been killed too. Or either she would have witnessed what you did and never been able to recover. There are a lot of scenarios in this that could have gone horribly. Don't linger on them.

"The decision you made was the best. Because of it, you got to meet your brothers and Priest. And not only that, but you also got to meet me, which should be the highlight of your life."

Her joke causes us to laugh.

"It is," I admit in my Milo voice. I use this voice more often when I am alone with Ari.

We had no idea we would ever find love. We didn't even plan on it. However, the day we first laid eyes on Ari at the receptionist desk, we fell for her. I'd never met anyone as beautiful as her.

Finally, being able to be with her and spend time with her has taught me that her value goes deeper than her good looks. Ariane is funny, loving, caring, smart, brave, encouraging, and the most giving being we've ever come across.

We don't deserve her.

"Approximately 70% of heterosexual unmarried relationships break up within the first year," Phyllis' voice says.

"If she tries to leave us, we will kill every man that touches her," Priest growls.

"Just love her and treat her right and she will never leave," Laura states.

Grabbing her hand, we place a kiss on her palm. "We will never let you go."

She giggles. "Aww, you thought you had a choice. I'm pregnant with your child, Milo. I'll kill you before I let you leave us."

She places a kiss on my lips before turning away from me.

"Alright, guys, it's show time. Zeke just arrived," Lucien's voice comes through the earpiece in my ear. "Turn the mics on from here on out. Many, I want this over quick."

Ari and I both take the devices out of our ear and switch on the microphone before placing them back in. Now we can hear the others and they can hear us.

"You got it, brother Lucien."

"Get to your spot," Lucien says. "Ari, get your dogs ready."

She chuckles. "They're always ready."

We stand, then help her to her feet. She places her arms around my neck and brings her lips to ours. We happily open our mouth for her. She rakes her tongue against ours deepening the kiss. Placing our hand on her ass we pull her into our erection. We feel her smile against our lips. We have not laid with Ari in the sexual intercourse since Papa Priest died. Up until now, we have not wanted to. We do now.

"Easy does it," Ari giggles. "We don't want to put on a show for your brothers."

"We do not want that," I say in my Priest voice.

"Please don't," Zel adds in my earpiece. "Nobody wants to see y'all's weird ass sex."

We pull away from Ari and jump down from the play set.

"Kraken, Hydra, go with Daddy," Ari says directing the dogs. They will only follow her command, so we had to fit the dogs with hearing devices as well.

Both dogs rush down the slide to stand at our side. With one final glance, we leave her at the playground. We rush to the running path and to the designated tree.

"I'm here," we say to the group.

We grab the lowest branch and swing our body up, using our legs to wrap around the next limb. We then right ourselves and use the rest of the tree limbs to climb as far up in the tree as we can get.

"Alright, Ari. Get the dogs in place," Lucien says.

"Kraken, Hydra, playtime. Wait for my command."

The two dogs move onto the track and start play fighting. We wait patiently.

Twenty minutes later, a tall man with a baseball cap, dark shorts and a white t-shirt approaches. He slows down once he spots the dogs. Kraken runs away, leaving Hydra behind. The dog picks up her paw and whimpers as she limps to Zeke.

Zeke stops and looks around. His eyes even scan the surrounding trees. We knew he would most likely be on guard, which is why not only did we climb as high as we could go in the tree with the most foliage, but we also wore all black.

"Hey, you hurt?" Zeke asks as he slowly approaches Hydra. His gaze still sweeps over his surroundings.

Hydra stops in front of him and sniffs his outstretched hand before lying her head against his leg.

"Good girl," Zeke says. "What are you doing out here?"

Slowly, Kraken approaches Zeke. He's so quiet, if we weren't looking at him, we wouldn't know he was coming. Before Kraken could get a good attacking distance, Zeke shoots to his feet, spins around and aims a gun at Kraken. He pulls the trigger, but Hydra reacts faster. She bites into his leg, sending him to the ground and his bullet whirling past Kraken.

Taking a deep breath, we leap from the tree. Tucking our body into itself, we hit the ground and roll into a standing position.

Zeke spins around and aims his weapon at Hydra. Grabbing our short spears out of our back holster, we toss one through the air stabbing him in his shoulder, causing him to drop the gun.

Zeke stands up, yanks the spear out of his arm and glares at me.

"I know you," he sneers at me. "You're one of those freaks from the Church."

We nod our head without replying.

"Did my bastard little brother put you up to this?" We don't miss the way Zeke's hand seems to slowly move behind his back. "This is his attempt at payback for killing his handler." He laughs. "You boys will never learn."

He brings out another gun, but we don't flinch. Kraken does his job. While Zeke was trying to keep me distracted while he went for his gun, we were keeping our eyes on Kraken.

The dog latches his teeth onto the arm holding the gun. Zeke yells as he tries to pull away from the dog's teeth. Slowly, walking over to the other fallen weapon, we pick up the Glock and weigh it in our hand.

Zeke finally gets Kraken to let go of his arm. He holds up the bleeding appendage and aims his gun at the dog.

Our bullet hits the back of his head before he could pull his trigger. He falls to the ground. We walk over to his body and place three more slugs into him.

"One down," We say into the silence.

"Seven more to go," Beast says through the earpiece. "Good job, brother."

CHAPTER TWENTY-SEVEN

Grieving

Summer

"Ooh, shit," I hiss as Gabriel reaches a depth inside my walls that has my toes curling.

"Open your eyes," he grits out behind me.

My eyes pop open. I stare at my reflection in the bathroom mirror. His large body stands behind me, his long hair draping down his shoulders. The hunger in his eyes as he gazes back at me through the mirror makes my body soften even more for him.

I was at the sink brushing my teeth when Gabriel came into the bathroom, lifted my leg up on the sink, and shoved my panties to the side before sliding into me.

The first night after Priest's funeral when he climbed in the bed with me and rolled on top of me, I thought it was a rare occurrence. However, lately I can't keep this man off me. He can look in my direction and get hard. It takes nothing to get him from zero to one hundred.

Gabriel wraps my braids around his hand and yanks my head back to his chest. He then sticks his tongue in my mouth for a sloppy kiss. I suck on his tongue as if it's his cock. He bites down on my bottom lip, gently pulling a moan from my mouth. He pulls away from the kiss and leans back as he starts to fuck me harder and faster. His pelvis smacking against my ass.

I scream at his deep strokes. My hand pushes against the glass in front of me. He uses one hand to open my ass cheek. With the other hand, he sticks his longest finger in his mouth before pulling it out and pushing it in my ass.

Biting down on my lip, I relax my puckered hole as he moves his digit in and out of me.

"Gabriel," I whimper. "I'm about to..." I never finish my sentence as I shoot off like a rocket.

He follows behind me, erupting inside me with a loud groan. He pulls out and backs away from me. His cock is soaked in my essence and the two orgasms I've had.

Lowering my leg back to the ground, I turn to face Gabriel. He tucks his dick back in his boxers and then takes a seat on the side of the tub. Walking over to him, I stand between his legs. He places his forehead against my belly.

"Better?" I ask, raking my fingers through his long hair.

It took me only a short time to realize this sex isn't about me. It's Gabriel's way of grieving. The moment he starts to think about Priest or more importantly, the day Priest died, he tries to run from the memory with my body.

It's only a temporary fix. He and I both know it, but I won't complain. Getting a dick down is never a bad thing. Plus, I will do anything to ease his pain, even if only for a short time.

Gabriel wraps his arms around my thighs, rubbing his hands up and down the bare skin.

"I just can't get it out of my head. One moment I'm good and the next I see him standing there before Victoria's gun goes off."

"Look at me," I say.

He lifts his head and looks up at me. "It's going to take time. You lost your father. And unlike the others, you actually witnessed the moment he was taken away from you. It's normal to replay it in your head, but you can't let it devour you. Priest wouldn't want that."

He grabs my hand and pulls it away from his head and places a kiss on my palm.

"You have been my rock, angel."

This is the sweetest thing he could have said to me. I love this man, and I love he loves me, but him telling me I'm his rock lets me know that he's seeing our relationship as something he wants to stick around for. He's finally seeing me as his partner and not just someone to protect.

"We should shower and head to the dining room." He stands and I take a step back.

"You just want to fuck again," I joke.

He looks at me and smirks. "Maybe."

We have another quick round in the shower before getting dressed. After dressing, we make our way into the dining room after grabbing some of Malia's blueberry muffins.

"Morning, everyone," I say.

Hawk and Brooklyn are here, along with Many, Ari, Fem, Maksim, Zel and Kyra.

"Morning," they all repeat in unison.

I take a seat across from Ari. Gabriel goes over to Maksim and Albany who are standing in front of the whiteboard. Not long after, Lucien and Malia walk into the room. Malia takes a seat beside me while Lucien goes over to the laptop near the head of the table.

"Still no word from Seth," I lean over and whisper to Malia.

We have not seen or heard from Seth since the day in that hospital room. Yes, I know technically Seth and Lucien are the same person, but I'm still used to seeing Seth walk around the house.

Malia shakes her head. "I'm starting to get worried. Lucien keeps telling me to not stress, it isn't good for the baby, but this isn't like Seth."

"Is there a possibility he won't come back?"

Malia explained that something traumatic happened to Lucien when he was a kid and that's how Seth was born. She didn't tell me what exactly happened, and I didn't need to know.

She looks at me and her brown eyes turn down. "I hope not. I love Lucien and he is more than enough for me, but I don't think I could live without Seth."

It sounded crazy, but I understood what she meant. Seth was an entirely different person from Lucien. She loved them both.

"Hopefully, he isn't gone forever, and he'll come back."

She smiles weakly as she turns to look at a disheveled Lucien. "I sure hope so."

"All right," Fem says. "We're all here."

I was glad that they started to allow us to sit in at these meetings. They took our opinions and input to heart. I finally felt as if I was truly contributing. It was my suggestion to hack into Zeke's security system to do the subliminal messages. I told them about one of the therapy sessions we had in rehab.

"What's D.O. E's report?" Fem asks the beautiful dark-skinned girl with the gray eyes.

Kyra taps at something on her tablet before the large computer monitor in the front of the room comes to life. There is a world map up and is covered in about fifty or so red dots.

"These are all the properties Corbyn owns."

"Damn," Zel says. "That's a lot of homes to destroy."

Kyra laughs. "We have our work cut out for us. As soon as we can eliminate these, Lucien and I will focus on those two unknown properties."

"Sounds like a plan," Fem says getting our attention back. "Who are we going after next, Maksim?"

Maksim turns to the whiteboard, already there is a slash mark through Zeke's name. It's been four days since they killed Zeke.

"I think we should hit Archie next."

"Tell us about him." Hawk says.

Maksim sighs. "Archie is smart. He won't easily fall for a trap, but he does have one weakness. He's a bit of a ladies' man. He's always on the haunt for warm pussy."

"That should be easy. We could get someone from D.O.E to lure him to a dark alley and kill him," Ari suggests.

"I doubt it will be that simple," Fem replies. "He's Corbyn's son. Which means he's rich, entitled, and white. Not only is he going to have a type, but he's going to be hard to corner."

"So, what do you suggest?" I ask.

She turns to Kyra. "I may need some help from D.O.E but leave Archie to me."

CHAPTER TWENTY-EIGHT

Ladies Man

Albany

"Alright, Angel. It's all on you now. We're right across the street if you need us."

Taking in a deep breath, I roll my eyes. Turning my back to my mark, I fake a sip of the Bourbon in my glass.

"Lucien, I can handle myself. Will you please stay out of my ear?"

Numerous chuckles come through my earpiece.

"Yes, ma'am," Lucien jokes.

I appreciate the way the guys have rallied around me these past few weeks. God knows I've needed it.

As soon as I think about him, my eyes burn and my throat feels as if it's closing. I have never had a pain like this. Knowing that the man you love, the other half of you, will never hold you in his arms again. The person you dreamed about growing old with for most of your life has left you here alone.

Clutching a hand to my heart, I take a few deep breaths. The only thing that has got me through this is the fact that I have Charlie. My baby boy needs me. Plus, I know for a fact if I were to end up on the other side with Nathaniel, leaving Charlie here alone, he would kill me all over again.

Shaking off the melancholy feeling, I lift my head and swallow my emotions. I have a job to do. I put my attention back on Archie. He's sitting three seats away from me. He's been flirting with two gorgeous blondes for most of the night.

From what I've gathered from the brown-haired guy with blue eyes and a chiseled jaw, I'm definitely not his type. He hasn't looked back at me since his initial assessment when he first walked in. He likes his women young, blonde, bubbly, and white. I can fake young, blonde, and bubbly, but my deep brown skin could never be white.

Getting him alone will take a little extra work. Thankfully, I'm always up for the challenge.

The handsome businessman in the white crisp shirt that has been eye-fucking me since he walked in stands up and makes his way over to me. He leaves his friend sitting alone at the bar.

"Do you mind if I sit?" Mr. crisp shirt asks with a charming smile.

Holding my hand out toward the empty chair, I say. "It's vacant."

He takes the seat, flashing his Rolex at me. His gaze rakes up and down my body. I'm wearing a red wrap dress that cuts low in the front and showcases my milk filled breasts.

"You are stunning," he hums.

"Yes," I reply glancing at him briefly. "I know."

He reaches into his pocket and pulls out his wallet. He places a black Amex card down in front of me.

"How about I buy you a drink?"

Glancing down at the card, I turn in my seat to give him my undivided attention. Tapping the side of my still full glass, I say, "Don't waste your money."

The guy winks. "Trust me, I have enough to splurge on you."

Keeping my eyes glued to him. I smile wide. I reach into my purse and pull out the same card he has and place it down on the bar.

"Would you like to measure dick sizes next? I don't have one, but I'm sure it could still rival yours."

He frowns, grabs his card and stands to his feet. He quickly makes his way back over to his friend. I chuckle at his quick departure as I place my card back in my purse.

"I told you not to try it," the business guy's partner says in a supposed whisper. "She shot James down two weeks ago. No one's bagging her."

When I look up, Archie's eyes are on me for the first time tonight.

I smirk at him. "Your attention seems to be lost. You may want to stick to the easier targets." I glance at the girls around him.

Archie rolls his bottom lip between his teeth and smirks.

"Don't even waste your time," the businessman snorts. "She must be a lesbian." He glares over at me. He and his friend quickly grab their things before tossing a few dollars on the bar and leaving.

"Alright, the game is set. It's all up to you now," Stuart, the businessman says in my earpiece. He looks over his shoulder and winks at me before he walks out the door.

I've been watching Archie for three days. I've had different members of D.O.E go to bars where he would be just to record him. I knew his preferred type the first night they recorded him. The next two days I spent trying to figure him out and my best chance at getting him alone.

I knew that if I were to show up to the same bar as him three days in a row, he would be suspicious. Which is why I had to get Kyra and other agents to help. Even Stuart and James, the other fake businessman, are on the payroll for the DOE.

Archie stands from his seat, tugs at his shirt and walks over to me. I watch every move he makes until he pulls the vacant stool out and takes a seat.

"I'll save you the trouble," I say. "My pockets are deeper, I don't have daddy issues, your dick size will not impress me, and I hate flowery words."

Archie shrugs. "I don't buy women, I have enough daddy issues for both of us, it's not my dick size you have to worry about, and I don't know flowery words."

I stare at him with a smirk on my face.

"Aurora Monroe," I say, holding out a hand to him.

He takes my hand and shakes it. "Archibald Corbyn."

Sitting back in my seat, I cross my arms over my chest.

"Just because you got my name, Mr. Corbyn, does not mean you have my attention."

He shrugs. "Well, I'm just appreciative of the name right now."

A beat of silence floats between us. His eyes roam over my body. I don't miss the sexual desire I see in his gaze, but I also spot the challenge there.

"You look like a woman that likes excitement."

I chuckle. "Considering your eyes have not strayed far from my tits, I find it hard to believe you read me so quickly."

He grins. "You do have nice tits."

"They are average at best. Not as full as your young friend over there." I point to the taller blonde that's now giving me the evil eye. Turning back to Archie, I grin. "You're missing your chance to get lucky with your little friends."

He looks at the girls and then back at me. "I think I'll be luckier here."

Running my tongue over my bottom lip, I shake my head. My goal is to give him the illusion that I am softening toward him. I can't give in too fast. Most of his attraction is due to the chase. The moment I make it easy he will lose interest.

I roll my eyes. "You're cocky. That's not really a turn on for me."

He grins. "Not cocky, beautiful, just confident."

I take a beat of silence to look him up and down as if I'm trying to get a better read on him. I didn't really need to read him. I knew everything I needed to know about him. "Tell me, Mr. Corbyn."

"Archie," he says cutting me off. "Mr. Corbyn is my father."

His eyes gleam, and his chest lifts as he speaks of his father. Everything I know about the siblings aligns with his actions. Twice he's brought his father into this conversation. Just then, when he mentioned him, pride filled his face. He is in awe of the man.

"Does Mr. Corbyn know his son is out here trying to pick up unattainable women?"

A huge smile lifts his face. He leans closer to me. "My father would be very proud. We both like challenges. He has never met one he could not conquer."

"Is that so?" It takes everything in me not to react to that statement. Even mentioning Corbyn in a roundabout way makes my trigger finger itch. The day we put a bullet in his head can't get here soon enough.

"It is."

"Your father sounds like a very interesting man. I wonder if his son is anything like him?"

Archie's eyes light up. Giving Corbyn even that simple of a compliment has Archie nearly drooling. I imagine his dick got hard.

"How about we head to my place, and you can find out?"

I give the appropriate amount of hesitation, allowing him to sweat it out a little longer. I'm keeping up the façade that I'm hard to get.

Without responding to him, I raise my hand to the bartender. He walks over to me with a grin.

"Close out my tab," I say but don't take my eyes off Archie. "And James," I turn to face the bartender. "Remember his face. If I'm not back in here at my regular time tomorrow night, call the cops."

Archie chuckles beside me. If he had been paying attention, he might have noticed the confused look on the bartender's face. Considering this is my first time coming here, and I knew his name without him telling me warranted his confusion. But I wasn't worried about him ratting me out. He knew I was using him as a precaution, like many women do when going home with a stranger. I needed Archie to think that I was a regular woman worried about regular stuff, like being raped or murdered.

Picking up my purse off the bar, I stand and run a hand down the front of my dress. Archie stands as well, holding a hand out for me to take. I keep him on my left side so that he won't notice the earpiece tucked down in my ear.

We walk out of the bar, side by side. The conversation remains light the entire ten-minute walk to his apartment.

We take the elevator instead of the stairs. He stands across from me, his back pressed to the left side. His gaze is intense as he stares at me.

"I'll have you know; I've never fucked a black chick before."

I smile, even though it doesn't reach my eyes. "Depending on how the next ten minutes go, you still may not."

He chuckles, before running a hand down his face. "I got you this far. I'm sure it won't take much longer to get you out of that pretty red dress."

I don't comment. The elevator dings and the doors slide open. He steps out first. I follow behind him. He stops in front of his door and looks back at me with a smug smile. When he opens the door, he allows me inside first.

I walk down a narrow hallway until I enter a wide-open room with an open floor plan. The large, picturesque windows give a clear view of the New York city skyline.

"Have a seat," Archie says right behind me.

I take a seat on the white sectional couch that faces the fireplace. I keep my eyes on him. Archie goes into the kitchen. He takes a bottle of wine down and pops the cork. He pours two glasses before coming back over to us. He hands me one glass. I take it and have a sip. His eyes follow the movement. He then tosses his back.

I place my drink down on the coffee table in front of me.

"The longer I'm in your presence, the more attractive I find you."

Raising a brow at him, I say. "And the more you talk, the less attractive I find you."

Thank goodness this man is a mark, and I wasn't actually interested in him. He's a completely deplorable human being.

He chuckles. "Then let me find a better use for my lips."

He leans in and kisses me. His lips are gentle at first before they become more demanding. I bite into his bottom lip, gaining a moan from him. He eases his way from my mouth down to my chin licking and biting. He sucks my neck and runs his tongue over the pulse point there.

"You taste fucking amazing," he groans. He licks back up my neck toward my lips, but this time I turn away from his kiss.

He narrows his gaze when our eyes connect. He goes to speak but stops suddenly. Leaning back, he brings his hands to his lips.

"My lips are tingling."

"Oh my goodness, are you okay?" I ask placing a hand to my chest.

He leans further away from me. His brows furrow even more, as his breathing becomes faster and more shallow. His eyes widen and his face flushes red. He's panicking.

His mouth drops open and he starts to claw at his chest. He gasps as he shoots to his feet. However, after three steps he falls flat on his face.

I pick up the glass of wine off the coffee table and finish it before I stand up.

"I spent three days watching you fuck every girl you brought to this home." I make my way over to him. Using my foot, I flip him over on his back. "You always start with the neck." I roll my eyes. "Very predictable, Archie. I don't think daddy would be pleased with that."

His eyes widen. It's about the only thing on his body he has control over.

I take a seat on top of the coffee table. His head is right by my foot.

"What..." he tries to get out of his mouth. I'm assuming he's trying to figure out what's happening to him.

"It's a body butter. The women at D.O.E created it. You can wear it without any harm, but if you ingest it, it causes paralysis. It's a slow and painful death. First your body goes numb, then your organs slowly stop working."

I couldn't walk into the bar with a weapon. Archie is trained to spot gun and knife holsters. He would have been on high alert had he noticed a weapon. Maksim told us that they were all taught to hide weapons around their homes. However, I couldn't guarantee that I'd be able to get to one without him noticing. The poison was my best option.

Archie makes a gurgling noise as if he's trying to talk. He has about thirty more minutes for the process to be completed.

"Why shoot them in the head?" The old conversation between Nathaniel and I pop up in my head. I shut my eyes to fight back the tears.

"Because taking a person's life isn't easy. Even when you think the person deserves it…... Giving out quick deaths helps maintain some of your humanity when this lifestyle tries to rip it from you."

Placing a hand over my heart, I take deep calming breaths. Every time I think of the man I lost, I get a pain in my chest. Opening my eyes, I stare down at Archie.

"I had planned to watch you suffer," I admit. "But he wouldn't want that for me." Sliding off the coffee table, I get down on all fours and look underneath the table. Just as I suspected, a Beretta is attached to the underside of the wood table. Pulling the gun out, I climb to my feet and stand over his body.

I look him in the eyes as I pull the trigger, ending his life with a shot to the forehead.

"Call the cleanup crew," I say out loud, knowing the guys in my earpiece will hear me.

"Zel's calling now," Beast says. "Are you alright?"

I shake my head as tears fall down my face. I'm broken, and until I can finish the job of getting rid of Corbyn, I will remain this way. But I'm thankful for the distraction, because if I ever sit down long enough to think about the fact that Nathaniel is never coming back, I won't survive.

"No," I answer honestly. "But we've got work to do." I toss the gun on the floor beside Archie. I'm not worried about evidence because the cleaning crew will wipe everything down.

I walk out of the apartment building the same way I came in. I don't worry about the cameras either. Lucien will scrub them clean.

Two down, six more to go.

CHAPTER TWENTY-NINE

Family

Beast

Summer scurries around the backyard, fixing the balloon arrangements she put up. She has been a much-needed light in this house. When all of us are locked in our grief, she finds some way to bring us out of it.

For instance, today she's doing a gender reveal party for Brooklyn and Hawk. They went for their ultrasound two weeks ago. Under the cover of night, we escorted them to Doc's where one of DOE's doctors was able to check her out. Even though Brooklyn was eight months already, that appointment was the first one where she got to find out the sexes.

Summer convinced them to get the sex of the baby put in an envelope so she could do something nice for them. No one argued because we needed this type of distraction. Only Summer knows the sex of the babies and she's not telling.

"What do you think? Is it a good mix of pink and blue?" she asks, coming up to me.

I look around at the backyard. One balloon arch sits behind two white chairs. Another arch is near a table full of pink and blue dessert. Four round tables are set up with white tablecloths and pink and blue flower center pieces.

I don't know much about baby gender reveals, but this was nice.

"I think it's perfect," I say, placing the very last folded chair under the round table.

Summer places her hands on her hips and gazes around at the yard.

"Do you think they will like it?" she asks, turning back to me.

"Yeah, baby. They will." Even if they didn't, I'd make sure they did.

"Wow, Summer," Ms. Reese says stepping out the door with a large cake in her hands. "You did a great job."

"Thank you, Ms. Reese." Summer goes over to Ms. Reese and takes the cake out of her hands. She carries it over to the dessert table. "What do you say, Ms. Reese? Pink or blue?" She holds up the pink and blue ribbons in her hands.

Ms. Reese taps her chin. "One pink and one blue."

Summer quickly hands the lady her ribbons before coming up to me.

"What do you think the sex of the baby will be?" she asks me.

I lift a brow at her before shrugging. "Never gave it much thought."

She giggles and I wrap my arms around her waist, bringing her into me. "Well, think about it now. Do you think it's two girls or two boys? Or a girl and a boy like Ms. Reese?"

I really didn't care what the sex would be. They would be my nieces and nephews either way. But it isn't about if it mattered to me, making a decision matters to Summer.

"Two boys," I say. "I'm not sure how I'd feel trying to protect multiple little girls. Emory is enough." I think over how tough Lucien and Seth are going to have it when Emory gets older and calls herself dating.

The moment I think about my brother, I get sad. There has still been no sight of Seth. I thought with the killing of Zeke and Archie, he'd show back up by now, but he hadn't.

"I can't believe I'm only one month away from being a new auntie," Albany says stepping into the backyard holding Charlie. She walks over to us. I immediately take Charlie out of her arms and toss him up in the air.

He giggles and slobs. He's starting to crawl now at nearly nine months. It's hard to keep up with him.

"If he throws up on you, I'm not helping you clean it up," Albany jokes.

Some of the guilt has eased up from seeing Charlie and Albany. I still feel the pain of their loss, but the guilt doesn't swallow me up. Instead of allowing it to keep me away from them, I use it to put in time with Charlie.

"Give me my brother," Zel says walking out of the house and taking Charlie from me.

Shortly after, we all gathered in the backyard. Summer once again did an amazing job distracting us from our pain. We've laughed, played games, and ate well. Now, Brooklyn and Hawk are standing in front of us with gender reveal smoke cannons. Each one holding a cannon to represent each child.

"All right," Summer sings. "On the count of three."

"Wait," Brooklyn says. "Let's do it one at a time. Hawk, you do yours first."

He nods obediently.

"Okay," Summer continues. "On three Hawk. One, two, three."

Hawk shoots his cannon, and blue smoke shoots up in the air. We all cheer.

"What color is it?" Hawk asks.

"Shit, baby. I forgot you're blind. It's blue," Brooklyn shouts. Hawk turns around and gently lifts Brooklyn up spinning her around.

"Did she just say he's blind?" Summer asks looking at me. "He's been blind this entire time?"

Maksim and Zel chuckle beside me.

"I was just as confused as you the first time I found out," Ari says. "Don't feel bad."

Seconds later, Brooklyn shoots her cannon, and more blue smoke pours out.

We continue to celebrate. I find myself in the corner of the yard staring up at the sky.

"You have two more grandsons, Priest. You would've had your hands full."

I hear her footsteps before she speaks. "He would've had so much to say about all this pink and blue, but deep down he would have been so happy." Albany steps up beside me.

We don't speak again for a long moment. Both lost in our own memories of Priest.

"Is it weird that I still feel this connection to him? It's like I know he's dead, but part of me feels as if my soul hasn't gotten the memo."

I turn to her, glancing down at her teary eyes. Placing an arm around her shoulder, I pull her into me.

"You lost your soul mate. Your soul is never going to get the memo. But we are here. For whatever you need."

She smiles up at me. "Look at you, tapping into your emotions. Priest would be so proud."

I shrug off her compliment even though it meant the world to me.

We spent the remainder of the night celebrating Brooklyn and Hawk's great news. At one point, we sat around the fire pit with Charlie, Emory and Gabe and shared stories of Priest. It was a good night. One we truly needed.

CHAPTER THIRTY

Baby Names

Brooklyn

I place a hand over my belly. The boys are active this morning. They've been that way a lot lately. I just turned eight months; they are probably running out of room.

I take the last tray of the muffins Malia made out of the oven. I love that woman, but I swear living with her is going to have my damn back so wide I won't be able to fit in the doorway.

Summer walks into the kitchen carrying a playful Charlie.

"Is that auntie's baby?" I coo at my nephew.

"It sure is. I heard him yapping in the room, so I went in and grabbed him."

Without a word being said amongst us, Malia, Summer, Ari, and I have all taken turns to help out with Charlie. My mom has been a godsend as well, but she's been back and forth with DOE a lot more lately. Since they are helping us track down Corbyn's homes, she's been at their headquarters helping out. I was glad she was able to make it to my gender reveal four days ago.

I know Albany loves her baby and doesn't mind spending as much time as she can with him, but with Priest gone, we try to lighten her load as much as we can.

"How was she this morning?" I ask.

Summer looks up at me before placing Charlie in his highchair. "She seemed fine, but..."

She doesn't have to finish that statement. Since the day of Priest's funeral, Albany has been like a robot. She's up every day ready to guide the guys on their next task and to track down Corbyn's crazy ass kids, but she definitely isn't herself. She puts on this face as if it's all business, but I can see all the pain she's hiding. We know she's hurting. If Walker died, I'd be completely inconsolable and useless. My sister loved Priest. She's loved him a lot longer than I've even known Walker.

Honestly, they are all still hurting. They're being strong, working together, and staying on task, but they are all in pain. Poor Summer has been a lifesaver, distracting everyone, but the distraction is only short-lived. They need time and they need to deal with their feelings.

I take two muffins out of the tray and place them on the plate, along with some fresh fruit and bacon.

"I'm going to go check on her. Do you need any help with Charlie?"

"No. I'm good. Go on," Summer says as she tickles Charlie and makes him laugh.

Taking the plate of food, I make my way upstairs to my sister's room. I knock before opening the door.

"I got breakfast," I sing.

Scanning the room, I don't spot her, but a sound coming from the closet has me heading in that direction. I place the plate down on the foot of the bed before walking into the closet. I pause at the door when I spot my sister sitting on the floor wrapped in one of Priest's shirts, silently sobbing.

I rush over to her, getting on my knees, I pull her into my arms.

"It's okay, I got you." I say stroking her hair.

"Why, Brook?" She cries. "Why did he have to leave us?"

I won't lie as if Priest was my favorite person in the world, but he had grown on me. And I know his impact on his family. He was their rock. But more importantly, he was the love of my sister's life. I know I may have given him a hard time before, but I know for a fact he loved Albany.

"I don't know why these things happen, sis. And I wish I could take your pain away."

I rock her in my arms as she cries. I don't know for sure how long we remained that way. Eventually, the sobs turned into whimpers before they became nothing but sniffles.

Albany sits up, wiping her face and nose with her hand. I remain seated beside her.

"Sorry about that," she says.

"Don't apologize," I say wiping her cheek. "You were due for a good cry. You've been so strong lately."

She chuckles and shakes her head. "Is that what it looks like? I've been a wreck. At least twice a day I have a breakdown in this closet. Every time I see his suits hanging here, it just….." She never finishes her statement.

I look around the large walk-in closet. So many black suits and white crisp shirts.

"Did the man own any other clothes outside of suits? He dressed like a mortician."

Albany snorts before laughing. I relish in her laughter. It's been so absent since the day Priest was announced dead that it sounds like a gift from heaven.

"I loved him in suits," she says.

"Of course you did. It fit your old man fetish."

She chuckles again before sobering. "I don't think I'll ever love again." She places her head on my shoulder. "No one will ever compare to him."

"If this is about to turn into a conversation about how good his dick is, I'm going to leave your ass in this closet."

Once again, she bursts into laughter.

"I'm serious, Brook. That man was everything to me. He knew me better than I knew myself. He loved harder than anyone I know. He gave so much of himself to those he considered his family. There will never be another man like him."

In that, she and I agreed. Although I've only known him for a short period, I can tell by the men he raised and the way they mourn him that he was a great person. Priest will truly be missed.

Rubbing a hand over my belly, I say, "I haven't told Walker yet, but I'm naming my twin Nathaniel."

Walker and I decided we would both get to name the boys. He got to name the first one, which is going to be a junior. If his twin had been a girl, he was going to name her Red. Not my favorite name, but I wasn't going to argue. I'd been indecisive about what to name my twin. I never could come up with a girl's name. However, after Priest passed, the decision became easy for a boy.

She lifts her head from my shoulder and looks at me with wide eyes. A tear slips down her cheek. She quickly wipes it away.

"Thank you."

I wrap my arms around her one more time for a hug before letting her go.

"I do have one concern. It's been on my mind for a while," I say. Her brows dip together as she stares at me. "Are the twins going to call you Auntie or Grandma?"

Once again, she laughs as she playfully shoves my shoulder. "Shut up, Brook." She sobers as she wipes her face. "Ugh, enough crying for now. We still have some more of Corbyn's spawns to track down." Albany stands and then reaches out to help me up as well.

Getting to my feet, I follow her out of the closet. I give her the breakfast I'd brought to her and leave her to finish getting dressed.

After checking on Summer and Charlie in the kitchen, I head back to my room with Walker. I walk in to find him sitting on the side of the bed, his head in his hands. He doesn't look up, but I know he heard me walk in. The man has damn near bionic ears.

"You haven't seen me since last night and you don't even look up when your whale of a wife walks in?" I joke.

Walker lifts his head and smiles at me. "My wife is no whale."

I scoff as I stand between his legs causing him to lean back to accommodate my belly.

"You only say that because you know I won't suck your dick if you didn't."

His shoulders shake with his laughter. He places both his hands on my round belly. He then pushes my shirt up so that he can kiss his boys.

One of the twins' rolls, causing my stomach to shift. Walker smiles.

"Does it look as weird as it feels?" he asks rubbing over the area.

"Yes. Yes, it does. It looks like someone trapped a cat in a bag and the cat is fighting to get out."

He chuckles a little before sobering. "Every day he would describe your pregnancy to me."

"What?"

"Priest," he explains. "I mentioned once that I was going to miss things. I told him I hoped that our kids wouldn't inherit my condition, and that I wouldn't even be able to witness your pregnancy or how our babies looked. So, every day he described how your body and face changed."

There is a lot to unpack in this statement. First, to know that Priest took the time to describe my pregnancy to Walker was so thoughtful. No wonder he would often ask me how I was feeling that day. The second part of his statement is what I decided to comment on.

"When were you going to tell me about your fears?"

He looks up into my face, his head tilting to the side.

"Are you afraid of the boys having my condition?"

I turn away from him, heading out the room. He leaps up from the bed and grabs my arm turning me back to him. There is significant enough light in the room to make out my shape, but he won't be able to see my features. However, the way he is looking down at me makes me believe he can see me.

"You're angry?"

"Damn right I am," I grit out. "How dare you ask me some shit like that. You think I'm that shallow and self-absorbed that I would care if my kids end up with the same condition of the man I decided to procreate with? Who do you think I am?"

He shakes his head and steps back. "I'm sorry, Brook. It's just, my parents—"

Holding up a hand, I stop whatever he was about to say about his deadbeat parents. "I'm not your mother, Walker. I won't run from my child or my responsibilities just because my kids aren't deemed normal by society. I don't care if they are deaf, blind, mute, or have two personalities."

Being in this house these five months has shown me what true love and family look like. Walker and his brothers are a collection of characters. Some, a little quirkier than the others, but they are my family. Even Many's weird ass.

He laughs. "Priest said the same thing."

Wrapping my arms around his waist, I hug him as best I can with my stomach.

"He was a good man," I reply.

"That he was."

"Which is why I'm naming baby two Nathaniel Priest Walker."

He grabs my shoulder and leans me away from him, looking down into my face.

"Are you serious?"

"Of course I am," I laugh. "He may have been an asshole sometimes, but he helped raise the man that I love. And I think that should be honored."

He shuts his eyes and sighs. "I love you, Brook."

"I love you too."

He bends down, pressing his lips to mine. He cups my face as he slips his tongue into my mouth. I moan at the intrusion. Being pregnant has sent my sex drive into overdrive. I think I've had more sex since I've been pregnant than I've had my entire life.

Walker reaches for the end of my shirt and lifts it over my head. We break our kiss just long enough to pull the shirt off. He tosses it somewhere behind me before going back to kissing me.

He walks backwards, taking me with him. He spins us at the last minute. The back of my legs hit the side of the bed. Getting to his knees in front of me, he tugs at my yoga pants, pulling them down along with my underwear. Once he works them down to my feet, he lifts my legs, helping me step out of them. He's face to face with my belly.

He drops a soft kiss on my navel before helping me sit down on the side of the bed. Keeping his eyes on me, he lifts one of my legs and places it on the bed, opening me up for him.

"Walker," I moan as he slips two fingers inside my core and strokes them in and out of me.

I should be embarrassed at how wet I am, but I'm too horny to care. He buries his face into my center, his tongue swirling around my nub like an expert while his fingers continue to drive me crazy.

I toss my head back as I place my hand on his head. "Yes, baby," I cry as he slurps up my wetness. My hips roll as he brings me closer and closer to my release.

"Don't stop," I beg. "Please don't stop." I shut my eyes so tight, spots appear behind my eyelids. My orgasm is fast approaching. I swirl my hips even more.

"Give me what I want, Brook," he demands before sucking my clit into his mouth.

As he knew I would, I erupted. I scream his name as my body convulses. He drinks me down without wasting a drop. He cleans me up so good, I spiral into another orgasm. This one has me pushing his head away because of how sensitive I am.

He stands up from the floor, wiping his face clean of my essence. His shorts bulge in the front. I reach for the waistband, wanting to taste him. There is nothing like his flavor. He knocks my hand away.

"You know what I want," He groans. "Slide back and lie on your side."

I oblige, scooting back into the center of the bed and turning onto my side. He takes off his bottoms and steps out of them. He tugs at his dick, causing a bead of precum to drip from his slit. My mouth waters to taste it. However, for some reason, Walker refuses to let me suck him off now that I'm pregnant.

He places one knee on the bed and slowly climbs up to join me. Since I'm so heavily pregnant, we have very limited positions we can do. This one happens to be both of our favorites. Walker lays behind me. Grabbing his length, he puts it to my center. I lift my leg higher. He runs the head of his cock through my wetness before slowly pushing into me. I gasp at the intrusion.

"Shit, you feel so damn good, Brook."

He hikes one arm under my thigh, lifting my leg higher. He pushes into me, hitting a spot deep. I cry out as I claw at the sheets.

"Fuck, you're deep," I complain.

He ignores my words, pushing my leg even higher until my knee is by his ear. He pulls out to the tip and then pushes back in.

I scream. He uses his free arm to slip under my head. He grabs my neck and turns my face to his before pressing his lips to mine. His tongue snakes its way into my mouth, swallowing my cry. He makes love to my mouth as he fucks my pussy. His hips move faster, his balls smacking my ass sounding like an applause. He breaks the kiss to place his forehead to mine.

"You are my world, Mrs. Walker," he whispers the words across my sweat slicked skin.

Leaning back, I look into his eyes and say, "I fucking better be."

He chuckles before going back to kissing me. He lets go of my leg and slips his hands down between our bodies. His fingers dance against my hardened nub.

I moan as I break away from the kiss. I look down toward my center, hating that I can't see over my baby bump.

"You're close," Walker growls. "I can feel your pussy pulsing around me. Are you ready to cum, Brook?"

"Yessss," I moan. "Fuck yes."

He speeds up his strokes and pinches my clit between his fingers. I cross my eyes as I come so hard it feels like my soul lifts out of my body and then plummets back to earth. All sound fades around me for a split second. By the time it comes back, Walker lets out a loud hissing sound as he releases inside me. His hips never stop moving as he fucks me through his orgasm.

When he finally finishes, he's breathing hard. We're both covered in sweat.

"Are you alright?" he asks, rubbing my belly.

I don't have the energy to muster up words. I simply nod my head. He can feel the movement against his arm.

He places a kiss on the back of my head before getting up from the bed.

"Come on," he says, holding out his hand. "Let's go shower."

I want to argue. The only thing I want to do is sleep right now. But I know I need to wash this sex off first. Walker pulls me up from the bed and helps me into the bathroom.

We have round two before finally washing off.

CHAPTER THIRTY-ONE

Spa Day

Hawk

I pull the cover up over Brooklyn's shoulders. She went right to sleep as soon as we got out the shower.

I stare down at her form, lying in the bed. The vision of her is too blurry to make anything out, but I still watch her.

I haven't been honest with her yet. It's a huge possibility that even if we do take care of Corbyn, and get the excommunication order withdrawn, I will still have to go back to the Church.

Asking Lucien, after all this, to go back and hide us again, is too much. I wouldn't want to put my brother through that. He has his own life and family to worry about.

If I go back to the Church, I might not be around to see my family. We've all had this conversation. Now that Priest is gone, we have no one to advocate for us. They won't be as lenient as before. Hell, they may put me in lock down like they did Beast or even retire me. Which basically means they will kill me.

Either way, at some point, I will have to walk away from my family. The thought of that kills me.

Turning from the bed, I head out of the room and toward the dining room. It's time for our morning briefing. I follow my well-known route throughout the house. When Priest had this house built, he did it with me in mind. Wide hallways, open spaces, and sufficient lighting in every inch of the house. He made sure I could navigate this house without any issues.

Walking into the dining room, I immediately make out the voices in the room. Lucien is here, along with Red, Many, Zel, Maksim, and Beast.

I take a spot against the wall beside Beast. I don't need my sight to know it's him. Summer's fruity scent is all over him.

"You alright?" he asks.

That seems to be the question that we're all asking a lot nowadays. I'm not sure about them, but I answer it with the same lie every time.

"Yeah, I'm good."

I wasn't. And it wasn't just because my father was dead. I wouldn't be good until we dealt with Corbyn, and until we figured out what we were going to do about the Church.

Unlike Beast, Zel, Many, and Seth, I had no desire to go back to my job as a deacon. I wanted my freedom. I wanted to wake up and go to bed beside my wife every day without fearing someone coming in and taking it from me. I wanted to hold my sons without always looking over my shoulder.

However, now wasn't the time to discuss that. So, my lie had to suffice. I wasn't sure if Beast believed it or not, but he didn't ask me any more questions.

"D.O.E has now eliminated fifteen of Corbyn's known residences," Red says briefing us. "They were all vacant at the time. He's still in the wind."

"He won't come out of the woodworks yet. There hasn't been enough pressure on him," Maksim confirms. "We need to continue to track down my siblings."

"Has he tried to contact any of them yet?" Red asks Lucien, who has been keeping tabs on the cellphones of the siblings we've killed.

The goal is to keep him from finding out our plan before we are ready to go after him. That's why we clean every crime scene and dispose of the bodies.

"No. As of right now, there hasn't been any attempts to reach out."

"Good." The sound of soft footfalls walking across the floor lets me know Red is moving. Tapping has my head turning in that direction. She's standing in front of the whiteboard in the room. Priest explained the layout when we first transferred the dining room into our makeshift headquarters.

Recently, all the names of Corbyn's kids were written on the board. So far, the only names that have been eliminated are Archie and Zeke.

"Okay, how are we coming along with tracking down Micah?"

Lucien lets out a deep sigh that precedes the sound of something solid clunking to the table. I'm assuming they're his glasses. I worry about him. I fear he's being stretched too thin. I also worry that we have not heard from Seth since we were in Doc's home. Although Lucien hasn't said anything to us about it, I think he's worried too.

"No word from him yet. I think our best option is to wait for Nolan to take our bait."

Last week Maksim explained that Nolan was a very high maintenance man. He spent thousands of dollars on facials, pedicures, waxes, tanning and massages. Lucien set up a free spa day at an upscale spa in the city. It's one of the most sought-after places. He made it seem as if Nolan had been chosen for a giveaway. He has yet to claim the award. The moment he walks into that spa, Lucien will be notified.

"Be patient," Maksim grumbles. "He's going to take the bait."

"Well, until then we need to move on to—"

Before Red can finish her statement, Lucien's phone rings on the table. There is a slight delay before I hear his voice.

"Hello?" he says. He pauses to wait for a response. "Thank you, Veronica." The phone clunks down on the table.

"That was the spa. Nolan is on his way."

That was convenient.

"Okay, we need to move fast. This needs to be a quick kill. In and out," Red says. "We don't want too much for the cleaning crew to clean up. It also needs to be quiet as possible."

"I'll do it," I say.

There is a pause in the room.

"Are you sure, Hawk?" Red asks.

I understand her question. There was a reason I'd left the Church. This killing thing wasn't for me anymore. But this was different. This was personal.

"Yeah, I'm sure."

Beast's heavy hand smacks me in the back. "Welcome back, brother."

This will be my first solo kill in a very long time.

"Alright, Maksim and Beast, you two take him into the city. Zel, you're going to be his guide. The floor plan isn't too complicated, but that place has a lot of twists and turns."

Standing to my feet, Beast joins me.

"I got this," I say.

Although it has been a minute since I've done this, there are some things you just don't forget.

Maksim and Beast let me out at the back of the building. The smell of trash is the first thing that catches my attention. Also, the absence of heavy traffic from the main road stands out.

I adjust the glasses on my face.

"These glasses make me feel stupid," I complain.

"Hey, as someone that wears glasses, I take offense," Lucien says.

The earpiece fills with laughter.

"Alright, Hawk," Zel says speaking up over the laughter. "I'll guide you through the layout once you get inside."

"And I'll be your eyes," Lucien adds.

I usually wouldn't need anyone to be my 'eyes' on a menu. However, this place has too many unknown variables. It's a public place during work hours. Not to mention, I don't know the layout. Because there aren't cameras in every room, I'll need Lucien's sight.

"Straight ahead is the entrance," Lucien says. "The key card I made for you will get you in. That service uniform and toolbox will also allow you to move freely. They recently had some plumbing issues, so you're there for that if anyone asks."

Walking up to the door, I swing it open and step in. The room I enter is bright enough allowing me to make out more shadows. Thankfully, the room is empty.

"They're leading Nolan downstairs," Zel says into the earpiece. "You're going to come out of this room and take an immediate left."

I follow his directions. There is much more traffic in the hallway. I weave through the few people I come into contact with. Sure enough, no one stops me or asks me any questions. This maintenance man cover up is brilliant.

"About ten paces ahead, there is an elevator to your right. You're going to take that down to the basement."

As I listen to Zel, I'm caught off guard when someone bumps into my side.

"I'm so sorry," the female says as I turn to face her.

"It's alright," I say as I try to continue walking.

"Wait, are you here for the plumbing?"

"Umm, yeah."

"Perfect, you can help me." She grabs my arm and starts pulling me in the opposite direction of the elevator.

"You could shoot her," Beast says through the earpiece. Beast and Maksim are parked a block away in the suburban, ready to intervene if things go wrong. They are using the camera view from my glasses to see what I'm seeing.

"No unnecessary bodies, brother," Maksim says, sounding exasperated.

"Maksim is correct," Red says through the earpiece. "Just see what she needs."

The female hauls me through a narrow door. I look around the dimly lit room, unable to make out anything. Soft music is playing in the background and the smell of incense floats through the air.

"You're in a massage room. Watch out, there's a table in front of you."

Just in time, I sidestep the table Lucien warned me about. Placing my hand on the soft surface, I run my finger along the edge to find where it ends.

"See," the female says. She isn't moving anymore so I stop too.

"It's a sink," Lucien explains.

"What's wrong with it?" I ask the obvious question any service worker would ask.

She doesn't answer, but I hear a movement in front of me. It sounds like a squeaking sound.

"The water isn't turning on," Lucien explains.

"Can you fix it?" She asks.

"Hold on, I'm googling it," Lucien says.

"We don't have time for this. Just shoot her," Beast says with a deep sigh.

"I can fix it," I say to the girl.

She touches my arm gently. "Thank you, handsome."

She removes her hand from my arm and then her footsteps start to recede letting me know she's leaving. The soft click of the door closing tells me I'm alone.

"You better be glad I know better, or I'd tell my sister you were flirting." Red says teasingly.

I scoff. "She'd know that was a lie. I only have eyes for Brook." Reaching my hand out to touch a flat surface, I find the counter in front of me. I place the toolbox down on top of it.

"Says the blind guy," Zel jokes.

"Alright, you're going to need pliers for this."

It takes me and Lucien less than ten minutes to clean out the aerator on the faucet. After replacing my tools, I head out of the small room and back into the hallway.

"Alright, he's still downstairs," Zel says, taking over the directions.

This time I make it to the elevators without incident. Once I climb on, I find the basement button and press it.

"When you step out of the elevator, go to your right. He's behind the second door on your left."

The elevator doors ding and I step out. The hallway is thankfully as bright as they are upstairs.

"You'll need both your hands," Lucien says. "In front of you is a table you can put that toolbox on."

I drop the toolbox on the table and head back in the direction Zel gave me. Stopping outside the door, I pause.

"There aren't any cameras inside that room. You're going to have to rely on Lucien and your instincts."

I don't respond. Instead, I pull my gun out of my back holster and look in both directions. I'll be able to see a shadow of a person coming. Thankfully, there is no one. Pushing the door open slowly, I walk in.

As soon as I enter, I take in as much as I can. The smell of sweat, the sound of movement to my right, and then the rapid sound of footsteps. I turn just in time to catch the impact of someone slamming into me. The glasses on my face fall off as I'm shoved into a wall.

"Shit, Hawk, I can't see anything," Lucien says in my earpiece.

I don't reply. A fist flies into my ribs, causing me to lean to the side. I aim my gun and fire off a round, but my gun arm is shoved to the right, sending my bullet in the opposite direction.

"Hawk, are you there?" a panicked Red shouts.

"A little occupied," I grunt as I dodge the next fist flying toward my face.

"Do you need us?" Maksim shouts in my ear.

Because of his interruption, I can't make out Nolan's next move and get kneed in the balls. I groan as I drop to the ground.

"Fuck," I gasp as I cradle my cock. "He kicked me in the dick."

Everyone on the other end of the earpiece hisses. My gun is then kicked from my hand.

"Now who are you?" Nolan asks. He's moving around me. "Can't be anyone that truly knows me, because this is too bold of a move." He chuckles.

"We're coming in," Beast says.

"No," Red argues. "Give him time. If you run in, it will draw too much attention."

"Will you please shut up so I can focus," I say as I push up from the ground.

"Focus on what?" Nolan laughs.

I take in my surroundings. It's obvious I'm in a sauna, which means somewhere on the wall are the controls for the steam. I slowly climb to my feet.

"I'm going to enjoy kicking your ass," Nolan gloats.

I'm shoved from the back into another wall. My hand hits something hard and square.

Well, lucky me. Finding the dial on the machine, I turn it all the way to the left. I'm then grabbed and spun around. Nolan shoves me into the wall again before he gives me a left hook to the face, followed by a right. I again drop to the ground.

Nolan grabs the back of my hair and hauls me back to my feet. However, he hesitates before swinging.

"What the hell?" he mumbles.

From the mugginess in the room, I can tell it's filling with steam. The sound of heavy footsteps moving away from me tells me Nolan is retreating.

"I can't see shit," Nolan fusses.

A slow smile spreads over my face. Closing my eyes, I focus on the sounds around me. The gust of wind blowing at me tells me exactly where he is. I send my fist into him, connecting with his jaw.

He grunts before hitting the wall behind him. I follow the sound, cornering him as I rain down blows on him. My knuckles split against his face, but I keep going.

At some point, he musters up enough strength to shove me off him. I stumble back, my foot hitting something solid. I smile as I bend down and pick up my gun.

Nolan's feet smack against the floor. He's moving in circles. The way the air keeps brushing against my face tells me he's swinging blindly.

"Where the fuck are you?" he yells, giving me his exact location.

Holding up my gun, I aim it and fire. The thud of his body hitting the floor is comforting to me. I feel around the ground until I find the glasses. I put them back on my face.

"Oh fuck," Lucien sighs. "He's alright."

"Thank goodness," Red says.

Squatting down. I feel for Nolan's body reaching for his neck.

"No need to check," Lucien says. "You got him right in the temple."

I still make sure he has no pulse. Once I'm satisfied, I stand back up.

"I'm getting too old for this," I say exhaling.

"Sounds like you got your ass kicked," Zel laughs.

"He definitely got his ass kicked," Beast adds.

I stumble out of the sauna, closing the door behind me. Retracing my steps back to the table, I grab my toolbox before heading to the elevator.

"At least the job is done. Call the cleanup crew."

"They are already there," Red says.

I climb into the elevator and push the button back to the main floor. I clutch my sore ribs as I lay my head against the wall behind me.

Yeah, I definitely can't come back to this shit.

CHAPTER THIRTY-TWO

Silence

Lucien

"You have to draw four, Hulk," Gabe giggles.

I look over to a fuming Beast. We've been kicking his ass in UNO. At this very moment he has close to twenty cards in his hand.

"I refuse to draw more. Maksim is cheating."

I fight to hold back my laughter.

Maksim shrugs. "I have no idea what you speak of brother."

I look up to find Malia and Summer at the island, fighting back their laughter as well. I think Summer knew how much trouble we would get into when she bought this game.

Beast tosses his cards down. "I want a rematch," he grumbles.

Gabe and Emory burst out laughing. I finally let my laughter out as well. It feels good to laugh. Feels like the house goes through long stints where we don't laugh at all. Even the kids sometimes lack laughter. It makes times like this so much more special.

"You're missing out, Seth." I say into the silence of my head.

I remember the days when I wished I could get rid of my brother, and now I worry about him. He has never been absent this long. I fear that he may be gone for good. I don't know how to handle that. He was my protector, a part of me. Yes, it took me a while to realize that. Now, I feel as if I've lost two people and not just one.

"Brother Beast, you have lost the last three games," Many says in his nasally voice. "Maybe you are the problem."

"Shut it, Many," Beast snarls. He turns to Maksim. "Stand up. I want to check your pockets."

"Babe," Summer laughs. "It's just a game. Let it go."

"No," Beast says crossing his arms over his chest. "I want answers."

Malia snorts and shakes her head as she rolls out the dough for the banana bread she's making.

I don't know what we would've done in this house if not for Malia, Summer, and Brooklyn. They have all been constantly by our side. They are the light in this house that keeps us going.

"I have no reason to lie. I will prove I am just better at UNO than you," Maksim stands up. "See, nothing." Suddenly a ton of cards fall from underneath his shirt. The kids laughter fills the room. Beast leaps up from the table. Maksim takes off running, laughing the entire time, out of the kitchen. Beast chases him.

Emory signs to Gabe. "Come on. Let's go see if your dad catches him."

"Okay," Gabe says, pushing his chair back and getting to his feet. In the past few months, the kid has learned a lot of sign language. No one has to translate for him anymore.

"Don't leave us," Many announces, tossing his cards down and following the kids out of the kitchen.

"I better go and make sure they don't kill each other," Summer laughs getting to her feet. She goes out after everyone else.

I'm alone in the kitchen with Malia. I stand from my chair and start to clean up the cards.

"That ended exactly like I thought it would," Malia says with a chuckle.

I look over at her, taking in her large belly beneath her shirt. She's seven months now. We found out we were having a boy a few days ago. With Brooklyn and Malia being so near their due dates, we've ramped up the doctor visits. We've even figured out the hospital the girls can go to when they go in labor. Thanks to our allies at the Church and D.O.E for making that possible.

"I know you will come back for that, brother." I once again try to entice Seth into coming out.

Again, there is nothing from him.

Looks like I won't have him or my father there to witness the birth of my child.

"What's wrong?" Malia asks getting my attention back. "You were smiling and then it turned into a frown."

She stares at me for a moment. "You were thinking about Priest, weren't you?"

I don't deny it. She wipes her hands on the kitchen towel and walks over to me. I turn to face her, grabbing her around the waist and pulling her into me. She places both her hands on my chest.

"That, and the fact that Seth has still been quiet." I admit.

She lets out a deep breath. "Don't worry, Seth will come back. He just needs time."

Running a hand through my hair, I lay my forehead to hers. "I'm scared, Baby. For the first time, I feel helpless. What if this new plan doesn't work? What if Seth never comes back, and we have to live our lives looking over our shoulder?"

Malia cups my face between her hands and lifts my head. Her brown eyes gaze up at me, as her brows pinch.

"What would your father say if he were here right now?"

I immediately laugh. Priest's voice pops in my head as loud as if he was standing in front of me.

"He would say, stop fucking whining and do what needs to be done."

Malia tosses her head back and laughs. "Then he'd pour up a glass of bourbon and go torture Albany in that sex dungeon."

At this we both laugh until my laughter dies down and the only thing left is the pain of missing my father.

"I miss him," I whisper.

"I know you do. He was an incredible man. And you need to remember he left behind four other incredible men for you to rely on." She leans in and pecks my lips.

It starts off sweet and gentle, but soon turns hot and heavy.

"We weren't even gone that long and already you two are about to contaminate the kitchen," Beast says in the doorway.

It wouldn't be the first time we contaminated a kitchen. I think back to Malia and me in her Grams' house. That seemed so far away.

"Why did you break it up?" Maksim asks with a grin.

I glare over at my newly adopted brother. "Don't make me kick your ass."

He tosses his hands up in front of him as if he's innocent.

Angel's voice comes over the house intercom system. "Guys, I need you in the dining room. TR has an update."

Maksim and Beast walk back out of the kitchen, leaving Malia and me alone again. I go back to kiss her, but she pulls her head away.

"Shouldn't you be going?"

"They can wait." I hadn't had sex in weeks. With Priest's death and Seth being silent, I wasn't in the right headspace for it. Finally, I was ready.

She chuckles. "Tonight." She places a kiss on my lips before going back to her bread.

"Ugh," I groan readjusting my cock in my pants.

I make my way into the dining room. Maksim and Beast are sitting down at the table. I take a seat at the head where my laptop is. Angel is standing up at the whiteboard. We now had three names marked out. It's only been three days since Hawk killed Nolan. We were moving quickly through the siblings. If we wanted to clear them out before Corbyn caught wind of what we were doing, we had to move fast.

Zel enters the room with Many on his heels. Hawk comes in a little later pulling a shirt over his head. He takes a seat across from Beast.

"Alright, TR," Angel says out loud. "We're all here."

"Your plan is working," Takar's voice comes over Angel's phone speaker. "Corbyn believes you guys are behind the house attacks. He has no idea you're going after his kids. However, he has been going around bragging about you boys chasing your tail."

"Which means he isn't desperate enough yet," Zel says leaning forward in his seat.

"No. Not enough to make a mistake," Takar confirms our thoughts. "I'm afraid you're going to have to go harder."

Angel sighs, racking a hand through her short haircut. "Alright, thanks TR. If anything else comes up, let us know."

"Will do." Her phone disconnects leaving us in silence.

"How many homes have D.O.E hit so far?" I ask.

"Last time Ari talked to Kyra this morning they'd taken down twenty-five of his homes," Many answers. "Still no sign of him."

Sitting back in my chair I let out a deep breath. "We knew he wouldn't be in any of those homes. I'm not shocked. I still say we continue the attacks."

"I agree," Angel says.

"Same," Beast and Maksim says at the same time.

"I agree, but I think we need to do more," Zel says. "He's not feeling the pressure yet."

"We're killing off his kids and burning his homes. What more can we do?" Hawk asks.

Yes, we are taking out his children, but he still doesn't know that. He has no idea the army he created is being slowly dissolved.

"A man like Corbyn isn't easily rattled," I say as I stroke my chin. "We need to hit him where it hurts the most."

"How do we do that?" Many asks.

"We hit his pockets," Beast says.

"Ummm, Kyra and I are good, but it would take months and a lot of time to take down a global industry like Corbyn Inc."

Don't get me wrong Kyra and the computer whizzes at D.O.E are fucking talented, but taking down a corporation like Corbyn's would take time. It would take us all working around the clock to bring it down and we didn't have that kind of time. Corbyn would have so many safety features in place that he'd be alerted as soon as we started digging.

"I'm not talking about his legal business."

My brows pinch as I stare at Beast. "What are you talking about?"

"Little brother is right," Maksim says, placing his elbows down on the table in front of him. "Everyone in the Royal Crown has two types of income. The legal and the illegal. The type of money it requires to make moves in the RC requires way more than your average salary could maintain.

"Corbyn, like every other member, has another source of income. Corbyn is an arm's dealer. If you wanted to hit his pockets, that's the way to go."

"Aright, so how do we do that?" Hawk asks.

"Adam," Maksim says. "We all had jobs for Corbyn outside of being his personal bodyguards and hitmen. I was the one that collected the money and debts from the members of the Royal Crown. But Adam was in charge of the money from the weapons."

"So, if we want the money, we go after Adam," Zel replies.

"At the end of each week, the money is all brought to a single location and counted before being shipped overseas to Corbyn's offshore accounts. I don't know the exact locations, but I do know he uses churches to count and hide his money."

"We need to find those churches," Many says turning to me.

I pull up google on my laptop and search the number of churches in NYC. "There are 6000 churches in NYC alone."

"Narrow the search down to catholic churches," Maksim says with a shrug. "He's catholic."

I do as he says, but I also cross-reference the churches with Corbyn's name as either a member or a donor.

"Bingo," I say. "It seems like Mr. Corbyn has a strong affiliation with about five catholic churches around the city."

"Put them on the screen," Angel directs.

I cast my computer screen to the large monitor in the room.

"Not bad," Angel says. "We can hit all five this week."

"Slight problem," Zel says. "If Adam is the money man, wouldn't we run across him? And if we kill him, it will alert Corbyn we are after his kids."

Zel had a good point. We needed to make sure he never figured out what we were doing.

"Not necessarily," Maksim says. "Lucien, I need you to track all movements of Adam while we hit the churches. If we kill Adam while robbing one of the churches it will look like a case of wrong place wrong time to Corbyn. He won't sweat over the loss of one of us dying in the midst of a robbery."

"I'll keep an eye on his movements. Is there any way we can find the schedule for the money drops? That will be the best way to figure out how to get to Adam." I say.

"I'll ask Kyra to look into it," Angel says. "She can go back through the camera systems of all the churches to see when the drops were made."

"I will advise you," Maksim says. "Adam won't be an easy take down. I, Zeke, Archie, Victoria, and Yohan all liked to work alone. But the other three have their own personal bodyguards. You won't just go up against Adam, you will go up against his men as well."

"I'll do it," Beast says shrugging. "When the time comes, I'll go in."

"Can't be you, brother. If we go into one of those churches on money count day, there will be guards all around that building. You look too much like Corbyn. Adam's men will recognize you immediately."

"He's right," Angel says. "When we go after Adam, we will need someone they won't recognize, is good with stealth, and is crazy enough to run headfirst into a church with guns blazing."

For the first time since Priest's death, I feel Seth stir inside me.

"Someone call for me?" he asks in my head.

A wide grin spreads across my face. *"About damn time you showed up."*

"Yeah, yeah. Let me out, nerd."

Speaking to the room, I tell them, "I know the perfect person for the job."

CHAPTER THIRTY-THREE

Money Man

Seth

"God sees all. He's coming back," I say as I stand in front of St. Augustine's Church.

For the last four days, the guys have been hitting every church Lucien found that was connected to Corbyn. They've stolen almost twenty million in cash.

Kyra went through with her research and discovered that this last Church was our best chance of running into Adam. Today was the day he delivered the money. And it was the first day I was making my reappearance.

"I'm glad to finally have you back, brother." Lucien says in my head.

I've been out here a couple hours now. I've caught a few nasty looks, collected about six dollars in change, and I've been provided two cups of coffee and a cheeseburger. However, I have yet to see the man I've come for.

I turn to look up at the large building built in 1893. There is a ramp that goes from the street to the front door. The ramp's tall retention wall doesn't allow me to see the front door or for anyone at the front to see me.

"How's it going, Seth?" Zel's voice comes through the earpiece.

Zel is on top of one of the buildings nearby with his M24. Beast, Maksim, and Many are down the street in a catering van. If things go left, they are all ready to help.

"Pretty productive day," I reply. "I made six dollars."

I hear a long sigh in my earpiece.

"They should've been here by now. Maybe Lucien got the wrong church," Maksim says.

"No," I answer. "My brother is never wrong."

The jury is still out on that guy. I know everyone else has accepted him, but I still don't trust him.

"You don't trust anyone," Lucien says in my head. *"Maksim has proven his loyalty. Plus, I've been monitoring his movements and phone calls. He's had no contact with Corbyn or his siblings."*

"Looks like I'm not the only one that doesn't trust him if you're tracking his calls."

Luc chuckles in my head. *"Yeah, well, Priest didn't raise a fool."*

At the mention of his name, there is a tightness in my chest. I shut my eyes to stave off the ache.

"I know it hurts, brother. You don't have to hold it in."

My eyes pop open and I shake my head. *"Get the fuck out of my head. I have work to do."*

"Look alive, Seth," Beast's voice comes through the earpiece. "We got action heading toward you."

Looking down the street, a line of black SUV's approaches the church. They look like the caravan we've been waiting for.

"Alright," Zel says. "Once you get inside the church, I will have limited view. When you get down in the basement, I'll be completely blind."

"Soon as you clear the entrance, let us know," Beast says. "We will come in behind you."

I knew the plan. We'd discussed it many times before we left the house. I didn't need the run down again.

"If one more person speaks, I'm taking this fucking earpiece out."

"Is he always this much of an asshole?" Maksim asks.

The resounding yes from Zel, Many, Hawk, and Beast almost makes me chuckle. Although Hawk and Angel aren't here, they are monitoring everything through the earpieces and from the street cameras around the building.

The line of SUV's pulls in front of the Church. I count seventeen men in ill-fitting black suits and one man wearing dark shades, a black trench with a dark gray shirt and jeans. He's tall, but nowhere near as tall as Maksim and Beast. He has the same color blonde hair as Beast, but his is cut short and styled like those pretty boys that make videos of themselves walking in slow motion at gas stations.

"I found Adam," I whisper into the earpiece. "I have to admit, little brother. I think you got the better genes out of all of Corbyn's cum drops."

"I really prefer the other twin," Maksim says with a sigh.

The priest, dressed in his robes, runs off the ramp and down onto the sidewalk.

"Adam," he says approaching the guy I assumed was the sibling. "We were expecting you hours ago."

Adam looks back and forth down the street. He glances at me, but quickly assesses me and then looks away.

"Corbyn's dealing with some pest. We've been having to move some shit around. A couple of our churches have been attacked."

The priest shakes his head. "Should we be concerned?"

"No, they only strike when I'm not there. They are not that bold to try it when I'm around."

He's a cocky little bitch.

"I'm going to enjoy killing this asshole," Zel says, feeling the same way I do.

"Well, come on," the priest urges. "I have everything ready to go."

Five of the men with Adam pull large duffle bags out of the back of the truck. Each man carries two to three bags at one time. Adam then directs his men, making two of them stay out front to keep watch. The others, I'm assuming, are going in with him.

Adam starts to walk off, but stops. He taps one of his men on the shoulder.

"Hey, get rid of the bum," he says before following the priest and his men up the ramp and into the church.

The guy appointed to deal with me starts walking in my direction.

"Show time, brother," Lucien says in my head.

"Aye, you, get your shit and get out of here," the guy says.

He shoves my buggy over, pouring out the contents onto the ground. I bend down pretending to pick up the stuff. He leans down and grabs my shoulder. I pull the knife out of my leg holster and drive the blade into the bottom of his chin. He gurgles up blood. I pull the blade out and then slice through his neck, finishing him off. He starts falling, but I catch him in my arms. Gently, I lie him down on the blanket I was using and then cover him up.

Taking off the dingy long winter jacket, I toss it down. Turning my head from side to side, I release the tension.

Here we go. Wiping the blade off on the coat, I make my way up the ramp toward the front door. Both men Adam left behind eye me suspiciously. The one on my left places a hand at his back as if he's going to draw his weapon. The one to my right approaches me.

"Hey, aren't you the…." I don't let him finish his sentence. I swipe my Bowie across his face with my left hand. Before the other could pull his gun out, I had mine in my hand. Putting a bullet between his eye, I then turned and shot the first man in the forehead, silencing his moans.

I step over their bodies and push through the church doors.

"He's in," Zel says through the earpiece. I'll pick off anyone that comes out or tries to enter."

"On our way," Beast announces.

I walk into the small foyer of the church. Stopping, I take a deep breath. From here on out, I need a clear head.

"You got this, brother," Lucien says in my head.

"This is not a got damn after-school special. Will you shut the fuck up?"

Lucien's sigh echoes in my head before I feel him slip away.

I walk into the sanctuary, quickly scanning the scene in front of me. Standing right at the door as I walk in is one man. He eyes me skeptically but doesn't move. The priest is in front of the altar talking to one of Adam's men. There is one guy sitting in the pews on the third row back on the left. Another guy is in the right pews at the very front. I look over my shoulder to see the guy up on the balcony, his arms crossed over his chest. One more guy is near a narrow door in the back, near the altar. I'm sure that door leads down to the basement where I will find Adam.

The priest looks up at me and smiles as I walk toward him.

"How can I help you, young man…"

I pull my gun out and shoot him in the leg and immediately take out the guy next to him with a shot to the head. The guy in the front pew stands, but my Bowie tossed into his chest sends him back to his seat.

Dealing with the guys outside, I realize that these men are slow to draw. Their guns are at their backs, which takes them longer to pull them out. I spent six months of training before becoming a deacon on working how to quickly draw a weapon.

"The time it takes you to pull your shit out can mean life or death. The fastest draw always wins," Priest's voice says in my head.

I shake off that feeling I get whenever I think about him.

The guy in the right pew runs toward me. I fire a round into his head before diving behind the pews. I moved just in time because a hailstorm of bullets whizzed into the wood over my head. The fucking guy on the balcony is a problem.

"Shit," I grumble.

"We have a problem up here," I hear one of the men talking loudly in what I think is a radio or earpiece.

"Talk to me, Twin? What do you need?" Zel says in my ear.

I peek around the pew and nearly get my head blown off by the guy on the balcony. Lying flat, I roll under the empty bench style seats.

"Do you have a clear shot into the balcony?" I ask Zel.

"No. The stained glass makes it hard to see."

The room goes silent, but I can hear the sound of heavy breathing, moaning, and footsteps. Peeking under the row of pews I'm under, I spot a pair of black boots. Aiming my gun, I shoot at the guy's ankles. A scream and then a thud proceeds the man falling to the ground. He turns his head just in time to spot me under the pew. I put a bullet in his right eye.

Bullets once again land into the wood over my head. I tuck and roll back in the opposite direction.

"I'm stuck until you get the guy in the balcony," I tell Zel.

"Let's Hawk it," Zel says.

I smile before lifting my head slightly to get a clear view of the balcony guy. I grasp his location before ducking back behind the pew.

"30-degree angle, from center, your right," I say to Zel.

"Got it."

A loud cracking sound, like when a rock hits your car window, proceeds groaning and then a loud thump. Lifting from my hidden spot, I see a small hole in the stain glass window. Looking down beneath the balcony stand is the body of the gunman.

"That was a damn near perfect headshot."

"Hawk, you would be proud," Zel laughs.

"I am," Hawk says through the earpiece.

I spin just in time to see the guy I hit with my knife standing behind me with his gun aimed at me. Shutting my eyes, I know it's too late. I think of Malia and my kids.

"Never lose count of your bodies," Priest words play back in my head.

The silent purr of a bullet leaving the barrel of a gun goes off and I wait for the pain. Yet, nothing happens.

I open my eyes to find the gunman lying on the floor, a pool of blood surrounding his head. I turn to find Many, Maksim, and Beast at the door. Beast lowers his gun and walks over to me.

"You good?" he asks.

"What the fuck took you so long? Did you take the scenic route?"

Many chuckles. "New brother, Maksim, misjudged the distance we were parked," he says in his deep voice.

Beast walks over to the guy he shot and yanks my knife out of his chest. He wipes the blood off on the dead man's suit before walking over to me. He eyes me up and down. At first, I thought he was checking for injuries, but the way he stares at me, I feel like he's looking for something else.

"Are you good?" He asks again.

Once again, I open my mouth to tell him yes, but I stop to think. He isn't asking if I'm physically hurt, he's asking if I'm mentally good. Staring down the barrel of a gun isn't new. I've had many close calls in this line of work. However, this time felt different. It felt closer. Before losing Priest, dying felt unreal. Even though we've been close to it many times, it almost felt as if we were superhuman. But after losing Priest, I've realized that we aren't immortal. For the first time, some of the things I've done, the decisions I made while doing this, seemed too risky. Staring down the barrel of that gun made me realize what my brother had been wanting for so long—to be done.

Finally, I answer Beast with the correct response. "No," I say looking into his green eyes. "But let's finish this."

He nods his head in understanding and holds out my Bowie for me. I take the knife and place it at my back inside the holster there.

"How many do we have left?" Maksim asks, making his way over to the moaning Priest.

"Eight, plus Adam," I say as Beast and I join him in front of the priest.

"You have no idea who you're dealing with," the priest snarls. "You will never again live in peace. He will..."

Beast puts a bullet in the priest's head.

"We don't have time for final words," he says, turning toward the door at the back of the altar. The one I believed led down to the basement.

He's right. I turn to follow him.

Just as we go to take the first step, the door we were heading to opens and two men step out, their guns aimed.

Beast fires the first shot, taking out the first guy. Simultaneously, I fire the second. The other guy drops to the ground, and we run toward the door.

"Is there another exit from that basement?" I ask Zel.

"Yeah, back of the building," he replies.

I turn to Maksim and Many. Before I could say anything, Maksim speaks. "We've got it covered." He taps Many on the chest and they head in the opposite direction of us.

I lead the way, stepping over the fallen bodies. Beast and I make our way down narrow stairs. We check before turning corners, our guns aimed in front of us. The closer we get to the lower level, the more voices we hear.

"I don't give a fuck," the voice I know to be Adam's shouts. "I want you to go check and make sure the job is done."

I look over my shoulder at Beast. Without saying a word, I ask him if he's ready. He gives a subtle nod. Reaching at my back, I pull out my Bowie. Let's get it done.

I walk around the corner and quickly scan the room. Behind a gated fence are three women sitting behind a desk. There are stacks of money on the table and in counting machines. On the floor in the same back room are the other duffle bags filled with money. Also, in the back of the room are two of Adam's men.

Standing in front of the gate is Adam and a taller man. I'm assuming that was who he was talking to. There are three other guys in the room. It took only seconds to scan the area.

Before I could fire the first shot, the man standing with Adam steps in front of him, blocking my view. I chose to shoot the guy closest to me. Taking him out quickly. Beast fires a shot into the gated room taking out the guy with the biggest gun.

One of the other guys in the room runs up to me. I toss my knife in his thigh, causing him to bend slightly. I quickly put a bullet in his head. A quick glance to my left and there is another body on the ground. I'm assuming Beast took him out. A shot whizzes past my head as I move through the room. The gunman is the second guy in the gated room. He's hiding behind one of the women, taking shots at me.

Does he think I won't shoot that chick? I laugh in my head.

I shoot the woman in the shoulder. She cries out before dropping to the ground. I then put a bullet in his chest.

While we were shooting, Beast and I were moving further into the room. At some point, Beast and the guy protecting Adam were in a hand-to-hand fight. The guy punched Beast in the face, but I wasn't worried about my brother. He'd be fine. I was more concerned about Adam. I knew he hadn't run out the door to the outside because it still had the padlock on it. Which meant he went back up the stairs.

I grabbed my knife off the guy I stabbed. "Going after Adam." I yell to Beast before rushing up the stairs.

I can hear Adam's heavy footsteps pounding up the stairs. Turning the corner, I spot him just as he got to the door leading back out to the sanctuary. I toss my Bowie through the air, and it lands right in the back of his thigh. He howls in pain but doesn't stop.

Adam shoves through the door. As soon as I rush out, I duck back in, narrowly missing the bullet he shot. I push the door back open to find Adam limply running down the aisle. I rush after him. He turns to shoot at me again, but I tackle him to the ground. We roll across the floor until my back hits one of the pew ends.

Adam kicks out his foot, connecting with my stomach before jumping to his feet. I grab his leg, sending him crashing back to the floor.

"Get the fuck off me." He kicks at me.

My grip loosens, allowing him once again to get to his feet. I jump up too, facing off with him.

At some point, I lost my gun in the scuffle and the knife at the back of his thigh is gone as well. Thankfully, he's without his weapon too.

Adam sneers. "You muthafuckers are like roaches. You just won't fucking die." He says as we circle each other.

A slow smile spreads across his face. "Well, except for your daddy. How was his funeral?"

The red haze slipped over me so quickly, my body heated up. However, before I could act, another lesson from Priest popped in my head.

I was fighting one of the other deacon trainees. The kid had been taunting me for months. The priest and the kid's handler finally decided to let us fight it out. I was a better fighter than the kid, but that day, he was kicking my ass. Priest pulled me to the side and thumped me in the head. I remember charging at him, but stopped short when he pulled his gun out and pressed it to my head.

"The quickest way to lose in any fight is when you fight blindly with anger. Fighting requires you to use your head. Had you been thinking straight and not pissed, you would have known my gun was in my hand when I thumped you."

I remember looking down at the weapon and realizing I missed a vital detail.

"Reign that fucking anger in, Twin. Then go out there and beat that kid's ass." I will never forget the smirk on his face after he said that.

Coming back to the present, I reign in the haze. Twisting my neck from side to side. With a smile, I look at Adam.

"At least I was able to see my daddy's funeral. You'll be on your route through a worm's digestive track by the time we put Corbyn's body in an early grave."

The smile on Adam's face falls. He charges at me while yelling. I shake my head as I take the beretta out of my second gun holster and put a bullet in his neck. He drops down right at my feet.

"Who the hell brings one gun to a shootout?" I ask no one in particular.

I swing around with my gun aimed as Beast walks into the sanctuary. He looks me over, then nods his head.

"We got a bloody scene in here. Zel, let the cleanup crew know to get it contained to the basement. We got nineteen bodies, one injured female and two other uninjured females," Beast says.

Unlike the other times we hit the kids, we needed Corbyn to find this scene. However, we needed it to look like a simple hit.

"Roger that. Cleaning crew is on their way."

Beast taps my chest. "Let's go collect the money."

We both head back down the stairs to gather the black duffle bags of money. Another one of Corbyn's cum stains down. Five more to go.

CHAPTER THIRTY-FOUR

It Hits

Seth

The car ride back to the ghost house was quiet. After letting Maksim and Many into the basement, we quickly loaded the money. I had intended to let the women live, but when one of them pulled a gun on Many. Beast took them all out. Maksim explained they were loyal to Adam and would have ran and told the first chance they got.

After showering in the downstairs bathroom, I make my way up to my bedroom with Malia. I was anxious to finally see her.

I push the door open. Malia is sitting up in bed reading a book.

"Hey, Luc, how was your…" her words die on her tongue when she looks up at me. "Seth." The sound of my name coming off her lips has my cock immediately hardening.

"Hey, Candy Girl."

Malia drops the book on the bed and rushes out of it. I have just enough time to open my arms right before she rushes into them. Her luscious lips seal to mine. I slip my tongue inside her mouth, dominating it as if it's mine. I grip her ass in both my hands and squeeze.

Malia cups my face and pulls away from the kiss. Her eyes shine with her tears. Slowly, they spill over her lids and fall down her face.

"I thought you left me."

Turning my head to the side slightly, I wrap my hand around her neck and use my thumb to lift her face. Our eyes connect.

"Don't ever let that shit sit in your head. I'll never leave you, Candy Girl."

I hold her in place as I bring my lips back to hers. I shove my tongue into her mouth and bite down on her lip before sucking the plump flesh. She moans. Letting her neck go, I place my hand on the back of her thighs, lifting her up like a bride on her wedding day.

She wraps her arms around my neck, never taking her mouth from mine. I walk her over to the bed and lay her down. She's wearing one of Lucien's t-shirts and tiny underwear. Lifting her shirt, I place my hand over her round belly. Knowing my kid is in there has my chest filling with pride.

"It's a boy," she says sweetly. "You're having a son."

"Why didn't you tell me?" I ask Lucien in my head?

"Because I knew she wanted to be the first to tell you. Congratulations," he says before quickly fading back into the background.

Pride swells my chest. Even though I didn't care if the sex of the baby was a boy or girl, I still feel the elation of knowing we were having a son. A tiny version of Luc and I.

Moving my hands down her stomach to her mound, I keep my eyes on her. She's so beautiful, it sometimes shocks the hell out of me that she's with us.

I slide the seat of her panties to the side, revealing her fat pussy lips. I hiss when my fingers connect with her warm, wet slit.

"Seth," she moans when I glide two digits into her heat. The slurping sound her pussy makes as my fingers move in and out of her has my cock rock hard.

"Can I taste it, Lia?" I ask, praying that she doesn't say no. "Can I have what belongs to me?" I wait for her answer as I still move my fingers in and out of her.

"Yes," she pleads. "Please, Seth, I missed you."

"I'm here now."

Getting to my knees by the side of the bed, I remove my fingers from Lia's center, then tug her underwear down her legs. I toss them over my head. She won't need them anymore tonight. I have no plans to sleep tonight.

I spread her legs wide and bury my face in her wetness, taking in her clean and musky scent. Flattening my tongue, I swipe it from her asshole to her pearl. She arches her back and moans. I suck her clit into my mouth before swirling my tongue around it.

"Ooh shit, Seth. Don't stop, baby."

Like I had any plans to. I work my tongue over her nub as I insert my finger into her tunnel.

She whimpers as she continues to roll her hips, feeding me her pussy. I pin her legs down, holding her to the bed so I can feast fully. Her cries grow louder as I continue to eat her out. My face is soaking wet from her essence.

Her body starts to shake, and her walls clamp down on my fingers, letting me know she's close to her release. I suck her swollen clit into my mouth. Lia screams and comes so hard her body shakes. I don't stop my assault. I lick and lap up every ounce of her juices until she tries to pull my meal away from me. Like an untrained dog, I growl. Wrapping my arm around her thighs, I drag her ass back down to my mouth.

"Seth," she screams as I bring her to another orgasm.

Only when I've had my full share of her delicious pussy, do I let her legs go and climb to my feet. I yank my shirt over my head and toss it. Lia lays on the bed, her legs hanging off the side. She hasn't moved since I let her go.

I take my shorts off next, along with my underwear. Tugging at my cock, I watch my girl.

"You know I'd never hurt you or our kids, right?"

She squints at me. "You know I know that."

"And you know I love you more than anything."

"Of course."

"Good," I say, lifting one of her legs and angling her center toward my cock. "Because I'm about to fuck you like I don't." I thrust into Lia until my cock is fully seated.

She gasps and moans. Pulling out, I slam back into her, making her claw at the sheets.

"Shit, baby. Right there," she whimpers.

Using the hold I have on her legs; I turn her to the side so that I can go deeper. I move in and out of her at a rapid pace, my balls slapping against her thigh with a clapping sound. I wanted to be so deep inside her my kid would have a playmate.

She chants my name over and over.

"Don't ever fucking doubt that I want this, Lia. I'll never let you go," I grit out as I lift her bottom leg further to her chest. It opens her up, allowing me another inch inside her.

"You feel so good. Ooh! Don't stop," she cries. "I missed you so much."

I know we're loud. But I didn't care if anyone else heard us. Pulling out of her, I flip her over to her stomach.

"On your knees," I demand, as I smack her ass.

She obliges, putting her ass in the air. I grab the pillow at the top of the bed and put it under her pelvis allowing a little relief from her belly.

"Look at me," I direct. She turns her head and looks over her shoulder.

Holding my dick in my hands, I guide it through her folds and push into her.

She hisses and moves up the bed. I bring my hand down on her ass, turning it red before rubbing the flesh.

"Don't you dare run," I warn before picking up my pace. I watch the way my length disappears inside her and reappears, covered in her essence.

"Fuck," I groan, tossing my head back. "This pussy has been on a different level since we got you pregnant. I'm going to keep a fucking baby in your womb." Wrapping my hands in her long hair, I pull her head back, arching her back even more, allowing me to sink in further.

"Aahhhhh," she screams.

"Do you hear me? Every chance I get, I'm filling you up with my cum."

"Yes, Seth. Yes, baby," she moans as she throws her ass back on my cock.

I smack her ass as I toss my head back and chuckle. She believed I was talking in the moment, but I had every intention of keeping her ass pregnant.

Lia's movements slow down.

"Don't you dare stop." Tugging on her hair, I lift her body up from the bed. Her back is pressed to my chest.

Turning her head, I kiss her sloppily, biting her lip and sucking her tongue into my mouth.

Pulling out of her, I climb onto the bed. Lying flat, I grab her hand and guide her on top of me.

"Ride me from the back."

She turns around, straddling my hips. I hold my dick up. She eases down on it slowly. Once she's settled, she rocks up and down on my length at a slow pace. Sticking my finger in my mouth, I suck on it. Pulling it out, I used my other hand to spread Lia's ass cheeks. Once her rosette comes into view, I smear my wet finger around the hole before slowly pushing my finger in. Lia stiffens on top of me.

She turns and looks over her shoulder at me. "Seth," she whines.

"Fuck me, Lia. Don't you worry about what I'm doing to this ass." I push my pointer finger in and out of her asshole.

She goes back to grinding on my cock. Her movements become more erratic, and her pussy soaks me even more.

"You like my finger in your ass, Candy Girl?"

"Shit," she cries. "Yes."

"Good, because after you have this kid, my cock is going in there."

Grabbing her waist, I hold her still as I fuck her from the bottom. She cries out with her head tossed back.

"I'm coming. I'm coming," she screams.

However, I didn't need her announcement. I could feel the ripple in her walls and the wetness of her orgasm. It felt so good, it pulled my nut from me.

I roar as my semen shoots out of me and paints her walls. It's so intense, I fold in half, lifting from the bed, I bury my face in her back.

Once the orgasm recedes, my body goes completely weak. I collapse back on the bed. Lia climbs off of me and tucks herself into my side. I pull her closer to me. She lays her head on my chest.

The only sound in the room now is our heavy breathing and the whirring of the ceiling fan.

Finally, I break the silence. "After we handle Corbyn, I'm leaving the Church. I'm taking you and our kids and I'm going off grid."

She lifts her head and looks down at me. Her eyes scan my face as if she's trying to determine if I'm really here.

"I expected that to come from Lucien, not you."

I have to look away from her as the memory of that gun being pointed at my face plays back in my head.

"My brother is right. We've lived our lives on the edge since we were eight years old. No care in the world about our wellbeing. Losing Priest." I stop talking to fight the burning feeling in my throat.

The urge to recede and allow Lucien to deal with these emotions is strong. However, I fight the urge off.

"Losing Priest has showed me that life is too short. No matter how good I am, and how prepared we are for a menu, it can all be taken away from you in the blink of an eye. And leaving you, tiny soldier, and this baby behind to mourn me the way Rose is mourning Priest doesn't sit right with me. So, I'm choosing you over the need to kill."

I look up at her when I feel something wet hit my chest. She's crying. I swipe her tears away.

"Baby," she stops and clears her throat. "Seth, I would've accepted you no matter what you decided. I understand your need to do what you do. You know that, right?"

I nod. "I know, Candy Girl. But, this," I point between the two of us before placing my hand on her belly. "This is what I want."

Her tears fall again. "Hearing you say you'll give it all up for our family makes me love you so much more. I promise to make it all worth it."

I pull her down, crashing my lips to hers. "You already have, Lia."

Rolling her underneath me, I part her legs with my knees and settle between her thighs. Reaching between us, I line my cock up with her opening and slide in. She purrs as I seat myself to the hilt.

"I fucking love you, Candy girl."

I spend the rest of the night proving those last words to her.

CHAPTER THIRTY-FIVE

Sex Club

Zel

The hot water from the shower rains down on my body, helping to clear my head. The visions of my childhood disappear to the back of my mind.

You are here.

You are safe.

They can't find you.

I repeat the words in my head over and over. It was the very first lesson I learned from Priest. The day he showed up at my parents' house and dragged me out of that box will be a day I'll never forget. Losing Priest has brought back many of my memories. Things I've worked hard to forget.

"As long as I'm alive, you will never have to fear them," his words from the day he rescued me play in my head.

Turning off the water, I climb out of the shower. I grab the towel on the hook beside me and wrap my lower half before going over to the mirror. My jet-black hair has grown over the last few months I've been here. Now the front hangs in my face.

"Zel, pull your fucking hair out of your eyes." I can almost hear Priest's voice as if he's standing here beside me.

Glancing down at my chest, I catch sight of the colorful artwork that adorns my upper body.

The vision of my eight-year-old self being held down as I'm tattooed for hours replays in my head.

"You belong to us, Kenji. For the rest of your life, you will belong to us." I shake the memory away, hoping it goes back to the deepest part of my mind.

Turning away from the tattoos, I head into my room to dress.

Before long, I'm heading down to the dining room to catch up with the plans for today. Before I walk into the room, I shut my eyes and take a deep breath. I shed my concerns and worries and plaster a smile on my face.

I walk into the room to find Lucien alone.

"I see class hasn't started yet."

Lucien looks up from his computer. "You're the first one here today."

I pull out a chair and take a seat, propping my legs up on the table. "Did you sleep at all last night?"

It's been a week since we took down Adam at that church. Yesterday, we realized that a little over a month had passed since we lost Priest. Last night, my brothers and I stayed up late reminiscing about the man that raised us.

"I got about three hours, but my mind wouldn't rest though. What about you?"

I smile. He doesn't need to know that I haven't slept more than an hour a night since Priest died. My problems are not my brothers'.

"Like a baby," I lie.

Hawk is the next to enter. He looks exhausted.

"I'm never drinking with you guys again," he grumbles as he takes a seat.

Lucien and I both laugh at him.

Many and Kimi walk in together. Kimi takes a seat beside Lucien. Many leans against the wall.

"We are not equipped for alcohol," he says, grabbing his head.

"No one told you guys to stay up drinking," Kimi jokes. "All of you are too old for late nights."

Maksim enters with a bag of frozen peas over his head. "All of you are too loud." He flops down in the chair beside me.

Beast is the last to enter, looking perky and relaxed. He didn't have a sip of alcohol last night. He explained that because Summer couldn't drink, neither would he.

Beast takes the seat at the other end of the table from Lucien.

"What's the latest?" He asks as soon as he sits down.

"DOE has moved diligently through Corbyn's homes. They're down to the last three on Maksim's list. They plan on hitting those three tonight. After that, it will be up to you, Lucien."

He nods. "I can handle that. I've also tracked down Micah. He's back in the states."

Micah has been one of the harder siblings to find. He does a lot of Corbyn's business overseas. He's rarely ever on US soil.

"If Micah is back home, keep an eye on the underground sex clubs. His favorites are Aces, Pearls, and the Red Dragon," Maksim says, laying his bag of frozen vegetables down on the table.

"I've heard of Ace's, but I've never heard of the other two," Beast says.

"Pearls is a lot like Aces, except only the very wealthy are allowed membership," Kimi explains. "Vito runs Pearls."

The funeral was the first time I met Vito and his brothers. We have yet to meet the one they called Mason, but they have been lending us their support this entire time. Guns, money, anything we've needed, they have offered. Even before Priest died, they were helping us and we just didn't know it.

"Now, Red Dragon is a different beast completely," she goes on to say. "It's a lot grimier, and they have a lot stricter rules than Aces and Pearls. Their clientele is mostly criminals, and I'm not talking about your petty thief. I'm talking about the type of people that have no problem dropping bodies in rivers."

"So not the type of place you want to run in with guns blazing?" I ask.

She nods. "Let's just say it would be much better for all of us if he goes to Aces or Pearls. It's easier to get into both of those with no negative outcome. Heck, I'm sure Vito would let us walk right in and put a bullet into Micah's head at Pearls."

We don't need any more enemies right now. We had enough to last us a lifetime. Best-case scenario, Micah goes to Pearls, we call up Priest's friend to set him up. One of us goes in and makes a quick kill. Worst-case scenario, we piss off a fucking crime lord and now we have a bunch of gangsters trying to kill us.

"Reach out to Vito now," Lucien says. "I'll go ahead and hack into all three of their databases. No matter where Micah decides to go, he will need to make a reservation."

Lucien starts typing on his computer.

Kimi pulls out her phone. She taps at her screen as if she's sending off a text. Only a few minutes pass before she speaks again.

"Vito says if Micah comes into Pearls, we have free range to do what we want."

We all nod.

"We still need to figure out a plan," Beast says. "I can take this one."

Maksim shakes his head. "Not a smart move. Micah won't be alone and if him or his men spot you, it's game over."

Word got out that we killed Adam in that robbery. Phoenix told us that Corbyn is pissed, but still doesn't suspect anything. Thanks to Phoenix, we now know that Corbyn is getting a little more desperate. He's been asking around about finding our location. He's finally scared.

"Welp," I say, shrugging as I take my feet off the table and place them on the ground. "I guess this one is mine."

"We will play it the same way we did with Nolan," Kimi goes on to explain. She's stepped right into the shoes of Priest as far as leading these meetings and directing us. "Many and Seth will go as backup just in case things go left. The rest of us will stay here and guide you. It will be easy to get in and out of Ace's and Pearls. Let's not make this one too complicated."

I dip my chin, agreeing with the plan.

"Fuck," Lucien says, getting our attention. He looks up at us. "He just made reservations for Red Dragon."

"Dang it," Kimi swears or at least her version of swearing. "That changes everything. Lucien, how fast can you make up a criminal profile for Zel?"

Maksim shakes his head. "The type of clout he will need to get into Red Dragon can't be on a resume. It has to be by word of mouth. His name must ring bells before they will allow him in." He scrubs a hand down his face. "I might have to bite the bullet and make an appearance."

"That's too risky," Hawk says. "By now your name is out there as being a traitor. They will either kill you on site or notify Corbyn and all this is for nothing."

Although I hear them talking, my head is swimming.

"You belong to us, Kenji. For the rest of your life, you will belong to us." The memory comes charging back to me.

I've spent all my life running from my past. Trying to distance myself from the woman that birthed me, and the man she recruited to raise me. They say you can never outrun your past. I guess it's true, because it has finally caught up to me.

"I can do it," I say, cutting into the debate that was going on around me.

The room becomes quiet.

"You're missing the point, Zel. You don't have a name in the underworld. We can't get you in."

I turn to glare at Lucien. "Tell them Kenjiro Isamu is coming."

"Who?" Hawk asks.

"Isamu?" Maksim says, leaning up in his seat. "As in Isamu-Kai the fifth largest Yakuza clan in Japan?"

This is part of my life I was hoping I could take to my grave. I always assumed this would never see the light of day. I guess once Priest was gone, I should have known it would come out.

"Yes," I sigh. "And I promise to tell you all about it, but if we're going to get into the Red Dragon we need to move fast."

"He's right," Lucien says, going back to his computer.

"You know that if you're going in as a member of the Yakuza, you will have to prove yourself. You can't just toss that name around," Kimi states.

Running my fingers through my overgrown bangs, I sigh. "I know."

Kimi looks at me skeptically. I wonder why Priest never told her the truth about me.

"You never have to worry, Kid. No one will ever know," Priest's promised words play back in my mind. I guess he meant what he said.

Kimi shakes her head. I assuming she's figured out I have this under control.

"Alright, you'll need bodyguards. Seth, Hawk, and Many you go in with him. Maksim, and Beast, will be your trail. If it goes left, you two will need to intercede. I'll stay here and be your eyes in the sky."

I nod as I stand from my seat. In order to don the persona of my old life, I need to clear my head and become someone I haven't seen since I was eight years old.

"Zel," Kimi calls out, getting my attention again. I turn back to face her. "There are rules in the Red Dragon. You're going to need to follow them. All of them."

Dipping my chin at her, I then turn and head out of the room.

Stepping into the crowded main room of Red Dragon at exactly half-past two in the morning, I glance around. Many, Seth, and Hawk, are behind me as my bodyguards. Beast is in the earpiece walking Hawk through the layout of the building.

The smoke-filled room is dimly lit. The neon lights make everyone seem extraterrestrial. All the furniture has sleek lines and is made of glass and metal. Each booth has a table equipped with a stripper pole and its very own stripper.

The main floor felt like any other strip club. Women in all different shapes and sizes filled the room, all vying for attention, looking for the biggest spender. However, to find Micah, I needed to be on the lower levels. Or the belly of the beast, as they call it.

As I make my way throughout the main floor, following the skinny Japanese girl that introduced herself as the hostess, I take in all the surrounding men.

It's obvious these men are part of the criminal world. The rugged looks, the number of bodyguards and guns I see attached to hips give them away. If that wasn't enough to tell me who they are, the way they glare at me is enough to warn me of their intentions.

"Okay, Zel," Kimi says through the earpiece in my ear. "You're going to meet Akito. He is the owner of the club. This part is going to be very crucial. You have to convince him you're there to sleep with one of his women."

We went over all this back at the ghost house before I left. In order to have access to the belly of the beast, you have to prove you are here for the reason of sampling a woman. Spectators don't get access to that level. Too much at stake to let just anyone down there.

I touch my left ear.

"He hears you and he understands," Maksims says, reading the signal off Hawk's glasses. Not only is it too loud in here for them to pick my voice up clearly over the earpiece without me yelling, it's also weird for me to walk around talking to myself. Too many eyes on me.

"Alright," Kimi says when we stop in front of a red door. "You're on your own from this point. Seth, you go in with him."

The hostess knocks twice on the door before a male voice tells her to enter in Japanese. The hostess opens the door and steps aside. I tug at the hem of my suit jacket before walking into the room. Seth follows behind me. The door closes and I'm in the room with the man I assume to be Akito.

He looks to be around my age. His black hair is shaved so low he's nearly bald. His tattoos cover his neck and hands. There are two other men in the room with us that I assume are his bodyguards. Akito sizes me up, taking me in from head to toe. I do the same with him. I don't speak. In the Yakuza society I grew up in, I am of higher rank than him, so he needs to speak first.

Akito nods his head in a casual bow. I return the greeting.

"Kenjiro Isamu," he says my full name with a grin. "I haven't heard that name in a long time."

"Ghosts don't have names," I reply.

Akito stares at me for a long moment before his grin spreads over his face.

"With all due respect, I hope you won't be offended if I ask for proof?"

I knew this was coming. This is what Kimi was warning me about. There was no way I was going to resurrect that name without showing my proof.

Instead of replying to him, I slip my jacket off. Turning, I hand it to Seth. He looks a little confused, but he doesn't say anything. Slowly, without taking my eyes off Akito, I undo my shirt. He watches me with a grin. Once my shirt is unbuttoned, I open it and slip it down my back and shoulders. I show him my chest and stomach first. His eyes widen as he takes in my marks. I then slowly turn so he can see my back. When I'm facing Seth, I can see the shock and confusion on his face.

When we were younger, I never went around my brothers without a shirt on. I was ashamed of my tattoos and the things I had to do to get these marks. The guys never questioned it. However, Priest knew what I was hiding.

Turning back to face Akito, I button my shirt back up.

"Proof enough?" I ask.

He dips his chin to his chest. "My apologies. What can I do for you?" his attitude and demeanor has changed.

Even though I have not been a part of Isamu-Kai for many years, my name still carries weight. Although, it isn't my name that he fears as much as it is the man that gave me the name. I push all thoughts of my biological father out of my head.

"I'm in town for a short time. I want to be entertained."

"And how can we entertain you?"

"I want access to the belly."

My request takes him by surprise, but he hides it well. "We would be honored to supply you with your entertainment for the night. And what type of entertainment would you prefer?"

"Girl on girl."

He nods before picking up the phone. "Send the new girl up to the office. I need her to escort a patron to the belly." When he's done speaking, he quickly hangs up the phone and stands.

"You're allowed only three guards into the belly. We ask that you be as gentle as you can with our…. products. But, if by chance one were to get damaged, please notify us as soon as possible and I will supply you with another."

The way he talks about women turns my stomach, but I don't comment. Hiroshi would never allow the mistreatment of a woman around him. However, Kenji was taught that women are nothing more than property and, if used correctly, income.

"Understandable," I reply.

He's silent as he walks over to me. "Red Dragon is considered neutral ground. I ask that there is no bloodshed on my property."

I chuckle, allowing the tension to build up between us. "Is that rule only for me or everyone?"

His nostrils flare. "Everyone."

I shrug. "Okay."

The door to the room opens and before I turn around, the sweetest scent I've ever smelled hits my nose. It's soft, yet warm and chocolatey. When I turn to find who the scent belongs to, I lose all ability to move.

Standing before me is none other than a goddess. Skin so dark and flawless it looks unreal. Her large afro stands out on her head like a crown. She's tall, in her heels she's just below eye level with me, and I'm 6'2". Her body is curvy, not as much as Malia's, but more than Brooklyn's. Her heart-shaped face emphasizes the slant of her dark brown eyes. I was drawn to her full, plump lips. She is fucking beautiful.

"Kenji, this is India. She will be your guide into the belly," Akito says, but I'm not paying attention to his words.

The moment he introduced us, the goddess smiled. Even though the smile doesn't reach her eyes, it is still stunning. The slight gap between her front two teeth makes her even more interesting.

"India knows all about the women and will help you pick the right ones for your enjoyment."

I watch the goddess the entire time he talks. I can tell she's new. It's in the way she smiles and the way her eyes have not yet lost the glimmer of innocence. I was taken from a place not much different from this before joining the Church. I know the eyes of a woman that has been in this environment too long. This beauty's eyes aren't as vacant as I would expect someone that is used to this line of work and has become numb to it, but they also aren't as lively as the females I noticed out front. Which leads me to believe she's here by choice, but she isn't happy about it.

"She can be of great service to you." This time when he speaks of her, he reaches out a hand and glides it over her exposed arm.

The subtle shift in her stance let me know the touch isn't wanted. But the fact she doesn't pull away or look disgusted tells me it isn't unfamiliar.

The urge to knock his fucking teeth out of his mouth erupts in me quickly. I twist my neck on my shoulder to fight down the tension.

"Remember why you are here," I remind myself.

"Shall we get to it?" I ask, my words coming out harsher than I planned.

Beauty's eyes flash up to mine. Not sure if the growl in my tone scared her or just shocked her. She quickly looks away when my gaze connects with hers.

"Absolutely," Akito says. "I'll charge all services to the card you have on your profile."

"Sure." I turn away from Akito.

Beauty leads the way to the door. My heart nearly stops in my tracks when I get a glimpse of her ass in her short dress. Damn.

We walk out of the room. Hawk and Many join us as she leads me to the elevator.

"Fuck me, look at her ass," Maksim says through the earpiece.

I take a step to my right, blocking Hawk's glasses's view. We're mostly quiet as we climb on the elevator. As soon as the doors shut, she turns and looks at me. When our eyes connect, she gives me a smile. This one is much more authentic than the one in Akito's office. When I return a smile of my own, she tucks her lips and looks down at her feet.

I think she's blushing.

"How long have you worked here?" I ask.

"Not long. Four months."

Her voice has my cock hardening even more than the view of her ass. It's sultry and raspy, like an old blues singer. I could listen to her talk all day.

"You like it so far?" I find myself asking as if she's working at Taco Bell, and not a brothel.

Seth clears his throat. When I turn to look at him, he's grinning like an idiot.

"Am I hearing this correctly?" Kimi says through the earpiece. "Is Zel flirting?"

"Is that what this is?" Maksim laughs. "You speak as if you're in high school. Tell her her ass is fat. Women like having fat asses."

"Do not tell her that," Kimi groans.

I ignore them as I place my attention back on beauty. The elevator doors open, and I am hit with loud noises and the smell of sweat, smoke, and body odor. The difference between this room and the main floor is night and day. Down here looks as if I walked into the den of sin itself.

Beauty leads the way out of the elevator. Men of all backgrounds crowd around tables of dazed women in all forms of debauchery.

Other than Beauty and the waitresses carrying the trays of food, no other woman here has on clothes. On one table a group of men with leather vests are triple penetrating a female with the deadest eyes I've ever seen.

On the next table, two chicks are being pinned down while a group of Italians take turns on them. The scene turns my stomach, but I remain stoic. My head stays high, and I keep my guard up.

"There, to Hawk's left is Micah," Maksim says. I turn to see a tall brown-haired man with a thick scar on the side of his face standing in front of a black door. He looks around the room, before opening the door and walking in. Two men stand on the outside of the now closed door.

"Excuse me," her voice brings my attention back to her.

A guy with a pointed nose and flat forehead is standing in front of beauty.

"I've never had dark meat before," the man says in a Russian accent.

"I'm not an entertainer," Beauty says before side stepping the guy.

He grabs her arm. Before she can flinch from the grip, I pull my gun out and slam the butt across his face. He drops to the ground. He turns to stand back up, but my barrel is pressed against his temple.

I don't have to look around to notice all eyes are on me. I can feel the tension seep into the room.

"Whoa. Whoa," Seth says behind me. "Ze….Kenji, maybe we should rethink this move."

"What the heck are you doing?" Kimi asks through the earpiece.

I ignore them all. My eyes are glued to the Russian. Was what I was doing stupid and risky? Yes, but my actions were damn near involuntary. I couldn't have stopped it if I tried.

Taking a deep breath, I pull back my gun and place it back in my back holster.

"She said she isn't an entertainer. Don't touch her."

The Russian climbs to his feet. "Who the fuck do you think you—"

"Isamu-Kai," I give my Yakuza name.

The Russian's gaze narrows before he takes a step back.

"All respect," he says, holding up his hands.

I acknowledge his truce, then grab beauty by the waist and steer her away. She leads us to one of those black doors on the left side of the room.

Once inside, I finally let her go.

"Thank you," she says, turning toward me.

"No need to thank me, Beauty."

She looks down, her lips tugging up in a smile. She's blushing again. "You'd be surprised how often that happens without anyone stepping in."

"I can imagine," I say.

She stares at me for a moment before looking away. "You can, umm, help yourself to anything in the room. Any preference for you two entertainers?"

Someone like you is on the tip of my tongue, but I hold the words back.

"No. I'll let you pick."

She blushes again. "Okay, enjoy yourself. I'll be back with your guests in twenty minutes, Mr. Isamu."

She walks out of the room, and I follow her every step, watching the way her hips sway in the dress.

"Fuck! Hawk, will you turn around and look at her ass?" Maksim groans.

I ignore him.

As soon as the door closes, we spring into action.

"Okay, Beauty said we have twenty minutes. We need to do it in ten," Kimi says.

I knew I would need to strip off my shirt in order to prove who I was, so I couldn't hide the things I would need on me. Many pulls the climbing rope out of his back and tosses it to me. Seth goes over to the chair in the room and drags it to the air vent in the ceiling. He climbs up and starts to remove the vent.

Hawk opens up his coat and pulls out the syringe he has placed there. This kill was going to be different. There is no way we could get a cleaning crew in here to get rid of Micah's body. So, we needed his death to look as natural as possible.

That's where DOE came in. They have a special drug they use for certain assassinations. Within seconds, it has the ability to stop a grown man's heart. I was more of the bullet to the head type of person, but we had to compromise.

Our plan still only works if Corbyn doesn't know what we're doing.

I take off my jacket and toss it to Many. Wrapping the cord around my waist, I secure the end with a carabiner.

"Alright, the vents open," Seth says climbing back down the chair.

I hand the other end of the cord to Many. He ties his end to the side of the bed, securing it with another carabiner. He then tugs it to make sure it's secure.

Hawk hands me the needle. The cap is securely in place. I stuff it into my pocket.

"Alright, do you remember the air vent layout?"

"Yeah. We're five doors down from Micah's room. It's a straight shot."

I climb up in the chair. Grabbing the ledge of the opening to the air vent, I use my upper body strength to pull myself up. Once I have most of my upper body in the vent, I pull myself further in. Once I'm fully inside the tight space. I settle down on my stomach.

It's freezing inside this vent, but I ignore the cold. I've been in much worse conditions for longer.

"Eight minutes remaining," Kimi says.

I army crawl my way through the vents. Moving too fast will make too much noise, so I take my time. I pass the vent to the first room. Glancing down through the grate, I find a man with tattoos all over his chest tied to a bed while a woman in black whips him with a belt.

Shaking the memory of the scene off, I keep going. I count the vents as I go so that I can find the right one. When I get to the vent above Micah's room, I stop.

Peering through the grate, I search for him. He's lying on a bed, stark naked. The speaker in his room is blasting some heavy metal song. Peering through the grates as best I can, I check to see if he's alone. So far, the room is vacant other than him.

"Six minutes," Kimi reminds me.

I easily remove the grate from the ceiling. It swings open into the room. But thankfully the music covers any noise. I situate my body over the vent so that I drop down headfirst. I'm hoping I measured this cord right, because if not, I'm falling into the room and possibly hitting my head.

Without delay, I fall out of the ceiling, my body dropping to the floor until I am merely inches away from the ground.

Thank goodness my measurements were accurate. Swinging my body up, I place my feet on the floor and unclip the rope from around my waist. The vent to the room is on his left and slightly behind him, but all it requires is for him to look over and he will see me.

Removing the syringe from my pocket, I creep over to the bed. At the last minute, Micah opens his eyes and turns to look at me. He darts out of the bed, charging toward me. We clash. He wraps his arms around my body, pinning mine down to my sides. He drives me back against the wall behind me, knocking the wind out of me. When he lets me go, he punches me in the ribs. Searing pain lights up my side. He throws another punch to my stomach that almost has my dinner making a reappearance.

When he goes to swing at my face, I move my head, causing him to punch a hole in the wall. Using that distraction, I slam my right elbow into his face. He steps back from the blow. I then kick him in the chest, sending him staggering back. He charges at me again. I drop low and sweep his legs from under him. He falls to the ground. Kneeling on his chest, he swings, but I dodge his blow. I flick the top off the needle and then jab the syringe into his neck.

He fights for only a second before his body starts to convulse.

"Four minutes, Zel." Kimi reads off the time once again.

Movement at the door has my head swinging in that direction.

"Fuck," I mumble. Flicking the top back on the needle. I stuff it in my pocket as I run for the rope.

"Pull me up," I say as I wrap the cord around my waist.

Immediately, I feel the tug. Using all my lower body strength, I leap up off the ground and reach for the grate. I manage to get a hold of it with one arm. The rope continues to pull me allowing me to swing my other arm up.

The door handle jiggles, alerting me someone is about to enter. I swing my body upward, barely getting my feet in the vent as the door opens. Thankfully, whoever entered the room was talking to someone behind them and not looking forward. I grab the grate and swing it closed, securing it again.

Wiggling my body as fast as I can, I make it back to my room. Before I drop through the ceiling, I hear the high pitch scream of a female.

"Come on, Zel," Seth shouts.

I wiggle my way down into my room from the vent, planting my feet on the floor. Seth climbs on the chair and replaces the vent. Many helps me untie the cord from around my waist.

We set the room right as best we can before my door opens. Two skinny half-dressed girls are standing in the doorway, their eyes wide.

"What's going on?" I ask casually.

"One of the patrons is dead."

Our night was cut short. Akito cleared the building to figure out what happened to Micah. We didn't put up a fight. As I was climbing into the blacked out Suburban we stole for this mission, I look to my left and my gaze connects with Beauty. She quickly looks away, but for a split second, I have her undivided attention.

CHAPTER THIRTY-SIX

More Family

Summer

Malia and I dance around the kitchen as we prepare dinner. The house is quiet today. Fem and most of the guys are out doing surveillance for Evan.

Ever since they killed Micah last week, they've been trying hard to get to Evan. I know part of the drive to finish the siblings is so they can get to Corbyn. We are all ready for this to be over. I can feel the energy in the home shifting.

Ari, Many, Charlie, and Ms. Reese are with DOE. Ari had a doctor's appointment with their doctor. She's twenty-eight weeks now. Her and Many have refused to find out the sex of the baby. They want it to be a surprise. This was just a regular checkup. Ms. Reese volunteered to take them. They even took the animals with them to get them out of the house.

Me, Malia, Brooklyn, Gabe and Emory were the only ones home at the moment.

"It will definitely be outdoors. I've always wanted an outside wedding." I answer Malia's earlier question.

"Me too," she hums. "I told Lucien and Seth that I wanted either an outdoor fall themed wedding or something under the stars."

"What about you, Brooklyn? I know you're already married, but you ever thought about renewing your vows and having a wedding?"

I look up to Brooklyn sitting on the stool across from me. I was dicing potatoes while Malia seasoned up some steaks.

Brooklyn frowns as she rubs her back. "I've never really thought about a wedding," she says.

"Are you okay?" I ask putting the knife down.

She sighs. "Yeah, my back's been bothering me all day."

"Oh no," Malia chuckles, joining me at my side. "Did you and Hawk have sex on the washing machine again?"

Brooklyn snorts. "Not this time." She straightens up and smiles. "Although we did have a quickie this morning before he left."

I laugh. I can't say anything because I rode Gabriel's dick for a while this morning. For some reason, I've been all over the man. My sex drive has skyrocketed. I know why he's been so eager to have sex. He's still chasing away his memories from that day, but I've taken it to a new level.

Suddenly, my phone vibrates against the kitchen counter. I don't even have to look at it to know who it is. My sister has been calling me nonstop for the last two days. I have yet to answer her call. I stare at it until it stops.

"Girl, that phone has been ringing every ten minutes since you put it down," Malia says.

"It's my sister," I groan.

"Oooh, sounds like family drama," Brooklyn says. "Why don't we like the sister?" She places her forearms on top of the island.

I laugh. I love that she immediately takes my side without even knowing the facts.

"Raina and I have never gotten along." I shrug. "I used to think it was because I was an addict. But it started much sooner than that. My mom had a lot to do with it. The last time we talked, we had a huge falling out and I have no plans to speak to her again."

"Do you think she is calling to make amends?" Malia asks, placing the seasoned steak in the fridge.

"I mean, homegirl has called you like twenty times in the last hour," Brooklyn says, rubbing at her back. "There has to be a reason. I love Albany to death but, I'm not blowing up her phone like that unless it's important."

When I told Trina about the phone calls yesterday, she said the same thing. They all had a point. As much as I didn't want to talk to Raina, there had to be a reason she was calling me back-to-back like this.

Suddenly, my phone rings again. I glance at the screen and sure enough, it's Raina. Sighing, I put the knife down, dry my hands on the dish towel, and then pick up the phone. I walk into the hallway before answering.

"Hello?"

"Finally," she huffs. "I've been calling you for two days."

"I know. What do you want, Raina?"

There is a pause on the phone. It's like she's talking to someone else or just distracted.

"Hello?" I say, getting her attention.

"Sorry," she says. "That was MJ. He uh…. asked about Gabe."

Crossing one arm over my chest while I hold the phone up to my ear with the other, I walk further away from the kitchen.

"Gabe is fine." I don't say anything else. I wanted her to feed this conversation.

"Where are you?" she finally asks.

"Out of the state," I lie.

She's quiet again. "When are you coming back?"

"Raina, is there a reason for this call?" I pinch the bridge of my nose. After the talk with Brooklyn and Malia, I was hopeful that this was a call that could possibly mend our relationship. But she just seems to want to chat about mundane stuff.

"I'm sorry for bothering you," she sighs. "I just wanted to know if you're okay."

Feeling slightly guilty, I change my tone a little. "Thanks for reaching out. I'm fine. Gabe is fine. I'm not sure when I'll be back. Maybe when I get back, we can—"

"Oh, Summer, I have to go," she says cutting me off.

I'm shocked by her abruptness, but it could be something serious.

"Okay. Well, I'll talk to you...." My phone beeps, telling me the call is disconnected.

The entire conversation strikes me as odd, but I shrug it off. I head back into the kitchen.

"How did it go?" Malia asks as soon as I walk in.

"Not how I expected."

We go back to enjoying our time. I don't think about Raina's call or the abrupt way she got off the phone again.

After getting everything prepared for dinner, the three of us went out to the back porch to watch Emory and Gabe play.

Nealy an hour had passed since that phone call when Brooklyn gasps and grabs her belly.

"Are you okay?" I ask leaning up from my seat.

She nods, but quickly looks horrified as she looks down at her lap. The seat cushion beneath her is a dark gray color. The total opposite compared to the light colors of the others. She climbs to her feet and a gush of liquid hits the floor. When she looks up, her eyes are wide.

"Oh shit, my water just broke. It's too soon," she says before her words turn into a moan.

Malia and I rush into action.

"You're thirty-seven weeks, you're going to be okay," Malia wraps one arm around Brooklyn.

Brooklyn groans as a contraction hits. "Fuck, this shit hurts," she complains.

"We need to get her to the hospital," I say.

"Emory, Gabe, come on," Malia calls out to the kids.

Both run up to us.

"Mama, did aunt Brooklyn have and accident?" Gabe whispers toward me.

"No," Emory's computerized tablet voice says. "Her water broke. The babies are coming."

"Yay, more cousins," Gabe cheers.

We make our way back into the house and toward the garage. Thank goodness for all the cars left behind. Not long ago, we all sat down and went over the birthing plan for this situation. The guys told us who to call, what hospital to go to, and what name to give when we check in.

"Wait," Brooklyn grabs my hand before we make it to the garage door. "I don't even have a bag packed. I wasn't prepared, we were going to pack this weekend."

"Okay, breathe, Brooklyn," I guide her. "Malia is going to take you to the hospital, I'll pack your bag. I still remember what you'll need."

"Oh my goodness, thank you....aahhhhh," she squeals as another contraction hits.

"They're about seven minutes apart," I tell Malia. "Call Hawk in the car on the way to the hospital. I will be behind you shortly with a bag."

"I got it. I'll take Emory with me," she says.

Emory opens the door, and we help Brooklyn into the black Porsche Cayenne. I get her situated while Malia gets in the driver's seat.

"I'm right behind you," I tell Malia. "Call Hawk."

Malia, Emory, and Brooklyn pull out of the garage. I head back into the house to pack Brooklyn's bag. Gabe helps me gather everything Brooklyn and Hawk will need, along with a few baby things. I load the two bags into the trunk of the Bentley Bentayga. I have never in my life ridden in a car this nice. But every car in this garage was nice. And although the Maserati and the Hellcat were appealing, this one felt like a safer choice.

I head back into the house.

"Okay, Gabe. Let's go?" I call out to my son. However, he's nowhere in sight. I walk into the living room and come to a complete stop. Sitting beside a man with the same face and eye color as Gabriel, is my son.

"Look mama, I got more family."

My heart nearly drops to the floor. There are two other people in the room. A tall blonde-haired woman is standing behind the couch Gabe and the man are sitting on. Leaning against the wall close to me is a younger guy with curly hair and caramel toned skin.

"So, you're the daughter-in-law?" The man beside Gabe asks with a smile.

He looks so much like Gabriel, it's scary. Maksim shares features with Gabriel that lets you know they were related. However, this man is Gabriel's twin. I know without a doubt, this is Corbyn.

"Gabe, come here, baby." I say, instead of answering him.

Gabe goes to stand, but the guy places a hand on his shoulder, sitting him back down.

"I've been dying to meet you, Summer. Although, not as much as I was to meet this guy." He looks over at my son and smiles. He glances back at me. "I didn't get the chance to raise Gabriel, but you have blessed me with the opportunity of a lifetime. And to think, I would have never found you if not for your sister's help."

The phone call comes back to mind. She wasn't calling to check on me, she was calling so they could track my phone. This was another sign that there was no salvaging my relationship with Raina. In fact, if I lived past this day, I was going to fucking kill her myself.

"Leave my son out of this," I plead.

The smile that spreads over his face is not at all soothing.

"No," he simply says.

The next few things happen quickly. The tall woman behind the couch pulls out a needle.

"What are you doing?" I spring into action, running toward my son.

The mixed guy in the room grabs me as the woman pricks Gabe's neck with the needle.

"Noooo," I scream. Gabe looks terrified before he collapses against the couch.

"Please," I sob, staring at my son's limp body. "What did you do to him?" I shout.

The guy chuckles. "He's just sleeping. This is my grandchild. My prodigy. Nothing will ever happen to him. You, on the other hand," he shrugs. "You, I can do without."

The mixed guy spins me around and backhands me across the face. I fall to the floor with a thud. He pulls out a gun and aims it at my head.

I cover my face as if that will help me.

"This time, my bullet won't miss," the mixed guy snarls.

"Easy Yohan," Corbyn says, climbing to his feet. He walks over to me and peers down at me. "If it was up to me, I'd let him put a bullet in your head so that my son could find your lifeless corpse. It's the least I should do after him, his treacherous brother, and his friends killed off my children," he sneers as he leans down and grips my braids, pulling my head back. I cry out at the bite of pain.

"But I made a promise to someone. For some reason, they want you. And if I'm going to make my grandson the killer that my son is, I need this person on my side." The man whispers down at me before letting me go and standing up straight. He tugs at the sleeves of his jacket.

"But you don't have to be in top condition." He grins.

Suddenly, blinding pain hits me in the side of the head. I remember nothing else after that.

Beast

Maksim, Hawk, Albany, Seth, Zel, and I all rush into the hospital. I pull out my phone and text Summer.

Me: Where are you?

I wait for a response. We were tracking Evan near an apartment complex when Malia called Seth and told him they were all headed to the hospital. We quickly dropped everything in order to be here with Hawk as his boys came into the world.

"Malia says they're in room 412," Seth announces.

Looking down at my phone, my brow pinches. How did Malia reply to Seth before Summer replied to me? I shrug my doubt away. Sliding my phone in my pocket, we rush toward the elevator.

"Relax, Hawk," Zel jokes. "You're not even doing the hard part."

We all laugh at Hawk's expense.

"I'm about to be a father," Hawk replies excitedly. "I'm fucking terrified."

I place a hand on his shoulder. "You got this. Parenting is the best job you'll ever have."

He smiles as he looks over his shoulder at me. "Thanks, Beast. You make this fatherhood stuff look easy."

Shrugging, I reply honestly. "I had a damn good role model."

The elevator goes silent as everyone reflects on the man that raised us. There is not a day that goes by that we don't mourn Priest. Losing him left a huge hole in all of our hearts.

The doors to the elevator slide open and we rush out. Hawk and Albany head to the room while the rest of us find the waiting room.

We're there for two minutes before the door opens and Emory runs in and straight to Seth's arms. Her hands are moving quickly as she signs to him all the things he's missed. Malia is right behind Emory. She goes into Seth's open arms. He places a kiss on her head as he rubs her belly.

I watch in anticipation for Summer and Gabe to walk in. After about a minute and a half and no one entered, I turn to Malia.

"Where's Summer?"

She looks startled, as if my question catches her off guard. She looks around the room.

"She didn't come with us. She stayed back to pack Brooklyn's bag, but she should've been here by now."

The first inkling of caution hits my stomach.

"How long ago did you guys get here?" Seth is asking Malia, but I don't pay attention.

I pull my phone back out of my pocket. Glancing at the unanswered text, alarm bells go off. Summer always texts me back.

I press her number on my phone and let it ring. It rings about four times before it's answered.

"Hello, son. It's been a while."

My world tilts and everything starts to fade as the sound of my heart racing thumps in my ears.

"Corbyn," I growl.

Everyone in the room turns and looks at me.

"I thought by taking your little daddy figure out of your life, it would put you in your place, but I see you don't listen. I can't fault you. You get that from me." He chuckles.

"Where are Summer and Gabe?"

"Put him on speaker," Seth urges.

Pulling the phone from my ear, I place the call on speaker.

"My grandson and your bitch are here with me." I close my eyes and take a deep breath. The voices in my head are all talking at once. Mother demands his blood. Priest wants me to be smart and listen, and the demon wants me to skin everyone within arm's reach. I have to fight to gain control.

Corbyn is still talking when I come back to reality.

"I caught on to your little plan before you could go after Evan. I hope you and your friends enjoy the little excursion he took you on today. I needed you away from your girl. I figured Yohan and Victoria would be the last on your list. The traitor would have told you that much."

"Bring my fucking family back," I roar.

"They no longer belong to you. The boy is mine now, and the bitch, well, she's disposable. You chose the wrong side, Gabriel. Face it, you can never defeat me. Have a good life." He laughs as the phone disconnects.

I roar out my frustration as I toss my phone across the room. It hits the wall. The two most important people in my life have been taken from me. I don't know where they are or if they're hurt.

"I can't....I can't breathe," I claw at my chest as it feels like my lungs are shutting down.

I drop to my knees as Zel and Maksim try to hold me up. Malia is holding Emory to her chest as tears spill down her face. The sadness and pity in her eyes tell me she believes my biggest fear. They won't keep Summer alive.

Seth runs a hand through his hair as he talks on the phone with someone. I have no idea what he's saying.

Maksim gets on his knees in front of me. "Look at me brother," I focus on his face. "We will get them back. I promise you will get them back. If I have to crawl to hell's door to do it, I will bring them back to you."

The door opens and Albany walks in. Her eyes immediately fill with tears when she spots me. She rushes over to me and wraps her arms around me.

"We got you," she promises. "We all got you."

In that waiting room, with my family around me and my world shattered, I made a deal with the demon in my head. From here on out, he and I worked together. We were going to kill my father.

CHAPTER THIRTY-SEVEN

Sins

Summer

I have screamed until my voice is hoarse. My throat and head hurt. Although I'm pretty sure the pain in my head is due to the knot on the side of my head. My body is exhausted. I woke up not too long ago and realized I'm chained to the floor in some type of basement. Near me, is a small cot in the corner of the room and a bucket that I'm too afraid to look in.

Not too far from the bed is a small rectangular table that looks more like a work bench you might find in a wood shop. Across from me is a set of stairs. From the way the basement is set up, a wall blocks my view from the top of the stairs down to the fourth step from the bottom. Near the stairs is a shelf full of cleaning supplies and other random things. My chains don't extend to that side of the room.

I have no idea where Gabe is. I pray that he's not hurt. Gabriel's father said that he wanted to turn Gabe into his next best weapon. I don't know what the hell that means. Hopefully, he doesn't intend to hurt him.

Noise from the top of the stairs grabs my attention. From the way the wall blocks most of the staircase, I can't see who is coming down. Still, I climb up from the cot. The chains around my ankle rattle.

I hold my breath as the stairs squeak with each step the person takes. I'm caught off guard when a tall woman steps off the final stair. She has a lean athletic build with wide shoulders. Her gray hair is pulled back from her face in a tight bun. She's wearing filthy overalls with a plaid shirt and work boots. A rifle is slung over her shoulder as she carries a tray with a bowl and kettle on it with her.

She eyes me with so much hatred, I question if she knows me from somewhere.

"Who are you?" I ask. I didn't have time for pleasantries. I needed to know who this woman was and where my son was.

She places the tray down on the wooden table. She doesn't speak until she turns to look at me.

"I can smell his impurity all over you," the woman sneers. "You're a dirty whore."

Clearly, this woman is insane. I pray my son isn't somewhere in the house with her unstable ass.

"Who the fuck are you, and where is my son?" I shout, but with as raw as my voice is, it doesn't come out loud at all.

She places her hands on her narrow hips. "You bore a bastard for the beast. God is not pleased."

She turns back to the items she placed down. Taking the bowl off the tray, she sets it down on the table. She then picks up the kettle and pours boiling hot water into the bowl. The water is so hot not only does steam rise from it, but it sizzles when it hits the bowl.

"I cannot have this filth in my home," she says, speaking to herself.

The woman walks away from the table over to the shelf near the stairs. She takes down a container of bleach, then walks back over to me. She pours the entire bottle of bleach into the boiling water. My nose burns from the smell.

I try once again to reason with her. "Please," I beg. "Just tell me if Gabe is alright? Is he here?"

She slams her hand down on the table, causing the things on it to rattle. She rolls her head toward me.

"My child is fine. He is upstairs sleeping."

Her child? What the hell is going on? I want to find comfort in her words, but the fact that she called my son hers is alarming.

Even though I've never met this woman before, something about her feels familiar. I don't know if it's the cadence in which she speaks or if it's something about her face.

"Do you know that when I gave birth to the devil's son, he ripped my body apart so bad that I bled out on the table," she goes on to speak, dropping a rag from the tray into the hot water.

"In order to save my life, the doctors had to take my uterus. I believed that it was Satan's way of ensuring I would never carry another child again. But God whispered to me that night in the hospital, he said be still my good and faithful servant. For I will make a way."

She turns to me with the freakiest smile I have ever seen. The feeling of familiarity strikes again. I try to rack my brain where I've seen her. However, nothing comes to mind. And I'm pretty sure if ever ran into her, I would remember her. She has one of those faces that's hard to forget, and not in a good way. She gives off Kathy Bates in *Misery* vibes.

"God has awarded me a second chance." She looks up toward the ceiling with a smile, as if she's seeing God's face. "This time, the child is pure and untainted by the devil despite his whore mother and demon father." She says the last part with an evil sneer to me.

It then dawns on me why she sounds and looks so familiar.

I gasp. "Your Gabriel's mother?"

"Yes," she chuckles. "He was my curse, but now I have a blessing."

Pure panic fills me. All the stories Gabriel told me about his mother and the things she did to him flash through my mind. The only thing I can think of is getting to my son.

"You bitch," I snarl as I charge toward her, hoping my chains allow me to get close enough "If you hurt my son."

She flips the gun around her shoulders and aims the barrel at me. I stop in my tracks. In my anger, I forgot about the weapon.

"Not so fast, whore," she taunts. "I have no fear of blowing a hole in your chest. In fact, I want to do it just to punish my son. I want to be the one that takes away his tramp. Don't make it an easy decision for me."

I take a step back, not wanting to trigger her anymore. It's clear that she's not playing with a full deck of cards. Even through Gabriel's stories, I knew that his mother was crazy. However, seeing it firsthand is an entirely different thing.

"Now, take off those clothes," she demands.

Her request has me confused.

"What? Why?"

"I told you, you're tainted. And this is the house of a servant of the Lord. You need to strip and cleanse yourself," she says the last part nudging her head toward the boiling water.

"Are you fucking crazy? I'm not cleaning my body with that shit."

She moved so fast I didn't see the blow coming. The butt of the gun cracks across my face splitting my lip and knocking me to the ground. I cry out at the impact.

"You will not use that filthy language in my house, whore."

I would've pointed out that her calling me a whore wasn't actually making her a saint, but the side of my face was too sore to argue.

"Get up and get those clothes off."

I stumble to my feet and take off my shirt. Tossing it to the floor. I remove my bottoms next. I do it all fighting through the pain in my face.

"Bra and panties," she growls.

Feeling vulnerable, I slowly take off my bra and panties. When I am wearing nothing but my birthday suit, I stand before her with one hand covering my mound and the other over my breast.

The woman looks at me as if she's staring at shit. Her nose is turned up and her lips are turned down.

"You're not much to look at, are you? Too skinny to hold on to. And you have the dullest brown skin I've ever seen. If the demon was going to go colored, he could have picked a prettier one."

I inhale and count to three. I so badly want to go off on this woman, but she has the upper hand. Not only does she have that gun, but she also has my son somewhere in this house. I needed to stay alive to keep an eye on him until I could find a way out of this.

"Go on," she says, pointing to the table with the hot water.

Slowly, I trek over to the bowl. Sticking my hands in the hot water, I hiss before yanking my hands back out.

"It's too hot. I can't touch it."

"It's no hotter than the hell you crawled up from. Now I said, clean."

Tears spill down my face as I reach back into the scalding hot water. I whimper as I wring out the rag. My hands burn from the heat and the bleach.

I drag the cloth over my body, the smell of the bleach burning my nose while also stinging my skin.

It takes me nearly twenty minutes to finish bathing in the awful water. And in all that time, the water never cooled off. When I'm done, I drop the rag back into the bleach solution.

His mother walks over to me, but I scurry away from her. I didn't want to be near her. She tosses me a long nightgown.

"Put that on," she demands. "In my house, you will dress respectfully."

I pull the thin fabric over my head and down my body. The bottom of the nightgown touches my ankles.

"Alright," I say once I'm done. "I've done what you asked. Can I please see my son? I just want to know he's okay."

She stares at me for a moment. She then pulls a box out of the front pocket of her overalls and tosses it at me. I catch it in my hands. My earlier fear returns when I see what it is.

"I'm not taking this."

Is there a possibility I could be pregnant? Absolutely. Gabriel and I have been screwing like rabbits the last few weeks. However, I really didn't want to find out right now.

"I wasn't asking you. The Devil wants whatever spawns you push out your loose vagina. So you will take the test."

"Please," I try pleading again.

She swings her gun around and aims it at me. Sucking up my emotions, I go over to the bucket in the room. I take the pregnancy test out of the box, pull up the long ass night gown, and squat over the bucket as I piss.

Please, for once, let Gabriel's sperm not work. After I finish, I stand up straight and lower my gown.

"What does it say?" she asks, never lowering the gun.

I close my eyes as I look down at the stick in my hand. I send up one more silent prayer that we didn't actually get pregnant and then open my eyes.

Immediately disappointment flows through me as I look down at the two pink lines. Any other time this would be good news, but all I could think about was being locked in this basement with this psycho woman, one child kept away from me, and another in my belly.

Gabriel's mother laughs. "No need to tell me, I already knew you were anyway. God already told me."

I toss the pregnancy stick to the floor. She chuckles and backs out of the room.

"For your sake, whore, you better hope its a boy. I don't much like girls." She turns and walks back up the stairs.

I'm left alone in the basement. My skin is burning and raw from the hot bleach bath. All I want is to see my son and have Gabriel hold me. I wrap my arms around my middle section, protecting the baby inside.

"Please, Gabriel. I need you to find us soon," I whisper into the empty room.

CHAPTER THIRTY-EIGHT

Maksim

"Ahhh!" the man tied to the chair screams.

"Chavis. Chavis," I say, calling his name. "You do too much screaming and not enough answering."

Chavis Alvarez is a longtime partner of Corbyn. He runs one of Corbyn's most lucrative illegal businesses.

It's been four days since Summer and Gabe were taken. While in the hospital that day, Lucien pulled up the video, trying to figure out how they got into the house without tripping the alarm. It seems Yohan cut the connection to the alarm system. We also watched the video of them taking Summer and Gabe. Seeing Victoria stick Gabe with that needle, and how Yohan kicked Summer in the head, had all of us boiling. We've been on a killing streak ever since. Anyone that has ever known or done business with Corbyn is in danger. We no longer care about enemies.

"Now, we are going to try this again." I stand up from the rolling chair and drag it over to Chavis.

His wide eyes stare at me in shock as blood dribbles down his chin. We are in the basement of the Ghost house. Priest had a very special room built on for an occasion such as this. I have to say, as much as Corbyn hates Priest, the man was brilliant.

"We are trying to find Corbyn. I know that you—"

He cuts me off. "I don't know where he is," he shouts.

"Aht Aht," I wave my hand in his face. "You're not listening. We know that you know how to find Corbyn. You bring in millions of dollars for him a month. He has a long-standing relationship with you."

"I don't know," He grits out.

I shake my head in disappointment. "I don't think you understand your predicament. Allow me to formally introduce you to my little brother." I hold my hands out toward Beast as if I'm presenting him to the world.

"He is, how you say, a little cuckoo in the head. But he is family, so we do not mock him. Anyway, Corbyn has taken his fiancée and son. My sister-in-law and nephew. And we are not happy about that. But you see," I lean forward. "He is much more pissed than I am. And right now, the only thing keeping him from brutally murdering you is me. I am his voice of reason."

I chuckle at myself, "And I know you're thinking, But Sim, how can you be anyone's voice of reason? You are just as crazy." I laugh heartily at my own joke smacking my knee. "I know. I know. It's weird. But this is my role. Now, I know you are thinking, he is already pulling out my teeth, how worse can it get?" I point to the two incisors and one molar on the tray beside him. "I assure you, my friend, it can get much, much, worse. So, you have a decision to make. If you give us some information leading to Corbyn, you can leave here a little bruised and without a few teeth, but alive. If not, I will walk out that door and leave my very angry brother alone with you."

"I don't know where he is," bloody spit flies out of his mouth.

I toss my hands up in the air and stand from my seat. "Alright, I guess—"

"Wait. Wait," he pleads, causing me to lower back in my seat.

"The accountant. Corbyn calls them every day. He checks on his money flow. Even when he's out of town or on a business trip, he will always call the accountant."

Shaking my head, I tell him. "We have already talked to William. He has no information—"

"William is his accountant for his legal business. He uses someone else for our stuff."

Rubbing at my chin, I think over how many moving parts Corbyn has. Even when I thought I was at the center of all his business dealings, I realized there was still so much I didn't know about him.

"Who is this accountant?"

"Her name is Julia Westfield. She works out of an office on the upper east side. You can track his phone call to his location."

"Very good, Chavis," I stand to my feet. "You did well. I'm proud of you."

Release washes over Chavis's face.

I look at Beastie. "Alright, I'm going to leave you two to it."

"What?" Chavis looks shocked. "I thought you said I could leave."

"Oh, I lied." I shrug. "Brother, enjoy." I turn my back and head out the room. Chavis' screams go silent once the door is shut. Thankfully, the room Beast is in is soundproof.

I make my way up the stairs and into the dining room.

"How did it go?" Lucien asks as soon as I walk in.

"I have a name, Julia Westfield." I quickly tell Lucien and the others what Chavis told me.

"I want you to see if you can hack into her phone from here," Albany says. "And check with Kyra to help. We need all hands-on deck."

"I got you," Lucien says.

"I'm reaching out to Kyra," Ari says, pulling out her phone.

We have all worked nonstop around the clock since Summer was taken. Even Hawk still comes and helps even though he has two newborn sons.

"Hey guys," Malia greets as she enters the room with a tray of food. She's designated herself as our very own chef. Making sure we eat every day.

She hands me a plate with a sandwich and chips. This woman is a godsend. Beautiful, full figured, and can cook. The twins should be lucky I am a loyal man. Malia tempts me.

"Thank you," I say genuinely, watching the way her hips sway as she walks away.

"Don't make me pluck those eyes out, Sim," Lucien says, looking at me over his computer screen.

I shrug. What does he want me to do? I'm an ass man. Taking a bite out of my sandwich, I put my attention on everyone in the room. When I went on this mission to find my long-lost brother, I never expected to find a new family. Being able to witness the way Priest loved his sons made it painfully obvious I never had that relationship with Corbyn.

Although it wasn't just fatherly love I noticed I lacked. Being amongst the guys and their women has made me realize everything I never had. The way Priest adored and worked alongside Albany was something to see. Seeing the Twins share Malia and Emory was inspiring. Watching Hawk love on Brooklyn as if she was his entire world was eye opening. Even the weird ass relationship Many and Ari have made me crave something I never thought I'd want. The biggest inspiration has to come from Beastie and Summer. Never have I envied two people more than I do them. Their love is beautiful.

While thinking about the couples around me, something sticks out to me for the first time.

"I've just noticed something." Zel looks up from his plate at me. "Did you all have a meeting to decide you would all end up with African American women, or was it by chance?"

Zel snorts in laughter.

"Wait, Brooklyn's black? I thought she was Asian," Hawk says jokingly.

The room fills with laughter. It may seem out of place, but the house has not been the same. We were slowly starting to find happiness after Priest died, but having Summer and Gabe taken from us pushed us right back over the edge. We needed this laughter now.

"How was he down there?" Albany asks stepping up beside me. She keeps her voice low.

"The same. Here, but not here."

Although we all believed that Beast would have a total meltdown once his family was taken, he had been quite the opposite. He's quiet, reserved, actually. He's in the room and present but feels miles away. The only thing he seems to do with any enthusiasm is kill. He and I hit the ground running. There has been so much bloodshed these last few days the streets could run like a river with it.

"We need to keep an eye on him. Until we get Summer and Gabe back, he won't be the same," she sighs. "Maybe I should bring Alicia back."

"I don't need Alicia," Beast says, appearing at the doorway. "I just need my family."

He's shirtless, but he has another one in his hands. I imagine the one he had on is probably ruined.

"Chavis?" I asked.

"Dead," he replies, taking a seat at the table. "Any luck with the accountant?"

"I'm tapping into her phones now. Kyra found a way in," Lucien replies.

"That was quick," Zel says what I was thinking.

We all enjoy our lunch as we sit around and plan our next move.

"If we can't get a hit on the phone, I'll pay the accountant a visit tonight," Albany says as she packs up her trash from lunch.

"I'll go with you," Beast adds.

"No offense, Beast, but I think I should do this alone. We want to scare her into telling us, not completely terrify her."

"She's right brother," I add. "I'll go with her."

Little brother is not in the right mind to be patient. And trying to get information from someone requires a lot of patience.

As Beastie opens his mouth to say something else, he's interrupted by Lucien's shout.

"I got him," he says, tapping on his laptop. Suddenly the room fills with Corbyn's voice.

"Julia," he chuckles, "How are my numbers for today?"

"Mr. Corbyn, as always, it's good to hear from you."

"Are you tracking the call?" Albany asks.

"Yes, it's triangulating."

"I may go silent for a little while, Julia. I have a bit of a pest problem that needs to be dealt with. This will be my last call for a few weeks."

"Oh, are you heading out of town?"

"Yes, tomorrow I will be boarding my private jet and disappearing for a short time."

"No problem. It looks like today your numbers are sitting right at two million."

"That's a good day," he chuckles. "I need you to clean out that entire account and have the money wired over to my offshore one by the end of the day."

"Will do," Julia says before disconnecting the call.

"Tell me you got that?" I ask Lucien. If we don't find where Corbyn is now, we will lose all chances tomorrow.

Lucien grins. "I got him. Looks like we're heading to Miami, Florida."

Pure relief washes over me. When I look at my brother for the first time in four days, I see life flash back into his eyes. I can only hope that when we find Corbyn, we will find Summer alive. I had no doubt that Gabe would be fine, but I worried about my little sister. Corbyn had no reason to keep her alive. And I know my father. He had no problem disposing of people he found useless.

"I'll arrange a jet," Lucien says.

"I'll get us weapons," Ari adds. She and Many walk out of the room.

"I need that address," Zel says. "I'm going to get blueprints of the house and surrounding area. Hawk is going to need to know the floor plan."

Albany nods her head. "We need to be moving out in the next hour."

"What about a plan?" I say. Even though we knew where he was, we couldn't go after Corbyn without a plan. We got one shot at this, it had to count.

"We will plan on the way," Albany says. "But tonight, we are taking Corbyn down."

CHAPTER THIRTY-NINE

Let's Go

Albany

"Are you sure you don't need anything else?" Mason Maxwell asks over the phone.

Beast, Maksim, and I are sitting in a pool cleaning van parked a few houses down the street from the Spanish style mansion where Corbyn is hiding.

"No. DOE already has the police department taken care of."

They hacked the phone system to 911 for this area. Anyone who tries to call in and report the commotion will be talking to a member of DOE. Any other calls will be rerouted to the real 911 operator. Once the attack starts, we have a full forty-five minutes to get in and out.

"All right. I'll leave you to it. The jet will be waiting at the pickup spot when you're done."

I say my goodbyes to Mason, placing my phone back in my pocket.

"What are we looking like?" I ask Maksim.

He's watching the tablet. Corbyn was smart not to have a camera system installed in his house, but a thermal reading on the building tells us that there are ten bodies inside the downstairs part of the house moving back and forth. We're assuming those are the guards. There are three others in a corner room that has not moved for a while. We believe those to be the remaining siblings. There are another seven guards upstairs and one lone person upstairs in one of the end bedrooms. Surrounding the mansion are another twenty or so guards.

"Everything looks the same. I think Corbyn is in that bedroom upstairs."

I also strongly believed that.

"Hawk, do you have that blueprint memorized?"

"Like the back of my hand," he says through the earpiece. Him, Seth, and Many are around the back side of the home waiting in the crop of trees behind the house.

"Remember," Maksim states. "If he gets to those tunnels, we will lose him for good."

Built under the house was a mile long tunnel that ended near a dock. Gassed up and ready to go was his very own boat. We didn't have enough of us to cover the dock as well as storm the house, so our best bet is to kill him here. We wanted to keep this job small. DOE offered a handful of my sisters, but we preferred they stayed back with Brooklyn and the others at the house.

"Don't worry. We got this," Seth says

It took us three hours from the moment we hacked that phone call to now, to get to this point. We have run down the plan and every possible scenario. It's now or never.

Tapping at the back of the van door has me moving to open it. Standing in front of me is Roberto and his mother, Louisa.

"What can you tell us?" I ask the pair.

Louisa has been cleaning and taking care of Corbyn's home for ten years. Apparently, he's an asshole of an employer and doesn't pay well. Unfortunately for him, it made it easier for us to get her on our side.

"The three children are there and Corbyn. But there is no woman with braids or child."

"Are you sure?" Beast asks, coming up behind me.

Roberto turns to his mother and asks her in Spanish, if she's sure she didn't see a woman with braids and a child in the house.

"No. I've been at that house every day for the last five days. There is no woman with braids or child," she answers him in Spanish.

I quickly relay her words to Beast. He nods his head. That isn't the best news, but if all goes well, we're hoping we can find a clue to their whereabouts either in the house or by prying it from Corbyn's mutilated body. It also allows us to go in heavy with gun power, not worrying about hitting Summer or Gabe.

Beast goes back into the van, before coming back out with one of those large black duffels filled with money we got from the church. He hands the duffle to Roberto. The man's eyes nearly pop out his head when he sees the amount.

"Thanks again," I tell the mother and son duo. They quickly clear out.

"All right," I say, so that everyone can hear. "The sun is going down. It's time to get to work. Summer and Gabe aren't there, so I need Corbyn alive until we figure out where they are. Set your timers to forty-five minutes." I set the timer on my watch, but don't press start. Maksim, Beast and I suit up, grabbing everything we will need.

"Many, Seth, and Hawk, start heading to the mansion. We are on our way."

Maksim, Beast, and I set off toward the mansion. It takes us no time to make it to the home. As soon as the house is in sight, I give Zel the signal.

"Zel, start us off."

"Sure thing, boss." Zel starts the countdown from ten in our earpiece.

A loud whistling sound shoots through the night. Seconds later, the front of the mansion explodes as the missile Zel launched goes through the front door.

"Whew!" Zel shouts. "I got to get me one of these shoulder rockets."

"Let's go," I shout as I hit start on my watch's timer.

Maksim, Beast, and I rush toward the mansion. We move quickly, taking down the guards in our path. The rocket blast helped eliminate some of them. It also helps that Zel and Kyra are taking folks down from the roof of the home across the street. We lucked up when we found out the house was empty.

I shoot a guard that's running toward me with a gun and before I can turn and aim my weapon at the second guard; he drops.

"I got you, Aurora," Kyra says through my earpiece. "Get inside. Hiroshi and I will handle the rest of these out here and make sure no one leaves the property."

Beast and I meet Maksim around the front of the house where the hole is. We step through together.

A guard comes out of nowhere. As soon as the three of us turn our guns in his direction, a harpoon flies through the air and pins the man against the wall beside him.

Turning around, I spot Hawk, Seth, and Many coming in through the back.

We make quick work moving through the guards downstairs. When it seems as if we can make it upstairs, four guards appear at the top of the balcony, looking over us into the foyer. They start firing off rounds. We all duck behind doorways and pillars.

I peek around the corner and fire off a round, hitting one of the guards in the chest. He drops to the ground. Hawk takes out two others. Seth gets the last one in the head. Before we could celebrate that victory, two more appear at the balcony overlooking the foyer. They have large machine guns. We all dive back behind the safety of our chosen hiding spots as bullets start to rain down on us.

"Victoria and Yohan are on the move," Maksim shouts.

I peek around the corner of my wall and see the tall blonde from the video from the house along with the curly-haired guy run up the stairs.

"We can't do anything with these two above us," Seth shouts. Bullets continue to rain down on us.

"Kyra and Zel, can you take them out?"

"Let me see," Zel says slightly out of breath. "No. The window only gives us a view of the top of the stairs. It isn't wide enough to view the entire upstairs area."

"Shit," Maksim shouts. "We're stuck."

"They have to switch the magazines in a minute," Many shouts. "When they do, cover us."

"You'll only have about thirty seconds," Hawk tells him.

"Yes, we know."

At that second, the bullets pause. We all slip around our hiding spots to shoot. The men with the guns take cover.

"Go, Many," I shout.

Many runs from behind the wall where he was hiding. He pulls one of his harpoons out of his back, extends it, and tosses it at the wall in front of him, all while in motion. The harpoon lodges into the side of the stairs. Many jumps up onto the bench placed against the wall, leaps on top of the harpoon as if it's a step and then do a back flip into the air. He pulls out his guns and, as he's falling back to the ground, he fires off two shots. When his feet hit the top of the stairs, the two bodies of the gunmen fall over the railing and down to the ground.

"That might be the coolest shit I've ever seen," Maksim says with his mouth wide open.

"Many, down," I shout as Evan steps up behind him with his gun at his head.

A gun fires, but instead of Many falling to the ground, it's Evan.

"I got your back, brother," Zel says into the earpiece. He took the shot from the foyer window that faces the top of the stairs.

"Keep moving," I say.

More guards come in from the first floor of the house. Many leaps back over the stairs and shoots one, while Hawk takes out another.

"I'm going upstairs," I shout as I move toward the stairway. I shoot my way past the guards as I take the stairs two at a time.

As soon as I get to the top floor, I shoot a guard that was aiming at me. A bullet whizzes by my head. I turn around and another guard is there, but he quickly falls to the ground with a shot to the chest. Turning back around, I find Beast coming up the stairs, his gun aimed.

"You good?" he asks.

"Yeah, let's spread out," I check my clip to my gun, noticing I have about ten more rounds in this one. "You go down that way and I'll go this way." He dips his chin. I turn and head in my direction.

With my gun out in front of me, I head down the hall. I peek around the corner into the first room and find it empty. Backing out, I push open the next door and ease inside. It's a bedroom.

The bed is in the center of the room. A patio is on the left side of the bed. I step into the quiet room. Moving through the area toward the open door, I believe to be a bathroom. A dresser is to my right with a mirror. Glancing into the glass, I spot Victoria coming up behind me. I turn around and fire, but she knocks my gun out of my hand, causing the bullet to hit the wall and the gun to slide under the bed. She aims her gun at my face. I spin around and bring my elbow up, hitting her in the face. I then grab her gun arm and bring it down over my knee, causing the gun to fly across the room.

She shoves me away. I turn around to face her. She wipes the blood away from her busted lip and then sneers.

"You fight like a woman scorned." She chuckles. "I wonder if it's because I killed your man?"

I glare at her before charging. We throw blows back and forth. I catch a right hook to the face, but return with an uppercut to her chin. She swings at my face again, but I dodge her blow before punching her in the throat. I run toward her as she stumbles back, tackling her to the ground. However, she uses her larger body weight to flip us over to where she's on top of me. She punches me in the face so hard, my head slams back against the floor. Searing pain explodes behind my eyes. She wraps her hands around my neck and squeeze.

"You will die," she snarls down in my face. "Just like he did."

That's the last time she will mention Nathaniel's death. I let the anger and the pain I've had inside me for the last two months boil up in me. Rage fills me.

I let go of her wrist and dig my thumb in her eyes. I press until I darn near slip my finger in the socket. She screams, releasing my neck. I push her off me. We both get to our feet quickly and face off again. Her eyes are red, but she can obviously still see.

"This will take forever," she chuckles. "We are too evenly matched."

I snort. "Bitch, you could never be me." Taking the blade out of my back, I toss it at her. It lodges right in between her chest and stomach area. She stumbles back before falling to her knees.

Her mouth moves, and blood sputters out. "You….you…."

I turn my back to her, and then back kick, pushing the blade further into her chest. I listen for the sound of her body hitting the ground. The thud it makes is music to my ears.

I grab my gun that slid under the bed. Walking over to her prone body, I fire two rounds into her head. Killing Victoria didn't bring back Nathaniel. But it felt darn good. I make my way out of the room.

Beast

I watch Albany as she slips down the hall. I turn away and head in my direction. In order for Corbyn to get to those tunnels, he had to go back downstairs. The last time the heat sensor picked him up, he was upstairs, and I know he hadn't been down those steps.

The sound of gunshots was still going on beneath me. Slowly, I creep down the hall, listening for any noise.

"Keep your head on the swivel, Kid," Priest says in my head.

"Slaughter the devil, boy," Mother encourages.

"Quiet," I tell them both.

Noise from the bedroom at the end of the hall has me heading in that direction. I stop at the closed door.

"Let me come with you," a male voice says.

"No. You will stay here and fight," Corbyn replies.

I kick open the door. Corbyn is standing in front of an opening in the wall. It looks like an elevator. It wasn't in the blueprints.

I fire off a round that hits Corbyn in the shoulder. He stumbles back into the elevator. Before I can fire again, the wall slides back into place.

"Nooo," I shout. Rushing to the wall, I beat my fist against it.

"Once it's been closed, you can only open it from the inside," I turn to face Yohan.

His hands are up in the air as he backs away from me. "I finally come face to face with the almighty Beast," He chuckles.

Lifting my gun, I aim it at his head.

"Wait," he says. "You mean to tell me I shot your girl and then kidnapped her, and you're just going to shoot me? I know you've waited for this moment. Do you want it to be over so quickly?" he nods toward the gun in my hand.

Looking down at the weapon, I think back over the moment Maksim told me Yohan took the shot at Summer. I remember running his face through my memory, telling myself that when I'm done with him, he will never look the same again.

"Show him what you're capable of," Mother hums.

"Let me out," the demon whispers.

I toss the gun to the ground. Yohan grins, dropping his hands by his side.

"Let the fun begin," he snarls before charging toward me. He swings at me, but his fist meets my Bowie. It slices through his flesh. The blade lodged in between the knuckle of the pointer and the ring finger.

Yohan lets out a gut-wrenching yell. I yank the blade out of his hand, then jab it up through his chin and out through his mouth.

He gurgles up blood. I release my hold on the weapon, and he falls to the ground.

"Smart, Kid. You don't have shit to prove to him. Go find your family," Priest's voice praises in my head.

I grab my gun off the ground as I head back out of the room. I spot Albany in the hallway.

"Corbyn?" she asks.

"Through the tunnels. There was a hidden elevator in his room."

We both run back down the stairs. When we get back toward the foyer, a guard runs from the back of the house toward us. Albany and I raise our guns, but a bullet splits the man's head. Hawk steps out of the shadows.

"Upstairs?" he asks, right as the others join us.

"Clear," Albany replies. "Corbyn is in the tunnels."

"What?" Maksim shouts. "I told you if he gets through those tunnels he's gone for good?"

Seth taps him on the shoulder. "Relax, brother. What do we know about Corbyn?"

Maksim looks confused, but answers. "That he's a patient and smart man."

"That he likes kids," I say, pulling out my phone.

I tap the screen until I get to the camera system I'm looking for. Holding the phone up, I allow everyone to see it.

"What's this?" Maksim asks.

"Just watch," Seth beams.

The view we are seeing is from a camera that's been stuck to a wall. In the frame is Emory and a dark tunnel. We all watch as Corbyn appears through the tunnel. He's holding his shoulder where I shot him, a gun down at his side. The moment he spots Emory, he pauses. Emory is on the floor with her knees tucked to her chest, whimpering.

"Hello," Corbyn says in a soft voice. "Are you lost?" he looks back over his shoulder before turning back to Emory. "How did you get down here?"

Emory looks up from her seated position. She stands up slowly, a headless rabbit clutched in her hands.

"Wait," Corbyn tilts his head to the side. "Have I seen you before?".

He makes the biggest mistake he could make, by turning his head and looking over his shoulder once again. Pulling her Bowie out of the body of the rabbit, she then drops the stuffed animal to the ground. Emory attacks. She runs toward Corbyn. He turns around at the last minute to see her coming. He lifts the gun in his hand to aim at her. She quickly dives on her stomach, sliding between his legs. She slices into his calf muscle as she comes out behind him. He drops down to his knees. She jumps up, runs back toward him and does a cartwheel over his head, planting her blade deep in his shoulder as she goes. She lands perfectly back in front of him, then kicks the gun out of his hand.

"What the fuck was that?" Maksim shouts. "You've had this kid sleeping in the same house as me all this time?"

Seth laughs. "Isn't she an angel?"

"Of death," Maksim grumbles as we all head to the bookcase we know that leads to the tunnels.

After sliding the bookcase open, we quickly make our way through the dark narrow walls. The moment we spot Corbyn and Emory, she skips over to us.

"Good job, tiny soldier." Seth high fives her.

I go to Corbyn. Grabbing him by the collar, I turn him around to face me.

"Where are Gabe and Summer?"

Corbyn grins. "I don't have many regrets. But you, you could've been my best pet."

I didn't give a shit about his regrets or what he thought of me. There was only one thing on my mind: finding my family.

"Where are Summer and Gabe?" I snarl, not in the mood for this conversation.

He laughs. "I'm giving you one last gift. He will be my greatest legacy."

His body goes limp in my arms. I roar as I slam his head against the concrete tunnel walls over and over. I don't stop until I feel hands on my shoulder.

"He's dead, brother. It's done," Maksim pleads.

I release Corbyn's bloody corpse and step away from him. My heart is racing, and my world is spinning. Even after all this, I don't know where my family is.

"We will find them," Albany says.

"Lucien will work nonstop until he locates them. With DOE helping, we will find them."

They all rally around me, but they don't understand without Summer and Gabe I can't go on. I can't face another day not knowing if they are safe and alive. It's been hard these last few days trying to keep the darkness away and to remind myself what's real and not. I won't be able to manage it much longer without them.

"Yes, give in to the darkness for good," the demon whispers.

"My greatest legacy," Maksim repeats Corbyn's words while looking down at his body. He turns and looks at me. "To Corbyn you were the greatest prodigy he had. It was why me and my siblings hated you."

"What are you getting at?" Hawk asks.

"He said he was giving you the greatest gift. Which means he's giving you, you."

"How would he do that?" Many asks.

Albany gasps. "By creating another Beast."

"So, Gabe's at the Church?" Seth asks.

"No," I growl as I realize what he meant. "He's with my mother." I take off back down the tunnels. We needed to get out of here and back to that jet. It's finally time I face my mother once and for all. And this time, one of us won't survive.

"Let's go kill that bitch once and for all," Priest says in my head.

CHAPTER FORTY

Like Father

Summer

Using the skinny nail I found on the floor, I fiddle with the cuff lock around my ankle. TV makes breaking into locks much easier than it is. I've been trying to get this lock open for the last three days.

"Come on, you stupid lock," I whine.

The squeaking of the basement door has my head turning in that direction. I quickly hide the nail under the covers on my cot. Standing to my feet. I wait for her to appear.

"Your wretched impurity has my basement reeking," Colleen says as soon as she steps off the bottom step. The god awful tray with the boiling hot water is in her hands.

She places the tray down on the table, then pours the boiling water into the bowl. This is a daily occurrence. Every morning, she comes down those steps with the scalding water, complaining about my impure scent.

"I don't understand how anyone could stand to be around you."

"If it's that bad, then let me and my son go."

The back of her hand flies across my face. The pain is immediate, but I've been struck by her so many times now, I'm kind of used to it.

"It's obvious I didn't teach the boy well. He should've corrected your mouth long ago. I will not have you sassing me in my own house."

I take a deep breath. I've never had to fight so hard against cursing someone out. I want to tell this psycho ass bitch she's the one that has me trapped in this fucking house.

Colleen walks over to the shelf to grab the bleach. She pours half the bottle into the boiling water. When she's done, she places the rag in the bowl.

"Undress," she states.

I go to pull the nightgown up in order to take it off. At that moment, the squeaking of the basement door has both of our heads swinging in that direction. Then I hear the sweetest voice ever. A voice I haven't heard in four days.

"Grandma, someone is calling. Can I answer and see if it's my mama or Hulk?" The desperation in his voice has tears appearing in my eyes.

I go to call his name, but it's almost like Colleen anticipated it. She swung around with a small gun in her hands aimed at me. I freeze. I haven't seen the rifle in the last two days, but I should've known that she wasn't completely unarmed. She places a finger to her lips.

"Go on and answer it, Gabriel," she says in a soft tone. One I didn't think her rude ass had. "I'll be up in a second."

His little feet rushing away from the door had my heart racing.

"What did you tell him?" I snarl at her.

She smiles. "I told him that you and the demon are away for a while and that you need me to watch him. After that one is born," she says, pointing at my midsection. "I'll tell him you both tragically died and left me to raise him."

Suddenly, I feel sick to my stomach. I knew this woman had nefarious plans for me, but I had no idea what they were. Hearing her so casually tell me she had planned to take my children and raise them had alarm bells going off in my head.

"Get cleaned up," she spits out. "I'll be back."

She slowly backs up toward the stairs and then turns and heads up them. I wait for the sound of the door closing before springing into action. Quickly, I go back to the nail under my sheets, and jump into action, trying to pry the lock open. With a new sense of urgency and desperation, I fight with that nail in the lock. At the sound of the soft click, the lock gives and the shackle around my ankle loosens. I gasp as fresh tears nearly spring to my eyes.

However, I fight the tears down. I needed to be focused. This was not the time for tears. I slip my ankle out of the shackles and rush over to the shelf in the basement. There is a hammer hanging against the wall. I pull the hammer down. As soon as I get it off the shelf, the creaking of floorboards near the basement door alerts me that Colleen is coming back. I rush back to my cot, the same spot I was in when she left me. I hold the hammer behind my back.

Colleen slowly walks down the stairs, each one creaking with her steps. When she gets to the bottom and looks over at me, her face scrunches.

"I told you to cleanse yourself."

Holding my head up, I look her in the face. "I want to see my son."

"No. Now, get undressed."

"Let me see my son," I shout.

She storms over to me. I imagine she's ready to backhand me and put me in my place again. The moment she's close enough, I pull the hammer out and swing it, striking her across the face.

She yelps and crashes to the ground near the table. Her head is bleeding, but she's not dead. I swing the hammer at her again, this time striking the arm she holds up to block me. I managed to swing the hammer twice more, hitting her in the face and chest. She finally goes limp. I toss the bloody hammer to the ground. My heart racing in my chest as I stand over her bloody body.

Seeing the blood causes bile to rise in my throat, I rush over to my piss bucket and empty my stomach. Wiping my mouth with the back of my hand, I stand on shaky legs.

Colleen has yet to move. I rush up the stairs. I nearly face plant on the steps in my rush to see my baby, but I fight to make it to the top. As soon as I do, I push the door open, walking into a sparse-looking kitchen.

I immediately catch the scent of freshly cooked bacon. A small circular table is in the middle of the kitchen with two chairs. Although the kitchen is small, it is clean.

In the distance, I can hear the sound of voices coming from a room nearby. It's the soft hum of a television show, something with a laugh track. I make my way toward the sound.

The moment I spot my son sitting on the floor in front of the old television, tears fall from my eyes.

"Gabe," I whisper his name.

He looks up from the TV and spots me. The smile that fills his face melts me to my core.

"Mama," he says as he leaps up from the floor and rushes to me. He wraps his arms around my waist.

I step back so that I can get eye level with him.

"Are you okay?" I ask, looking him over.

"I'm fine. Grandma said you and Hulk—"

I shake my head. "Listen to me, that woman was not your grandma." Technically, she was, but I didn't feel the need to explain that.

Gabe's brows furrow. "She's not? Is she bad?"

Before I could respond, my hair is nearly ripped out of my head, and I'm dragged away from Gabe. I grab at the hand clutched in my hair.

"You filthy whore," Colleen yells as she continues to pull me across her floor by my hair.

"Let go of my mommy," Gabe yells.

"It's okay, Gabe," I shout, trying to calm him down. "Go sit down." The last thing I wanted to do was get him worked up and he somehow angers her.

Colleen loosens her grip on my hair. I tug away from her and try to crawl. She quickly grabs me back and flips me over before punching me in the face. My mouth fills with blood.

She kneels on my chest and wraps both hands around my neck. "For the wrath of God is revealed from heaven against all ungodliness and unrighteousness of men." Her voice is void of any emotion and her eyes take on a distant look.

I dig my nails into her wrist, breaking the skin.

She blinks as if she's waking up from a trance. A smile lifts her cheeks.

"I must not harm the baby," she whispers, climbing up from my chest.

I gasp for air, my lungs burning. She opens the basement door. I had no idea she'd pulled me that far away from Gabe. I fight to get away from her. She yanks me back down and places her boot on my chest.

"The moment that new bastard is out of your belly, I'm going to put a bullet in your head," she says with a cheerful smile.

"Leave my mama alone!"

Colleen and I both look over to Gabe. He's standing in the hallway, a small gun in his hands as he aims it at Colleen.

"Gabe" I squeal. "Baby, put the gun down."

He holds the weapon up, his little arms shaking.

"My sweet boy," Colleen coos in that tone I've only heard her use with Gabe. "Put the gun down. God is watching you."

"You hurt my mama," Gabe says without lowering the gun.

Colleen looks back at me, before turning to Gabe. "She misbehaved. And remember what I told you about God? He talks to me and tells me when I need to discipline those that are not good. I'm only doing the Lord's work."

Colleen takes a step toward Gabriel. "Now, put the gun down, sweet boy."

"Gabe," I call out. "Put the gun down."

He glances down at me before looking back at Colleen.

"No," he says, breathing hard.

Colleen takes another step toward him. "You're not listening. The lord said that children should honor and listen to their parents. You are being very naughty right now."

"Don't you touch him," I shout at Colleen as I slowly get to my hands and knees.

"Shut up, whore," she spits out at me before turning back to Gabe. "Listen to your grandma, sweet boy."

"No," Gabe says. "I'd rather listen to my papa." The gun goes off and I scream.

My entire world seems to come to a screeching halt. Did Colleen have her gun on her? Did the crazy bitch kill my son?

Right before my eyes, Colleen's body falls to the ground, hitting the floor with a thud. A bullet wound in the center of her forehead. It was a perfect shot.

I rush to Gabe, getting on my knees in front of him. I reach for the gun. He hands it over to me without saying a word. I toss the heavy metal to the floor.

Cupping his face in my hands, I watch his eyes. I look for any sign of trauma. For anything to show me that this will live with him for the rest of his life.

However, instead of seeing fear or disturbance, a slow smile slips over my son's face.

"I did it," he cheered. "Just like papa Priest taught me."

I wrap my arms around him and bring him in for a hug. I can't even be mad at Priest for teaching him how to shoot. It saved our life. I will forever be thankful to that man.

Pulling away from my embrace with Gabe, I climb to my feet.

"We have to get out of here," I explain. "Is there a phone somewhere? Ahh,"

I scream when the front door splinters open. I quickly put Gabe behind me. My heart racing in my chest. Standing in the door with his hair hanging in his face, his shirt bloody and torn and a menacing look in his eyes, was Gabriel.

"Daddy," Gabe shouts as he rushes past me.

Gabriel scoops his son up and hugs him to his chest, yet his gaze never leaves my face. I imagine I look insane with this long ass gown on, my braids tangled on top of my head from where Colleen nearly ripped them out. My face is most likely bruised and bleeding.

Gabriel holds out a hand toward me. "Come here."

I rush to him. He wraps his arms around me and buries his face at the top of my head.

"I'm sorry," he repeats over and over.

Suddenly, Sim, Zel, Seth and Many step into the house. They all look as if they've been running. The sweaty bodies and panting give them away. They move into the home, their guns up and ready. I lose sight of them.

"I found Colleen," Seth calls out. "She's dead."

Gabriel lowers Gabe to the floor and removes his arm from around me. He walks into the hall where we left Colleen's body. He stands over his mother without saying a word.

"Nice shot," Seth says, smiling at me. "You hit her dead center. Haven't seen a hit that clean since Priest."

Maksim looks around at the walls. "I don't see any other bullet holes. Was this your only shot?"

I hold out my hand for Gabe. He places his small one in mine.

"Yes," I say in answer to Sim's question. "But I didn't kill her. Gabe did."

Everyone, including Gabriel, turns to look at Gabe.

"How?"

"Papa Priest taught me," Gabe says with a huge smile and his shoulders back.

I don't think I've ever seen a room full of prouder men.

"I think that earned you a nickname, kid," Seth says. "What do you think, Beast?"

Gabriel smiles, as he looks down at his mother and then back at his son. "You take after your grandfather. It's only right we call you Preacher."

H.E.A

Beast

It's been five months since we killed Corbyn and found Summer and Gabe at my mother's house. Since that time, the family has grown. Seth and Lucien are now the parents of a four-month-old baby boy they named Anthony Calogero Gramble. They also made their relationship with Malia official when they got married three months ago.

Dominique kept his word. He made the call and withdrew his signature on the order. We still have not heard anything from the Church. Although the attacks on us have died down tremendously, they have not made an official announcement about the order. They also still have yet to assign a new Pope.

"How do I look, Hulk?" Gabe asks, looking up at me with a smile on his face.

I look down at my son in his little tuxedo that is the exact replica of mine. "You look good, son."

"Yeah, Preacher," Lucien says. "You look like the best ring bearer I've ever seen."

Gabe's chest pokes out. Nothing makes him prouder than being called his nickname. After everything was settled, I decided to continue Gabe's lessons. I'll never let him sign his life over to the Church like we did, but I will train him to be just as good as a member of the Church.

"Charlie put that down," Many says.

We took our promise to Albany to heart. There isn't a day that one of us doesn't have Charlie with us. We are all still at the ghost house. At this point, we're staying just because it helps with the healing.

Priest's absence is still felt. We've had to rely on each other to get past it.

I grab little Charlie and lift him up. The kid has been all over the place since he learned to walk. He's one-year-old now and I know Priest would be so proud of him.

Charlie giggles as I toss him in the air and catch him. I plant him back on his feet in front of Gabe.

"Take your uncle to Ms. Reese so he can get a snack before the wedding."

Today, I was marrying the woman of my dreams. I made a promise to Summer that I planned to keep. Today, we were making that promise in front of our family.

Gabe grabs Charlie's hand. "Come on, Charlie. Maybe we can get granny Reese to get us a cookie."

I watch him lead Charlie out of the room.

"How are you feeling, Beast?" Hawk asks. He's sitting on the bed, his back against the headboard as little Nathaniel sleeps on his chest.

I turn back to the mirror, looking at my reflection. I tug at my tie.

"Nervous," I admit. My weekly meetings with Alicia have taught me to not only recognize my emotions but also get comfortable with speaking about them out loud.

"You're nervous because this is wrong," Mother's voice says in my head. *"You don't deserve to marry the whore."*

The voices in my head are still there. Alicia explained that the voices may never go away. I've had them for years. She has taught me how to understand them.

"She chose to marry me," I answer to her voice. *"Which means I deserve her."*

"Don't be nervous," Lucien explains. "Marriage is beautiful."

Zel laughs. "You've been married three months and now you're the marriage expert."

Lucien waves Zel away. "I can't wait until you find your other half. I hope she takes you through the ringer."

Although we all laugh, Zel does not. He cuts his gaze away. I wonder does the look have anything to do with his weekend disappearances? We have yet to find out where he's going.

Maksim claps me on the back. "There is no need for you to be nervous. Plus, it doesn't matter. Nervous or not, I'm getting your ass down that aisle. It is my job as best man."

The others in the room scoff. Since I announced that Maksim would be my best man, he has not let my other brothers live it down. It was not an easy decision. I in fact was more inclined to have Seth as my best man. But he is the one that pointed out how happy it would make Maksim. He said he didn't need me to prove to the others he was my favorite. I think they all knew that if Priest was alive, he would be the one standing beside me.

"I swear, when I renew my vows to Brooklyn, I'm making your ass an usher."

I laugh at Hawk's annoyance.

"We should be heading out," Zel looks down at his watch and announces.

I turn away from the mirror once more. My heart beating rapidly in my chest. I've been dying to see Summer in her dress.

"Let's go get you married," Lucien says, getting to his feet.

Hawk slowly climbs from the bed cradling his son.

"You good?" I ask him.

"Oh yeah," he says. "The lights are bright enough."

He makes his way to the door. We all follow him out of the room and toward the stairs leading up to the main living area. Suddenly, all of our phones chime alerting us of a text. I pull mine out of my pocket and read the message.

"What the hell?"

"What is it?" Hawk asks.

"By decree of the newly instated Pope, it is declared that Hiroshi Zel Tanaka, Killian Hawk Walker, Luciano Seth Twin Gramble, Milo Many Beckett, and Gabriel Beast Taylor, have been cleared. The excommunication order is null and void. Furthermore, Killian Hawk Walker and Luciano Seth Twin Gramble are no longer employed by the Church. Their contracts have been fulfilled and canceled," Zel reads the text out loud.

"When did the Church start canceling contracts?" Many asks in his deep voice.

Never. The answer is never had they ruled a contract fulfilled. Even when Hawk was released, his contract wasn't canceled. It was just fulfilled by Albany which is why he got called back in when she was supposedly killed.

"Wait," Hawk says. "That means we're free?"

"Sounds like it," I say.

"Hulk! Mama! Everybody! Come quick," Gabe shouts through the intercom system of the house.

Summer

"Best friend, you look amazing," Trina says as she secures the last hairpin in my halo braid.

Glancing at my reflection in the mirror, I smile. My make up is light and natural. Gabriel made only one request about this wedding and that was that he would be able to see my freckles. Trina did my makeup and hair. My edges are laid, and my thick course hair is braided around my head.

The diamond drop earrings look perfect with my A-line deep V sleeveless dress. I felt absolutely beautiful in this gown.

"You look stunning, Summer," Malia says, placing little Anthony in his bassinet. Although I love all the women I have met during our stay at the ghost house, I have to admit that Malia and Brooklyn have become like sisters to me.

Especially since there will be no reconciliation between Raina and I. A month after Gabriel rescued me from Colleen's, he took me to my mother's house to have a word with Raina. Fem went with us. Mother admitted she had no idea what Raina had done. She told us that Corbyn had first tried to convince her to get me to come home, but mama wouldn't do it. He then approached Raina.

She had no problems setting me up. Gabriel wanted to kill her, but I talked him out of it. MJ needed his mother. However, I did have other plans. Because I was pregnant, Fem did the honors for me. She beat the dog shit out of Raina. Brooklyn volunteered, but she was still recovering from the birth of the twins. Trina is mad I didn't record it so she could watch. Although I appreciate what Fem did, once I drop this baby, I'm getting my lick back.

"Thankfully, you're pregnant, Summer. If not, your tits wouldn't have been enough for that dress," Ari says, taking a seat on the foot of the bed. Her baby boy, Itadori Zelis Beckett is strapped to her chest.

They named their first child after an anime character. We were all a little confused by that, but we just call him little Zel and keep it moving.

"Thank you, Ariane," I say, glancing at Malia, who shakes her head.

No matter how random Ari is, we love her to death.

"Yes, my poor goddaughter is working overtime," Trina says, placing a hand over my belly.

I was so excited to find out I was having a girl. However, no one was as happy as Gabriel. He turns into a complete sap anytime my stomach moves. She's going to have him wrapped around her finger. The only person slightly happier than Gabriel is Maksim. You would think this was his child.

"Alright," Fem says walking over to me. "Time for the veil." She adjusted the clip of the veil into my hair and then fans the tulle out over my shoulders. She steps back and smiles.

Fem and I have a unique relationship. Although she is only a year older than me, she feels more like a motherly figure.

"Aren't you glad I didn't kill you five years ago?" she whispers in my ear with a grin.

"Very," I chuckle.

"Alright," Brooklyn says, walking into the room. "KJ is down for his nap. Mom is watching him. I am free to be of assistance." She stops and stares at me through the mirror. "You look so beautiful."

Immediately, tears form in her eyes.

"Oh no," Trina says, grabbing a tissue for me. "You're going to start a chain reaction."

Emory walks into the room in her flower girl dress and everyone coos at how cute she is.

"We should be going," I say. "We don't want to keep the guests waiting."

"Girl, you got three people in that audience," Trina chuckles. "They can wait."

She wasn't lying. I didn't have any real family. Even though my mother didn't rat me out to Corbyn, I still chose to distance myself from her. The only friend I have outside of Trina is Shay. Thankfully, she and her husband showed up. James is the third person sitting outside and not in the wedding.

"We should be going." Malia gets to her feet and grabs Anthony out of the bassinet.

Emory signs something to her. I only catch a few of the signs. I'm learning sign language now.

"You sure can hold him," Malia says, handing Emory her brother.

Albany holds out a hand and helps Ari off the bed. We all head for the door when suddenly Gabe's voice comes over the intercom.

"Hulk! Mama! Everybody! Come quick." As fast as I can, I rush out of the room. We all head into the living room where we pull up short.

I can't believe my eyes.

With a huge smile on his face, Gabe says, "Look, Papa Priest is back."

Pope

I would have never guessed what Dominique wanted to speak to me about that day in his office.

"You're going to need to take that earpiece out for this part."

Although I still didn't trust him, I wanted to hear him out. I pulled the device out of my ear and clicked it off.

He took a seat back in the chair he was sitting on and held out a hand for me to do the same.

I retook my seat across from him.

"You were right. There is something else I want from you." He leans back in his chair.

"And what is that?"

"I want you to run the Church."

If my eyes could have popped out of my head, they would have. I did not see that coming.

"I have to admit, I wasn't expecting that. There are protocols—"

"Fuck those protocols." He waved me off. "Right now, Corbyn has nearly 60 percent control over the Church."

"And you want that control?"

"No. I want you to have it."

I'm completely fucking lost. There is no motive here. Why would he want me to control the Church.

"I'm struggling to follow this, Dominique. What do you get out of all this?"

He grins. "I become partners with one of the most powerful men in the world. You see, unlike Corbyn, I have always admired the Church. But I won't lie as if it doesn't have its flaws. For instance, the no outside connections thing is stupid."

"I agree," I admit.

"Good, then we're on the same accord. You will run the Church. I will make sure you have total and full control over the organization. I will even supply you with the means to find legitimate cash flow. But I want it gutted. Take it down to its studs and rebuild it. I believe you are the only man that can do that."

"I'm hearing you. And I'm for a change in the Church. But I'm no dummy. No one does anything like that without wanting something in return."

Dominique shrugs. "I want what anyone in my world would want. Complete access." He held up a hand to stop me. "Don't worry, no women and children bullshit." He spins the ring on his finger subconsciously. It looks like one of those old class rings. In the center of the red stone is a capital R with a thorny crown.

"In my circle, I meet some of the most dangerous people in the world. People that would watch the world burn just for money and respect. I am offering a partnership. I give you the true scums of the earth and you run the Church."

There is no mystery that the Royal Crown has access to people that I'll never have. And I know what money and power can cause people to do. However, what he's asking won't be easy.

"How would this work? Trying to take down the Church is like trying to take down the Royal Crown."

"You can do it, but Nathaniel Otella has to die."

"What?"

"In order for this to work, you have to become someone else. That means leaving everything behind, if only for a short while. We will give you a name and put you in front of the Royal Crown. But no one can know. Not even those you trust."

"How long?" I ask. How long am I supposed to leave behind everyone I love?

Dominique shrugs. "I don't know. Could be months, could be up to a year or more. It depends on you and how persuasive you are."

I'm silent as I think this over. Now is not the time to disappear. My boys need me. My son needs me, and leaving Fem would damn near kill me.

"I'm going to give you time to think it over," Dominique says, getting to his feet. "But know this. You need to make a choice, Nathaniel. A hard one. How important is running the Church to you?"

When I left that office, I was pretty sure I was going to turn the role down. But I thought of changes I could make not only for my boys, but my grandkids, and future kids that would come into the organization. The morning I got up to hold that meeting before we went after Corbyn, I had already made my decision.

"What the fuck, Priest?" Zel shouts.

"You were dead," Gabriel says. "We buried you."

"We fucking mourned you," Lucien adds.

The room is in an uproar, and although I know my sons are hurting and deserve my attention, my sight stays on Fem. The tears streaming down her face with the anger in her eyes tell me I have a lot of explaining to do.

"How about," Summer says, interrupting everyone. "Trina, you take all the kids outside and let the guests know there will be a slight delay."

Trina rounds up the kids. She takes little Nathaniel from Hawk. Gabe takes Charlie's hand and leads him out of the room. Emory carries her brother out. Only one left is little Zel still strapped to Ari's chest. I wait until the kids are all gone before I speak.

"Where do I start?"

"Why?" Fem asked. "Why would you do that to us?"

Sighing, I quickly fill them in on mine and Dominique's conversation.

"So you had to fake your death? You couldn't just disappear?" Zel fumes. "We were lost without you." He pounds his fist in his open palm.

"I didn't fake my death," I explain. "Not fully. In that operating room, I died. Twice actually. But doc is a very talented man, and Dominique's a very powerful one. By the time we went to that fundraiser to attack Corbyn, I had already notified Dominique of my decision. He made the call to Doc the moment I was shot. He knew it was the best time to make me disappear. When I woke up, you had already buried the silicon body replica."

"It looked just like you," Fem argues.

"It should've. Dominique got some of the best in the industry to create it. It had to look as if I was truly dead."

"If that's the case, what have you been doing all this time?" Hawk asks.

"It took a while for me to recover. The bullet almost paralyzed me. Thanks to Beast's fast reaction and my reflexes, we dodged a huge setback. While I was healing, Dominique hit the ground running. He always knew you guys would handle Corbyn. He recreated an image for me and talked me up to the right people. It also helped that I had a few allies on my side."

I can never thank Mason, Vito, Kaz, and Nico enough. They came through for me in the best way.

"By the time I was ready to step in, most of the work was done. They quickly moved me up to Pope and I now fully run the Church."

"You're the reason Hawk and I have been released?"

"Yes."

That was one of the first changes I made in the Church. No one is tied down for life. That one change had twenty percent of our members resign. They left with the understanding that if they ended up on our radar, we would not see them as family. We would kill them.

The other change I made was to the no outside commitment law. Every member of the Church is now capable of having their own family.

The changes to the recruitment process was one of the toughest changes to get passed. We no longer recruit. The Church Home for Misplaced Kids was now being built. We weren't taking kids from their families and making them killers. Now, we trained kids that had no home. We provided them with a family and a bond of brother and sisterhood.

"So, you got what you wanted?" Fem asks wiping the tears from her eyes.

Reaching behind me, I grab the onyx cane with the crystal end. Slowly, I place my weight on the stick and rise from the chair. I didn't come out of all that unscathed. It took me nearly two months to walk again. And I still cannot fully manage without a cane.

I hold my arm out at my side. "Not everything I wanted. If I'd had my choice, I wouldn't be needing this fucking stick. But to set my boys free so that they could enjoy the lives they wanted, to create an organization where young kids can find a home and a purpose without selling their souls for it, and to live my life with the woman I love more than anything in this world without having to look over my got damn shoulder every second, I'll take this stick in a heartbeat."

Beast is the first one to break the ranks and approach me. He wraps his arms around me and hugs me tight.

"I'm glad to have you back," he says as his voice cracks.

Lucien is next to join our hug. Many, Hawk, and Zel come shortly after. I'm surrounded by all my boys. Every decision I made was for them. I'd give them the world if I could.

They step away from me, giving me space. I wait for the one person I needed to forgive me. Fem watches me, tears still in her eyes.

"Are you still mine, Fem? Even though I'm an old crippled man?"

She looks away and wipes her eyes. "I should kill you," she says. She turns back to me.

I don't speak. Time seems to slow at a snail's pace as I wait for her to tell me where we stand.

Finally, she let out a deep breath. "So, what's my new last name?"

I smile as I hold out a hand to her. "Monroe. You are Mrs. Charles Monroe."

She rushes into my outstretched arms and buries her face in my chest. I have missed this woman more than anything in the world.

"Ugh," Brooklyn says, cutting into our moment. "I can't believe I named my son after you." She wipes her eyes, causing everyone to chuckle.

"Now," I say. "We have a wedding to attend." I turn to Summer with a smile. "I would be honored if you allowed me to walk you down the aisle to my son."

She grins. "Absolutely."

The night ends peacefully. Summer and Gabriel said 'I do' in my backyard. Everyone danced and laughed and enjoyed the evening. And when the sun had fully set, we put the kids to bed, and we all fucked like rabbits.

The End

ACKNOWLEDGMENT

Well, it's done. I started this series in 2020. Honestly, finishing this book is bittersweet for me. I lost a lot along the way to completing this series. Things and people I will miss dearly. However, I also gained a lot. Like many of my readers. You guys found me from Hawk and stayed with me until the very end. Thank you all for sticking with me on this journey. I can't wait to meet you on the next one.

To Nanny, my guardian angel, I'm still writing.

To my husband, who has stuck around for my crazy, I love you.

And last but never least, to my babies. All I do, I do for you.

ABOUT THE AUTHOR

Tiya Rayne is an avid reader and writer. She has an unhealthy relationship with coffee and is known to enjoy a glass (or two) of wine on a regular basis. When she is not reading or writing—which is rare—she's trying to master this thing called parenting. She's married to her high school sweetheart, and they live in North Carolina with their three—subjectively wonderful—children. Tiya also writes Young Adult Paranormal under the pen name KC Connor.

Thank You

Wait, there is more to come! You can stay up to date with my latest releases, and learn more about me, the author by subscribing to my newsletter at www.TiyaRayne.com

If you enjoyed Beast: Part Two, I'd love to hear your thoughts and please feel free to leave a review. And when you do, please let me know by emailing me at TiyaRayne@gmail.com or leave a comment on Facebook https://www.facebook.com/AuthorTiyaRayne/ or Instagram @AuthorTiyaRayne

Until the next time.
Bye!